I hadn't seen Damon in nearly two weeks.

I hadn't had sex in so long, I didn't even want to think about it.

And Justin was doing one thing guaranteed to make Damon's brain shut down.

"You know, this is what happens when you hook up with a shifter, Kit," Justin said, pushing up onto his elbows. His black T-shirt rode up, baring his flat belly. "The animal kicks in too easily, shuts down the brain. Now, me? If we were still together, I wouldn't be all that worried if your bedroom smelled like another man."

"That's because you can't scent another man in my bedroom, you asshole."

He shrugged. Crossing his feet at the ankle, he said, "He knows we're done. I just—*hey!*"

Justin glared at me from the floor.

I let go of his ankles and smiled.

"You were saying?"

He cocked his head. "Well, the view is nicer from down here."

"You're ridiculously juvenile," I said. Shaking my head, I turned away.

After grabbing my gear, I ducked into the bathroom.

"You're sure you didn't leave any signs behind?"

"Justin…I'm not new at this." Dressing in short order, I moved out of the bathroom to find him at the window. He was staring outside, arms crossed over his chest. "Don't worry so much."

"It's my job," he said easily. Then he turned around. "So…speaking of jobs…"

EDGED BLADE

THE COLBANA FILES

J.C. Daniels

Edged Blade

J.C. Daniels

ISBN-13: 978-0-9894605-6-9

Also by J.C. Daniels

Blade Song

Night Blade

Broken Blade

Bladed Magic

DEDICATION & ACKNOWLEDGEMENTS

As always, dedicated to my husband and kids. You're my everything.

By special request...also dedicated to Haley, Aspen, Jess, Trinton, Caimen, Heather, Dev, Cam & Em. A rowdy, rotten bunch of kids... I love you all.

Thanks to Sara R., editor extraordinaire and my beta readers, Tori, Teresa and Jennifer.

A special thanks to Charles Andrulis. Thanks for your bid in the Brenda Novak auction! Enjoy your incarnation in Kit's world.

A HUGE thank you to all the Kit lovers out there...all of your support astounds me.

Chapter One

Prep could be a pain in the ass. All the things necessary to get yourself ready, this shit is a nuisance that I would love to live without.

Sadly, the kind of life I lead sometimes calls for prep.

Not that you can *prepare* for my life.

Not that *I* can prepare for my life. The few times I tried, life went and kicked me in the face.

I'm slowly learning how to kick back.

I wouldn't be doing much kicking in the shoes I'd just slid onto my feet, though. My balance is stellar, but it's just plain stupid to go kicking at something when you're standing on a spiked heel not much bigger than a toothpick.

Heels.

Shoot me now, I was wearing *heels.*

And what would probably be considered something sort of...dressy?

Maybe?

I don't know.

It was a costume.

I'd never been to a costume party and if I was smart, I wouldn't have even suggested going, but impulse sort of drives my life.

I'm Kit Colbana and I'm a...troubleshooter, of sorts. Or troublemaker, depending on who you ask.

On just about any other day you could find me in a pair of battered jeans or black BDUs, a T-shirt and my vest. My vest—man, I felt naked without it. I'd seen an old Swiss Army knife in a junk store once and although the blade on it hadn't been shit, the tool itself had been full of useful little gadgets. Maybe not useful in *my* line of work, but for somebody who wasn't crazy? Yeah, pretty useful. Scissors, screwdriver, tweezers, corkscrew...you never knew when you'd need a corkscrew. The knife reminded me of my vest.

I could pull almost any damn thing out of my vest.

But it didn't go with sparkly green. And it was unlikely I'd need weapons.

Unlikely. That didn't mean *impossible.*

I was going to a party. More to the point, I was going to a party with *Damon.* Damon was leader of the area's dominant shifter faction, which pretty much made him the top dog. Or the top cat. He was the Alpha of the Southern Cat Clans, a region that spanned from Mississippi to the Carolinas down to the far reaches of Florida and the Keys. I guess in a way, I *did* have a weapon. He just walked and talked and grew fur and fangs.

Nerves fluttered in my stomach.

I was going on a date with Damon and I was wearing a dress and I wasn't taking my weapons.

Panic seized me and I lunged for my trunk. No way, no how could I do this without *some* kind of weapon. My hands fumbled with the clasp and it only got worse as I thought about where the party was going to be, who—not a *specific* who but a who nonetheless—would be there.

It was a party thrown by the Assembly. There would be vamps there.

I wanted to puke. What in the hell had I been thinking?

Answer: I hadn't. I'd just acted.

Something red caught my eye. Power zipped up my arm and I hissed, instinctively jerking my hand back, only to pause and reach for the dagger more slowly. It was a pretty piece and even years after its bearer had died, you could feel the power inside it. Druids were rather famed for creating pieces of magic—relics even—that carried their magic inside them for decades, even centuries, after their deaths.

Most Druids worked with more…natural…mediums. Wood, for example. I'd once seen a Druid's staff and I'd coveted it so badly, I had sketched out plans to steal it.

But it was on display in the Smithsonian.

I'm greedy, but I'm not stupid.

Supposedly, the Druid had given the staff as a peace offering at the end of the wars between NHs—non-humans—and humans. I wasn't sure I believed it. Most Druids didn't part with their creations. They'd leave them behind, but part with them?

I don't know.

This one had been given to me. I'd done a job once and I'd done it well enough that my employer had given me a bonus—this blade. I don't know how he had ended up with it. He wasn't a Druid. That detail hadn't kept me from accepting it, though.

The blade had silver in it, making it effective against most supernatural baddies out there, and the hilt was encrusted with jewels. I'd stroked and petted it like a child with a new pet and after a few days, I'd put it in my trunk and promptly forgotten about it.

Now, several years it had been given to me, the dagger sat in my trunk, like it was waiting for me. Lips pursed, I studied it and then I shifted my focus to the various rigs I used for carrying my weapons. I'd have to jury-rig something, but I was almost as good at improvising as I was at impulsivity.

It took thirty minutes. I could have been done in less, but since I wanted the rig to *look* nice, I had to take a little more time. This wouldn't work for the long run, but I didn't need long run.

If I'd thought it through better, I would have found a pair of sparkly boots— boots were *fantastic* for concealing weapons—to wear with the sparkly dress, instead of the silly heels, but this worked okay.

The leather was inky black against my skin and stark, but in a way, it balanced me more, I decided. The bright and cheerful sparkles hadn't exactly clashed with the tattoos that twined across my chest and neck, but the leather thigh rig that now held the lovely, lethal blade gave the whole thing more of an edge.

I returned to my trunk and took a few more minutes, finding a few more items that would work.

The woman staring back at me from the mirror was almost unfamiliar.

"Who *are* you?" I murmured to her. Her cheeks were pink, flushed. Not that I'd admit I was excited.

Okay, screw that. I was excited. Scared. I shot a look at the clock and groaned. The butterflies in my stomach turned into tiny little dragons with razored wings.

Damon would be here in a few minutes.

Here, at my house, and I'd be alone with him for the time it took for us to get to the ball, thrown at an estate just outside of the city. I hadn't been *alone* with him in…forever.

As the Alpha of the Southern Cat Clan, Damon Lee pretty much had a standing invitation to any of the big soirees the Assembly threw, but to my knowledge, he didn't attend.

At least not until tonight.

Our first *real* date in…forever. If you could call a ball thrown by the Assembly a *date*. I mean, one wrong move, one wrong step and it could result in an interspecies feud.

Man, what was I *thinking*?

A couple of months ago, we hadn't even really been talking. Then we had started having the occasional dinner at Drake's. Nice, safe. Plenty of other people around.

There'd be plenty of people around tonight, too. In just a short while, I'd be surrounded by shifters, witches…and vamps.

I needed to quit panicking. Needed to quit brooding and working myself up.

And I needed to quit staring at my reflection. It was too late to change my costume and it was too late to do anything but brazen my way through the rest of the night.

Slipping out of the bathroom, I smoothed my hand down the sequined green skirt of my costume. As long as I didn't bend over, everything would be fine.

And if I did bend over, I'd made sure to wear matching panties.

Not that it would matter. If I found out I'd been flashing people, I'd probably die of embarrassment.

A flash of green in the hall mirror caught my eyes and I stilled, only to realize it was me, in my bright green sparkly dress.

● ● ●

Behold, Kit Colbana—assassin, thief, jack of all trades…and I looked like Tinker Belle.

Panic grabbed me by the throat—the feminine kind of panic. I looked like an *idiot*. I looked—

A heavy hand hit the door and I gulped.

Too late now.

Damon didn't knock again.

He just waited.

He wasn't the patient sort, but he could outwait anybody I'd ever known, including me.

With hands that had gone damp with sweat, I moved to the door and opened it.

A saturnine smile creased his dark face, even as his lids drooped and he raked me over with a glance.

"Well, well, well," he murmured. "You play a perfect little pixie, Kit."

I sniffed. "I'm not a pixie. Tinker Belle is a fairy—there's a difference."

He lifted a brow.

"Fairies are deadly." I grinned at him as I picked up the wings that went with the costume. "If you find yourself trapped by them, you're screwed."

He opened his mouth, then closed it and asked, "Fairies are real?"

"Yep." Unfazed by the question, I let my smile widen. There were plenty of creatures in the world that most people were unaware of, even now. "So are pixies and trust me, you'd much rather have a pixie. Too bad they're almost extinct."

He ran his tongue along the inside of his teeth. "You're never boring, Kit."

Then, in the span of one moment to the next, the lighthearted atmosphere vanished. Heat replaced it as he moved in closer. Not too close—he'd been walking on eggshells around me for months. I was so tired of it, but at the same time, I didn't know how to tell him to stop. I couldn't just say I was okay, because I wasn't. Sometimes I thought I'd never be okay again.

His gaze slid over me, the intensity of it almost a palpable caress. When he reached up and trailed one finger across my bare shoulder, my breath lodged in my chest. "You sparkle," he murmured.

● ● ●

"Ah…" I swallowed. "It's just some sort of glitter spray. Washes off."

He didn't respond, just continued to trail his finger across my skin, along my breast bone, leaving a trail of gooseflesh in its wake. He went to lower his hand and I caught his wrist.

His gaze shot to mine.

When I stepped up to him, I don't know who was more surprised, me or him.

A soft groan escaped him as I pressed my mouth to his. Even in the heels, I wasn't tall enough to reach his mouth, but he dipped his head and I clutched his shoulders, clinging to him as his tongue slid past my lips.

I'd missed this…

Heat swam through me and I clung to him tighter, straining against the warmth of his skin.

Something cold trailed across my back and I hissed.

He broke away.

"What is…"

He let me go and I saw his left hand.

Abruptly, I started to laugh.

"Really?" Looking at him, I cocked my head. "What are the odds?"

"Not good." He brandished his hook, a shiny, polished curve of real metal—silver, if I was right. "I could lie and say the idea just came to me, but I asked Colleen."

I made a face at him. "That's cheating."

"Well, Captain Hook's a pirate…he would totally cheat."

"Riiiiggghhhhttt…." Head cocked, I studied him. The burgundy velvet frock coat suited him far more than I would have imagined possible. He had a gold hoop in one ear, although it was either one of those faux piercings or gold over silver. His body would have just rejected any metal but silver. Shifters and piercings just don't mix. He wore black breeches tucked into knee boots and the breeches were snug enough that I thought I just might have to hurt some women tonight. The entire picture was topped off by the black cloth he'd tied over his head.

"I guess this suits you better than green tights would have," I said.

A faint grin curved his lips. "I don't think anybody would ever buy me as the boy who never grew up, kitten."

"True. Still, Damon…green tights…"

The party was in full swing by the time we arrived.

It was something of a spectacle, attending a Halloween party thrown by creatures that were once thought to exist only in myth.

The senior Assembly members were responsible for the event and wow, did they know how to do it.

The ball was set on the estate of Amund, the oldest vampire in the southern states. One of the oldest in the world, truth be told. Amund sat on the local Assembly, and had for centuries. He didn't have a last name. Or maybe he did, but nobody knew it.

He was the head of the powerful Amund vampire family and he ruled with an iron fist shod in a velvet glove.

I'd once heard that he'd come to America as a Norse explorer, but I don't know if I believe that or not.

He *looked* like a Viking—big and blond; his hair cropped short, penetrating blue eyes under a heavy brow.

This wasn't the first time I'd met Amund, either.

Absently, I reached down and stroked the blade riding in a sheath on my thigh. That job I'd worked? It had been for him. One of the first really *big* jobs I'd ever done.

Amund was…odd. He didn't have that baiting cat-and-mouse attitude many vampires had and the only way I could honestly describe him would be to call him *bored.*

Bored with life, bored with the people around him, just bored.

I guess if you've seen ten or twelve centuries, life gets rather dull.

He moved through the low-lying mist that twined on the ground with grace and control. It wasn't my imagination that people moved out of his path in an unending ballet. Whether they knew it or not, people stepped out of the way for Amund.

Me, I preferred to just *stay* out of his way.

His, and any other bloodsucker.

I don't like vampires. I used to not much care one way or the other, but I've…developed a quirk. I figure I'm entitled.

After all, just under a year ago, one of Amund's cohorts had kidnapped me, dragged me across the country and imprisoned me in a frozen fortress perched on the edge of a mountain.

The vampire's name wasn't on the guest list tonight, and wouldn't be for the next five decades, but I still couldn't breathe easily around vampires. Not all of them were like Jude Whittier, a fact I well knew, but what my brain understood and what my body understood were two different things.

It didn't help that some of the vamps from his house *were* here and I'd received everything from withering stares to knowing smirks.

Feeling eyes on me, I looked up. My skin crawled as I saw another from Whittier House on the edge of the crowd. *Son of a bitch*. If I'd known they were going to play this not-fun game of let's-freak-Kit-out, I think I would have kept my mouth shut when Damon had said something about the ball.

But the vampires were one of the reasons I'd come.

I needed to learn to be around them again without losing it.

The dark-haired vampire looked nothing like Jude, but he wouldn't. They were family in the way vampires were—they'd shared a sire somewhere up the line.

This guy was newer, though.

Newer—and stupid, because he decided to move my way, ignoring the fact that Damon was a towering presence at my side.

My hand dropped to the knife and it was drawn before the vampire had even taken his second step.

Silver—I already knew how much silver was *in* the blade, too. It wasn't pure silver. Few weapons were. It wasn't the best metal for weapons, but if you blended it with steel, it was damn effective. This one was the perfect mix. I could try to shred his heart—a chancy thing with the small blade and a vamp's speed—or...I frowned, watching as somebody slipped between the vampire from Whittier House and me.

It was one of Amund's guards.

Damon's hand slid from my back up to my neck, a light caress—and it was his hand, not that hook.

"Damn," Damon said, sighing almost theatrically as the guard politely—but firmly—escorted the vampire away from me. "I was hoping nobody would notice."

"Poor Damon," I said. My voice sounded rusty. Slipping the knife back into the sheath, I shot him a look.

A faint, cynical smile curled his lips as he followed the path of the two vampires. I could no longer see them, but then I stood five-foot-nothing.

"Kit."

I tipped my head back and met his eyes. There were a thousand questions, a thousand comforts, a thousand promises in that single utterance of my name. He brushed his fingers down my cheek and I caught his hand. "I'm fine."

His lids dropped low, shielding his eyes. He had amazing eyes. Okay, *Damon* was amazing. A powerhouse of a man, he stood a few inches over six feet and he was nothing but muscle from the soles of his feet up. His mixed ancestry was apparent in the pale gold skin, the high slash of his cheekbones. His hair, when he didn't crop it close every few weeks, was inky black and tightly curled. More often than not, his hair was shaved close to his skull, leaving nothing to detract from the arresting power of his face.

His eyes, though, his eyes had always floored me.

Pale gray, ringed with a darker rim of near black, those eyes could cut right through a person. In my case, they could steal the breath from my lungs.

He reached up—the hand with the hook—and the cool silver brushed over my cheek.

"This is...an event," I said, focusing on him instead of letting my gaze slide away to a clutch of vampires gathered in one area.

"Yeah, the Assembly likes their parties," he said, his voice low. "Are you having fun?"

Translation: Do you want to leave?

The nerves inside me screamed, *Hell, yes!*

There were more vampires here than I'd been around in…well, forever.

But there were others, too. The air was bright, a sensation that came from having a large group of witches in one area and there was laughter and low voices on the air.

"I'm good." I forced a smile. I was going to get over this. I *was.*

I was fine—or as fine as I could expect to be.

I looked away from him, concentrating on the ebb and flow of people around us and caught sight of a few vampires, drifting off to follow a path that led through the wispy fog up to the house. Must be dinnertime, I thought before I could stop it.

And I was likely right.

A few minutes later, that group of vampires returned, their eyes glinting with a vivid light, their cheeks with far more color than before.

A few more moved toward that same path as Damon introduced me to a man that all but dwarfed him. His name was Matthew and he was almost as big as Goliath, a friend of mine who lived about an hour south of East Orlando.

But this man didn't have the gentle humor in eyes that Goliath had.

In fact, when he held out a hand for me to shake, I had the impression that he was dissecting me, bit by bit.

"So you're holding the fort up in northern Georgia," I said, as he continued to watch me, expectantly.

"There is no fort," he said, his voice a flat monotone.

"It's an expression." I tugged on my hand and he let go. I resisted the urge to swipe my hand down my abbreviated skirt. His touch was like dry, desert bones—all smooth polish and death.

He continued to watch for a moment and then shifted his attention back to Damon.

As he did, I eyed him narrowly. I had the image of a large, tawny cat, high up in a tree. Ready to drop down on his prey.

Cougar, that quiet voice of mine murmured. *He's a cougar.*

● ● ●

Yeah. That fit. A cougar…and a snake.

Oh, he didn't change into a reptile. There were a few reptilian shifters, but they were all native to the African continent and they didn't like to leave.

"So this is your mongrel pet," Matthew said and the disdain in his voice was so thick, it all but dripped on the floor.

I tensed.

The heat of Damon's fury lashed the air for one split second—and then it was gone.

Pet?

Matthew's eyes cut to me, a smirk on his lips.

Want a reaction?

I smiled. "Meow."

Damon rubbed his thumb across my spine and I moved in closer, partially angling my body toward his. *Don't*, I tried to tell him. I don't know what I was telling him *not* to do, but whatever this piece of shit was up to, it wasn't worth it.

A dark form separated itself from the crowd and came toward us.

I looked away from Matthew to focus on the sleek shadow moving our way.

The death mask he wore covered his face completely. He wore black from head to toe. I couldn't even see skin at his hands—he'd worn gloves as black as his clothing.

But I knew him.

"Wow, Chang. You really went all out for this event," I said, tucking my tongue in my cheek as he slowed to a halt. "You bought a mask to wear with your all-black ensemble."

Chang's black eyes glinted back at me. "I wouldn't wish anybody to waste time noticing me when there are ladies as lovely as you."

Damon's hand flexed. I could feel it where it rested low on back. A subtle tensing of his palm before he relaxed. "Chang." A hard smile curved his lips. "You remember Matthew, don't you? Out of Georgia?"

Chang turned his head, lifted a brow as he studied the other man. Matthew dwarfed him by probably a good foot. Chang was only a couple of inches taller than I was and Matthew pushed seven feet.

And I watched as fine lines formed around Matthew's eyes the moment he locked gazes with Chang.

"Matthew…" Chang narrowed his eyes as he said the name, drawing the syllables out. "Oh, yes. I remember." He gave a sharp smile. "How's the leg?"

Reflexively, I looked down at Matthew's leg.

Damon chuckled as he turned his face into my hair. "Old history. Matthew was trying to climb up the chain before he left the state, years ago. Challenged Chang—got his leg ripped off for his trouble."

A low growl rumbled out of Matthew, but he wasn't looking at me.

"Are we now in the habit of discussing clan business with outsiders?" he asked.

Damon's black brow winged up. With a lazy curl of his lips, he said, "I'm in the habit of discussing whatever the blue fuck I want to discuss. You don't like it…" His arm fell away from my back and I was none too subtly nudged behind him. "There is one way to shut me up."

While the two of them glared at each other, Chang cordially took my arm.

He *was* more subtle about it as he tucked my hand into the crook of his elbow and guided me a few steps—what he must have decided was a safer distance—away. "Kit, you are looking rather lovely. Captain Hook and Tinker Belle fit together surprisingly well."

I glanced back over my shoulder to see that Damon and Matthew were still locked in silent combat.

Matthew would lose. But it still did something to my gut to see my guy out there, this close to what could be a fatal battle if Matthew decided to push it.

Nothing to be done for it. I loved a warrior. This was the cost of it.

Chang's hand covered mine and he squeezed. I looked away.

Forcing my attention away from them, I gave Chang a smile. "I told Damon he should have gone for the Peter Pan look. I'll never recover from missing my chance to see him in green tights."

Chang blinked, looking vaguely disturbed. "Well. I'll never recover from you putting that image in my head." With a sidelong look, he murmured, "Thanks for that."

I laughed. Some of the tension in the air shattered and I realized everybody around us had been holding their breath. In the next moment, conversation resumed. I looked back, but Damon wasn't there.

Neither was Matthew.

That was probably a good thing.

I think.

Feeling eyes on me again, I faced forward and smiled at Chang.

"You're looking well, Kit," he said after a few seconds and I had the distinct impression he'd been studying me, taking me in. Evaluating.

I'd gotten that a lot tonight.

I think people kept expecting me to run or hide or cling to Damon's arm.

It was insulting.

But many of the people here had been present when the Assembly put Jude Whittier on trial. I'd been forced to recount what had happened in front of two dozen strangers and I hadn't held it together well. They'd looked at me and seen a victim.

First impressions are lasting ones and too many of the people here had only that memory of me.

If I could cut that image to shreds, I'd be more than happy to.

A shiver of energy raced up my spine in the next moment and I breathed a sigh of relief as Damon came to stand next to me. Chang relinquished his hold on my hand and I bit back a smile. Chang's manners were more than a little old fashioned.

"Is everything okay?" I asked, pitching my voice low.

He dipped his head and rubbed his cheek against mine. As he did that, he murmured, "Yes. But stay away from Matthew."

"Wasn't planning on asking him for tea and cookies."

"That's because you don't share your cookies."

With a snort, I grinned up at him. He reached up, brushed the back of his knuckles down my cheek.

● ● ●
19

Something warm and sweet shifted inside me under his touch. It had been so long…

Unconsciously, I moved closer and sighed in satisfaction as he slid an arm around my waist.

My skin prickled in response to the nearness of him. It was like standing in the middle of an electrical storm—exhilarating and terrifying.

Keep waiting, I'd told him.

He'd done just that, waiting patiently for me to sort my head out, although I still hadn't done that.

So. Just how did I tell him I didn't want him to just *wait* anymore?

"Should I contact Scott?"

The sound of Chang's polite voice tugged me back to the here and now. Curling one hand into a fist, I closed my eyes. Damon's response rumbled out of him as he answered. I barely heard the words.

Can we just stop the waiting…

"You still have the blade, I see."

I stilled that sound of that voice.

Slowly, I looked up and met Amund's pale eyes—pale like arctic ice under the noon sun. He stood three feet away, head cocked as he studied me.

"Ah…"

His gaze flicked to the knife strapped to my thigh.

"Yes." I managed a polite smile. I fumbled for something to say but came up empty.

Amund took another step toward me. "I apologize for Roberto. He is…young."

Roberto. The vamp from Whittier House. I tucked the name away and inclined my head. Okay, civilities. I could manage that. Probably. "There is no need to apologize."

"He wished to upset you. We both know that." He continued to watch me with penetrating eyes. "Many of Whittier House would see you…upset."

The minute pause sent a spike of fear up my spine. *Upset?* I wondered. *Or dead?*

"Plenty of people have wanted to *upset* me." I let myself pause before the word as well. Then I smiled. "I'm not in the habit of giving people what they want."

His gaze strayed across the room, lingered. "What of the Alpha? Do you give him what he wants?"

"Ah…"

Those pale eyes came back to me. "He's a strong protector to have at your side. It would stand to reason that you would do much to keep him there."

Blood rushed hotly to my face. I don't like to think of myself as hot-tempered—scratch that. I don't like *being* hot-tempered and as I stood there staring at the ancient son of a bitch, I had to swallow down any number of furious replies. "I don't suppose anybody has thought about the fact that I was doing just *fine* on my own *before* I met Damon. *Before* he became Alpha."

"I've thought about the fact." His gaze flicked to the knife once more before returning to mine. "You sound insulted."

"Do I?"

Silence had fallen and none of the people around us even made the attempt to pretend they weren't listening to us. Amund ignored them. I wish I could do it so easily, but the weight of their gazes made me even more uncomfortable.

"I mean no offense," Amund said, lifting a shoulder in a shrug. "It's been something I've wondered about."

"How about you just *ask* what you're wondering about instead of insinuating…whatever you are insinuating?"

Amund offered me a formal half-bow. "It's hardly necessary. It's easy to see you are still your own person, Ms. Colbana."

He straightened and turned, disappearing into the crowd just as Damon emerged from it.

I was petty enough to wish I'd taken the knife Amund had given me and jabbed the son of a bitch with it. It wouldn't kill him. Hurt, yes, but not kill. But you don't pull a tiger's tail if you're not prepared to handle his teeth.

Swallowing, I rubbed at the scars hidden in the tattoos on my neck.

Damon drew even with me, a thunderous look on his face.

I flashed him a brilliant smile. "Wow. Some party, huh?"

The skimpy green dress I wore left little room for anything other than me—and underwear.

The deadly little toys I'd found to accessorize with went rather nicely with my costume and I was pleased to see I wasn't the only one who'd gone that route.

I was also pleased to see that my weapons were the prettiest. The silver band that coiled up my arm had been designed to hide a garrote in the intricate design. This was the first chance I'd ever really had to wear the arm band.

I'd secreted another blade on me, one tucked into a sheath designed to ride between my small breasts. Every time I moved, I felt the cold, reassuring weight of its presence.

I liked them, yes, but I hadn't been prepared to need anything.

After all, we were at a party where the presence of the attendees was like a sting in the air, they were so powerful.

Who would be *stupid* enough to try and get into a fight here?

Answer: *Me.*

In my defense, I hadn't *planned* on the fight.

It was the crazy-eyed shifter who'd crashed into me at the buffet—*she* started it.

The buffet was loaded with everything from raw cuts of meat—for the shifters—to the most beautiful sugar-spun pastries you could imagine. I was staying far away from the area where things were still bleeding and focusing on the sweets. The sparkly little ball of puffy dough should have looked too pretty to eat.

I'd eaten five of them before I could stop myself and was pondering a sixth when she moved in front of me.

She was so close, I could feel the ripple of her energy on my skin—*way* too close and I didn't like it.

I backed up two inches before I realized what I was doing and then I wanted to kick myself.

I already recognized the feel of shifter—and the feel of bitch.

A smug smile curled her lips and I knew I'd just broken one of the cardinal rules when dealing with shapeshifters.

Never back down until they throw you down or your life depends on it.

I could brazen it out, though.

I can brazen my way through anything. With a bright smile, I met her gaze. "Hello."

She just continued to stare.

A chill raced down my spine, but I ignored it and selected another sweet, this one a delicate cake that resembled a miniature pumpkin—complete with the grinning jack o' lantern.

She caught my hand before I could pop the cake in my mouth.

"You weren't raised very well, were you?"

Her voice grated across my nerves.

The words, too, rubbed me raw, but while I can't lie and say I've accepted my less than desirable upbringing, I *had* come to grips with the fact that it wasn't *me* who screwed up.

With an easy smile, I said, "Nope."

Then, moving into her grip, I waited and when her grip slackened just the slightest, I twisted away. People never expect you to move *in* when you're being forcibly restrained.

Once her hand fell away, I backed up—fast.

She'd already tried to grab me again, but now there was five feet between us—and eyes on us.

Instead of advancing, she flared her nostrils and scented the air. "Human," she pronounced and she said it the same way I might say *dead mouse*—with utter distaste.

"Guilty." I gave her a wide grin. "At least, partially guilty. There's something more in the bloodline than just human."

"All that matters is the human," she said, shaking her head. "No wonder you have no manners. I'm curious just what the Alpha sees in you."

A few more gazes slid our way. Most people only glanced out of curiosity before looking away, but more than a few started to watch us and the low murmur of voices in the immediate vicinity went quiet.

"I don't know." I still held my plate. I dragged my finger through the sugary powder that had fallen onto it, and then, still watching her, I popped my finger into my mouth. "Maybe he likes *human*."

"For meat." She all but purred it.

Meat. What the more asshole shifters called those they considered *prey*.

"If that was what he was looking for, I think he would have moved on by now."

"Oh." She gave a condescending laugh. "Precious, it's only pity that holds him. Pity. Fascination. He'll tire of you."

A heavy, familiar tread came to my ears and I knew he was near. Near enough to hear us both and it sent a twist through my gut.

"He'll tire of you," she said again and now she smiled. "You can't even satisfy his hungers now. Your fear is like a stink in the air. You aren't even a woman."

"Alice," a low voice said.

It wasn't Damon.

I didn't bother to look from her to Chang. I just put the plate down and leaned closer.

"Maybe I'm not a *woman*, but at least I'm not a hyena," I said, curling my lip at her.

A low, ugly growl escaped her and I saw Chang catch her arm. "Enough," he said, his voice a biting command. "You will leave."

She tensed, like she'd ignore him, but then she inclined her head.

I saw the promise of retribution in her eyes, though, as she headed down the buffet, her back turned to both me and Chang. That was a look that promised pain.

I guess that's why I wasn't surprised when she circled the far end and slid me a cold smile—then she lunged.

Her body was still melting from human to cat and I caught her, feeling fur sprout and muscles reform and bone break.

It was habit and instinct that had me shoving my forearm into her face. If she wanted a chew toy, the arm was better.

As she sank razored teeth into my arm, I shoved my free hand down and caught the jeweled hilt of my blade.

I tore it from its sheath and twisted my body at the same time.

Her teeth clamped down around my arm. I could feel the pain even as I processed how her body had tensed, ready to shake me like a dog with a bone.

I swung out with the blade and drove it into her neck.

Blood fountained out, and her garbled howl echoed like thunder.

Her body was gone in a moment and I rolled away, coming to my hands and knees—well, one hand.

The other, I cradled against my chest as I shoved upright, staring at the convulsing body on the ground in front of me.

My pulse thudded hard, too loud, and I tensed, well aware of the fact that I was suddenly dripping the very substance some of the guests craved like a druggie needed his next hit.

Four bodies surrounded me and I sucked in a desperate breath.

CHAPTER TWO

When Doyle brushed against my arm, I had to bite back the low whimper of pain that was climbing up my throat.

"Allow me."

I glanced at Chang and then down at my arm.

Part of me wanted to tell him *not here*, but I was oozing blood and all but advertising lunch. I knew none of the vampires were likely to take that offer, but if any of them were lacking on control, I didn't want to be the thing that pushed them over.

Without comment, I held out my arm.

Fabric ripped and I gritted my teeth as something black and soft wrapped around me.

I glanced over and then did a double take when I realized he'd simply shredded his shirt.

Skin like gold-dusted silk stretched over tight, compact muscles as he dealt with my arm. I looked away, breathing through my teeth in order to combat the pain.

A low whine came to my ears and I shifted my attention to Damon just as he ripped the knife from the back of the woman who'd attacked me. "Who is she?" I asked, keeping my voice low.

Chang shook his head. I don't know if that meant *not now* or *I don't know*.

It was a chore to just stand there, breathing shallowly as the pain chewed its way up my arm. Damon leaned down, studying the woman with narrowed eyes. The skin in her throat had yet to start knitting back together. She wasn't a dominant shifter and she wasn't a strong one on any level. The silver would slow the healing. Give her time, though, twenty minutes or so, and she'd be ready to turn me into a chew toy again.

● ● ●

I was damn tired of being bitten.

"Just how quickly do you want to die?" Damon asked.

Her whimper, still wet and thick, wasn't much of an answer.

"Weren't expecting her to know how to handle you, I guess," he said, his voice unsympathetic.

He shot out a hand and I couldn't stifle my flinch at the brutality of his next action. He caught her around the neck, his palm slamming against the silver-wrought wound and squeezing. It would be like shoving blades into the pulp of her throat, the pressure on her wound.

She couldn't even scream now.

"Release her." The word was a harsh growl.

When the cat Damon had introduced me to earlier stepped through the bodies, I wasn't surprised.

Irritated, yes.

But trouble and hate had danced in the air around him. I should have expected *something*.

"Stand down, Matthew, unless you want to catch the bad end of my temper, too," Damon said, his voice flat.

"That's my cat you're abusing," Matthew said with a sneer. "Harm her and I'll file a formal complaint."

Damon looked up then, dangerous humor flicking across his face. "A complaint?" He slid a look toward us, his gaze lingering on me for only a moment before he looked at Chang. "Shit, Chang. He's going to file a complaint. What do I do now?"

"Kill them both?" Chang finished wrapping my arm and looked up with a serene smile that belied the light of battle in his eyes.

"Yeah." Green-gold flashed in Damon's hard, flat stare and he nodded. "I like that idea."

He rose, though, facing the cat across what just might become a battleground.

"Is she yours?" Damon asked gently.

"She is." Matthew inclined his head.

● ● ●
27

"Then I'll make this clear. She attacked the woman I call *mine*." A low growl punctuated the air. "And she did it on *my* turf. If she's lucky, all I'll do is kill her."

"Yours…" Matthew's low, sneering chuckle echoed in the air. "That runt? She was a fool and challenged my companion. If she's injured, then it's because of her own foolishness."

I managed not to drop my jaw, managed not to gape.

I did not, however, manage to be silent.

"Yeah, you're right." When a dozen—no more—gazes flew my way, I held out my arms. "I'm battered and tattered now. Somebody will have to scrape me off the ground here in a minute." Then, with an evil smile, I added, "But I can wait until you're done scraping your…companion off first."

Damon's eyes flashed to me and I saw the demand there.

Be quiet.

I huffed out a breath but looked away as he moved between Matthew and me, cutting me from the other cat's line of sight.

"Your *companion*," Damon said, twisting the word so it fell like a curse from his lips. "Made the first move. If I want her blood for it, I'm clear to take—"

"Enough."

The word was a sliver of death. All but Damon turned to watch as Amund drifted into the circle. And *drift* was the only word for it, for how he moved. He was grace and menace personified.

My gut cramped with fear when I saw the look on his face.

Amund no longer looked bored.

"If she had attacked off my lands, then you would be justified to act as you chose, Alpha Lee," Amund said, his ice-blue eyes avid. "But she did it on my lands. Therefore, I decide what happens."

"Councilor—"

Amund flicked a hand. "Be silent or you'll be removed—with force, Alpha Lee."

Damon's jaw went tight and his dark look promised retribution. Had *I* been in Amund's shoes, I'd be worried.

● ● ●

But Amund wasn't worried.

He looked *amused*.

Raking the fallen woman with a look, he said, "Get up."

Damon came to stand beside me and I felt the tension and anger as it vibrated in the air around him.

So much for our nice, fun night.

The woman rolled to her knees, coughed up blood and then stood.

"Your name."

She lifted her head, but didn't look at Amund.

She stared at me. "Alice. I'm Alice." The words were thick and wet.

"And who do you run with?"

A poetical way to ask what pack or clan a shifter called their own.

"I'm of Matthew Dahl's line," she said calmly.

"The laws were violated. You attacked a non-shifter at a peaceful gathering." He circled around her.

Her gaze never left me.

Where the hell was my knife?

Silver glinted in the pool of red and I could have hit something. It was on the far side of her, where Damon had dropped it.

Son of a bitch.

Amund continued smiling. His voice was soft, but I heard him loud and clear as he said, "The consequences are simple. You die…or accept my challenge."

I let my hand drop. The cool silver of Damon's hook brushed the back of my hand. He'd yet to take it off. Instinctively, I tugged on it. A moment later it was in my hand. I don't know how he did that, but whatever fitted it to his hand was gone.

Amund slid his gaze my way and smiled but his words were for Alice.

"You wanted her death badly enough to risk your own. Kill her and you may live."

Damon snarled.

Hands went to grab me, but I was already moving.

So was Alice.

Time slowed down, dragging to a crawl as I took in everything. Poison still tainted her blood, poisoned her, slowed her down. She rushed in without taking any time to evaluate.

My best weapon lay too far away.

But I had that silver hook—

I spun it around and found that it went on my hand almost like a glove, albeit a large one. The cuff of it concealed the grip buried within where the body of it flowed into a hook.

I closed my hand around it, still watching—

At the last second, I spun to the side.

Silver arced through the night as I slashed the hook across her throat, the wicked tip catching and severing her spinal cord.

Her eyes, wide and shocked, locked on mine. I gave another vicious pull and the light in her eyes died.

The body toppled to the ground, the head connected only by a few strips of meat.

Looking away, I let go of the silver hook.

It fell to the ground as I locked gazes with Amund.

The bastard was *smiling*.

I was offered the use of a shower within the house and clothing.

I refused the shower and used the outdoor guest house to change.

When I emerged, my skin damp from the hurried bath I'd given myself from the sink, the grounds were all but emptied.

Amund stood with his people, while Damon echoed his posture some yards away.

And Matthew lingered.

His eyes burned hate at me as I strode toward Damon. He still wore the waist coat of burgundy and the piratical look suited the thunderous expression on his face.

"I'll see you *dead*," Matthew snarled at me.

"Yeah. She thought so too," I shot back at him even though I knew it was stupid. Alice had been a weak cat. Matthew was stupid but he wasn't weak. "Next time, pick a better fighter."

Damon's hand came up and rested on the back of my neck.

The tension coming off him slammed into me and I managed to bite back the rest of what I was going to say.

It wasn't easy, though.

I was so pissed off, I was shaking.

Literally *shaking*.

"You will be escorted out of Orlando," Amund said, his deep voice cutting through the air as he came to stand between Damon and Matthew. "Alpha Dahl, while I cannot prove it, I believe you were behind this…farce."

Amund looked up then, his eyes seeking me out. He still looked amused.

So glad to have provided your entertainment for the evening, asshole.

His eyes narrowed.

Well, fuck.

If he turned out to be one of the mind readers, then I might have just insulted him. Normally, I'm a little more cautious than that. But normally, I don't have blood leaking from my arm or fever starting to rage through me. Not to mention the temper.

The fury chewing at me had sharp, jagged teeth.

"Master Amund—"

"Do not bother to lie to me," Amund said, turning his head back to stare at Matthew. "I have no desire to listen to whatever inanity you may wish to offer. As I said, I cannot prove you were behind this, but I suspect you were. It would be wise of you to stay out of Florida for the time being."

Matthew's jaw went tight. "We have business with the Assembly in the coming months."

"Send an emissary." Amund waved a hand. "For the next two years, you are banned from my territory."

He smiled then. "I heard that you lost a leg when you fought the Alpha's current second. Face me and you'll lose much, much more…and you'll live long enough to regret your foolishness."

Matthew bowed his head. "Of course. I'm happy to do as the Assembly wishes."

As he straightened, his eyes slid toward me and Damon.

Death lingered there.

"Alpha Lee, I assume you and your men can attend to escorting Alpha Dahl from the territory…safely?"

I whipped my head around to stare at Amund for a long moment.

But…

"Of course."

But…

Crestfallen, I tried not to droop as I stood there. I wanted to, though. I really wanted to.

So much for telling Damon I wanted him to *stop waiting*…like *tonight*.

Chapter Three

It had been almost two weeks since the Halloween party and I hadn't had a good night's sleep since then.

Now, a dark pool of oblivion awaited me, beckoned to me.

I stumbled toward my bed, water still dripping off me from my shower, more exhausted than I could recall feeling in a very long time.

All I wanted was my bed.

Okay, Damon lounging in my bed—naked—would be better, but as long as I had my bed and silence for the next five hours straight, humanity could survive.

I crashed facedown onto it and lost the world.

I don't remember anything until a long, loud wolf whistle split the air.

I grunted and twisted away from the noise.

It came again, along with the sound of my name.

Shoving my head under a pillow, I tried to escape, but that didn't help because the pillow—and my blankets—were jerked away.

Only my speed kept me from crashing onto the floor, the way that son of a bitch ripped the bedclothes out from under me.

"Kit, I gotta say, you're still one of the most gorgeous women I've ever met."

"Justin." I said his name through gritted teeth as I glared at him through my hair. "I'm going to kill you. Slowly."

He held out his hands. "Hey…I'm here on a mission of mercy. I need your help. Also, you weren't answering your door." Something grim flashed through his eyes. "I was worried."

"Justin. I'm going to kill you," I said again. "*Slowly.*"

He chuckled and moved to the end of the bed. "Well, you might want to get dressed before you do it."

A shirt came flying my way and I snatched it out of the air. Since I didn't want to commit murder naked, I pulled it on. I looked at the clock. I'd gotten three of the five hours I needed in order to recover from the job from hell.

"Have you been in town long?" I asked conversationally.

"Yep. Got back two days ago."

Justin's been in and out of the area for the past few months. We work together when he's here—sometimes—but he's been gone a lot. I think he's searching down leads and info on the hospital—a.k.a. *prison*—where he'd once been told he'd go if he didn't be a good little soldier and fight the good fight.

It's not much of a hospital.

It's the human version of the roach motel for us—we go in; we don't come out.

I'd ask him later if he'd learned anything. He'd beat around the bush. We had a rhythm. But for now… Shoving my hair back, I pinned him with a direct look. "Have you paid any attention to the media lately?"

"Yeah." He twisted his dreads back into a long, heavy knot, leaving his too-pretty face unframed. "Some sick schmuck was actually acting out some of those old horror movies. Been at it for years, sounds like. He's done…son of a *bitch*." He planted his hands on his hips and stared at me. "That was you."

I gave him a tight smile. "I haven't slept in three days."

"How did you do it?"

"Nova." I shrugged. "He knew who the guy had picked out for this year and he called me."

Nova was a psychic—and psychotic with it. I'd once accepted a job to kill him, only to discover the guy who needed to die was the one who'd ordered the hit on him. So that's what I'd done. *Assassin* isn't one of the jobs I advertise, but I can, and have, killed.

The man I'd killed last night was a man who'd needed to die in the worst way.

He was also human, so if I was ever discovered, I had a one-way ticket to the chopping block—any NH discovered to have murdered a human gets the guillotine, assuming the non-human community doesn't deal with the offender on their own. Losing the head is the surest way to kill any NH—and it's bloody and spectacular. I think that's why humans do it. We have teeth and claws and magic and they have giant silver blades.

"He was human," Justin said, echoing my thoughts.

"Only on the outside." I shrugged. "He was a monster, through and through." Smiling thinly, I added, "The media is hailing his suicide as an act of cowardice. No doubt the victim who'd somehow escaped would have been able to identify him."

"She says an angel saved her." Justin's eyes gleamed now. "You got wings I can't see, Kit?"

I flipped him off.

He laughed and dropped down on my bed.

I frowned.

He lifted a brow. "Problem?"

"Damon's coming over tonight."

Now Justin grinned and laid back on the bed, linking his hands together behind his head and stretching out.

Sighing, I rubbed the back of my neck.

"Are you trying to make me hurt you?" I asked. "Because trust me, I'm frustrated enough to do you a lot of damage."

Frustrated didn't touch it.

My plans of inviting Damon back home after the Halloween Ball had fallen through and he'd spent the next few days dealing with some sort of clan politics. It turned out that the clan in northern Georgia *seriously* had business—the kind that came with a major *B*— that needed to be discussed with the Assembly and now that Matthew wasn't allowed in the area, they were fumbling to come up with a plausible arrangement, because Amund wasn't rescinding the ban. And nobody could *make* the millennia-old vampire rescind it.

All of it made my head spin. If I thought about it too long, I'd have a migraine. All I wanted was *one night* with my guy. One night.

Then, just when I was thinking I'd go join him at the Lair, I got the call from Nova.

It had taken almost a week of running leads down before I'd managed to find the woman Nova had seen in his vision and I almost hadn't made it in time.

I hadn't seen Damon in nearly two weeks.

I hadn't had sex in so long, I didn't even want to think about it.

And Justin was doing one thing guaranteed to make Damon's brain shut down.

"You know, this is what happens when you hook up with a shifter, Kit," Justin said, pushing up onto his elbows. His black T-shirt rode up, baring his flat belly. "The animal kicks in too easily, shuts down the brain. Now, me? If we were still together, I wouldn't be all that worried if your bedroom smelled like another man."

"That's because you can't scent another man in my bedroom, you asshole."

He shrugged. Crossing his feet at the ankle, he said, "He knows we're done. I just—*hey!*"

Justin glared at me from the floor.

I let go of his ankles and smiled.

"You were saying?"

He cocked his head. "Well, the view is nicer from down here."

"You're ridiculously juvenile," I said. Shaking my head, I turned away. Since he clearly wasn't leaving, I needed to get clothes on.

After grabbing my gear, I ducked into the bathroom.

"You're sure you didn't leave any signs behind?"

"Justin...I'm not new at this." Dressing in short order, I moved out of the bathroom to find him at the window. He was staring outside, arms crossed over his chest. "Don't worry so much."

"It's my job," he said easily. Then he turned around. "So...speaking of jobs..."

"Disappearances."

My gut clenched as I said it. Sometimes Justin came to me with jobs that were just a walk down easy street. Other times, they fell into the *what the bloody hell* category.

We were in the *bloody hell* zone. I knew it without asking even a single question.

We were no longer alone in my apartment.

Padraig, a witch both Justin and I knew, had joined us and he sat on my sofa, his dreamy blue eyes cold and hard as he stared back at me. "Aye, a fair amount of them, too."

"Are they…" I hesitated, choosing the words carefully. Over the past couple of months, there had been some odd happenings. One small wolf pack had been all but eradicated and the survivors claimed they'd been attacked by friends—by their own *Alpha*, one who'd gone missing some months earlier.

There were rumors of several small Houses—witches who worked and lived and trained together—facing similar attacks. One house—a strong one, though somewhat small—was gone. Every witch who'd lived inside the walls of that House had disappeared.

I rubbed my temple and met Justin's gaze.

His eyes were hard and flat and his face was haggard.

"You're still digging into things about the hospital," I said. "Is this connected or is it something different?" My mind veered down a particular road…*something different*. It left me cold. I'd worked a *something different* before.

Damon's adoptive son, Doyle had been kidnapped. That was how we'd met, when he'd hired me to find the boy. We'd found him, but I still saw the echoes of nightmares in Doyle's eyes.

We hadn't been able to save everybody, though. And they'd been kids. Teenagers, most of them Doyle's age.

"We don't know," Paddy said in response to my question. "These disappearances, there are no reports of violent echoes, like what was discovered in the Clearwater House."

I looked away as he spoke. Clearwater had been the home of that one House. A House they now called silent. No surviving witches.

"These are all random disappearances, too," Justin said. "No connections."

"How many?"

"A fair number, I'm afraid. I know two witches personally," Paddy said, leaning in. "One was a mate of mine. The other…I didn't know her, but I knew of her. She wasn't the sort to just disappear and she's gone. Both of them, just gone. I've heard of others, though. Clearwater, then this…it's enough to make a man worry, Kit."

"Are we talking five? Ten?"

Padraig sighed and reached up, rubbing at his face. For a moment, he pressed the tips of his fingers against his eyelids, hard. "I talked to an old friend at Banner. They've been watching, although watching is all they are doing. They've had thirty reports…of witches."

"What aren't you saying?"

When Paddy didn't answer, Justin did. "Other NHs have gone missing. This is some of the information I've been tracking. Lone shifters, they just disappear. One small pack in Alabama—it's like Roanoke. No survivors. I've even heard tales of a few vampires here and there."

He hesitated and then added, "The most recent vampire disappearances have been from here. One of them was Roberto Whittier."

I tensed.

Justin looked down at his hands, palms facing each other, fingertips pressed together. "I heard you two almost rubbed shoulders not too long ago."

"I wouldn't call it that," I said softly. "He was trying to stare me down at the Assembly's Halloween thing. It didn't go very far. He was asked to leave and…" I shrugged. Blowing out my breath through my teeth, I shoved my hands into my pockets. "He's missing."

"Yeah."

Somebody is nabbing vampires?

"How is that even possible?" I stared hard at them. "Vampires have that whole hive-mind thing going."

Justin smiled. "It's not a hive-mind thing, Kit."

"Close enough." Wrapping my arms around my middle, I looked away. Vampires were connected to every member of their blood family. It was a distant connection, but if they chose to reach out, they could. If one of them was in a blood frenzy or maybe out trying to turn an entire town into their personal feeding ground, the family, as a whole, could, and sometimes had, worked together as unit to bring the lone vampire down. Nature's—or maybe Pandora's—protection against that particular species wiping out too much of its food supply and therefore going extinct

* * *

itself.

Vampires weren't a compassionate race, but they were a cunning one. Sometimes they had bad eggs. Bad eggs didn't bode well for them. Sadly, *their* idea of a bad egg and everybody *else's* idea of bad egg didn't exactly align.

"We have a…contact," Justin said. "He doesn't exactly work for Banner, but he's been known to take on contracts and he gets good intel. I've spoken to him."

Without turning my head, I slid my gaze back to him. "A vampire."

He didn't answer that, just continued on with what he was saying. "He's in the line of one of the missing bloodsuckers. He says there's just a disconnect."

I shook my head and frowned. "A disconnect?"

"Yep." He looked around and then grabbed the notepad on the corner of my coffee table. "Here."

Justin sketched out a series of circles, connecting them by lines. It reminded me of…well, of a chemical formula more than anything else. Inside the circles, instead of elements, he'd scrawled names. A few of them, I recognized. Most of them didn't cause much reaction, other than my now-instinctive dislike of vampires, but others would have made my heart lurch in fear, if I had allowed it.

"This is the direct line and the closest relation for my contact."

I saw the name. Immediately, my spine stiffened. Allerton.

Abraham Allerton.

"I know him," I said softly.

Paddy looked up as Justin continued his sketch. "D' ya now? He's not a bad man to have at your back in a fight."

"I'd rather stick a knife in my own back," I muttered.

Justin looked up and met my gaze then. Jamming my hands into my pockets, I averted my eyes. It took another thirty seconds before I was sure I had the wild fear inside me under control, but thirty seconds was better than thirty minutes—and I hadn't even broken out into a sweat or had a panic attack this time.

"I'm waiting on the lecture, Professor," I said, my tone coming off more caustic than normal.

Justin just nodded after moment. "This. It's the direct line," he said again, and then he drew a circle around Abraham's name. "I've known Abraham for going on…I guess fifteen years now. One of the first vampires I ever had more than a five second conversation with—most of them, I'd just as soon shove wood through, but he's not a bad one."

Maybe one day I'd get over the dislike and fear Jude had bred into me. Today wasn't that day.

I continued to stare at the lines and circles and names, so hard they started to blur together. Paddy crouched down next to Justin and reached out. "This is the missing vampire," he said as Justin continued to watch me. "His name is Icarus. He's two generations ahead of Abraham."

Justin looked back down, watched as Paddy tapped another name on the sheet of paper before him. The name went red, standing out from the rest of the ink. "This is Jedidiah Allerton—he was the first of the Allerton line to settle here."

The way vampire 'families' worked was confusing as hell. Some decided to adopt a new name when they came over—that seemed especially common if they'd been leaving a particularly pathetic or sickly life, or if they'd just had a really lame name—but one thing *all* of them did was adopt a second surname. They took on the name of the familial line who'd sired them.

It was their protection, their status, their identification in their world.

The Allerton vampire family went back centuries and they had sects in several places in North America and the United Kingdom. They weren't a large sect here in Florida, but their name was a powerful one. Powerful enough that I didn't see people fucking with them just to fuck with them. Maybe they weren't on par with the Amund family, but they weren't small fish, either.

I studied Jedidiah's name as I riffled through my mental file, trying to figure out if there was anything else I knew about them. Well, other than the fact that Damon had offed somebody in the line before.

"Jedidiah was sired about the same time as this woman—Ruth." Padraig tapped another name and the woman's name flared and became a paler, less vibrant shade red and then, slowly, the line lit up and it trailed its way down to Icarus—the name Justin had initially pointed out.

• • •
40

"So, from Icarus, up through all the vampires between him and Ruth, then to Jedidiah, then down from him and all the vampires made between him and Abraham," I said slowly.

Paddy winked at me. "Remember—the connection between Ruth and Jedidiah is that they were created by the same vampire—not sure, but I think his name might have been Charles. But, yeah…that's the connection."

"I've got a headache just thinking about it." I rubbed my temple. "How do they live with everybody in their heads all the time?"

"It's a matter of shuttin' the doors," Paddy said with a shrug. "Remember, this is a species that loses bits and pieces of their souls over time. The connection to the younger ones helps the older ones stay grounded, while the control from the older ones helps the younger not to get lost in the blood frenzy. Truly, if they weren't made like this, think of the slaughter they'd do. It's what keeps them sane—or as close to sane as we can expect them to be."

But too many of them *weren't* sane—that was the problem. Paddy was busy staring at the diagram and didn't see me as I reached up, rubbed the scars hidden under the ink on my neck.

Justin did, though.

Curling my hand into a fist, I lowered it back to my side. "So, about Icarus?" I asked.

Justin reached out and stroked a finger over Icarus' name.

The lines connecting him to everybody else vanished. His name was still there, but he was cut adrift.

"There's a disconnect," he said again, but the words seemed…grimmer. And I studied the diagram. There had been lines and links and connections under him. The ones that were higher up remained solid. But there were a few, farther down, that were fainter—and the very bottom line of names were *vibrating*. As I watched, Paddy flipped the diagram, so that the older, stronger vampires were the ones on the bottom of the odd little family tree. "Once a vampire has a few decades on him—or her—they're old enough and strong enough for that feedback to start supporting the young ones. Usually, the smaller lines are the ones where you tend to see more…trouble children."

I flicked him a look.

That was such a polite term for *psychotic killer*. But he was right. If a newly turned vamp was going to go batshit, more often than not, it happened with the smaller houses—this made sense. I knew this, in general, but the *why* of it? I'd only speculated.

"So they all actually need each other for survival—or at least sanity," I said softly.

"That or a fresh supply of warm bodies," Paddy said. I think he liked vampires about as much as I do. "Blood, they can get by on synthetic, but they need that other mental connection. Now, Icarus was how they originally noticed their problem. Even though all vampires can *make* other vampires, some are just better suited. They are stronger and can anchor a new one better—few people outside the families know it, but that's what they call the better ones—*anchors*. See how some of these names will have a few offspring, while others have double or triple? The ones with the higher numbers are anchors. Icarus was an anchor. When he disappeared, the youngest in his line lost stability." Padraig tapped what I assumed was a younger vamp—he was at the far end of the spectrum from old Jedidiah himself—the father of the local Allerton house.

"This boy." A sneer curled his lips. "He decided he wanted to be called Spike."

Slowly, I looked up. "Spike."

"Yeah." He shrugged. "You have to admit, it's better than Vlad."

"Is he at least blond and hot?"

"As you're my version of blonde and hot, love, I'm not a good judge." Paddy grinned.

Justin chuckled.

Paddy ignored my dark look and went back to his explanation. "Now, our boy Spike won't be watching Buffy or anything else for a good long while, assuming that's where he picked out his name, assuming he survives. Assuming anything. Back to Spike and Icarus—Icarus was pretty choosy about who he brought over, but his offspring, less so and it devolved from there. It's not uncommon."

● ● ●

He looked up at me. "During the war, vampires were hit hard—they won't give up numbers, but some estimate they lost hundreds of thousands at the minimum. Population estimates are hard to pinpoint. Roughly, we figure the world population of vampires, before the war was about two million. The war wiped out a quarter of that, at least. Vampires hunt alone, but they rarely travel or live alone. So as things settled down, they went about rebuilding their numbers fast."

It made sense. In a way. "So they were looking for quantity over quality?"

"In a sense." Paddy looked back at his sketch. "Spike had only been dead about thirty years, would have been among the first to be brought over. He's quiet, low key. A drone, basically. Then he loses it. Was driving through Orlando and apparently the hunger hit him. He went after a woman—mortal—and the only reason the she's alive and Spike doesn't have an EOS on his ass is because there was a shifter in the same area. The wolf—one of Dair's—grabbed him before Spike could lock his teeth on the girl and he threw him through a plate glass window. Then he gave chase and ran him back across the boundary into East Orlando."

I rubbed my brow, wondering when all of this had gone down. Well, since the EOS—execute on sight—hadn't gone out, Allerton House had probably been able to keep it contained.

Justin cut in. "For his trouble, the wolf had to spend a day in custody and he was fined for destroying the window. The girl intervened on his behalf, though. She's with that activist group, TAP2. I think the cops let him out just to shut her up."

TAP2—I wanted to groan. The group was a pain in the ass—granted more for human authorities and the anti-NH groups out there than for us, but sometimes they just *got in the way*. TAP2 was short for *They Are People, Too*—and guess who the *they* is?

I don't guess anybody bothered to explain to them how insulting that was, but what can you do?

"Okay. Dair's wolf got let out, Spike is on the run, Abraham went after him, and...?"

"Spike is under lock and key." Padraig's voice was grim. "From what I'm hearing, nobody can reach him. If they can't find Icarus, it could be years before he's stable enough on his own."

"Years?" I hissed out a breath, my gut twisting as a wave of nausea hit me. *Years?* Held as a prisoner? Memories tried to assault me, but I shoved them back. Spike's confinement was for different reasons—and he hadn't been brought in solely for some psychotic asshole's amusement. Still…

Softly, I said, "He'd be better off dead."

"He chose to get bitten. He had inoperable brain cancer—one thing humans still can't fix. He had a fifteen percent chance of surviving the bite and according the information I read up on him, the drugs were making him sicker every day." Justin shrugged. "Death isn't an option for some people. Now…"

The word trailed off and we all looked at his name.

Abruptly, Justin grabbed the sheet of paper and wadded it up. He threw it into the kitchen and I heard the recycler kick on, chewing up the bit of paper. "Nice aim," I said absently. "So this guy loses it and they figure it out then?"

"Basically." He shrugged. "It's all about that door—the one Paddy told you about. Vampires keep their mental doors closed. The feedback they need from each other is subconscious. They have to actively seek each other out otherwise. When they started tracking up this guy's line to find out why he went unstable, they couldn't find Icarus."

"Nobody reported him missing?"

"Nope." Justin settled back on the couch, his face grim. "Apparently, he's known to go into seclusion for short periods. The vamps he's closest to, his servants, they all assumed he'd taken some *me* time."

Puffing up my cheeks, I blew out a breath. "Okay." I thought back to what Justin had said just a minute or so back. *Death isn't an option for some.* Blocking back the fear that tried to build up inside, I stared hard at the name of the missing vamp. "So this…anchor is gone. How do they know he's not dead?"

"They'd feel it." Paddy's gaze came back to me. "There's not a *void* there. It's a disconnect. A death feels different, and they can adjust. It's how they work. The power flow works around it—the same way a river would adjust to rocks pilling up to block the flow—or those rocks being yanked out the way. They'd adjust—stronger vampires would feel and stabilize the younger ones. But there was no warning, no backlash, no surge to warn them of Icarus' disappearance so nobody knew to stabilize the younger ones."

"Are they looking for him?"

Paddy nodded. "Abraham's been off on a search for over a month." He gave me a thin smile. "That was when I heard about this—for the record, his hunts have never lasted more than a week. He's just that good."

"You sound jealous."

Paddy chuckled. "I can't help but admire the man's skill. But…" He sighed. "I like having a pulse."

"A pulse is nice." Brooding, I stared down at the floor. "Is it the same with the vamp from Whittier?"

"Nope." Justin flicked me a look. "That one's dead. Missing—but dead. Isaac Whittier reported his disappearance and subsequent death to the Assembly three days ago."

"No idea where he is?"

"Just that he's dead. They all felt it. Nobody lost it, though, from what I heard." Justin shrugged and rose to pace. When he passed by me, there was speculation in his eyes, but I pretended not to notice. I hadn't killed the idiot. If I was going to kill a vampire, it would be for something more important than him staring at me.

"Any guess on how many shifters have gone missing?" I asked, focusing on the next matter.

"That's harder to say. And…." Paddy's brown eyes moved to Justin.

Justin had stopped by the wall, studying my weapons, but when I shifted my attention to him, he looked at me.

Arms crossed over his chest, he pinned me with a hard, direct stare.

"You're not the only one who's been in touch with Nova lately, Kit. I hear tell a couple of cats went missing in Georgia." His eyes gleamed. "I need you to talk to Chang for me."

I gaped at him.

"*What?*"

Justin shook his head. "He won't talk to me, you know that. All I need is some concrete info on where they were, where they were going and I can move forward. *We* can move forward."

"You woke me," I said slowly. "You came here and woke me up all so I could go and talk to Chang?"

"Well, no. I woke you up because we need you on the job." He gave me a charming smile and added, "Come on, Kit. He'll talk to you. You know he will."

"No." Hands on my hips, I glared at him. "I *don't* know that."

He cocked a brow.

I shoved my hands threw my hair.

He was wrong. Mostly. I didn't know that Chang would talk to me. I think he would if he *could*.

Justin, though, was shit out of luck. Chang would toy with him the same way he'd toy with any other outsider.

CHAPTER FOUR

Chang had a last name but nobody used it.

Although, to be honest, not that many people used his name at all. Chang was one of those men who got *yes, sir'ed* and *no, sir'ed* unto death. Half the people who talked to him met his eyes for all of five seconds before looking deferentially down at the floor, hands folded meekly in front, or tucked away behind in a military fashion.

He was a shapeshifter, but I'd yet to figure out what.

That was one thing that drove me insane.

I could usually peg a shifter's animal within minutes—sometimes within seconds—but Chang had me stumped. He was some sort of cat because he was one of Damon's lieutenants, but I had absolutely no idea *what* kind and it both annoyed and intrigued me.

I was pretty sure he knew this—and I was equally sure it amused him.

At any given time, Chang could be found at the rec center. When I pulled up in front of the place, one of his men was already moving to meet me. I didn't bother asking if Chang was around. Of course he was.

I don't think he slept here, but any time I'd come looking for him, he was here. It wasn't really a picture that fit, this elegant man presiding over the rough and rowdy lot of shapeshifter children, but over time, I'd come to realize why.

Chang was the self-appointed guardian of the reckless shapeshifter youth in the city. The rec center was a place where both the wolves and the cats hung out, although there were more cats than wolves. The cat clan outnumbered the wolves almost two to one here, but the relationship between the two factions was guardedly friendly, more so in the past year and a half since the previous cat Alpha had died.

Most shifter parents kept their youngest close to home—close and protected—but as they got older, the youth became...restless. It wasn't just the hormones that any teenager would face—they had *those* hormones, plus the hormonal surges that would eventually precipitate the change that led to their first shift between their human forms and their animal one.

The aggression would come spilling out, but it rarely came coupled with common sense.

The club was a safe place for them to let all of that aggression out, without getting into trouble.

It was also a place where they would be protected.

I'd never seen less than fifteen dominant shifters on guard here. That was practically a platoon in human terms.

One of those guards had escorted me to Chang's office—I'd been surprised when I'd seen her. I'd been here too often and in all my visits, I'd never seen a wolf standing guard at the gate. It was unusual enough to have me questioning Chang about it—or I would as soon as he got off the phone.

His conversation was inaudible, which told me he was speaking to a shifter.

He had yet to give anything other than a polite nod and smile when I came inside, but that didn't mean anything. I'd *like* to think it meant he wasn't talking to Damon and saying something like: *Oh, shit, she's here and asking questions, what do I do?* Actually, I was almost positive Chang wouldn't ask anything like that, but something more…urbane? *Kit is here. If she starts asking questions we don't want to answer, do I stonewall her or just wait for you to arrive?*

Another three minutes passed before he wrapped up the conversation, but I didn't let it get to me. He was the second in command of one monster group of shapeshifters. Clan business would always come before anything else. He tugged the earpiece out and gave it a distasteful look before putting it away and rising from the desk. I rose to meet him as he came to stand in front of me.

"Hello, Kit."

"Chang." I cocked my head. "Sorry to crash in like this…sounded like serious stuff. Am I interrupting?"

Chang had an innate courtesy. He'd brush it off. *Of course not. How are you, would you like some tea—*

• • •

To my surprise, the only response he made initially was to sigh.

It was a soft, heavy sigh, one that carried a world of weariness. "I had to call a family up north with grim news. An awful sort of call to make."

"I…" I stopped for a moment. "I'm sorry. Are there…problems?"

An odd question to ask, maybe, but the look on Chang's face wasn't one that spoke of somebody who'd lived to see a ripe old age and then died peacefully in his sleep.

From the corner of his eye, he watched me. There was a strange expression to his features, as though he wanted to say something, but then he sighed and said, "No. Sit. I'll fix tea. You'll tell me why you're here."

There was no point in arguing.

Chang had fallen back on his role of courtesy.

There was no getting out of it now—and no chance of tugging out any details about that phone call, either.

I waited until I had my tea in hand—tea was a personal addiction of mine, almost as bad as the soaps and lotions and other girly things I bought obsessively. Breathing in the sweet and spicy scent, I sighed. I doctored it with sugar and cream. I liked my tea, with just a little more sugar than most people. Or a *lot* more sugar.

"How you can drink it that way confounds me," Chang said. "I keep trying to break you of that habit, but it doesn't work."

"To each their own." I shrugged and took my first sip. Perfect.

Chang had a look of amusement and revulsion on his face.

"When you spend a good ten years of your life scrapping just to get enough water and food to fill the hole in your belly, you develop odd cravings." I shrugged it off.

Chang's eyes fell away.

I scowled inwardly, wished I hadn't said anything. I'd dealt with more abuse in my life than most people had ever heard of—I'd come to grips with what my family had done and generally dealt with it, in my own unique sort of way.

Sometimes, I was even able to not be ashamed of it. But it made other people uncomfortable. Honestly, that's just plain stupid to me—it happened to *me*—if I can deal with it, then why can't they?

But then I had to deal with people looking away, or lapsing into silence…or just…fading away.

"Sorry," I said, my voice tense.

"Why?" Chang said quietly.

I stared at him, opened my mouth—then snapped it shut. "Fuck it. Never mind."

But he was too insightful, by far. Unlike many shifters I knew, he didn't just go by what his senses told him. He *looked* at people. Saw beneath the surface. Sometimes, he saw so deep, it pissed me off.

"I'm not aggravated with you for speaking of your childhood," he said softly. "In a way, it…humbles me. I know you don't always speak freely of your past, Kit."

He rose.

The languid way he moved couldn't be called pacing, not by any means.

But Chang rarely made wasted moves and the way he moved from the window at the back of his office to his wall of weapons then to his desk to straighten the non-existent clutter there before repeating the circuit was nothing *but* wasted movement. And it was done with all the elegance, grace and speed he did everything else with. "At the same time, the thought that any soul could treat a child as I know you were treated makes me…"

He looked up.

For the first time in all the time I'd known him, I saw a faint glow roll across his eyes.

The flash was gone so fast, I couldn't even place it—just a glow of color too light to belong in that dark gaze, and then it was gone. "It angers me. Children should be treasured."

"That's how the world works sometimes."

His eyes held mine. "And sometimes, the world sucks."

"I've found myself thinking that a lot lately."

"Yet another reason I like you, Kit. You are a wise woman."

At that, I snorted. "I'm a lot of things—wise isn't one of them."

He chuckled and the tension in the air passed. He returned to his seat and faced me. "Let's discuss why you're here. Not that I'm not delighted to see you, of course."

He'd never say it, but I suspected he had things to do, secrets to pass on and people who needed to kill or be killed.

That was his job, after all.

Since I respected that, I didn't beat around the bush.

"I'm tracking down—or trying to track down—some information. I could use your help."

He arched a brow as he lifted his tea cup to his lips.

He'd help if he could. I knew that. Just like I knew he'd stonewall me if he couldn't.

"NHs are disappearing. I need to know about any shifters who have gone missing...specifically some in Georgia. I need information and if anybody has it, it's you."

The cup froze at his mouth.

Without taking a sip, he lowered it. Then he put it down and moved behind his desk to stare out the window. "Who have you been talking to, Kit?"

I started to move my knee back and forth. "Am I going to sound terribly childish if I say I asked you first?"

"Sound as childish as you want. But you're more likely to get answers from me if you cooperate." His eyes narrowed ever so slightly. Then a faint smile appeared on his face. "You can always ask Damon. However, if you wanted to do that, you would have. You often end up in messes that worry him, a fact I'm sure you're aware of. This is likely why you came to me instead."

"You're telling me this because..." I drummed my fingers on the arm of the chair as I stared at him.

"Only two people possess the information you're looking for—or possess an in-depth knowledge of it. That *I* know of. Damon hasn't spoken to you—he wouldn't, not about this. If somebody has spoken to you..." He let the words trail off.

"If you're worried my source might be behind these disappearances, you can draw your claws back in, Chang."

"My claws aren't out." A brow lifted. "Yet."

"I'm terrified," I said dryly. Putting my tea down, barely touched, I moved to the wall. Giving into the urge, I closed my hand around the grip of the katana. "May I?" Even I heard the wistful note in my voice.

"I've been wondering how long it would take you to ask."

I looked over my shoulder at him.

He inclined his head. "By all means. I enjoy blades but I hardly do them justice."

A thrill raced through me, muted because I couldn't hear the katana's song. My race has an…affinity for weapons. They speak to us, sing to us, murmur in the backs of our minds like treasured friends. But the bond I'd had with my sword had been shattered by a witch back when Jude had kidnaped me. Yet another thing to hate the bastard for.

There was an odd, empty void at the back of my head. I'd been aware of it for a while now. At first, when the weapons hadn't whispered to me, I'd only felt an ache and I don't think that was physical. Just something I felt with all my soul.

This void, though, I'd almost swear if you looked inside my skull, you'd see some tiny, pinprick of emptiness.

I'd grown used to it, though, and I was able to swing the blade through the air, smiling at the weight, the balance. "He was made by hand, wasn't he?"

"Yes. By a true master of the art."

I swung it again and again until it became a blur in front of me. Through it, I could see Chang's eyes on me.

"I relieved him of the blade when he tried to use it to relieve me of my head."

I stopped, mid-swing, and stared at him.

Chang cocked his head, something that might have been feral amusement dancing in his eyes. "It was almost a shame to kill him—he was nearly as good at using blades as he was at crafting them. He had a feel to him like your friend, Justin. Some sort of magic in his blood. Might have been why he almost succeeded in his mission."

"An assassin?"

"I have my suspicions. Never could confirm them, but as I was hunting down certain people who didn't want certain secrets revealed, it made sense." He moved to stand in front of me, holding out his hand.

I held the katana out in front of me, balanced on my palms.

He took it, angled it so that it reflected the light back at us. "Tell me what's going on, Kit. I can't help you unless I know more."

"How do you know I'm not trying to help *you?*"

He studied me and I had the impression he might be praying for patience—or counting to ten. Or ten thousand.

"Why don't we help each other?" he suggested after a moment. "I'll tell you what I can, after you tell me what I need to know."

"Damn cats." I'd muttered this to myself more times than I could recall ever since a certain one of those damn cats had strolled through the door of my office. As Chang's dark eyes glinted at me, I turned away. I settled down in the chair I'd vacated, watched as he continued to angle the blade, studying it as though it held the answer to some great mystery. "My *source*, or sources, if you want to call them that, are a couple of witches."

"Ah…" Chang's nostrils flared. "And how is Justin?"

"Causing trouble."

With a gleam in his eyes, Chang said, "Then he is well. And the other…source?"

"A friend of ours, a witch by the name of Padraig. He's affiliated with Banner. We trust him."

"You trust him. Under many circumstances, that would count for a lot," Chang said.

"I've trusted him with my life."

Chang turned to face me now and the blade, he studied me, eyes narrowed. "I'm still listening."

Hard ass.

"Justin needs my help on a case…the missing NHs in Georgia. He says there

• • •
53

are some cats missing—and he's got good, solid info." I was winging it here—I hoped Chang wouldn't push, because Justin hadn't told me what Nova had told him. "But he needs confirmation and as much information as he can get before we go in."

"Go in." Chang's eyes narrowed and he leaned forward. "The three of you plan to *find* them?"

"You're smart. I admire that about you." I smiled, hesitated for a moment and then sighed. I leaned forward as well and met his eyes. "Look, witches are disappearing, too."

Something flashed in his eyes. He waited.

"We're hearing the same about vampires."

When he didn't say anything, I got up and started to pace. I found myself thinking of that time, more than a year ago, when I'd found myself standing in here, looking to interview one of the young cats. That was how I'd gotten dragged into the world—I'd only danced along the edge of shifters then, taking courier jobs, and I'd been just fine with that, too. Shifters were *trouble*. Especially the cats, although then, it had been because their Alpha had been crazy.

That case that had brought me here had changed my life. Most times, I think it was for the better. But when my nightmares screamed too loudly, I have to admit, I do wonder what would have happened if I'd just told Damon to take his case and shove it up his ass. Then I choked on the guilt.

"It's not like the games," I said softly, finding myself at the window where Chang often stood. "Padraig and Justin knew some of the witches that have gone missing. A couple were warrior-born. Tough bastards. One witch of Justin's skill could stand against a platoon of human soldiers if you put him in the right place." I paused and then said again, "It's not like before."

"No."

I turned to see Chang standing just inches away.

His face was grim. "It's not."

He gave me five names, five dates, five routes. I noted them all down on a piece of paper while he gave me the stats and other information that wasn't on the computer.

The latest was going through Georgia—via Atlanta—and the cats who'd gone missing had been seen there.

"She was the most recent," he said quietly, bringing up a picture of a trim brunette. He looked up at me. "She went missing only five days ago. She could still show up in Orlando, but it's not looking good. The others, however, are officially counted as missing."

I studied the woman on his datapad. Shanelle Maguire. "Why was she coming here?"

"Several reasons." Chang looked back at the screen. "I'm sure you recall the unpleasantness at the Ball. Shanelle is from the clan in northern Georgia. They call themselves the Claw, by the way." He smiled, as if it amused him.

"The Claw." It made me roll my eyes. "Sounds like a cheesy TV superhero villain."

"Doesn't it?" The smile faded as he hit a key. The image faded out of view, replaced by a stark, staggering display of mountains, the sun rising up low over the mists. I don't know where that picture had been taken, but the beauty staggered me.

"Shanelle had dual goals when she announced her intentions to come to East Orlando. She'd volunteered her services for business that is ongoing between the Assembly and the Claw." He paused and then added, "And she has petitioned Damon to rejoin the clan once her job for her current alpha is complete. She lived here years ago, but left. There were…reasons." His voice was so smooth, I barely noticed the pause.

Barely noticed. But I did notice it. Noticed, filed it away. "Okay, so she left." I smiled thinly. "I assume it had something to do with Annette. Annette's dispatched—now she wants to come back and this Assembly job just came up at the right time. How convenient."

"You noticed that as well." Chang returned my smile, thin and just barely there. "You're smart, Kit. I admire that about you. Saves time when I don't have to connect the dots." Now he looked away. "Shanelle notified the clan—as courtesy dictates—

that she was on official business for the Assembly and then she filed the official petition stating her desire to rejoin the clan and take reclaim her official position."

"Which was…?"

"She had been one of the lead enforcers." His voice was neutral.

Too neutral. There was something he wasn't telling me.

"What *else* was she?"

The door opened and Chang's eyes cut to the left.

As Damon came inside, I had a sinking feeling I already knew.

"What, I don't get invited to tea these days, Chang?" He studied me before shifting his attention to his second.

I folded up the slip of paper and tucked it inside my vest, keeping the movement casual. Damon took note of it—he took note of *everything*.

I imagined he also noticed the tension in the air and the way my heart jacked up before I got it under control. I could attribute that racing heartbeat to any number of things—I hadn't seen him in over a week.

Hadn't touched him—*really* touched him in far too long.

I could attribute it to nerves.

Maybe even a bit of jealousy, because I knew as sure as he stood there that there was a woman—a shapeshifter—who'd been heading this way to take back her place as an enforcer *and* as his lover.

But really, just looking at him was enough to make everything in me sigh.

Can we stop waiting already?

"I would have invited you, but you hate tea, Damon." Chang's calm voice shattered the silence when all I could do was just sit there and stare dumbly at the man in front of us. "Kit wanted to know if I had any information about an on-going case."

Damon shifted his gaze my way.

Chang might be a picture of masculine beauty, but Damon was pretty much the living, breathing personification of power. Up until he'd steamrolled his way into my life, I'd tended to avoid powerhouses like him, just because I didn't like to feel that surrounded.

• • •

56

He was gorgeous and headstrong and intimidating and sarcastic.

And...still mine.

"Well." Chang cleared his throat, the gesture pointed. "I think I'm going to attend to some matters out in the club. Kit...if you can, check in when you have information about your case."

"Uh...yeah." I barely glanced at him.

"Hmmm." The dry amusement in his voice was evident. But he didn't head toward the door.

Rising, I swiped my hands down the sides of my cargoes, looking away from Damon before I somehow embarrassed myself even more. "So...ah...I..."

"Here."

Chang cut me off before I managed to even stammer out a greeting to the man still watching me with intense eyes. I looked at Chang, then looked again.

He held the katana out in front of him, sheathed.

Slowly, I lowered my gaze to the katana and then back up to him. "I can't..."

"The blade needs somebody who would appreciate it—" Chang corrected himself. "*Him* as a weapon. I appreciate the effort that went into creating him, and I appreciate the artistry. But I have no need of the blade. You would do his maker justice."

"You said his maker tried to relieve you of your head," I said.

"And I repaid him by taking his." He continued to hold it. "Take it, Kit."

Greed raced through me and I couldn't stop myself another moment. Reaching out, I closed my hand around it and took it. "Thank you."

Chang, instead of replying, gave me a small bow.

I returned it and he left without speaking.

The door closed behind him a moment later and I lowered my gaze to the gift he'd given me.

"If he wasn't my best man, I'd be tempted to hurt him for putting that look in your eyes."

I shifted my attention up and met Damon's gaze.

"Ah...hi."

CHAPTER FIVE

Even now, more than a year after I'd first met him, looking at him was enough to steal my breath away.

When he asked me out on a date—a for-real, actual *date*—a little over a month ago, my instincts had been to say no. My heart had kicked my instinct in the balls and screamed *yes*. My response had been a slow, almost stammered, "Sure." Since then, we usually saw each other once a week, but we met at a designated place.

He didn't come see me.

I didn't go to the Lair.

It was always in a public place.

The one exception had been the night of the Halloween Ball and my plans of seducing—or at least telling him I wanted to stop waiting—had gone screaming out the window.

But now we were alone.

I couldn't exactly call this a *date*, of course. He'd shown up in Chang's office, not knowing I'd be there, although he would have seen my car, and to be very honest—he'd probably realized I was here before he even hit the grounds. Shapeshifter senses are funny like that.

His nostrils flared.

"Justin's back in town," he said, his voice neutral.

"Yeah." I hitched a shoulder in a shrug.

His nostrils flared again, lids hanging low. I braced myself because I knew what he was doing. Damon was a shifter and that meant he could smell things no human or half-human could possibly pick up. He was analyzing the scent layers on me. "Somebody's dead, Kit."

"Somebody needed to die, Damon." I gave him an innocent stare. Son of a bitch. I should have spent another thirty minutes in a shower—or a steam bath. Determined to make him think about *anything* other than the fact that I smelled like human blood, I said, "You haven't seen me in almost two weeks and you're more interested in other people than me."

He came in a little closer and I froze as he dipped his head, breathed in.

Then, as his breath drifted over me in a soft sigh, he murmured, "No...never. I just don't like thinking about what could happen if somebody found out you'd killed a human. I'd have to slaughter the world, Kit."

Now he lifted his head. While his eyes swirled and the intensity of his emotions beat against me, I eased back.

"Ah..." I blinked. "That would be a bit of overkill. And relax. I know what I'm doing."

He sighed. Then, with a gentle touch, he smoothed a finger over my brow. "You got sick from her biting you. The virus...it lingered." He smoothed a finger across my brow. "It made you sick."

"What...oh." I shrugged as I remembered the debacle with Alice at the ball. "I'm fine. It was just a fever. No big deal."

His gaze roamed over me and I knew he was looking for some sign of injury, but I was standing there all but *burning* and it didn't take long for him to pick up on it.

His lashes drooped as he drew in a deep, slow breath and his big body seemed to ripple—everything in him drawing tight.

When he looked back at me, I felt it as intimately as if he'd stroked his hands over me.

"I...um..." My brain tried to kick in. "Look, I should go."

He took a step toward me.

The list of names Chang had given me was burning a hole in my vest and I wanted to demand Damon tell me who Shanelle was, and why she'd been coming here. I don't care that I'd had Chang's explanation. There was the *official* explanation and there were the reasons a woman would give a former lover—and she'd *stay* former.

• • •

Will she? That sly voice murmured in the back of my mind and doubt slid in.

Before it could take root, though, Damon reached out.

His fingers slid up my cheek, tangled in my hair.

"I was going to call you when I left here," he said, his voice low.

"Were you?" Heat skittered and danced in my veins.

"Hmmm. Am I still coming over tonight?"

I turned, my answer on my lips. But then it died...faded away, as his mouth covered mine.

Why would I want to talk when I could be kissing him?

"Stop."

A rush of heat and hot skin and hunger later, Damon caught my hands as I went to shove his shirt up.

His chest was heaving, his skin hot under my hands. When he tried to pull back, I just followed his mouth with mine. Stop? Why in the world would I want to do that?

Damon groaned and reached up, cupping my face in his hands. His arms were now an effective barrier between us, too.

Damn it.

"Kit...baby girl. Stop..."

I groaned.

He dropped his head on my shoulder.

The ragged rhythm of his breath on my skin, the heavy brush of it all over me was enough to have my nipples drawing tight. I clutched at his hips, desperate hunger clawing at me.

In the next second, Damon was by the door and I was gripping the desk to catch my balance.

"Damon...?"

He dragged his hands down his face. "That's...okay. Enough. I have to be able to walk out of here."

Involuntarily, my gaze dropped lower and then I turned away because I was tempted to rush him. Sex up against a wall—it wasn't an unknown for us. Even as some part of my brain was wary, the rest of me was all for crashing ahead at full speed.

"Yeah. Um. I don't think I could face Chang if we…" I looked at his office and my face went hot and red. Ohhhhh, no. I'd die of embarrassment. I wasn't particularly shy, but Chang would know in a hot second if we had sex up here. Hell, he'd probably know how close we'd come to having sex up here and that was already pretty bad.

A hand brushed down the back of my hair. A kiss ghosted over my shoulder.

I would have caught his hand, but he was already sliding through the door.

"You're coming over tonight, right?" I asked, knowing he'd hear me.

"Still want me to?"

I licked my lips. "Yeah. I'll be home…probably late. See you there."

There are some people who could get in trouble with a wet bag and a rubber ducky.

I know.

I'm one of them.

There I was, standing with a wet bag, eggs oozing out of it, half of my groceries for tonight all over the ground and a rubber ducky in my hand. I'd dropped one of the bags when a small tornado had almost bowled me over. I'd held onto the other, although thanks to the smashed eggs, the stuff in it was probably ruined.

Sighing, I looked down at the bag and then the ducky.

Said duck belonged to the little girl cowering at my feet.

Or maybe not…

"This doesn't concern you."

The words were delivered in a cloud of garlic and undercooked meat as a man came storming my way. He went to snatch the duck away and I whipped my hand out of his reach.

"She stole it," he said.

"I'll pay for it," I said calmly. "Just tell me how much it is."

"I'm not selling it to you." His lip curled and he glanced down at the girl. He went to grab her. I dropped the rest of my groceries and shoved my hand against his chest.

He went flying back.

I took advantage of the momentary distraction to pick up the girl and put her in my car. I'd only barely had the chance to shut the door when he came rushing at me. Magic sparked around him as he swung out at me.

Splintered power danced in the air around him. An untrained witch, probably watered down—just enough ability to light a fire—or make him feel tough.

Ducking under the punch, I slammed my fist into his gut and spun away.

He lumbered after me.

I caught the next punch.

His face went red as I started to squeeze. I heard bones break.

As he started to squeal, I flung his hand away.

"Well. This is entertaining."

With a disgusted sigh, I looked up as Megan Banks came striding up.

Megan was the second in command for the local wolf pack. She looked like a soccer mom, cussed like a sailor and had a jaw like a brick wall. I'd broken my hand on that jaw of hers. As I caught sight of the amusement in her eyes, I relived that moment. It had been worth it.

Blowing out a disgusted breath, I looked at the groceries I'd dropped when the little girl had plowed into me. The eggs were a lost cause. "Hi, Megan. Long time, no see. Oh, you're in a hurry? Sorry to hear that. See ya."

She chuckled as she knelt down next to me. "I'm here to speak with the man you made cry like a baby." She picked up a packet of steak and held it out. "Planning on having company?"

I just stared.

"It's been a while since I've seen the Alpha. Perhaps I should swing by and just touch base. It's a courtesy...from the pack to the clan."

"Come by my house tonight and die," I said.

She threw back her head and laughed.

Trying to ignore her, I stacked up the groceries that weren't ruined. I'd need another bag.

"Don't worry. I'm here to pick up a cub. You're safe...I'll be playing mama." Her voice went soft then.

A cub...? I looked up, watched as she rose.

I did the same, fighting the urge to glance back to my car.

"I thought you were here to talk to him." I jutted my chin at the man who had finally gotten to his feet, although he was still clutching his mangled hand.

"I am." Distaste thickened her voice. "Maurice called and said he had a stray kid in the store—was positive she was a wolf. We pay rewards for anybody who finds a youth."

Narrowing my eyes, I looked over at him, thought about the way I'd seen him going to grab her, the fear in her eyes.

"How long ago did he call you?" I asked softly.

She frowned. "He left a message—it's been about two hours or so. He said she was secure. I couldn't get here immediately. I was tending to...a problem."

I fought the urge to snarl. "You might have another one."

"What?"

I pointed to my car, and she turned just in time to see the tiny child duck into the back, hiding.

Terrified.

"Now, see here...that's not fair!" Maurice jabbed a thumb at his chest. "That's *my* reward."

"You had one of *my* wolves locked in a *closet*," Alisdair MacDonald said. The words sliced through the air, vicious and feral.

"The kid tried to run! She bit me! She stole my merchandise!"

I started to laugh.

Dair cut me a cold look.

"It was a rubber duck," I said. The child was currently sound asleep in the other room—with the rubber duck. We could see her through the open door—or I could. The raised voices didn't disturb her at all, so either she was that exhausted or she was used to them. Either scenario tugged at my heart. "She took a rubber duck. She's five years old, if that, and she was scared."

"She's a thief." He jabbed his splinted hand at me. "And you...*you*...I'm filing a complaint against you."

"I'm quivering," I drawled.

"Do it," Dair said, his voice silky. "And I'll have you before the Assembly on charges of child cruelty."

Maurice froze.

Megan said, "Alpha, I'm sure Maurice doesn't realize that locking her in a closet counts as child imprisonment." She gave Maurice a polite smile, but the look in her eyes said the opposite—she was sure Maurice *did* realize it...and he didn't care.

I was pretty sure of that myself.

"She tried to run away!" Maurice shouted again.

"Then you should have let her." Dair lifted a shoulder. "You'd notified us. We could have tracked her. Instead you chose to manhandle and traumatize her."

"If she ran, I didn't get paid—"

He snapped his mouth shut, but it was too late.

Even if he hadn't spoken, Dair already knew. *I* knew. I'd known the moment Megan had mentioned a reward. "You don't get paid now, do you?"

He waved a dismissive hand. "Megan, see him out."

Maurice looked like he wanted to argue, but he followed Megan. Just before she would have opened the door, Dair said softly, "Maurice, I expect to still receive phone calls from you should another young wolf end up in your establishment. You know this."

Maurice gave a jerky nod and then he ducked out, moving like his ass was fire.

I was left alone with Dair.

"I'll have Megan issue you the fee."

"Don't." Jamming my hands into my pockets, I glared at him. "She was a scared kid. I didn't do that for money."

Before he could argue, I asked, "Does that happen a lot? You get calls about kids randomly showing up with no parent?"

"No." He blew out a quiet breath and tipped his head to the sky. "No, thank God, we do not. But…it does happen."

"How?"

Intense dark eyes leveled on me. "There are no easy answers to that—and at the same time, the answers are ridiculously easy. My pack is stable. We have few fights outside those for advancement within the pack, but the same can't be said for others. Travel a hundred miles from here and you'll encounter another clan where they'd kill their neighbor simply because they didn't like the man's shoes. Children are most often ignored in such fights, but then they are left to fend for themselves." He shrugged. "Sometimes they end up here. Sometimes…they end up dead."

He looked away then, weariness seeming to weigh down on him. "That's simply one explanation. Another…I cannot tell you how many wolves I've known who've just decided to end it. They leave behind husbands, wives, children, mothers, fathers…"

My mind flashed back to the day I stood on a cold, steep gorge, only moments away from flinging myself over the side.

Dair's voice dragged me back. "Sometimes they see no other outlet."

He said nothing else and a strained silence spread between us. Clearing my throat, I rose from the chair. On my way to the door, I swiped my hands down the front of my trousers.

"Thank you for helping the child, Kit."

"No problem," I said.

"If there's anything I can do…"

I paused, then.

"Well, yeah." Slowly, I looked back at him. "How about some information?"

Chapter Six

Bed.

The promise of bed and oblivion awaited me yet again.

Except...

I groaned as I remembered.

Damon.

He was coming over and my food had been trashed.

I'd been planning on a big dinner, followed by...well, hopefully sex.

Once I'd decided to take the child to the wolf den, I'd just ditched the food. The little girl hadn't wanted to come out of my car—and the car smelled bad now. I don't think the poor thing had had a bath in weeks.

I was halfway to my condo before the air cleared and I had another workable menu in mind. It wasn't red meat, which meant Damon would grumble, but oh well.

The sun had slid below the horizon by the time I pulled into the parking lot.

I didn't let myself worry.

I was getting better about that.

I couldn't live my life behind locked doors every time the sun disappeared.

Or maybe I could.

Cold wind brushed down my spine, even though I still sat in my car—my locked car. And the air was still.

That wasn't the source of the energy, though. It was the vampire.

I couldn't see him, but I felt him.

Fear screamed through me. Instinctively I flexed my hand. My palm went hot and tight—but there was nothing there. No blade came to my call and the music in my head was gone.

That's fucking *fine*. I grabbed the katana Chang had given me and climbed out, drawing it and tossing the sheath back into the car. My other blade was tucked in behind the passenger seat but I wasn't about to ignore the threat long enough to get it. Casually, I rested my hand on the firearm strapped to my left thigh. The Glock XT23 was strong enough—and fast enough—to put a hole through a vampire.

All I had to do was…

Shadows gathered in front of me.

A good thirty feet separated me from that cluster, but it was still too close.

I had the Glock leveled by the time the shadows cleared and his face emerged.

The sight of Abraham Allerton didn't make me feel *any* better.

Penetrating gray eyes stared at me. His hair, thick, black and straight, flowed back from a widow's peak to his shoulders. He was tall and slim and he carried himself with military bearing.

His gaze landed on the Glock and he cocked his head.

"Do you intend to use that?"

I smiled. "I'm thinking about it."

"Then I'll stay here until you've made up your mind. I recall how fast you are."

Ah. Yes. He'd seen me use a gun before—right before I blew the brains out of a friend of his. My finger tightened convulsively on the trigger and I forced myself to let up. "Why are you here?"

"I'm looking for Justin Greaves." His lids drooped. "You've seen him today."

"And you know this…how?"

A second later, I was ready to kick myself. I shook my head. "Never mind. I dunno if anybody's ever pointed this out, but the smell thing is *annoying*."

"Your lover is a shapeshifter. His sense of smell is keener than mine." Abraham lifted a shoulder, looking unconcerned. He lifted an elegantly arched brow, his expression patient.

Perfectly patient.

Like most vampires, his expressions were *too* perfect. Practiced almost.

The only time I'd ever seen what seemed to be *real* emotions from vampires…

Don't go there, Kit, I told myself, wrapping a choke-chain around my memories.

"Have you seen Justin?"

I stared down the barrel of the Glock at him, debating. Slowly, I lowered it. Not because I trusted Abraham, but because I trusted Justin and Justin trusted Abraham.

I wasn't going to stand there all night with a weapon pointed.

I kept it unholstered there, hanging at my right side, while I gripped the katana in my left hand.

Abraham's gaze slid from one weapon to the next, lingering on the blade.

Just as I was about to respond, he murmured, "I know that blade."

I think I hid my surprise better than he hid his. I *think*.

"Yeah?" I angled it, letting the streetlights dance off the surface. There was only one way he'd know this particular blade and that would be if he'd been in Chang's inner sanctum. My skin crawled at the thought of it, but Chang was Damon's top man. He was going to have odd bedfellows.

His gaze slid to me and if I wasn't mistaken, he looked somewhat disgruntled. "Yes." Eyes narrowed, he said, "I offered a fair sum to buy it from Mr. Tanaka."

"I guess it wasn't fair enough." Mr. Tanaka—Chang—wasn't going to sell his toys.

"I'll pay double." His gaze rested on the blade with a covetous greed that I could completely understand and I found myself relaxing. Odd, that. He was all but drooling over a deadly weapon and that made me breathe easier.

"I didn't pay him anything." I smiled as I said it and watched as the expression ripple over his face.

We were interrupted before he could formulate his response and I mentally chanted: *Steady...stay steady...*

The last thing I wanted was to have one of the top vamps for the Allerton family squaring off with my lover because Damon didn't like how edgy I was.

The loud rumble of his engine went silent as he pulled up and parked next to me. Casually, I shifted my body and slid my Glock back into the holster although there was nothing to be done about the blade.

Abraham's face went blank, smooth as glass.

Damon could be as silent as he wished—when he chose. If he wanted, he could move without making a sound and when he came at you, you wouldn't know until it was too late.

On the flipside, there were times when he damn well wanted you to know he was coming.

This was one of those times.

The door to the classic Dodge Challenger closed with slow deliberation. I didn't look away from Abraham, but the sound of Damon's booted feet striking the ground sent a thrill rushing through me. Or maybe it was a chill. His mood had slid into dangerous territory—all at the sight of Abraham Allerton.

His shadow fell across mine, swallowing it.

I slid him a glance.

"Hey." My smile was firmly in place.

His lashes swept low, shielding his eyes for a long moment and then he flicked a look at Abraham. "You're keeping strange company, Kit."

"I can't say he's company." I lifted a shoulder. "Abraham came by looking for Justin."

Abraham inclined his head. "Alpha Lee."

Damon took one step forward. "Greaves isn't here, as you're perfectly aware. Get lost."

Abraham's gaze moved back to me. "Miss Colbana, if you will let him know I need to speak with him, I'd appreciate it."

"She doesn't need to be passing messages along for you, leech," Damon said, his voice dropping into a low growl.

I pushed past him and caught Abraham's gaze. "I'll let him know, Abraham." As the shadows wrapped around him, I shot Damon a fulminating look. "You do *not* speak for me." He opened his mouth and I whirled on him, driving my finger into his chest. "*Ever.*"

Teeth bared in a snarl, he bent his head.

I rose up on to my toes and shoved my face into his, jabbing him once more for effect. "*Ever,*" I said again.

Then, with a disgusted sneer, I moved to my car and gathered up the rest of my gear. Storming over to my front door, I mentally cursed the damn cat that I couldn't seem to live without.

I didn't hear him, but I knew he was following. I ducked inside before he could touch me, but I didn't slam the door in his face, as much as I was tempted. If I'd thought about it for another five seconds, though, I might have.

Especially once the intensity of his anger jacked up.

Standing in the middle of my bedroom, the katana in one hand, my blade in the other, I stared at the floor and cursed Justin in one breath, Damon in the next. It was faint, but Justin's scent still lingered. If I could smell it, so could Damon.

"Kit…"

Ignoring him, I placed both blades near my bed and moved over to the table where I kept my other weapons. Glock, dagger, throwing knives—

Hands came down on my shoulders.

I tensed.

"Kit."

"That's me."

A headache pounded between my eyes. Putting the garrote down, I focused on the wooden surface.

"You want to tell me what's going on or do I just go kill him?"

Shrugging out from under his grip, I moved over to my bed and sat on the edge. "Seriously, you're really going to kill Justin because he came into my bedroom?"

My plan had been to unlace my boots.

I hadn't even been able to bend over.

Damon was suddenly looming over me and my heart lurched up into my throat.

Green-gold swam in his eyes as he bent over me, his hands coming down to pin me in place. "No, I'm going to kill him because I smell him all over your bed."

I was going to kill Justin—for being a pain in my ass.

Reaching up, I laid my hand on Damon's cheek.

He froze.

"But you don't smell him on me, do you?"

Closing his eyes, Damon ducked his head. "That's not…Kit, I didn't think…"

"I know." Lifting my other hand, I cupped his face in my hands. The dark crown of his head was bowed and I leaned in, pressed a kiss to his scalp. "He's just being evil. I mentioned you were coming over later and he flopped his ass down on the bed just to get under your skin."

His head came up then.

"It looks like he's done just that," I said softly.

His hands flexed on the sheets next to me. "I'm going to get under *his* skin. Literally."

Leaning in, I pressed my mouth to his.

He groaned.

I all but held my breath…waiting.

The soft, gentle kiss wasn't what I wanted.

It wasn't what I needed.

My heart raced and my body begged…and he soothed.

While that edgy need climbed higher and higher, I twisted my arms around his neck and hooked one knee around his hip.

He broke the kiss immediately.

As he put the width of the room between us, I clenched my hands into fists.

Maybe the only way to do this was to get naked.

The idea had merit.

Yeah, he'd probably try to coddle me through it—and maybe I'd end up needing that—but at least he'd get the point.

"Why was Allerton here?"

The question was a splash of cold water.

Jerking my head up, I met his gaze. The grey was a warm haze of smoke and his jaw was a rigid line, but the words had been delivered in a cool flat tone. *Interesting segue, Damon.*

I ran my tongue across my teeth and immediately wished I hadn't because I tasted him on me. His gaze dropped to my mouth and I shuddered. A muscle pulsed in his jaw and he looked away.

"Fuck this," I muttered, shoving upright.

I moved toward the door, my sock-clad feet silent on the hardwood.

Damon moved out of the way—away from me—like I carried some sort of contagious disease. I wanted to grab him and shake him and beg him to touch me. How did I tell him that I needed it?

Just do it.

But the words lodged in my throat, trapped.

"Kit."

Shooting him a dark glare, I continued into the kitchen. I needed chocolate or a drink or a huge pot of tea—or sex—but clearly, I wasn't going to get the option I really wanted, so I had to make do.

"He was looking for Justin," I said. "Just like I already told you."

He was quiet as I opened the fridge. Milk. There was milk. I grabbed it and opened the cabinet next to the fridge. Perfect. A half bar of real chocolate. Hot chocolate—not quite sex, but almost as good.

"And why was Justin here?"

"Because we're gearing up for a job." I focused on heating up the milk instead of looking at him. I wasn't quite ready to talk about that job just yet—or Shanelle. Not considering how pissed off I was getting.

"What's Allerton got to do with this?"

I jerked a shoulder. Breaking the chocolate into pieces, I added it to the milk. One piece went into my mouth and I hummed in appreciation.

Heavy arms came around me, surrounding me.

My body reacted to the nearness of his. Heat grabbed me, shimmering through me. I turned to face him, one piece of chocolate still in my hand. Lifting it to my mouth, I stared at him as I licked it off my fingers.

His eyes flared.

"I don't know what he wanted from Justin," I said, deliberately choosing those words. I had a bad feeling I knew exactly what Allerton wanted with Justin, but I wasn't going there right now. "He just wants to speak with him."

Damon's gaze stayed on my mouth.

The taste of chocolate lingered.

I wanted the taste of *him*.

Licking my lips, I shrugged casually. "Now…can you back off?"

Instead, he reached up and touched his finger to the corner of my mouth.

I felt that touch jolt through me from head to toe.

I turned my head and caught his finger in my mouth and sucked on it.

He was on the other side of the room in a blink.

Swearing, I spun around.

The milk was starting to steam, but suddenly, I didn't want it. Hot chocolate wasn't going to do it. I hit the button to turn off the heating element. Fury pulsed, twisted and pounded within—but it wasn't just fury.

He'd treated me with kid gloves the past few months. Yes, part of me had appreciated the patience…at first.

But I was coming out of my skin and I *needed* him. I didn't know what to do about it, though, and this indecision was killing me. I didn't know how to handle it— or him.

"Kit, I…"

"Don't." The word ripped out of me with a viciousness that stunned me. "Just *don't.*"

I spun on my heel and stalked toward him. "You know what?" I slammed the heel of my hand against his chest. He didn't even budge. I did it again and my lack of ability to make him move infuriated me. "Just get out. You hear me? If you can't stand to be around me and treat me like a real person then just *get the hell out!*"

The fury inside me was a beast and I couldn't make sense of it.

Damon's eyelids flickered.

He inclined his head and then turned on his heel.

"Yeah," I sneered at his retreating back. "You go ahead and run."

I sounded *insane*. I'd just told him to go.

He stopped right where he was and dropped his head. "You told me to go. I'm just doing what you want."

"You don't know what I want!" I shouted.

With a half-scream, I turned away and left the room before I made myself look anymore the fool. I was going to blister my skin off in the shower. And maybe try to relieve some of the pent-up frustration in there as well, since Damon still didn't know how to handle touching me.

But when I went to slam the door, a heavy hand stopped me.

My breath caught in my throat as Damon came inside.

"It seems to me that you want to fight," Damon said after I'd backed myself up against the sink.

"Do not." Oh. *That* sounded mature. I folded my arms over my chest and jutted my chin up. "Well, maybe I do, but you only have yourself to blame. You have no business interrogating me over things that connect to my work."

His eyes narrowed as he reached up and cupped my chin. "No right…" His thumb swept over my bottom lip and it sent a shiver through me. He noticed, too. His pupils spiked. "You got any idea what it did to me to see you standing in the parking lot here, alone with a vampire, baby girl?"

Under that flat tone was a world of pain and my heart clenched.

"Abraham wasn't here to hurt me," I said, reaching up to curl my hand around his wrist.

"Oh, I know that. Allerton's one of the few that I don't immediately want to skewer. Well, not until I saw him near you. But it still put me in a bad place, Kit."

Closing my eyes, I pulled my chin out of his grasp. "I can't live the rest of my life worrying about whether my job will put you in a bad place, Damon." I was having a hard enough time not getting in a bad place *myself.*

He was so close I could feel his breath mingling with mine and the scent of him swam in my head, making me drunk.

Too much…too much.

Unwittingly I opened my eyes and found myself staring at his mouth. In self-defense, I spun around and stared at the woman in the mirror in front of me, the one who I sometimes still hated. A year ago, I could have turned to the man behind me and reached for him. That was the one thing I wanted to do—the one thing I needed.

"You said I don't know what you want," he murmured, his mouth now pressed to my ear.

● ● ●

I suppressed a shiver.

"I think I do know. I'm just not sure if I know how to give it to you anymore."

The uncertainty in his voice made my throat knot up.

"I just want you," I whispered.

His patience was killing me.

His patience.

My fear.

I focused on the woman in the mirror, the woman who so often still seemed like a stranger. Tonight, it was even more so. Her green eyes were over-bright, her skin flushed and there was a set to her face that was a mix between mutinous defiance and need.

A harsh, low growl ripped out of him and in the next moment I was surrounded by him, his hands coming down to bracket me in against the counter, his front against my back. He managed, somehow, to pin my body there and still let me feel like I could break away.

One hand came up, pressed against my belly.

He dragged up my tank and I hissed out as he pressed his palm against my skin. The rough callouses, the pads of his fingers, I felt every nuance.

It was overwhelming.

"You don't always have to handle me with kid gloves. I'm not going to break, Damon."

"No. I'm afraid I might." He lowered his mouth to my neck and I whimpered, free hand braced against the counter. My legs threatened to give out. Need was a primal scream inside me and I forgot about everything but him.

His hands turned me and I rose on my toes, seeking out his mouth with mine. The brush of his lips was a teasing, taunting caress and it wasn't enough.

I broke away and forced my eyes to open. His eyes spun between gray and green-gold and the sight was enough to send a shiver racing down my spine. That was need there. A hunger he couldn't fully hide and I wished he'd stop trying.

He pressed his mouth to my neck, brushed a line of kisses down it. His teeth scraped over one of the scars. Scars hidden under ink, scars left on me during the weeks I'd spent on a mountain, a prisoner with little chance of escape.

I couldn't help it—I tensed and a moment later, he was out of the room and standing in the hall, hands flexing as though he kneaded the very air.

"You wonder why I handle you with kid gloves," he said, his voice harsh.

I swore and spun around. With a scream, I drove my fist into the mirror. Glass shattered. Pain sang up my arm and blood dripped from my hand but I didn't care.

"I don't want you to be sorry!" I shouted, spinning to face him.

His eyes were all cat now, glowing as I went to him. "I am *tired,*" I whispered, striding toward him. It was easier than I'd hoped and I was able to take another, then another until I could reach out and hook my fingers in the waistband of his jeans. "I'm tired of waiting. I go to bed lonely. I wake up lonely…and scared and empty. I'm tired of it. I'm tired of remembering how it used to be and wishing to feel that way again. I just want—"

His mouth cut off the rest of the words.

Skin that had started to go cold was hot now, pressed against the solid wall of his chest, the heavy muscles of his thighs. His hands stroked down my back and I whimpered, arching closer.

I couldn't get any closer, even if I tried, and I did. I tried so very hard.

Hooking my arms around his neck, I all but wrapped myself around him and then he caught me by the hips, boosting me up until I could do just that. The rub of denim against my inner thighs had me shivering and his palms, rough and callused, stroking up my sides and back had me arching in his grasp.

The bathroom door was hard against my back but it groaned ominously as he moved against me. I didn't care. Arching against him, I shuddered with a mix of relief and delighted as I felt him throbbing against me.

I tugged him closer, greedy, desperate. His mouth met mine and I could have answered that growl of his with my own as I gorged on his taste. I smoothed my hands up his chest, felt his heart thud against my palm. His skin was scorching hot. Desperate for air, I tore my mouth away.

He caught my wrist, forced my hand to his mouth and I tensed as he licked the blood away. The skin was already knitting together, the blood slowing to a trickle.

Tugging my hand away, I wrapped my arms around him and arched closer.

Damon caught my chin and pulled me back in. "More," he demanded.

I sank my teeth into his lip.

"Get naked," I demanded.

"Not so fast." Damon tangled his hand in my hair, licked my mouth and then started to move lower, leaving a path of heat in his wake. "Easy…easy, baby girl. We have all night."

"I don't want easy…I just want you." I needed to feel it, that hunger I sensed burning inside him. Wanted to feel it burning me, chasing away the shadows, the cold spots, the emptiness.

"You can have me. Always. Just…" His hands framed my face as he brushed a feather-light kiss over my lips.

Heat pounded, pulsed inside me. Too much heat, too much sensation and too much need building inside, threatening to burn me alive. That need, Damon's body, all of it was driving me nuts and he wanted *easy*?

I untangled myself from him, nudging him back. He went and I scraped my nails down his chest, watching as he shuddered.

A groan rumbled out of him when I reached for his belt.

Damon went to catch my hands. "Kit…

"I don't want to be gentled or babied right now," I said, holding his gaze as I dealt with the heavy buckle, then, still watching him, popped the button. His hands fell away and he watched me as I dragged the zipper down.

I pushed my hand inside his jeans and found him naked. Naked and hard, pulsing against my hand as I closed my fingers around him. He throbbed and despite his insistences about *easy*, when I dragged my hand up, then down, a snarl escaped him and he shoved himself into my caress, once, then twice, before his body went rigid and his eyes flew open. Green-gold spun with grey as our eyes locked. "We…fuck," he panted. "Let's go to your room."

"I don't need my room. I just need you." I squeezed him, rotated my wrist, and watched his gaze go unfocused. "I'm tired of waiting."

"I don't want to scare you—hurt you."

Leaning in, I caught his lower lip between my teeth and tugged. "If I freak out, I freak out. We'll have to deal with it. But right now, I need you…don't make me wait."

His chest rose in a ragged, harsh rhythm, his lids drooping down to shield his eyes.

A second later, I was caught up against him and the room spun around him. "No waiting," he muttered. Then he flicked a look around the bathroom. "But not here. Glass…"

I couldn't even process that and it didn't matter. I nuzzled his throat, caught a patch of skin between my teeth and bit him, delight a sweet haze in my brain as it made him shudder.

Something crashed. From the corner of my eye, I saw him sweeping his arm out and realized we were in the narrow alcove just between the bathroom and the main living area.

The small table that I used as a desk was now empty. A few seconds ago, it had been littered with folders, a few daggers and who knows what else. Now I was stretched out on it as Damon moved between my thighs. He bent low over me, one hand braced by my shoulder, the other under my waist to tug me to the edge of the table.

I reached for my shirt, but he nudged my hands away and stripped me naked, clothes ripping when they didn't come away fast enough for him.

My hands curled into fists, I watched him as he straightened and shoved his jeans down. He didn't take them off and I was just fine with that—I couldn't have taken it if he'd left me any longer than necessary.

"You look at me," he said, his voice rough. He dragged his fingers down my chest, the roughened pads lingering on the vivid tattoos, the scars hidden under the elegant ink. "You think only of me."

Then he bent his head and I gasped as his mouth closed around my nipple.

Heat and pleasure slammed into me, devastating me. Teeth raked against sensitive flesh—I hadn't *ever* felt anything this intense. His touch was just on the edge of pain before he shifted his attention to the other breast. His lips caressed the lines of the leopard that crouched along my breastbone, rising up just below my shoulders before the tangle of flowers—every last one of them poisonous, hiding more scars in their petals and vines. Damon found every one of them, his teeth matching the marks placed on me months ago, covering each faded scar with a kiss. He repeated the process over and over until he'd found them all and when he'd finished, I turned my face to his, seeking out his mouth.

It wasn't until I felt the wetness on his face that I realized I was crying.

He kissed the tears away as well.

His hand smoothed down over my belly and I tensed.

"Kit..."

"I'm fine," I gasped, squeezing my eyes shut.

Memories of a stone floor, a mocking voice tried to creep up on me. Laughter, cold and cutting.

Warm hands cupped my face. "Look at me."

The words were a hard slap, echoing through the room.

With a shudder, I dragged myself out of the past and locked onto Damon.

His hand tangled in my hair. "Look at me," he whispered again, his thumb stroking over my lower lip. "Look only at me."

As though I could look anywhere else.

"Please..." I panted the word out against his lips. I didn't entirely know what I wanted. Did I want him to stop? Did I want the memories to stop? Did I want *this* to stop?

I didn't know.

I really didn't know.

But Damon didn't seem to have the same confusion going on.

I gasped as his weight settled between my thighs. Just there, though. He kept his upper body braced on one hand. Between my legs, I could feel the heat of him and he caught my wrist, dragging my hand down. "Take me in," he ordered. "If this is what you want..."

If...?

Some starving, desperate part of me screamed in female demand. *If?*

● ● ●

It was that part of me that reached down and wrapped my hand around his cock. That part of me that tucked him against my entrance and that part of me that whimpered as he slowly sank inside me.

The rest of me was almost frozen—it wasn't fear, not really.

But I didn't dare breathe.

Not even as he stroked completely in the first time, and then withdrew.

My chest was aching on the second thrust, and I was dying for air on the third.

"Fuck, Kit…" the groan rumbled out of him and reflexively, I reached for him, my hands digging into his muscled hips, feeling the flex and glide as he rocked inside me.

I felt exposed, too exposed—my skin far too sensitized and every breath tripping out of me could have been my last, I was so vitally aware. I felt every nuance of his cock as he moved with me, felt every pulse, the glide of his skin over mind.

A gasp broke out of me. It was too much—*too* much—

Feel him, a voice inside me whispered.

Feel him.

No. It wasn't too much.

It was what I needed.

This was Damon and *he* was what I needed.

He stretched me and bruised me. Just past the panic trying to slither in, that beautiful pleasure started to ripple through me as that part of me that wasn't cut off by panic reveled in being with him.

I wanted to feel more like her. The woman I'd been—the part of myself that remembered pleasure and love and just…this.

I arched against him and he stiffened. *Oh…*

Feel…

That was all I had to do. Just *feel…*

That soft, beckoning voice whispered to me as Damon's hand glided up my side, along my neck to cup my face. I met his eyes, my pulse hammering in my throat, my ears. "Kit…"

Feel…

* * *

I focused on him. Just on him.

And the fear, the panic that tried to grab me fell away.

Chapter Seven

"Bed."

"Um. Shower first." I snuggled against Damon's chest and sighed as his arms came around me. "But…do we have to?"

Bed sounded good. And I needed that shower, but I didn't want to move.

He laughed a little and tried again. "Kit…You've got a nice, soft bed fifteen feet away."

"I'm comfortable."

"No." He sat up, cradling me against him and then a moment later, I found myself snug against his chest. Well, this wasn't a bad place to be, either. As long as I didn't have to move.

When he put me down in the bathroom, I glared at him through the tangle of my hair. He just grinned. "You wouldn't sleep until you showered anyway, so why not shower then move to the nice comfortable bed?"

I didn't really want logic. Just…him.

But since he'd moved, I might as well get it done. I glanced around, my gaze bouncing over the shattered mirror.

"You're getting in."

Frowning at the command, I arched a brow.

He was looking at the floor. "There's glass. I'll clean it up and then be in with you."

I hadn't even started washing my hair when he joined me. He took over the job. Strong hands kneaded my scalp and neck until I was all but purring with pleasure and then, after he'd nudged me under the water and rinsed me clean, I found myself sighing in sheer contentment as he wrapped himself around me.

His chin tucked against my chest, his arms enfolded me. Closing my eyes, I lost myself in that one moment.

If only I could held onto that moment, that feeling…forever.

That feeling lingered, something that might have been peace sliding through me as we settled down in bed. My bed wasn't as big as his and he ended up half-wrapped around me.

I didn't mind that at all.

I hadn't felt this…easy in a long time.

It wouldn't last—couldn't. Under the mask of my calm, there was that underlying tension about what lay ahead—disappearances, Justin…my family.

His lips pressed against my temple. "This…" he muttered, his voice a deep, sleepy rumble. "This is what I missed."

"What? Me, naked?" I smiled, even though I knew that wasn't what he was talking about. "That's because you're a man, ergo, you're a pervert."

He laughed, but it sounded hoarse.

We lay there, like that, just like that, for a long time.

It seemed like I'd lived with a cold, aching knot inside me for too long. Ever since the day I'd collapsed against my car with a tranq dart in my chest and a wrong witch in front of me.

That knot was gone now. I just felt happy.

His hand stroked down my side, rested on my hip. "I miss smelling you on my skin. It didn't matter if it had been two days since I'd seen you. I could still smell you on my skin. I missed it more than I thought possible." His hand shifted to my belly, spread wide. "Missed seeing you."

He hesitated for a moment and then said, "I know we've been seeing each other some, but it's not the same. I don't let myself touch you. I miss that, being able to touch you and hold you and knowing I'll have your scent on me when I'm done. I missed that smart mouth of yours…missed everything about you and I came so close to you just being…gone. Forever. And it was my fault."

Well. That peace hadn't lasted as long as I'd hoped.

Slowly, I uncurled from his arms. He didn't seem to want to let go, but I couldn't have this conversation without looking at him.

I watched him go to his back and then I sat up. Looking into his haunted grey eyes, I reached for the words. In my head, we'd already had this conversation. In my head, it was over and done. But that wasn't reality.

"What happened…" My voice caught and skipped, tripping over the next few words. "When Jude grabbed me, that wasn't your fault. It wasn't my fault. It wasn't anybody's fault but his."

"If I hadn't been such a fucking idiot, then you wouldn't have been alone." His arms came around me and when he moved, sitting upright and dragging me onto his lap, I let him. I needed the connection, his touch as much he needed mine. "I…fuck, I was ready to come chasing after you the minute I walked, but I had to calm down. There was something wrong, I knew it and I was ready to kill somebody over it—it didn't matter who it was, I was ready to kill over it. I had to…"

His eyes slid away. "Because I was so fucked up in the head, because I wasn't thinking straight, you were alone."

Looking into his eyes, feeling so vulnerable and exposed, it made it too hard to think. So I did the easy thing. I buried my face against his neck. It shouldn't matter, those words. So what if he'd been ready to come back after he'd left my office—it didn't take back the words that had left me bleeding. It shouldn't undo any of the misery, but it felt like one of those deep, ripping gouges in my heart started to heal.

Because I couldn't trust my voice to be steady just then, I gave myself a minute and focused on the scent of him, the warmth of his skin against mine. Then, finally, I murmured, "If he didn't try it then, he would have tried later. Doyle found me, but the reason you all were able to get to me so fast was because of Justin. Justin is used to working with people who track—specifically…people like me. What would have happened if Justin hadn't been around? If it had been just Doyle and nobody here could help the way Justin could? Sooner or later, it was going to happen. The way it played out…I guess it was my best chance of surviving it."

Damon's hand tangled in my hair.

"I should have…"

Lifting my head, I pressed my fingers to his mouth. "We can't undo it. It's already done. I'm learning to live with it—or trying to. If we have any chance at all of making it, Damon, you'll have to do the same. And that means we can't constantly play the maybe game, the should-have game. It's done."

He caught my wrist, kissed my fingers, his gaze intent on mine.

Silence fell between us.

"I love you." He reached up and laid his hand on my cheek. The emotion churning in his eyes was enough to break me open. "I have to tell you—you didn't want to hear it before and I won't say it again after this, but I'm sorry for what I did. I hate myself for not being there."

Slowly, I let out a breath I hadn't known I was holding.

"Okay." I nodded. "Okay. Now…we just…can we just move on from here?"

His arms came around me, tight, so tight I could barely breathe. But I didn't complain.

"This is what I missed," I whispered. "Being like this. With you."

It shouldn't have been a surprise, the nightmares coming on the way they did, not then. Even though some part of me was vaguely aware that I was still in my bed, even vaguely aware that Damon held me, I could feel it pulling at me.

They'd been getting worse lately. Not that I had them more often, but Jude's voice was getting stronger in my head. It seemed like the easier it was for me to push his touch away in the day, the harder it was to break free in my dreams.

I could *hear* him.

Sometimes I thought I could even smell him, feel him.

He's not coming for you.

Jude might be in a box for the next fifty years, but in my head, he was still free. No. He stood right *there*, beside my bed and as I tried to roll away, he reached out and tangled a hand in my hair.

I froze, the memory of all the pain rising back up. Teeth sharper than blades shredding my skin. Blood pumping out of me. His body ripping into mine. Bones breaking.

Broken already?

"You're not here!"

I shouted it at him. Or tried.

He smoothed my hair back, his voice oddly gentle. *Oh, Kit,* he murmured, his voice kind. *I'll always be here. Don't you know that?*

And then he drove his fists into me, my face, my belly, my ribs. Bones broke under the blows and I tasted my own blood yet again.

Nobody will save you.

I broke free, because even in dreams, I always do. I could see the blinding white as I hurtled toward the chasm. Snow stung my skin, my hair blinded me.

Even that will not free you, little warrior. Little weakling.

The cliff lay ahead, the dark abyss a promise.

The only way to escape is to die—

To be free, all I had to do was jump. The gorge was right there. I could see it, all but taste the oblivion I'd find once I jumped.

That's it, darling Kit. Just jump...just jump, Jude crooned in my ear.

"Kit!"

Hands closed around my arms.

I swung out. I had to—

A roar shattered the cold air and then—

"Wake up." Warm, hard lips pressed to mine. A familiar scent flooded my head. "Wake up, baby girl."

"You're not here," I whispered. "Not here...he said you wouldn't come."

Hot hands caught my face. "Open your eyes, Kit. I did come. We all came."

Damon's mouth pressed to mine, the taste of him shocking me out of that weird twilight sleep. Jerking back, I stared at him, breath sawing in and out of my lungs.

A dream.

Just a dream.

"Damon." I started to shiver.

He pulled me in close, but even the heat of him wasn't enough to warm me. "You're okay," he whispered. "You're safe."

I clung to him, waiting for the echoes of the dream to fade. Waiting for the feel of *him* to fade. In the back of my mind, Jude lingered, almost like he lived inside my head.

Son of a bitch, that had been a bad one.

That nauseating reality of what that might mean left me wanting to puke and I turned my face into his chest. I shivered and Damon stroked his hand up my back. "It's over," he whispered.

Was it?

How could something that felt *that* real be over? I could still feel the bruises, the ache of broken bones, the lingering pain between my legs. I could still taste the blood and feel the biting cold from when I'd torn out into the snow.

"Come back to me," Damon murmured, his lips brushing over my brow.

I huddled against him. Under my cheek, Damon's chest was hard and warm, rising and falling with every breath he took. I spread my hand wide against his skin, the inky black of his tattoo so dark under my hand.

"Sorry," I muttered. I hated this, how vulnerable—how *raw* I still felt. "Shit. I hate this. *I hate it*—"

"Don't." His hand tangled in my hair as he spoke the word against my temple. His voice was low, raw, like he had to force it out. His chest shuddered on a ragged breath and then he spoke again, "We all have nightmares. Don't apologize for yours."

"It's…" I squeezed my eyes closed, focused on the beat of his heart. "It's not just the nightmares. It just…Damon, these feel…" I stopped, shook my head. I wasn't explaining this in front of him. I needed to talk to somebody, yes. But not Damon. Not now. "I can't explain it."

His hand smoothed down my back, gripped my hip. "Try."

Of course he wouldn't just let it go. But there was all sorts of wrong I could detail without lying. Blowing out a sigh, I forced myself to open my eyes, staring out into the dim room. "They won't stop. If the nightmares don't stop, maybe I'll never

• • •

feel like me. If they'd just stop…"

I let that one fear out. It was a true fear, one that choked me, haunted me. Even as it left me, I wanted to pull it back. Would he even understand?

"You're going to beat this," he said when my voice trailed off. "You're too strong not to."

Closing my eyes, I turned my face back into his chest. It seems like he almost always understood. A sigh shuddered out of me.

"What scares you?"

It came out of me without me realizing I even wanted to know.

His odd silence had me looking up but his gaze fell away from mine.

I stroked my index finger over his lower lip and waited.

A sigh rumbled out of him and he looked back at me, caught my wrist. "A lot of things. I've got my own nightmares, Kit. Losing you—I can't tell you how many times I've woken up remembering the nights you were missing, how it felt to see you on that cliff. I relive it over and over. And there's…"

He stopped, looked away.

"There's what?"

Now he did look at me. "I can't even remember a lot of it. There are nightmares, but they started when I was a kid. Back when I was too young to remember."

Something clicked. *It's the story of me…what put me on the road that made me what I am—*

The tattoos…

"Does this have anything to do with your family?"

A shudder fell across his eyes. "You see too much sometimes." Then he pressed his brow to mine. "I don't know."

Before I could even ask, he pressed his thumb to my mouth. "There aren't any answers. Chang found me—I was maybe four or five. He'd been out hunting with his kin, smelled…decay. Me. I was close to dead. I was too young, too weak to tell him anything. I have no idea. I'd been alone so long—he figured the food had run out a few weeks before. The water supply had dried up a few days earlier. If I would have left, I might have been okay, could have been found sooner. But I wouldn't…"

The words trailed off.

"You wouldn't leave."

He looked back at me. There was a haunted look in his eyes, one I'd never seen before. "I couldn't. Chang told me he had to drag me out of there, even as weak as I was. As sick as I was. I kept—"

He stopped, eyes closing. When he looked back at me, long moments had passed and suddenly, I didn't want to know. "He thinks it must have been my father. The body was too decayed for him to tell—Chang said he must have been dead for months. There wasn't anybody else there."

"You were alone there for months."

His gaze slid away. "We lived in the mountains. Sometimes I remember that. Mountains, with the sun rising up over them. I can remember the mists rising up as the sun rose. There were caves, and trees, and paths we'd walk."

His lashes fell down, hiding his eyes. "We were in a cave. That's where he found me. The body was in the main cavern—they were man-made. Like somebody had cut them out of the rock. There was a little room…Chang said he'd found the remains of supplies, food up there. That's where I was. With my father."

There was nothing to say to that.

I wrapped my arms around him. He tucked his head against my breasts and just held me.

"I understand nightmares, Kit. I've had almost forty years to come to grips with mine. Yours are still raw and you remember them all. They don't make you weak…they're just part of who you are." His lips skimmed across my skin as he spoke.

A sigh shuddered out of me and I lay against him.

Moments passed, one hand sliding up and down my back while the other flexed on my hip, kneading the skin there.

As the tension slowly drained out of him, I curled one arm around his neck. Desperate to chase away the dark memories—both his and mind—I stroked my fingers up and down his skin as I said, "Forty years, huh? You're an old man,

● ● ●
90

Damon."

A grunt escaped him and then he rolled.

"That a fact?" he asked as he tucked me beneath him.

It was still dark. Morning hadn't even kissed the horizon, but I didn't need light to see him. Something that might have been the first edge of humor lit his eyes as he threaded his fingers through my hair.

"Probably too old for me." I pretended to mull it over. "Geez, you're like…eighteen or nineteen years older, practically."

"Give or take, hard to say since nobody knows exactly how old I was when Chang found me." He caught my thigh in his hand. I gasped as he settled against me. His mouth found mine. "Do I feel too old now?"

I couldn't say anything as he drove inside me.

Instead I just wrapped my arms around him.

It wasn't a bad way to chase away the nightmares—mine or his.

Dawn came sooner than I liked.

I drifted back into a twilight sleep, although I don't think Damon did.

I didn't rest much longer. As those faint rays of dawn crept up along the horizon, my body came to completely wakefulness. *Get up, Kit. No more sleep for you.*

I was warm lying there, Damon's arm around my waist, his scent surrounding me, the heavy weight of his thigh pinning mine to the bed. Turning my face into his neck, I breathed him in, tried to remember the last time I'd felt this…whole.

It had been months. Too many months.

In a few more weeks, it would be a year. My throat tightened. Pushing that thought away, I squeezed my eyes closed and lay there another moment.

But that peaceful, easy feeling was gone.

My belly twisted into a tight, hot knot and my mind was…buzzing. *I* was buzzing, I realized. I went to twist away and Damon's arm shifted, freeing me. I slid him a look from the corner of my eye, saw him studying me from under his lashes.

There was an intense look on his face.

He reached out and trailed a finger down my arm as he watched me.

I bent over him, pressed my mouth to his—hard and quick before I rolled out of bed. I would have liked to linger, but…

There was something nagging me, something in the back of my brain that wouldn't let me.

Damon must have recognized the look because he rolled out of bed with feline, easy grace, a resigned expression on his face.

Unable to resist, I said, "You move pretty well for a man of your advanced years."

"Keep it up, smart-ass, and whatever has you so twitchy just might have to wait." There was a gleam in his eyes.

It made my belly burn and I almost went to him.

It felt…good. *I* felt good. I almost felt like me.

But I turned away, crossing the bedroom to my dresser. It was the old fashioned kind—a lot of people had gone to the built-in organizational units that took up less room, but I liked *stuff*. Came from too many years of not having *stuff*. The old dresser had been warped and needed a lot of love and work. Sanding, painting, refinishing—things I'd had to research and teach myself, but I liked the way it looked.

I wasn't even able to drag clothes out of my dresser before the phone rang.

For a split second, the sound of the Imperial March froze my blood.

Justin.

It wasn't just my blood that froze, either.

It was *everything*. Damon didn't breathe, I didn't breathe and that odd buzzing in my head went silent.

Then life lurched back into rhythm and I had my phone in hand before I even recalled moving.

"Colbana."

He didn't even bother with a greeting. "You going to be ready to roll?"

I looked over at Damon. He sat on the edge of the bed, staring at me with grim intensity.

"Yeah. You figure out where we're needing to go?"

"Bet your ass." He paused a moment and then, voice going sly, he asked, "So how did last night go?"

"Tell him I said hi." Damon's voice was a low growl.

Justin's laugh was quick and bright. Rubbing the back of my neck, I tried to decide just what had happened—what I'd *done*—in my life to have these two at odds like this. There weren't two men that meant more to me than them and they practically looked for reasons to rip each other apart.

"Hi back, pussy-cat," Justin said.

Damon's hand curled into a fist.

I turned my back. "Justin, do we have a job going down or not?"

He sobered fast.

"Oh, yeah. There's a job."

"What's going on?"

I gave Damon a blank stare in the mirror. I had ten minutes to shower and dress, twenty minutes to pack my gear. *No* minutes to argue with my boyfriend. "What do you mean?"

"Something's up." Damon stroked a thumb down his stumbled chin, his gray eyes gone to flint. "You're worrying on something. So's the asshole, although he's hiding it. I heard it in his voice. Has it got anything to do with whatever you were talking to Chang about?"

I tensed. It was only for a split second, but that was about two split seconds too long, because Damon knew me far too well for that to go by unnoticed. In a casual voice, I said, "I just needed a few questions answered."

Damon sighed, the sound heavy and drawn. "You're dodging me."

"No. I'm not." *Yes, I am.*

He threw his legs off the edge of the bed and strode out of the bedroom.

I caught up with him just as he dug his palm unit from the tangle of his jeans.

"What are you doing?" I asked warily.

"Calling Chang." Unlike me, he sounded completely fine. "If you won't talk, he will." He gave me a sidelong look. "He might not like it, but if it's an order…"

"Fine." Teeth gritted, I spun on my heel. He'd hear it sooner or later anyway. If I told him, then I controlled what he learned. And maybe I could figure out more about Shanelle. "But you'll have to listen while I shower and dress. I don't have much time."

Damon's silence as I showered didn't do a damn thing to calm the butterflies in my gut.

I stepped out and he met me, holding out a fat, fluffy towel. Slowly, I lifted my arms. As he wrapped it around me, I said, "And that's about all I know."

"Why didn't you ask me instead of Chang?"

Scowling, I said, "Because I'm working a job. You worry too much about me anyway." I jerked my shoulder in a shrug. "Besides…half the time he's hearing stuff before *you* do."

He stepped back and turned away. "I could have told you just as much about the cats who've gone missing. I want them found."

"Would you have told me about Shanelle?"

The muscles in his shoulders went tight, rigid as a length of steel. "What's there to tell?"

"How long were you lovers?"

He tensed. Just as quickly as the muscles in his shoulders tightened, they relaxed and if I hadn't been *looking* for some sort of reaction, I would have missed it. But I saw it.

I'd been right.

"Well?" I asked when he didn't respond.

"Lovers?" He shrugged, almost lazily and glanced back at me. "I don't think you could say we were *lovers*, Kit. We had sex. We worked together. It was not a romantic relationship."

He strode to the door.

I remembered what he'd told me once—I was the only one who'd ever had his heart.

But had he ever had anybody else's?

Softly, I asked, "Did she feel the same?"

"What does that matter?"

"Because she's planning on taking her former *position* back…whatever that means." I moved up behind him and slid my arms around his waist. "She's not getting you, Damon."

His hands covered mine. "No. She's not. There was nothing but sex there, Kit."

"On your part."

"I…" He stopped and sighed. I pressed my cheek to his back as he lifted his head to the sky. "Yeah. On my part. I can't tell you what she thought or wanted, Kit. But you don't need to worry."

I snorted. "Yeah, I tell you that about Justin all the time."

He turned then and I gasped as he caught me around the waist, lifting me up until my weight was supported by his body. "One big difference. I never loved her. You can't say the same."

He kissed me, hard and fast, and then put me down. "I know it's over—or at least on your part. But he still has feelings for you and you two work together. I deal with it, but don't expect me to like it. Now… just what is going on with this job in Georgia?"

Chapter Eight

To my surprise—and disgruntlement—I wasn't the only backup. If we needed others, that was fine, but the woman riding in the backseat was...surprising.

On any number of levels.

I'd only met the witch a couple of times, but Tate wasn't anybody I would have picked to watch my back.

I wasn't going to question Justin's decision—this job was his baby, whatever it was, and if he thought we'd need that kind of firepower—and I meant that literally—then, fine.

But I didn't have to *like* it.

"So you going to tell me what's going down?"

"You already know, unless you weren't paying attention the other day." He drummed his fingers on the steering wheel. "Rescuing some cats and a witch or two. Maybe a vampire. Didn't get any confirmation on that one."

I waited a few seconds for him to elaborate. He didn't. "Okay. You going to give me any more information than that?"

When he didn't answer me right away, I slid him a look.

I didn't much like the expression on his face. It was...worrisome.

There were just times when I thought life would be easier if he wasn't in it. No, I didn't *think* that. My life *would* be easier if he wasn't in it. But I could say the same for all the people who mattered to me. Life was better because you had people who mattered, but they were also the reason life got messy.

Right now, though, Justin was being more complicated than I liked.

"What did you find out from Chang?" he asked.

Tongue tucked against my teeth, I stared at him. He still hadn't answered my question. I debated a minute and then shrugged it off. He'd talk when he was ready to. He just better be ready to sometime *well* before we hit our target. Wherever that may be.

"Chang confirmed several disappearances. Damon did, too. Neither of them went into detail, but…" I hesitated and then added, "I get the feeling it's a bigger problem than they want people to know."

"Well, yeah. I'd assumed unexplained disappearances *are* a big problem," he muttered.

"No. Not in that way. It's…" I frowned, searching for the right way to explain what I meant. "I think maybe they've lost a lot more than they are admitting."

Justin's hands tightened on the steering wheel. "People from the clan?"

Shaking my head, I murmured, "No. I can't say if it's local people or just loners. I just think there is more they know, more they haven't told me."

"Loners?" Tate asked from the back.

I met her gaze in the rearview mirror. "Shifters who don't run with any pack or clan. Kind of like Justin here—he's got independent status. It's not as common among shifters, but sometimes you'll have one who just doesn't play well with others."

Justin snorted. "I play just fine with others."

"Yeah. It usually involves threatening to play with their entrails," Tate said.

It startled a laugh out of me. "Wow. You know him well, don't you?"

"They're just threats," Justin said, ignoring me. "And they're effective."

"Most people aren't going to want to *play* with anybody who threatens to use their liver as a loofah." Tate's voice was wry.

"A liver as a loofah. How lyrical, Justin." I shifted in the seat and rolled my head on the padded headrest, watching as the large *Welcome to Georgia* sign loomed closer. "You surprise me."

"I'm full of surprises, Kitty-kitty."

"Don't call me that." Watching the holographic peach flash across the welcome sign, I fought the urge of unease swelling inside me. Georgia was one of those states.

There were some places that you just don't want to be if you're not fully human. To be fair, if you're fully human, there are plenty of places you probably

* * *

don't want to go—like East Orlando. You'd be safe enough, but that doesn't mean you'd *feel* safe…or welcome.

But for a non-human, some places were an invitation to harassment, threats, imprisonment. The Middle East was a place you couldn't *pay* me to go. I'd sooner eat my own intestines than step one foot over the border into North Korea. On the flip side, Argentina, Australia, Lithuania and Germany weren't just *receptive* to non-humans—they had *waiting* lists for those wanting to emigrate. In time, they might have more NHs than humans.

Canada was actually becoming more tolerant, too, and there were a few cities in the US were they were struggling to become less…ass-aholic. Sadly, none of those cities were in Georgia. No, in fact, the cities in Georgia clutched tightly to their pearls and all but fainted at the *mention* of accepting those of us who weren't human. The election this year had been a huge, ugly, mud fest, all because the woman who'd been up for re-election had recently been outed as a sympathizer to the non-humans. Apparently, her daughter had married a guy who had witches in his blood and the mom actually loved her daughter enough to *not care.*

She'd lost her seat in the Senate and her competition's entire platform had been about how the woman had *betrayed* her own kind by accepting the unnatural relationship.

Yeah, this wasn't the place I wanted to be. *Relax. Maybe you're just driving through. On the way to Tennessee or the Carolinas—*

Oh, no…not a good thought, that one. In the past six months, supposedly they'd made strides on the vampire infestation that had plagued the state for several years, but who knew if they'd ever get the upper hand.

I was almost positive Justin wouldn't attempt to go anywhere near there, not with me in the car.

Still, my hands were slick with sweat and my shoulders had turned into a hard, knotted mess.

"Where are we going?" I asked, staring at the open expanse of the marked sky road in front of us. The air traffic pattern cluttered up the clear, blue bowl of the sky, but at least there was sense to the traffic—cars weren't shooting off in every direction.

Justin's jaw tightened for a moment and then he flexed his hands, deliberately loosening them before looking over at me.

"Savannah."

I'd been prepared for anything up to South Carolina. I'd thought.

But hearing the name of *that* city had me jerking upright, my hands fisted in my lap as I gaped at him. "Savannah…are you *kidding* me?"

Justin was unperturbed. "No."

From the back of the sleek little sports car, I heard a snicker, but I didn't look back. If Tate thought it was a grand plan to walk into one of the few cities where NHs were sometimes shot on sight, then hey, good for her. It wasn't my idea of fun.

"Why?"

He reached between us and popped open the center console, withdrawing a palm-sized computer. "Read up."

With dread creeping through me, I powered it up. It was a case file, the kind I'd generate if I'd taken a job on, but the word *sketchy* didn't even describe it. There was a location—just outside of Savannah and then information on four people.

There were four images in the information—two had no names, just descriptions and races. White male, vampire. Female, race undetermined—that probably meant she was an offshoot. Then there were two shifters. My gaze bounced off one—black male, skinny, young—who looked like he was barely out of his spike and the age seemed about right. Nineteen.

The fourth name made my hands clench on the datapad.

"Kit?"

Shaking my head, I focused on the picture.

She was even more striking in this picture than the one I'd seen in Chang's office.

Shanelle Maguire was beautiful. That wasn't surprising.

There was a glint of intelligence in her eyes and the information definitely backed that up. She was an engineer, had a job at one of the few companies that openly hired NHs, and not just for muscle. She'd be strong, though. I had no doubt of that.

If she was a former lover of Damon's, strength was a given and not just because she was a shifter.

Damon wasn't into damsels, not matter how often he thought about putting me in a tower.

Shanelle Maguire wasn't the kind of woman who'd need a tower—or even inspire those thoughts. Even from the picture, she looked like a force to be reckoned with.

Before my thoughts could get any darker, I forced myself to keep reading.

I finished, still focused on breathing—and controlling the emotions raging inside me.

Tate tapped my shoulder and I passed it back to her as I looked over at Justin.

"That didn't tell me jackshit."

"It told you plenty." He gave me a curious look. "I think it told you more than it told me. What did you see?"

"Nothing." I lied without blinking an eye and if we'd been outside, I would have turned my back on him. "What are we doing?"

He let it go. But his next words completely floored me.

"They are due to be transported to the hospital within the next week." His eyes gleamed and a cold, vicious smile twisted his lips. "We're going to make sure that doesn't happen."

The hospital. There was a lurching sort of fear inside my belly, the kind that left a cold sweat in its wake. As a metallic taste formed in the back of my throat, I took in a deep breath. "You're sure? Is this from Nova?"

"Yeah."

Well, that would explain the avid glint in his eye. Justin was on a blood trail. He wouldn't let it go for anything now. "Lovely." That processed, I asked, "Don't suppose our friendly, neighborhood psychotic psychic gave you any idea of whether or not we'd survive, did he?"

"Odds are good." Justin's nostrils flared as he sucked in a slow, deep breath. "He wanted me to tell you that you did good. I wasn't sure what he meant until you told…"

I shot him a silencing look.

He smiled. "Well, you did good. He's quite satisfied."

"My life is now complete," I said dryly. I settled deeper into the seat, letting the specs of the job settle deeper inside.

It was just a rescue, I told myself.

I'd done them before.

This would be easy.

No sweat.

"Enjoy your stay. Please be advised that an extra twenty percent will be added to your bill, in accordance with NH safety regulations. Magic of any sort, shapeshifting and violence are forbidden on this property and violators are subject to fines and imprisonment."

I curled my lip as the politely delivered message ended and Justin's key for the pre-paid motel room was dropped out of the slot.

"Twenty percent? That's insane," Tate said.

"Complain to the state liaison." Justin hefted his bag as he strode up the walk, searching out our unit. "Georgia state law allows business owners to decide their own hazard charge, as long as it's not applied to any humans."

"You know, we *could* have just gone straight on to Savannah, avoided being ripped off by paying for a squalid, filthy room and just done our job and gotten the hell out of Dodge," I said helpfully.

"We *could* have, I guess." Justin swiped the chip in front of the lock. It made a low, electronic hum and the locks disengaged. "But we didn't. Look, we need to sleep and I'm meeting a contact."

A contact.

Great.

As he disappeared into the room, I lingered on the porch, my bag hooked over one shoulder. Staring out over into the night, I focused on the uneasiness that spread through me with every passing second.

"This contact had better be important," I said after a moment. "And prompt."

Justin stood near one of two beds. Neither of them were particularly clean looking. He'd taken the one closest to the door and the quilt was a revolting shade of green, one that made me think of bile.

As I stared at him, he checked the time. After a moment, he finally seemed to realize I'd said something—and was waiting for a response. "Yeah, it's important. And…prompt? Why?"

"Because we don't need to *be* here," I said.

"Meaning…?"

I shook my head. I couldn't define what I felt any better than that.

But Justin knew me well enough to hear the unsaid things. He closed his eyes and started to swear, long and loud.

Tate sat on the edge of the other bed, apparently unconcerned by the fact that the quilt looked like it hadn't been cleaned since the war. "Why don't we need to be here?" she asked, her brow wrinkling. "Is this some of your crazy *aneira* shit?"

"Sure." I gave her a wide smile. "Just like setting things on fire is your crazy witch shit."

I moved back to the door, drawn by some unseen threat and a faint voice in the back of my mind, one that whispered: *Hurry hurry hurry*—

"How many people knew we'd be here?" I asked, resting one hand on the butt of the Glock.

"Only my contact." A grim smile slanted his lips as he added, "And the online reservation service I used to book the room, but I don't think that counts since it's a *what* and not a *who*."

I stared hard into the darkness. "Who is…"

The words lodged in my throat as a cool presence drifted across the edge of my consciousness.

Justin moved to join me.

I murmured his name softly.

"Well, fuck." Mouth in a tight, grim line, Justin lifted his eyes upward.

A shiver raced down my spine as my conscience brain acknowledged what my instincts had already figured out.

• • •
102

"Kit?"

I shook my hand, trying to ease the gut-wrenching nerves. "Yeah?"

"It's going to be okay," Justin murmured.

Then he moved forward, right as the pale, dark-haired form emerged from the darkness.

Abraham Allerton stood there, studying us. He stared at us. We stared back. I had the feeling he was holding himself still only because he was giving us—*me*—time to adjust to his presence.

"If he's your source, Justin, couldn't you have met in East Orlando?"

Justin scowled. "He's not my source," he said, frustration underscoring his voice. "What are you doing here, Abe?"

A flicker of distaste crossed Abraham's face, but it was gone quickly, like a ripple over a lake. "I'm looking for you." A benign smile curved his lips. "We agreed to share information, after all. I shared. Now it's your turn."

"I'm sort of in the middle of a job," Justin said.

"No." Abraham looked around, his expression bored. "You're in the middle of a trap."

I tensed.

Next to me, Justin's posture lost its easy languidness. "What?"

"A trap," Abraham said. Then, helpfully, he offered, "It's when you're in a position to be captured by bad people who wish to do bad things to you. It's not a place you want to be, Justin. I'm sure Ms. Colbana and Ms. Prescott don't wish to be in that position, even if you are somewhat careless."

Justin strode forward.

Abraham was either one tough bastard or stupid. I'd seen people die when Justin had that look on his face. He stopped just inches from Abraham. "Explain—and do it fast."

"I shall, because fast is all we have time for." The lazy amusement faded from his face. "You need to leave—all three of you—and you must do it immediately. This establishment is...problematic."

"That's not explaining."

His hair fell to the side, brushing his shoulders as he explained, "In the past two years, seven non-humans have disappeared from this motel. None of them were ever seen again. In the past two years, only nine non-humans have ever stayed here. Those numbers are troubling."

"Uh...*yeah*," Tate said, snorting.

Abraham didn't even look at her. "And aside from that is your...source. He's even more of a problem. He's a skin trader."

I hissed out a breath. Tate gasped and Justin's spine went poker-straight.

Skin traders are pretty much the scum of the earth, and that's being polite. They were NHs who sold their own kind out. It didn't matter who it was, or what was going to happen to them. What mattered was the bottom dollar and the bigger that bottom dollar was, the happier the skin trader was.

"You're fucking with me," Justin said, shaking his head. "I know him."

"As do I." A thin smile curled Abraham's lips. "And I'll be sure to keep that acquaintance in mind when I hunt him down and rip out his jugular. Trust me, Justin...Saul Tremble is a skin trader. He's one of the best. He flies so low on the radar, nobody ever recognizes him. He's one of the men I've been hunting for years...and I never even realized it was *him* I was hunting until seventy-two hours ago."

Justin turned away. His gaze connected with mine before bouncing away. He was pale, almost as shaken as I'd ever seen him. "You're sure?" he asked, his voice low and rough.

"I'm afraid I am," Abraham said quietly.

Justin nodded and said nothing for the next couple of minutes.

I looked at Tate. "Pack up."

By the time Justin had finished wrapping his mind around what he'd just learned—or at least shoving it into a box until he was ready to deal with it—we were ready to go.

"We're just going to have to drive through the night," Justin said, tossing his bag into the car.

"I have a place," Abraham offered, walking alongside me.

It was somewhat disconcerting to realize his nearness didn't bother me. It wasn't any more disturbing than having Scott standing next to me, or Chang.

"We'll make do," came Justin's terse reply.

"You should let me help you," Abraham said, his voice flat. "You agreed to share information with me. I've shared information. You've withheld it. That's not like you, Justin. I can be of help and you know it."

Justin opened his mouth only to shut it without saying anything.

Abraham pushed his advantage. He looked back at me, then at Tate. "Three of you. You intend to do this with only three of you."

Justin lifted a shoulder. "With the plan I have, I could do it with two, but I like to be prepared."

Abraham lifted a brow. "A fourth would be better. I know where you're going. Don't be foolish."

"I got this." Neither of them looked at me as they argued.

That pointed avoidance had me narrowing my eyes, because I had a feeling I knew why Justin was refusing the offered help.

"We have a mutual interest." Abraham was one stubborn son of a bitch.

"Yeah, we do." Justin opened the door, but lingered, eying Abraham. "Look, you wanted us gone, so we're going. But listen up, I've worked with too many vamps before. Once you get the man you want, you're just as likely to bail and I plan on getting *all* of them out."

"I will help you with that—you have my word."

"Not the issue." Justin went to climb inside.

"Justin."

He stilled.

"Do we need another set of hands?" My own hands were slippery with sweat.

"We can handle it," Justin said. The words were completely and utterly devoid of emotion. He didn't sound confident but he didn't sound doubtful. That worried me more than anything.

"That's not what she asked," Tate said quietly, moving to stand at my shoulder—not a place I'd *ever* expected her to be.

I didn't look at her. "Yes or no, can we use more hands on this?"

• • •
106

Chapter Nine

My newfound sense of calm melted when I realized Abraham wasn't going to fly the friendly skies as vampires tended to do. Nope, he was going to *ride* with us. In Justin's car.

The idea of being trapped in the confines of a car with him was beyond nerve-wracking and my stomach wanted to twitch and heave. I fought to calm myself as we sped down the highway.

I'd ducked into the backseat as soon as I'd realized what he planned to do. No way did I want a vampire at my back, even one who didn't make my skin crawl. We'd been heading north down the country highway for maybe ten minutes when a black truck drove by us, driving in the opposite direction. I couldn't explain why, but I looked back and noted the license plates, committing them to memory.

Then there was another black truck, followed by three black sedans. There was another truck—a utility vehicle—and although we were speeding by, I sensed the presence of numerous people inside it. Curling my hands into fists, I said, "Justin...we have to *move*."

"Yeah. I figured that."

"There were twenty men in the truck," Abraham said and I watched as he turned his head slightly, watching as the last of the cavalry drove by—three identical black vans. The tint on the windshield was so dark, I could only make out the roughest of features and there were no other windows.

"You can tell that?" I asked softly.

"Yes." He didn't elaborate further.

"Think that was for us?" Tate asked softly.

"I'd lay money on it." Slumping in my seat, I continued to stare down the road. It wouldn't have been enough, not for me, Tate *and* Justin. Add Abraham into the mix—assuming he didn't take to the skies—and the only ending wouldn't have been a happy one. Not for us or the people we would have ended up killing.

"Think they'll turn around and come after us?"

Justin grunted and reached out, flipping a few switches. The move from road to air was seamless and then we were wrapped in darkness as he turned off the lights. "I'm almost betting on it. But we won't be there for them to find."

His magic started to ripple in the air. "Is that smart?" I asked.

"Public roads and public airspace, Kit. As long as I'm using non-offensive magic, I should be cool." Then he met my gaze. "But even if I'm not, we're not hanging around here."

"Talk."

Just over an hour later, we'd reached the house Abraham had offered. We'd all had a chance to eat and change.

Tate had disappeared and I don't know where Abraham was.

Taking the chance to corner Justin, I followed him into the room Abraham had offered him, shoving past him when he tried to shut the door.

"It's late, Kit," he said. "We need to rest up and get ready for tomorrow."

"*You* need to tell me what's going on—who Saul is and why you're not explaining this job in better detail." I punctuated the last few words by drilling my finger into his chest.

He grimaced and caught my wrist, nudging it down. "Stop trying to skewer me. And…" He stopped abruptly, heaving out a sigh. He spun around and threw his fist out, smashing it into the wall. "*Fuck!*"

I simply waited.

I'd known he was angry. I might have even been waiting for this.

When I smelled blood, I wasn't surprised.

Blood was welling from his split skin as he pulled his hand back and I sighed. Turning away, I moved toward his bags and opened a small black one, rooting around until I located the first aid kit he carried.

With an ease born of practice, I pulled out the items I needed and moved back to him. "Tearing up Abraham's place isn't going to help you feel better," I said quietly.

"What will?"

I looked up at him. "I don't know."

His eyes connected with mine. Rage and misery danced in his eyes.

He reached up and touched my cheek. "Kit…"

Oh, shit.

I caught his wrist. "Don't," I whispered.

His lashes swept down, shielding his eyes. A humorless smile curled his lips. "Well, it was something that would have made me feel better."

I focused on cleaning his hand. The cut was small and shallow. Thanks to his hyped-up DNA, he'd be healed within a week, unless he decided to speed it up even more. As I finished wiping away the blood, I said softly, "It wouldn't make you feel better. You only think it would."

Justin pulled his hand away. There was still blood on it, but the sudden stiffness of his body kept me from arguing. "Don't think for me, Kit. I know what I feel, what I want."

Heat suffused my face. Awkward now, I gathered up the supplies. The things that weren't reusable, I threw in the fireplace. Witches—and creatures like me—tended to burn anything that had body fluids on it, rather than just throw it away. Especially blood.

"Justin…"

"Kit, it's okay. I can handle it. Just don't tell me what I think, what I feel."

From the corner of my eye, I saw the long line of his spine. He was facing the fireplace now, hands braced on the mantle as he bent over it, the heavy weight of his dreads falling to shield his face.

An ache settled inside me and my voice was husky as I said softly, "Okay."

Neither of us spoke for what felt like an eternity and I was just about ready to leave when he finally turned from the fireplace and looked at me. "So." Crossing his arms over his chest, he blew out a breath. "About the job…"

There's only one rule. Don't kill or cause any lasting harm.

That was what Justin had told us.

That was what was going to make this job a total bitch, although not undoable.

It required that I do something I didn't particularly like to do in front of people, even the ones I was supposed to be working with. There was only one here that I truly trusted and my secrets were safe with him.

Tate and Abraham were a different matter entirely, but the entire plan—so simple, it just might be stupid enough to work—depended on one of those secrets. Now, as I faded out, right in front of Tate, Abraham and Justin, I hoped I didn't have any reason to regret this. Very few outside the *aneira* race knew of our ability to go invisible. It was a handy trick for a race that made a living as assassins and bounty hunters. Or, in my case, a general jack of all trades.

I'd studied the blueprints of the building, memorized hallways and corridors and then I did the same with the outbuildings.

We were going in blind—and fast. No time to prep, which meant I'd have to follow my gut once we got there. My gut said they wouldn't be in the house, but they'd be damn close.

The most likely option was the oblong building a few hundred yards from the big house. There was a swimming pool and the rest of the space between the house and the building was open ground

No cover.

Wonderful.

I studied the map but time and again, my gaze returned to that one building. Okay, then. I'll start there first.

Mind made, I focused on the less likely methods of departure. Hopefully, none of those would be necessary. The reason Justin and Tate were there was to provide a distraction when I was ready.

All I had to do was send a single message.

Simple.

While they watched from their position a quarter of a mile away, I moved in. I'd like it if they were closer, but the security here was tight. Cameras picked up any and all movements and until I was able to throw them offline, nobody could risk moving through the trees with me.

I had to take it slower than I liked because while the cameras wouldn't capture *me*, if I broke a branch or brushed up against something, whatever I touched would be seen.

Crossing that quarter mile seemed to take hours.

My brain told me it had taken roughly fifteen minutes, even moving at what felt like a snail's pace to me.

I reached the gate that rose up around the compound and circled slowly, looking for the best way in. The wall was ten feet high. I could climb easy but I wasn't about to touch it. Although the security information we'd received said nothing about the gate being touch-responsive, I wasn't taking that chance. There was a way in, though. There was always a way in.

This time, it proved to be via a tree, one with a long, heavy branch that ended just a few feet away from the gate. I spent five minutes working out the best path, one that would most likely go undetected by the watchful eye of a camera if somebody should notice a branch moving this way or that.

It put me more than fifteen feet up in the air and I stared down over into the surrounded yard.

Landscaped within an inch of its life, the nicely manicured lawn spread out in every direction with absolutely no cover. Guards patrolled the house inside that massive fence and light shown from almost every window.

And there were a lot more guards near that building that had caught my eye. Twenty of them, I thought at first glance, but there might be more.

This was listed as a private residence.

My ass.

I made the jump that took me from the tree to the ground. It would be trickier getting out, but that was just something I'd have to deal with.

Crouched in the grass, I held my breath and waited.

One guard passed by, only ten feet away—so close, I could see the lines age had carved into his face, forming grooves around his mouth and eyes. The weapon he held was one that could put very big holes in me—or anything else. It was loaded with silver.

He also had a blade more than a foot long strapped to his left thigh, set up for a cross-draw. I made out four other weapons on him before he moved out of sight.

Wonder how many of *them* I'd have to avoid tonight.

Between me and the house? There were six.

There were another dozen inside the house—and I had to go inside first. Disabling the cameras was vital.

That would actually be the easier task and I knew it the moment I got inside.

They hadn't soundproofed the rooms good enough and I could already hear the faint whine electronics gave off. Humans couldn't detect it. I'd grown used to that background noise until it was nothing more than static. Focusing on it now, I let it guide me.

The room where the security was monitored was spacious, on the lower level and done up in a way that made me think of a spaceship. Sleek and shiny and high tech.

And it was manned by all of two men.

With a pleased smile, I got to work.

Getting to that outbuilding was more problematic.

I entered the house when I slipped in behind a man who'd gone outside for his break.

I exited the same way, trailing after another guard, one who stank of tobacco and sickness. I wonder if he knew he had cancer, but I decided it wasn't likely. It was early, just barely noticeable under the smells of smoke, sweat and everything else.

● ● ●

He moved off into the direction of a small grouping of chairs but paused a few feet away, turning around to study the area around him.

His gaze tripped right over me.

The odd look on his face made me uneasy—he'd sensed something. Soldiers usually had good instincts. But he was like almost everything else out there—he believed what his eyes told him and his eyes told him nothing was there.

Still, I held my breath and waited there until he had settled himself down with a cigarette in the sheltered spot I could see waiting in a pool of light. Once he was busy with his cigarette, I continued my way across the grounds.

The next objective was to learn where the NHs were being kept. They were here. The air was static with their energy and I was getting closer.

I was still several dozen yards away from the outbuilding, trying to filter a scent out past the chlorine from the pool, or a sound.

A low, powerful roar drifted through the night. It was cut off abruptly, followed by a pained whine.

And...laughter.

"Damn...she's got tits even when she shifts! Look at the crazy-ass shit!"

Demeaning, mocking laughter.

"Nice ones, too. I wouldn't mind having a piece...except I don't want to turn into a damn monster."

"Remember that wolf..."

I'd heard everything I needed to know.

In a sprint, I raced over the ground, dodging the guards, cataloging away the ones who turned their heads, almost as if they heard me. They hadn't, but it was like the soldier from earlier. Some were just sharper than others.

When I came to a stop, my heart was racing—from anger, not from the run. Pressing my back against the wall, I eased around until I could peer inside the building.

Nothing.

I moved to the next window.

Nothing.

The next was shuttered—and barred. Barred, inside and out. I couldn't see the bars on the inside, but through the narrow slit between the wooden shudders, I could see the thick iron.

Showtime.

I sent word to Justin, a coded message sent via the mic fixed to the inside of my vest.

And then, with one last look around, I pulled out the remote inside my back pocket.

Justin was a genius with all sorts of offensive attacks, from spells to charms to bombs.

What lay inside the security room, with all those cameras and telephones, was a mix of the mundane and the magical and once I hit the button, a slow burning fire would start.

Two minutes later and the house descended into chaos.

The explosive had been the catalyst to a powerful hallucinogenic, one of Justin's charms. Screams started to echo from the house, and men came rushing out of the building behind me.

I eased past the one who still stood half inside the door, shouting into his radio with ever-increasing urgency.

When the screams turned to cries for help, the men shared grim looks and then the man in the door—clearly in charge—barked orders.

Nine guards went running. I'd placed myself in the corner behind the door and watched as they all came rushing in. Almost half of them left for the house, which left me with ten more men, including the grim one who still guarded the door, a hand on the pulse blaster at his side.

That thing wouldn't put a hole in me, but the electric charge it put out could put a rhino on its ass.

Keeping him in my sight, I started down the hall.

Justin and Tate would be doing their thing while Abraham kept watch from the skies. Time for me to get moving.

I heard the first blast before I even made it out of the main hallway, but I didn't turn back.

Two more guards waited at the first door—a sealed one.

With a silent swear, I moved as close as I could to study the locking mechanism.

It was a bio-lock. I didn't see a retinal scan, but that didn't mean much. Some of the new tech was a serious pain in the ass.

They spoke, a low, terse exchange that convinced me of a couple of things—these weren't green recruits and they weren't going to leave their post of their own accord.

Fine, they could leave on *my* accord.

Whoever ran this place liked the fancy shit even here, in their prison cum torture chamber. They had definitely been doing some torturing. The stink of burnt flesh and blood hung in the air like a bad perfume, totally out of place with the fine furnishings and the elegant painting that decorated almost the entire length of one wall.

A small, beautifully carved table rested next to the other wall and on it was a bowl of exquisite crystal. Tracing one finger along the lip of the bowl, I told myself it was for the greater good.

I still winced as I knocked it off the table and sent it flying to the floor.

I darted around the one who came over to inspect the bowl. Both of them were staring all around, eyes wide. They'd already drawn their weapons but they had nothing to aim at.

I did, though.

I wasn't allowed to cause any harm or kill anybody.

But the dart now protruding from the guard's neck wasn't going to cause *harm*. Just heavy, crazy dreams.

I plucked the dart out before he could fall and I spun to face the other one.

He turned at the sound of his partner falling to the ground. The other dart found its home and then I was alone.

I dealt with the bio lock. It required the palm print of the man at my feet and then the ID tag he wore around his neck. It took under a minute and I was sweating from the nerves by the time I was done.

Please let that be all…

The door unlocked and I froze.

There were two guards.

One of them held a weapon trained on the door, but this wasn't one of the annoying pulse weapons.

It was an old school UMP9 and I'd bet my eyeteeth it was loaded with some sort of silver ammo.

Considering the NHs restrained in various forms around the room, silver was the best weapon to pack. There were more than the four we'd been looking for— Justin had said there might but I hadn't been prepared for almost double that number.

Considering what they were dealing with, the UMP was probably *under*kill, but it could still cut me in two. The same could be said for the witches.

I doubted the shooter would be fast enough to use it on a shifter or vamp, though.

I hit the floor and rolled, coming up in a crouch near the feet of one of the witches.

She knew I was there.

She couldn't see me, but she'd sensed me—heard me, smelled me, something.

The female cat shifter knew I was there, too. Shanelle. From the corner of my eye, I saw her nostrils flare as she drew in a deep drag of air. As she let it out, a faint smile curled her lips.

That smile made me uneasy.

Deal with the problem at hand, then with her.

"Where is it?" That came from the second guard. He stood in the middle of the room, a knife in one hand and a limp body in his arms.

A witch.

Her eyes were open, but dull and glazed and even when he pricked her neck with the knife, she didn't react.

I readied another dart.

It hit its target as the man jabbed her harder with the knife. "Who's here, you little…"

He stumbled.

The woman fell to the floor, limp, her neck bleeding. Her wound wasn't fatal.

The first guard spun, watching as his partner staggered and then went to his knees.

In the split second I had, I took him out, too.

A collective breath left the monsters around me and I stiffened as first one, then another, and another turned my way. There were seven of them in there, not the four Justin had believed.

"Are there more?" I asked softly.

"Not yet." The words came from the female shifter. "But there will be. *Hurry.*"

Wasn't planning to dawdle, sweetheart.

Working my way around the room, I freed the witches first, then the oldest of the two vampires. "Are you Icarus?"

He stared at the empty air—or what he thought was empty air—for a brief moment. "I am."

"Abraham has been searching for you. He's waiting."

He just inclined his head and without asking, he moved to the wolf straining to free himself. The wolf was big, bulky and despite the snarl tightening his features, he was gorgeous.

Skin a dark, deep brown and through heavy dreadlocks, I could see eyes the color of gold. He growled as Icarus freed him.

I saw his plan in the subtle tensing of his body.

"No!" I shouted.

He didn't even slow.

Icarus caught him and threw him to the ground.

"Off me, leech," the shifter said, his voice a low, dangerous snarl. "I want blood."

Icarus didn't move. "You'll have to get it later. We have no time."

"I'll just slaughter them all," the wolf panted.

Hurriedly, I freed Shanelle and then as she moved away from the wall, I ducked behind her.

Behind the shield of her taller, curvier body, I let the invisibility fade and then I moved back to face them.

She hissed and leaped away, landing on her hands and knees nearly ten feet away. It would have been funny if I had the time to appreciate it. "We can't kill any of them," I said, striding forward and placing myself between the wolf and the two unconscious mortals.

He tossed his head, throwing the dreads from his eyes—no. *Eye*. I hadn't seen the injury until that moment. He only had one eye and despite the puckered scar where his other one should be, I had a sick feeling that wasn't an old wound. "We won't kill anybody. *I* will kill them."

"No." I twitched my wrist, letting a blade fall into it. "None of them can die."

He snarled and lunged—I was snatched back before I had a chance to react, cold arms binding me to an even colder body. I tensed, fighting the fear that choked me. The vampire who held me still hadn't spoken. Icarus eyed him for a second and then looked at me.

"Alejandro, you may release her. My dear, round up the others," Icarus said, his voice smooth and unperturbed.

The silent vampire behind me freed me right as I found my tongue—ready to lash out, cut, fight, bite—anything to get away.

He said nothing at my obvious fear and moved to join Icarus, who stood as a wall between the wolf and the guards.

"Drake."

It was Shanelle who spoke. The wolf—Drake—tensed as she picked up the UMP on the floor. Her small hands looked almost comical on it, but she held it with confidence.

"We're leaving and you're not going to interfere. If you try, you can stay here…in pieces."

Damn. Too bad I'd already decided I wouldn't like her.

"Where is he?"

It was the first words any of them had spoken since Justin had appeared out of the darkness with what looked like a work van too battered to even run. But it purred like a big cat and cut through the night like a dream.

From my position in the front seat, I asked, "Who?"

Her nostrils did that funny flare thing again as she scented the air. Her gaze locked on me.

"The man who hired you. Where is he?"

Justin chuckled. "You're looking at him, sweetheart."

"But I—" Shanelle stopped then, an assessing look in her eyes. "You're working for somebody then?"

"Nope." Justin sounded almost cheerful and I watched as his gaze flicked to the back. The corner, I thought, where three female witches huddled together. They hadn't spoken; they barely seemed to realize we were there. After a moment, he shifted his attention back to Shanelle. "You were in the right place—wasn't going to leave you there—but you weren't who we went in after."

Looking out the window, I stared at the night as it sped by.

"Kit?"

"Yeah?"

When Justin didn't respond right away, I looked over at him. He opened his mouth, but then after a few seconds, closed it without saying anything. He shook his head, clearly deciding against whatever he'd been about to say.

Sighing, I rested my head on the padded cushion of the seat. I was exhausted.

I was also ready to be done with this and get back to East Orlando.

To Damon.

Because even though she was off-base about why we'd rescued her, I knew why she'd made the assumption.

I could still smell Damon on me. No doubt she could, too. She'd just made the wrong assumption…and now we had the next couple of hours for her to figure out the *right* assumptions.

● ● ●

Maybe I had a little of that insane possessiveness Damon was always displaying, because all I wanted to do was get back to him—mark my territory.

CHAPTER TEN

I didn't go home.

My body screamed for sleep, but I had Justin take me to the Lair.

Fortunately, he'd taken Shanelle to the Assembly first—Shanelle, Drake, the others. Since their kidnapping and captivity was somewhat of an issue, as Justin had called it, he'd decided it would be better if they all spoke with the Assembly first, filed their formal complaints and all that bullshit. Complaints—after being kidnapped and tortured.

Even if they knew who'd done it, nothing would be done to them.

But if they had the complaints filed, they'd have something of a defense if the people who'd done it attempted to come looking for them again. At least if it happened here in Florida. The laws here, at least, were slowly getting better and we had some protection.

While she was tending to that, I had every intention of finding Damon.

Sadly, he wasn't around when I got there.

Voices went quiet, briefly, as I climbed out of the car. Justin joined me at the curb, looking almost as haggard as I felt. He held my bag out and glanced around for a moment. "What's up between you and the female?"

He didn't clarify *which* female.

I didn't need him to.

Chewing on my lip, I debated on what to tell him and finally just gave him the truth—or the abbreviated version. "She used to have a thing with him."

I didn't clarify *which* him.

Justin didn't need me to.

His brows went straight up and he dragged his hands down his face. "Well, shit."

"Yep."

His gaze came back to me. "Are…" He hesitated, clearly searching for the right words. "Are you…back?"

Although I hadn't told Justin the personal details of what was going on between Damon and me, I think he knew me well enough to guess. "Yeah." I shrugged self-consciously. "There was never a question of it, really. I…I love him. I just needed time."

Justin reached out and this time, when his fingers brushed my cheek, I didn't move.

Maybe he did still have feelings for me, but first, last and always, he was a friend. "After what you went through, if you *didn't* need time, I'd think there was something wrong with you."

"There are all sorts of things wrong with me," I muttered. I caught his hand as he went to lower it and gave it a quick squeeze. "But…yeah. I needed time. He gave it to me."

He gave me too *much* time, but that didn't matter now. "We're fine, though. And she…."

I pursed my lips for a moment. "She was coming down here because there was business between her clan and the assembly, but also because…" I blew out a breath. "She's got this idea that she can come back and reclaim her *position*."

"Reclaim." His green eyes glittered like glass. "So she was here before. With Annette, I assume."

We were speaking in low voices due to all the shifters around, but at the mention of the former Alpha's name, I glanced around. Nobody seemed to pay us any attention. The operative word there—*seemed*. "Yes, she was."

We left the other part unsaid. *And Damon.*

My hands curled into fists. "She thought he sent me after her." Slipping Justin a hot look, I said fiercely, "She *can't* have him."

He laughed. "Kit…I don't think that's even an issue." He leaned in and kissed my brow. "I've got to go. The witch…"

As he straightened, I tried to figure out which witch. I couldn't.

He looked away. "Lila."

Lila. The one they'd grabbed when I went in. She'd been catatonic the entire drive back, making no sound, no response, no matter what anybody had said or done.

"She's the one you were really after," I said softly.

"Yeah."

"Why?"

When his gaze came to mine, the green was all but blazing. "Because she's the only one I've ever known to have escaped the hospital."

Those words punched the air right out of me. "Escaped…"

"Yes." The air around him sparked, a sign of his agitation, too much energy rolling through him. "She escaped. But somehow they found her."

For the first time in months, I strode into the Lair and I was stained with soot and smelling of smoke and sweat. We hadn't taken the time to stop on our way out of Georgia and my skin all but itched with the need to wash up.

Yeah, I knew how to make an entrance.

Nobody spoke to me as I made my way inside, but I wasn't given the *eyes-on-toes* treatment I'd gotten when I'd first returned to the Lair after my kidnapping. It wasn't until I was nearly to Damon's quarters when somebody fell into step with me.

Scott looked like he'd just stepped off the cover of a men's fashion mag, dressed in a collarless white dress shirt, his custom-fit suit a deep, steel gray. I looked even more ragged next to him. "Hello, Kit," he said, his voice polite.

"Scott." I flicked him a look. "Where is he?"

I didn't have to ask to know he wasn't here. If Damon had been in the Lair, he would have met me before I even stepped inside.

"Attending to some business." He reached the door to Damon's quarters before I did and opened it, allowing me to precede him inside. He lingered near the door as I moved deeper inside. "If this is urgent, I can notify him."

I almost said, *Please…*

But it wasn't urgent that I see him right that moment. Maybe I wanted to, but I didn't have to.

"No." Looking around the broad, open space, I asked, "Is it okay if I wait, though?"

"Of course." He opened the door. "Shall I have somebody bring you some food? You look as if you've had an eventful day."

"I..." I almost refused and then I stopped. "Yeah. I can eat. Anything is fine...as long as it's no longer bleeding."

He chuckled. "I'll make sure the food is cooked, Kit. I promise. Perhaps a burger and fries? You're fond of fries, if I recall correctly."

He recalled correctly. Once he'd been my shadow and I bet he could even tell me all the places where I was known to enjoy fries. "That works."

"I'll see to it. And I'll make sure the burger no longer bleeds." He winked and slid outside. I turned in a slow circle, looking around the room.

I hadn't brought anything with me other than the gear I carried in my bag. There was an extra set of clothes in there, but I didn't want work clothes. I wanted something warm and soft against my skin as I cuddled up on the lake-sized bed that took up almost a quarter of the opposite wall.

Ducking through the door that led the shower and his office, I moved into his closet. There was a built-in set of drawers and I tugged open the top one, staring down at the clothes I'd left here more than a year ago.

Everything was still in there.

Jeans, panties, bras, shirts, the spare work clothes I'd brought just in case.

I took out underclothes, a pair of soft cotton pajama bottoms and a faded T-shirt that had *Memphis* scrawled across the chest.

Exhaustion beat at me as I stumbled into the lavish bathroom. It was done in earth tones with gold accents, more elegant than you'd expect from a guy like Damon.

The only thing that kept me from falling asleep in the shower was the fact that I knew I'd drown if I did. Once I'd washed the soot, blood and sweat away, I fell face-first onto Damon's big bed. It was soft as a cloud and I grabbed the pillow, bringing it to my chest.

It smelled of Damon.

Smiling, I closed my eyes.

It was a surprise when I woke up curled around Damon.

The feel of his hand curved over my ass was a surprise after so many nights alone. A surprise, yes. But a welcome one. Snuggling deeper into him, I murmured, "I don't want to move. Ever."

His hand smoothed gently down my spine and his lips brushed over my brow. "Good morning, Goldilocks."

"Somebody's been sleeping in your bed."

He laughed softly. "My favorite somebody."

He moved and I caught my breath as he pulled me on top of him.

"You smell like smoke."

"Job got hot," I said, reaching down to trace my finger along his cheek. His skin was warm, five o'clock shadow darkening his jawline.

"What time is it?"

"A little before three. Scott said you've been here since ten."

I yawned and my jaw cracked. "Yeah. Spent most of it sleeping."

He nodded at the tray on the table across the room. "He sent food, but it's cold by now. I'll call for more."

I sat up, eying the burger and fries. I hadn't even heard Scott come in. It was unsettling, but there was nowhere I was safer than in Damon's quarters, whether or not he was there.

"I need to call Justin—check in and see if he got everything wrapped up."

"You need food." His voice was flat. "Kit, you're exhausted."

I grimaced as I threw my legs over the side of the bed. It was so tall, my feet didn't even touch the floor.

"I'll eat." I *was* exhausted. Sighing, I looked around, searching for signs that anything had changed.

"This job…"

I looked at Damon. His nostrils flared as he breathed in the air.

Nerves clenched inside me. "Yeah?"

"What exactly were you doing?"

"I…ah…" Shrugging, I looked away. "I told you about it. NHs were being held against their will. We busted them out."

I felt his reaction more than saw it. Because I wasn't ready to talk about Shanelle yet, I turned back to him, crawling across the lake of a bed until I could bend down and press my lips to his.

I bit his lower lip and he groaned, pulling me to him.

I'd missed this more than I'd thought possible.

As he cradled the back of my head, a wave of emotion flooded me, left me feeling stupid with love. *Wow…*

That was it.

Just…

Wow.

The last of the walls I'd unconsciously erected between us started to topple. I could feel myself surrendering completely to the need and love that still burned inside me. I was tired of being away from him, tired of the fear that wouldn't go away.

Breaking the kiss, I lifted my head to look down at him.

I'd hidden from all of this for too long while I struggled to come to grips with everything. Now that I was ready to deal with it again—deal with *us*—I was back in that crazy area where what I felt for him was constantly throwing me off balance.

Emotions had never been my strong suit and what I felt for him was too big. But that didn't mean I'd give it up. And if some sexy shifter with a need to take back her place in his life tried to come between us, I'd cut her down.

"What is it?" he asked quietly.

I shook my head.

"Don't lie to me," he said. "You're worried about something."

I made a face at him. "I didn't lie. I shook my head. Difference." Shoving the tangle of my hair back, I thought about Shanelle, and the million questions that still burned inside me.

● ● ●

126

"Kit…"

"You have a couple of silver hairs popping up on your head. I never noticed." I grinned at him.

"You probably caused every one of them." He studied me. I felt the warmth of his breath ghosting along my skin as he tugged me closer. "Come on, Kit…"

I blew out a breath. "Look, I was…"

There was a hard knock at the door. "Go away," Damon shouted.

The knock came again.

Sighing, he let me go and I rolled away, eying the door with a mix of gratitude and sympathy. Damon didn't like it when his orders weren't followed.

He had the door open before I even made it off the bed.

"Sometimes I think you have a death wish, Chang."

"It's important," the other man said.

Damon stepped aside, allowing his second in. Chang's gaze came straight to me, his mouth tight. He looked harder and colder than I'd ever seen him. "Where did you find her?"

"Ah…"

Damon's gaze cut to me as he closed the door. His eyes narrowed speculatively and I saw the very *second* he figured it out.

My response was interrupted by another knock.

Chang's eyes narrowed, a low growl in his voice.

"I told her to *wait*," he said.

Damon continued to stare at me for a long, long moment. Then, without saying a word, he turned and moved to the door.

I wasn't surprised, not really, when I heard her voice.

"Damon…"

From where I stood, I could see as she went to move in. I was doing the same thing—moving in to knock her *away*.

It wasn't necessary, though, because Damon had already moved out of her reach.

Her face fell, although the expression was gone almost as quickly as it came.

She smiled. "What…no hug?"

"Shanelle."

He shot me a look.

Shanelle glanced my way and then back to him. Then her head whipped back in my direction

"You…"

She had big, brown eyes and as she stared at me, the heat that had been in her eyes faded to ice. "So he didn't *hire* you, huh?"

"Nope." I shrugged and dropped down on the couch. My sword was now in reach. Not that I expected I'd need it, but in a moment, she'd stop thinking about getting in Damon's pants and connect some dots and come up with the right picture.

One that included the fact that *I* was the only one who'd be getting into Damon's pants.

"Shanelle. You were expected over a week ago," Damon said, drawing her attention back to him. "Where have you been?"

"Where…" She stopped and shook her head. "What do you mean, where have I been? Didn't you…"

The words trailed off as Damon moved closer to me.

"Hire her?" he offered as he settled on the couch next to me. He kicked his legs up and put his feet on the polished surface of the table. "She just said *no*." He slid me a look. "We're going to talk about this job, Kit."

I ignored him, my attention focused on the woman across from us.

"You don't know," she said quietly, her voice tight. "You *didn't* know. You didn't send her after me?"

Damon curled a possessive hand around the back of my neck. "Would be hard to do since I had no idea where you were."

She didn't even seem to hear him. She was staring at the hand he had on my neck and the tension in the air spiked.

"Shanelle."

Chang's voice was low and the authority in it was undeniable. Still, it took the woman several moments to drag her eyes from me—and Damon—to look at the slender man across the room. "You were told to wait," he said when she finally looked at him.

She angled her chin up. "I was. I didn't."

Something that might have been temper snapped in Chang's gaze, but it was gone too quick to say. I was kind of surprised to see that she was getting under Chang's skin.

I didn't know that was possible.

"Chang updated me on your petition and I understand you're in my territory, regardless of that petition, for as long as it takes you to conclude the business you have with the Assembly. But…" Damon paused and although he didn't change position, didn't move a muscle or even alter his expression, everything about him changed, from his demeanor to the very feel of the room. The power level punched up so high, the hair on the back of my neck stood on end. "Remember…you *are* in my territory. You'll follow the laws or you'll suffer the consequences."

"Of course." Shanelle made it sound as if she lived to serve.

And she just might…if it suited her needs.

Damon's eyelids drooped low. "About the petition, that's still under consideration. However, if you're looking to return to the clan, then you better figure out a couple of things fast—and I mean *really* fast. Number one thing to figure out is that there's a new way of doing things now, Shanelle. If you're given an order, it's *followed*. I don't make allowances for old friends or bend the rules because it suits me at the time."

Color flooded her cheeks. "Understood." Her gaze skittered to me and then back. She inclined her head. "If I may…Alpha?"

Damon waved a hand. The gesture was casual. Everything about him was casual at the moment—a big cat stretching out to relax. But it was a façade. I could feel his tension even if I couldn't see it or sense it any other way.

"As you clearly pointed out," she said, her voice deferential, "things in the clan have changed. Ten years is a long time. Clan business is best discussed within the clan."

Amused, I settled more comfortably against the couch. "Is that your subtle way of trying to get Damon to send me away?" I asked. With a restless shrug, I added, "I'm not much on being *dismissed.*"

Heat burned in her dark brown gaze. "You should show more respect in the presence of the Alpha."

Damon skimmed his fingers along my neck and from the corner of my eye, I saw the way his mouth twitched, as if he was trying not to laugh.

"Perhaps you should concern yourself with *your* actions, instead of hers," Chang said. The words were mild.

Shanelle went stiff as they were said. She bowed her head. "I mean no disrespect, but clan business belongs within the clan."

"Yeah." Damon nodded, drawing his hand away. The absence of his heat made me sigh.

He flicked a look at me as I shifted and curled up more comfortably on the couch. This wasn't going to end up with either her or me bloody so I'd sit here and pretend to behave. For now.

"Clan business belongs with the clan." Damon moved one big shoulder in a shrug. "Outsiders have no place here, but Kit isn't an outsider. If I wish to discuss clan business in front of her, then that's what I'm going to do. Tuck that into that *things have changed* file, Shanelle. Kit's ours."

He paused and slid me a look. His lids drooped, shielding his gaze. "She's mine. Outsider rules don't apply to her."

The door shut behind Shanelle as she left. She ended up being dismissed out into the hall to cool her heels while Chang and Damon spoke

Right before she'd closed the door shut behind her, Damon had said softly. "One more thing, Shanelle. This section of the Lair is mine. Only me and my lieutenants can freely come and go down these halls. Stay out unless your presence is requested." He paused and then added, "Kit's the only exception. She can go wherever the hell she likes here."

Her eyes had gone flat and she'd given him the nice, polite subservient response, but anger tinged the air around her.

Now, as the echo of her passing faded, Chang stood there, head bowed, hands folded together in front of him. He seemed to be struggling with something.

Finally, he lifted his head and stared at us.

"I apologize, Kit, Damon." Chang's eyes held as much emotion as I'd ever seen. "If I'd known she wouldn't wait, I would have put a guard on her."

"It's not on you," Damon said, shaking his head. "She's the one who disobeyed the order, Chang."

"I'm the one who didn't realize she was so foolish." Chang's face was implacable.

"You two can toss this back and forth all you want, but Damon's got the right of it," I said, interjecting. If I left them to it, they'd snipe until they were growling at each other. "She's a cat—she knows how clan authority works and she chose to ignore it."

Chang narrowed his eyes while Damon smirked.

"Now that we've got that settled..." I gave them a brilliant grin. "What are you planning on doing with her? Can you send her back? We can put a pretty little bow on her head and say she didn't work out, request a replacement."

Chang covered his laugh with a polite cough.

Damon didn't look quite so amused. In fact, he looked outright disgusted. "No."

"Damn." Leaning forward, I braced my elbows on my knees. "I was afraid you'd say that."

"You could have just left her where she was," Chang said.

"No." I looked away. "That wasn't ever an option."

The weighted silence stretched out between us, shattered by the low rumble of Damon's voice when he said, "Why don't you tell us what happened, Kit?"

Restless, I rose from the couch and started to pace.

My stomach chose that moment to rumble and I eyed the food, now cold, waiting for me on the table. I picked up a cold fry and nibbled on it.

"Kit, I'll get you something hot," Damon said, irritated. "Just tell me what's going on."

With the taste of cold fry in my mouth, I shot him a look.

He stood by the couch, where he'd been for the past five minutes. Chang stood closer to the fireplace, languid and relaxed, as though he were at a cocktail party. There was nothing languid about Damon, though. His gaze, his posture, everything about him was a stone wall. *He* was a like a bloody stone wall—unmovable, unyielding.

He yields for you…

The soft voice in the back of my mind had me going still.

He did. Damon yielded for me. Everything else that came at him just crashed into him, usually stopped in their tracks or else they just submitted. But for me…

Closing my eyes, I took a deep breath. Then I said, "Justin. It was Justin who tracked her down…but he wasn't looking for her. It had to do with a witch he was looking for. She was just a bonus, I guess you could say."

"A bonus," Chang said. "What a lovely…bonus."

Damon said nothing, not for a long while. But finally, he spun away and muttered, "Now why in the hell doesn't *that* surprise me."

When I finished, the two of them shared one of those silent communions they seemed so fond of. After about sixty seconds of that, I said, "Would you like me to leave so you two can continue this in private?"

Chang frowned. "Continue what?"

"This…" I sketched my hands through the air. "Whatever you do. When you both say a million things to each other without saying a *damn* thing."

Damon's brow went up while Chang gave me a bemused smile. "If we're saying things without saying them, then why would we need you to leave?"

"Because it's *annoying*." I enunciated the word very slowly.

"So what you really mean to say is that *you* want to leave." Damon moved to the door just as somebody knocked.

I frowned when he opened it to reveal Scott—and a fresh tray of food. "When did you call him?"

"I sent him a message." Damon shrugged and stepped aside as Scott came in and put the tray down next to the other one.

"Will you please eat it this time?" Scott asked. He looked me over from head to toe. "You're losing weight."

"Women don't like it when people comment about their weight."

He rubbed his jaw. "I thought that was a human thing."

"It's a female thing."

He looked at Damon. Damon looked at me. "Eat the food and stop losing weight and it won't be an issue."

"How about you both shut up and it won't be an issue?" I suggested. If my stomach hadn't been all but dancing because of the scents coming from the plate, I would have told Scott to shove it. But I'm not much for cutting my nose off to spite my face—or my stomach. I dropped down in front of the plate and pulled the cover off. A huge burger, a double order of fries this time and he'd included a strawberry milkshake.

"Is the shake a bribe?"

"It's calories." Scott slid his hands into his pockets. "I'd say why, but females don't like it when people harp on it."

"Ha ha." I was too hungry to care that much so I focused on the food as the three men started to talk.

It wasn't until I heard them say *Maguire*—that I looked up. Maguire. As in *Shanelle Maguire*.

Damon's gaze slid to me and the conversation went quiet.

He ran his tongue across his teeth and then said, "We'll finish this up another time."

Scott and Chang said nothing else and in seconds, we were alone.

I popped a fry in my mouth as he prowled across the floor toward me.

"It makes me feel all nice and secure when you shut up all because I looked up when you said her name."

Lids drooping low, Damon dragged a chair close to mine and sat down. He was so close, he all but surrounded me. That *really* made me feel all nice and secure. Well, maybe *nice* wasn't the right word. *Nice* rarely described what I felt with Damon. *Naughty. Needed. Necessary.* I could probably go through the alphabet and come up with a whole slew of words, but *nice* wasn't one of them.

"It's clan business, Kit." He stole a fry, winking at me when I glared.

Rolling my eyes, I muttered, "And *that* line makes me feel even *better.*"

He stopped chewing for a moment and then resumed, swallowing and then he went to his knees in front of me.

It was a sight that staggered me, floored me, to see him so easily do something like that and I suspected he didn't even think about it—or the magnitude of it. Perhaps to him, it had no magnitude. Not with me.

"Do you need to know?" he asked.

"I…" The question startled me. Clan business was just that. It didn't matter if Damon told others that I wasn't an outsider. I might fall into some odd place where I wasn't exactly *clan* yet still not an outsider, but that didn't mean I had the right to know what Damon was doing within the clan. What he was doing with his people.

He leaned in closer. "Do you need to know?"

"It's not my place."

"Your place is with me. Just like my place is with you. If you need to know to feel…better…about everything that's going on now that Maguire is here, then tell me. I don't want secrets between us, baby girl." His eyes searched mine and then he pressed a kiss to my cheek, high, near my ear. "She used to be an enforcer, but she never really earned the spot. She wasn't always fair with it. She wasn't overly cruel, but she could be…petty. That's why we worked together a lot. I figured I could minimize her damage if she was with me, because I outranked her. I'd be the one making the judgment calls. Since she's claiming she wants to retake her place, she's going to have to prove she's capable. That means…facing Scott."

I blinked.

Then I smiled.

"Can I watch?"

He laughed and rose to his feet, moving away.

My gaze dropped to admire the view and then I scowled. "So when did you two start sleeping together?"

He stilled. Then, over his shoulder, he said, "Kit...it was just sex."

"And just how long did this...*just sex* last?"

He turned now, facing me from across the room. "We hooked up off and on for a few years. The last few months she was here, it was very much...off."

I jutted my chin up. "It's staying off."

He went from the middle of the room to kneeling in front of me again in the blink of an eye, so fast, it left my head spinning. I held my breath as he caught the front of my shirt in his hand, holding me in place as he dipped his head. His lips brushed my ear and the warmth of his breath was a teasing, taunting caress. "Trust me, baby girl...not an issue."

He rubbed his mouth over mine. When he would have pulled away, I caught his head in my hands. Our gazes held as I captured his lower lip between my teeth and bit. His body shuddered and heat sparked inside as he laid his hands on my thighs.

I pulled back and when he would have followed, I reached up, pressing my thumb to his lips. "You know she came for *you*—just as much for *you* as anything else."

"She's wasting her time." He pressed his brow to mine. "I'm yours. You know that."

"Does *she* know that?"

"If she's got a brain, she does by now." His eyes were flat and hard.

"Well, I don't know her. *Does* she have a brain or do I need to make her a sign?"

A short, hard laugh escaped him and then he sighed, rubbing his hands across his face. "Shit. I don't know. She gets an idea in her head...look, I'll make it clear that it's over."

"Do that."

"Consider it done." He moved back to me, all dangerous grace and deadly beauty. "But you need to understand something—I can't wash my hands of her completely. You asked if I could send her back and if things hadn't gotten fucked up, I'd do it. But she was kidnapped when she was coming to the clan. To me. That puts her under my protection. It happened under *my* watch. I'll get to the bottom of it."

"It's not just cats." The heat of his anger danced along my skin. "It's a lot deeper than a few of your minions going missing."

He was quiet a second and then he said, "Minions?"

"Yeah." I stroked a finger down his cheek. "You growl. They scramble to obey. Sounds very minion-ish to me." Hungry now, I nudged him back and bent over my food.

"Kit."

"Um?" I had just taken a bite of the burger when he spoke.

"Look at me."

I did, only half focused on what he was saying. At times like this, I understand why he and Chang and Scott and Doyle always insisted on putting food in front of me—it tasted so damn good.

"I'm going to figure this mess out." Damon leaned against the table next to me. "With your help, preferably....but I'll do it without your help if I have to."

My help?

I swallowed the chunk of beef before it became lodged in throat. Swallowing, I stared at him. "My help."

He inclined his head. "You and Justin are involved in this. You went after them in Georgia, after all, right?"

"Yyyyeeeaaaahhhhh…" I drew it out, uncertain whether I wanted to commit to anything else. I'd done the Georgia job, yes, but I hadn't signed on for anything else.

He bent over me, one hand braced on the back of the chair, the other on the table.

"So are you going to help me or not?"

Clearing my throat, I asked softly, "Are you talking about hiring me…again?"

"Why not? It worked out pretty good the last time." He flicked at my hair. "So…what do you say?"

"Eesh."

I crammed another bite of burger into my mouth so I didn't end up saying what I *really* thought:

I'm so fucked.

Chapter Eleven

I needed to talk to Justin and I knew he hadn't left town—yet.

Since he wasn't answering my calls, I decided I'd hit his usual haunts—the Market first, the communal hall where a lot of the freelance agents hung out next and when I struck out there, I tried Drake's.

When I saw his bike, I couldn't say I was surprised.

Although it was the middle of the day, the last job had been a rough one. Rough in more ways than one. First, Abraham lays out that we'd almost walked into a trap and then Justin finds out that one of his contacts is a skin-trader. I didn't even know the bastard and I wanted to string him up. Justin had to be feeling like he'd been sucker-punched.

After all of that, the rescue gets underway and we found exactly what we'd been afraid we'd find. I guess that shouldn't be surprising. But we'd been hoping for the best—hoping that it was all rumors and that nobody had been hunting NHs just to turn them over to the hospital.

So much for hoping.

"So. Saul." I dropped down on the seat next to Justin. "What's the deal there?"

Justin slid me a look. "What do you mean?"

"Abraham told you he's a skin-trader. Guy's been working with you for a while, seems like, and it sounds like he was trying to set us up. That pisses me off." I jerked up a shoulder in a shrug and waved down Drake for a beer. "Seeing as how he almost put *my* ass on the line, along with yours, I want to know what's going on. You wanted a connection to the hospital…you found it. Now what are we going to do about it?"

Justin stared straight ahead. He had a tall glass in front of him, nearly half-empty. As I sat there waiting, he reached out and picked it up. He took a healthy swig and then put it down. I continued to wait on an answer. That was fine. I wasn't going anywhere until he talked. "Saul... is not a pleasant person. But he is... no, make that *was* useful. Now, he's going to be a dead person." That familiar sly grin lit his face as he glanced at me. "Problem solved."

I wish it could be solved that easily. But if he had been setting us up, he hadn't been doing it on his own. There were others involved. Was he connected to whoever had kidnapped Shanelle? Shaking my head, I said, "Not good enough. Not good enough by a long shot." I gave him a hard look when he went to argue. "Look, you dragged me into this. I'm involved. You'd be the same way and don't tell me otherwise."

Justin muttered something low under his breath.

I chose to ignore him.

After another moment, he swiveled on the barstool to glare at me. "You know, you're finally back with your fur-boy. Why don't you just focus on your life and let me handle this mess?"

I was tempted to grab his glass and dump the contents onto his head. Maybe that would wash away the smug-ass attitude. But I was never one to waste good alcohol.

"As I already said, you and I are involved in this. You ensured that the second you asked me to help you on this." When he tried to argue this time, I leaned in and jabbed him in the chest with my index finger. "And maybe this hasn't occurred to you, but it has to me—that hotel was probably under video surveillance. So whoever showed up after we left already knows I was with you, as well as Abraham. If Saul goes missing as quick as that, we'll be the first place they look. This is something that requires stealth. And Justin, honey, you don't have stealth." I gave him a brilliant smile. "That's my domain."

He opened his mouth, then closed it.

I knew I had won. I gave him a moment to adjust before giving him the other sucker-punch. "Now, for the really good news, Damon wants to hire us."

He stared at me blankly. Then he shook his head, reaching up to rub his ear like he was trying to clear it. "What did you just say? Could've sworn..."

"I said, Damon wants to hire us," I repeated, drawing each word out.

● ● ●

139

Justin slid off the stool and walked to the door of Drake's. He opened it up and then leaned outside. Curious, I followed him. "What are you doing?"

"I'm looking to see if the moon's turned to blood or if frogs are falling from the sky. I could've sworn you said Damon wants to hire us, or some crazy shit like that."

I burst out laughing. "I don't think the world's ending. At least, not right now. Since we were already involved in tracking down the missing NH's and getting them home, he wants us to help with the next step. He wants to know who's involved and figure out who kidnapped Shanelle and the other cat. And why and how." The door squeaked softly as it closed behind Justin. His sigh was soft and low. He turned to look at me and I met his gaze soberly. "He's going to be looking into this anyway. He's got good people and somebody is going to unearth something, probably Chang. We can help each other or just fumble around on our own. Why not work it together? They've got a vested interest in it, just like you do."

Justin slid his tongue across his teeth as he studied me. Then, jerking his head in a 'come-on' motion, he ducked into one of the back rooms. He didn't bother to ask permission, but then again, Justin rarely did.

Drake wouldn't say anything.

A few months ago, I'd found out that Drake had been with Banner before he had decided to go back into the civilian life. Of course, before he had been with Banner, he had been in the Special Forces. He had been human right up until he had been bitten. That had been the end of his career in the military.

As the door swung shut behind me, Justin moved to stand on the far side of the room. "Just what is your interest in this, Kit?"

I had to fight to keep my jaw off the floor. He was serious. When I didn't answer right away, he turned to look at me. He must've seen something on my face. "What do you mean, *what is my interest in this*?'" I took a step closer to him, struggling to vocalize the rush of emotion inside me. "My interest? My interest is you, you dumbass. And now that I know they're going after the cats and witches, my interests are my friends as well. They're targeting people I care about. Why shouldn't I have an interest in it?"

Justin sighed. "Kit, it's not like they've declared open season on all of us.

They've been selective. They haven't gone after Colleen and they're not coming after me." Then he shrugged. "Well, they might have been. But Saul got his plans thrown off. Right now, honestly, they're going after people nobody will miss. There's no rhyme or reason to who they're grabbing. But they aren't grabbing anybody who's hugely important in our community."

"That doesn't matter," I snapped. Frustration bubbled inside. I shoved a hand through my hair and fisted it, hoping it might lessen the tension building in my head. "You think this is connected to the hospital, Justin. That hospital needs to go down, and we both know it. I haven't forgotten what they threatened you with. Even if there is no other reason, I'd be involved for that and that alone."

"Why, Kit. You still care." A curious smile curled his lips.

My heart gave a funny bump against my ribs and I had to fight the urge to squirm. "Justin, don't be any more of an ass than you already are."

"Just how much of an ass do I have to be? I like to know my boundaries."

I looked around for something handy to throw at him. Sadly, the room was lacking in projectiles. Something shifted in the corner of my eye and I looked up to see Justin less than a foot away. I tensed, bracing myself. After a moment, he reached up and brushed my hair. I reached to catch his hand, but he took it away. "Kit, I don't want you involved in this. I realize you feel obligated—"

"Obligated?" I bit the word off. I no longer wanted to throw something *at* him; I wanted to throw *him*. "Obligation has nothing to do with this. Justin, you're my friend. You're one of my best friends. If you need me or if you have a need, then I want to help."

"But Kit, that's just it. The things I need, you can't help me with." He gave me a sad smile and then cut around me. As he headed to the door, he said over his shoulder, "I'll get back to you about the deal with Damon. As for Saul, I'm going to handle him. You've already done enough."

If Justin thought I was going to let it go, the son of a bitch had another think coming. There was no way I was going to let him get involved in something like this

● ● ●

on his own. Apparently, I wasn't the only one thinking that, although I can't say I was happy to see who else was thinking along those lines. When I got to my office, there was a vampire waiting for me. The unwelcomed scent of the undead tinged the air. The unwelcomed feel of his presence skittered across my skin like dry autumn leaves on an isolated country road.

He stood in the shadows, but it was rather clear that the late afternoon sun had little effect on him.

Abraham Allerton was one powerful son of a bitch. With deliberate slowness, I climbed out of my car. I took my time taking my weapons out and settling them into place. If I lingered a little longer on the katana I had chosen to take that day, who can blame me? Abraham's gaze flicked to it, but there was no change in his expression.

I took my other blade from the back seat, and out of habit, I stroked my fingers across her hilt. She warmed under my touch.

"The sign says closed," I pointed out. "You can call and make an appointment if I'm not in."

Abraham inclined his head. "I had the time."

You had the time, but do I have the patience?

"Is this business related?"

He inclined his head.

"Okay." Pasting a blank smile on my face, I said, "It's your dollar."

A few minutes later, we were within my office. My skin didn't crawl in his presence and I considered it a win. Every time I could be around a vampire without freaking out, I'd call it a victory. Considering that this guy was younger than Jude, but just as powerful—or *more*—this was one mega victory.

As I settled my swords against the desk, Abraham strolled around the office. He lingered by the weapon wall and I could see him studying each of the swords. "You have a fondness for blades."

"Ya think?"

His lips twitched. Softly, he said, "You're not the first weaponsmaster I've ever come across. I don't think I've known anybody who is as…gifted as you are." He slid me a sidelong look. "And I've known a great many."

I lifted a shoulder and dropped it. "Well, I imagine you haven't known a great many who have it running through their DNA. Literally." Since he'd opened the door, I decided to walk through it. "How old are you? A hundred twenty?"

He cocked a brow, a surprised look on his face. "Very close. I died one hundred and twenty one years ago next month." A thoughtful look crossed his face. "How could you tell?"

"It's just a knack of mine." I leaned against my desk. My blades were still behind my desk, but oddly enough, I didn't feel the need to keep either of them close. I still had my Glock and numerous knives. I didn't think I'd need them. Now that I'd let myself relax—or now that my body had *let* me relax—I'd realized I'd found a kindred soul here. Deciding to go with my gut, I spoke the truth. "You should know that as a rule, I can't be around vampires without hating them on sight."

Abraham studied me for a long, quiet moment as he thought over his response—and he *did* think it over. I could see a hundred words flitting through his gaze before he finally settled on what he chose. "If you didn't hate them, then I would think you lacked brain cells, Ms. Colbana."

"Kit." I frowned at him.

"Kit, then. If you'll agree to call me Abraham." He gave me a distasteful look. "And it *is* Abraham. Justin has an annoying habit of calling me *Abe*. That is not my name."

"Well, then. Abraham it is." Absently, I stroked my hand down one of the sketches of ink on my neck. "*Annoying* is one of Justin's strangely endearing qualities."

"If you insist." He looked amused. "As I was saying…or perhaps I hadn't quite reached that point…" He took a step toward me, his expression somber. "I might be crossing a line here, and I do apologize if I am, but I feel the need to tell you…." He paused, looking almost lost, then said, "Have you ever researched how I was changed?"

I don't think he could have caught me any more off-guard if he tried. "Why would I have done that?"

"Why wouldn't you have?" He lifted one shoulder in a lazy shrug. "You would not have been the first. Not by a long shot."

● ● ●
143

"Frankly, Abraham, you haven't come on my radar enough. I'm not looking to kill or rob you. There's no reason for me to know that stuff about you."

He angled his head to the side. "Yet another reason you puzzle me. I've known so many with an insatiable sense of curiosity. You seem to have none."

"Oh, I'm curious about a lot. I just don't go prying where I have no right to pry."

An embarrassed expression crossed his face. "I see. I didn't expect that of you. I guess that's unfair. You have much of you that is human. I'm not used to that—respect, you see—from humans." A look of shame crossed his features. "Forgive me. That is unfair. I was human once, as well. Perhaps that is my failing. It was my curiosity that led me to what I am now."

Now it was my turn to look lost. I held out my hands. "You've gotta help me out here. I don't know what you're talking about."

"I realize that." His expression was reluctant.

"Look, if you don't wanna talk about this, that's fine." I was starting to feel reluctant myself. He had secrets he felt the need to share, but I don't know if I wanted to hear them. I had more than enough pain on my own.

"As strange as this may sound, Kit, I find that I do want to talk about this. And how odd is that?" He looked pensive.

"Ah… I dunno. Why don't you tell me?"

He laughed softly. "If you only knew. I haven't spoken of this… in, well ever." Moving over to the sole chair in front of my desk, he hitched up his trousers and sat down, each movement languid, graceful—yet you could still see the predator. Death incarnate. I had death incarnate in my office.

And he wanted to tell me about *his* death.

"I was twenty-eight when I died," he said, his gray eyes still focused on the weapons that hung on my wall. "When I was still mortal, interest in the occult was all but unknown at that time. I was ostracized by my community for my interest. But I was convinced that there were other creatures out there besides humans. I don't know exactly what I believed existed out there, but I knew there was something else. So I looked…investigated. Searched. People thought I was a charlatan, a fake, or simply crazy. The few who didn't think I was insane or a fraud wanted nothing to do with me. So naturally, anytime someone was willing to listen, I cleaved to them like ivy to a tree. When she came into town, I was enchanted."

Immediately, my skin went cold. Ice replaced the blood in my veins. Pushing away from my desk, I went to the window. The word *stop* rose to my lips, but I bit it back. Maybe it was because I recognized what it was like to have poison inside you.

This was Abraham's poison.

"Eve was unlike any other woman I had ever met." Abraham looked at me now and I saw it there, that poison I'd sensed. "I lived in a small, backwater town in Oregon. My father was the town's only doctor. I was expected to follow in his footsteps, but I had no desire to. The only one who seemed to understand me was Eve. She was this bright light in my dark world. And when she listened to the things I had to say, it was life-changing. I spent more and more time with her and found myself getting caught up with her, everything she did and said. And when she asked me to come away with her, saying no was unthinkable."

I turned then. He was staring at the floor. As though he sensed my gaze, he looked up and met my eyes.

"If only I'd known how right I was."

I don't know if he was even aware of the fact that he had reached up to stroke his throat.

"You are aware, I'm sure, of some of the vampiric abilities?"

I scowled. "Which ones?" A thousand unflattering things sprang to my lips, but I bit them back.

The look on Abraham's face told me he heard every one, nonetheless. He didn't look offended. "At the time, I was completely unaware that I had been under her thrall, almost from the time I had met her."

My heart slammed against my ribs as a chill settled in the air. It sent a shiver up my spine, but I clenched my teeth together to keep them from chattering.

"Do you know what it's like to be under a vampire's thrall?"

"No." I stared at him. "Honestly, I'm immune to most things. Unless, of course, you're talking about being overpowered. That can be done easily. All of you are stronger than I am."

"Are we?" Abraham tucked his hands into his pockets. "You've survived things that would have shattered the mind of any number of people."

That direct stare made me want to flinch, but I refused to look away.

He inclined his head. "Perhaps your physical strength is less than mine, but there is more to being strong than the ability to lift a car."

I had no idea what to say to him. Turning away, I focused on the weapons on my wall. "One skill I don't possess is the ability to read minds, so I don't know what it is you want me to say."

The soft sound of his sigh filled the air, a sound that conveyed too many emotions to even list. "It wasn't until I had been a vampire for several years that I realized I had all but been her slave from the very beginning. I never knew it until it was too late. By then, my life was no longer my own."

His voice was faint. Almost too faint for even me to hear. "Now when she changed me, I knew I didn't want it. I was aware of that, but I could not fight it." Abraham laughed softly. "Even if I had wanted too. Unlike you, I was unaware of the difference between a human's strength and a vampire's. Until the first night she drank from me, I didn't even realize what she was. Even then, at first, I did not know if she was a demon, a monster… or both. Sometimes, I still wonder."

There was a world of things unsaid in those simple words. As the silence stretched out, I processed all those unsaid things. As he remained quiet, I asked him, "How long did she keep you?"

"Two decades." He looked at me, haunted. "By the end of that time, I well knew what I was. Nothing but a toy. Her blood-whore. Her bed-toy, when she wished it. Her whipping-boy, should it please her."

The word *blood-whore* made me flinch. I couldn't stop it. And I knew then why I felt *like* I understood him. *Like recognized like.*

He'd been a toy, a pawn…a *thing*. Just like I had.

I moved closer to him, stopping just a few feet away. I had to angle my head back to meet his eyes. The nearness of him did not make me uneasy, but I wasn't surprised by it now. He was no longer just the undead. He had faced the same things

I had. Oddly enough, that made him more human than anything else. I wonder if he would laugh at me if I said that.

"When did it stop?"

"When Ezra Allerton killed her. Eve was of his line and he discovered that she had been feeding too freely of the humans in her territory." He shrugged dismissively, as if the past was of no concern to him. "She had moved us to Salem. The disappearances had become noticeable, but she didn't care. When Ezra came to speak to her, she laughed and brushed it aside. She insinuated that people would look to Boston for those who had gone missing, or that nobody would care. Ezra said she missed the point. He cared, and if he cared, others would. If she would not get her appetite under control, he would do it for her. The next day, she killed a newlywed couple. She was dead before the sun rose."

I found myself respecting Ezra Allerton more than I wanted to. I knew little of the man, other than the fact that he was the current head of Allerton House. He'd stepped in when Jedidiah Allerton died. I say *died* when the truth is that he decided to kill himself. I hear they do that sometimes.

"Why did Allerton take you in?"

"He chose to. Tradition dictates that a vampire who kills another vampire may deal with one's flock as he chooses. He could have killed us all, or taken us in. He chose to take us in." Once more, he reached up and touched a faint scar on his neck. It was nearly imperceptible. It was two neat bite marks. They were almost surgically neat, but I knew what they were. They were the marks Eve would have given him when she first bit him.

"For that, I am forever grateful. I did not choose this life, but I also did not choose to end mine."

Taut, heavy silence fell, weighted and thick, nearly smothering us both. Uncomfortable with it, I moved behind my desk and sat down. "I'm sorry."

I laid my hands flat on my desk. I wanted to reach for one of my blades. The need to have something in my hands that was strong, but it seemed inappropriate. "I wish I knew what else to say. I just don't."

Abraham studied me. "You did nothing wrong."

"What happened to you sucks. If I didn't feel bad about it, I would be messed up."

"Perhaps this is why I like you, Kit. You are human, yet… not."

"Feel free." I settled more comfortably in my chair and watched as he did the same, practically sprawling in the chair across from mine. I would have expected him to sit rigidly. After a moment, he made a soft, sighing sound. I rarely heard vampires breathe. They had no need to, but it was almost out of habit. This was almost as if he needed to relax more than anything else.

"You need not apologize to me. It was my own foolishness that put me where I was. And I ended up far better off than many who made the same mistakes that I did." He gave me a weak smile. "I was not Eve's only blood-whore. Yet, I am the only one who still survives." He leaned forward then, pinning me with a stare so penetrating I wanted to hide. "Perhaps you can understand me when I say that there are certain things that do not sit well with me. Would you like me to elaborate? Or… what is the phrase, 'Do you know where I am coming from?'"

I tensed. "Please. Don't."

"Understood." The intensity faded from his face, though some remnant of it lingered. "Bits and pieces of us die with the soul, Kit. There is no changing that. But memories do not die. And they will fade only if we let them. And those memories hold our salvation, perhaps even the essence of our soul. I remember. Many of us do."

In the next moment, the phone rang.

CHAPTER TWELVE

There were any number of ways we could have played it when Justin announced he would be meeting me at my office. He didn't know that Abraham would be joining us, but what he didn't know would help me.

I hoped.

Justin had done some thinking, he'd told me, and decided that maybe the best way to handle the abductions of the clan was to just work with me on it. After all, he'd drawled, he still had to get to the bottom of it and he could try to do it on his own but the job offer had already been extended toward me and he knew I'd get a more than fair payout.

Why risk getting maybe a third of that and getting stonewalled at every other turn?

Translation: He'd already been trying to do just that and doors were getting slammed in his face.

The clan was secretive as hell, something I'd learned back when I was trying to find Doyle all those months ago. I'd had a giant Damon-shaped shadow at my back and I'd *still* been pulling teeth.

Things were different now—for me, at least—thanks to that Damon-shaped shadow and the doors that Justin was banging his head against would open on oiled hinges before I even lifted a hand to knock.

Justin would know this.

Sometimes, he could be smart.

The silence lingered as I pondered that phone call. I hadn't mentioned Saul and neither had Justin. He knew it wasn't done, but if I knew him, he was going to hope he could handle it during the down time on this job. Or in all likelihood, while I was doing the legwork for the clan case, he'd be doing the face-work for the Saul case—

as in smashing Saul's face in.

"You don't intend to let it go with Saul."

I looked at Abraham. Canting my head to the side, I said, "No. No, I do not." Closing my hand over a dagger I kept on my desk, I started to toss it, letting it dance in the air until it became a blur over my fingers. Abraham's gaze flicked from the dagger to my face and back. "Justin's so caught up in this, he can't see the forest for the trees, but once he lets himself look, he'll see it. It's too connected. Too tied up together. You can't separate the strands of a thread and not expect it to unravel."

Abraham leaned back, his gaze thoughtful.

I continued to play with the dagger.

He continued to watch me. The silence was…odd. I didn't feel uncomfortable in his presence, something that made more sense to me now.

Still, it was strange. Almost every person I knew in my life, almost every person I called friend was somebody I'd known for an extended period of time and we'd gotten closer after they'd somehow…*proven* themselves to me.

Even Damon, in a way.

Doyle, too.

But this odd kinship I felt for a *vampire* was…bemusing. It wasn't anything remotely romantic. That idea was laughable. I couldn't deny the fact that I felt comfortable with him, though.

"Allerton House needs to know what is behind the abductions, Kit," he said, interrupting my contemplation.

"Understood." I caught the dagger by the handle and put it down. Shifting in the seat, I leaned forward and met his gaze. "Let me guess…when Justin gets here, you want me to tell him that I'd already agreed to work with you on this."

He slid a hand inside his jacket. It was heavy weight, something with the sheen of real velvet and it moved with his body with supple fluidity. It was an old world affair and put me in the mind of afternoon teas and walks in the gardens. From an inside pocket, he pulled out an envelope. I sighed at the sight of it.

Some of the biggest headaches of my life had come in the form of written missives.

Not everybody dealt in written correspondence anymore. So many things had gone electronic, but in a world where many creatures had been around before such inventions had come to be, the tried, true and traditional were still in use.

"This is from Icarus, and it's co-signed by the head of my house, Ezra." He placed the heavy-weight vellum on my desk. "It's for five hundred thousand dollars, Kit. Should you choose to work with Justin, then you may split it equally with him. You may work it alone. It is completely up to you."

Hot greed lit inside at the fee he'd laid out. So many zeroes…

Wow. I could pay off the new car. I could buy my condo.

I could maybe buy my office—or screw that. A *new* office.

But…

"Why do they need me? You seem to be their go-boy on all of this. Justin's friend Padraig all but wept tears of envy at the sound of your name."

"Did he?" Lips twitching, Abraham settled back in his chair. "I'm good at what I do. I always have been. But there are doors you can open that I cannot. And to be blunt, you impressed Icarus. You impressed me. I think you will see things I won't. We want answers, Kit."

Answers. Grimly, I stared at the envelope waiting for me to open it.

"What happens if I don't solve it?"

"The money is yours simply for taking the case." He leaned forward again, holding my gaze. "There are risks associated with this, as you already know. You must agree to tell your lover of the case, and of the risks. We will not risk war between our house and the clan. But I believe your lover wants answers as much as we do." A look passed over his face, as though he waged an internal war. Then, after a moment, he nodded.

Decision made.

"I know of Samuel Allerton, and I know of the actions he made—*mistakes* he made. Samuel was always a greedy, power hungry bastard."

At the sound of that name, my blood went cold. My heart froze in my chest and my mind spun back to a day when I'd watched Damon striding away from a vampire's home. He'd killed said vampire—because said vampire had supposedly been willing to talk to my grandmother. Nobody knows just what he'd told her, because Damon had killed the son of a bitch.

He'd also killed a number of other high-level NHs.

That was also the day I'd been kidnapped by Jude Whittier. Another vampire.

I could tell by the look on his face that Abraham was aware of that day's timeline of events. Samuel's death. My abduction and disappearance. He didn't know the events that took place between them.

I could remember them, each and every minute, carved into my heart—etched into me. Those old scars on my soul.

And while I had a feeling I could like Abraham, even apart from this weird connection I felt with him, there lay a complicated mess between Allerton House and the clan. Samuel might have been a greedy, power-hungry bastard as Abraham had called him—I couldn't say, I didn't know him. But his death at Damon's hands wasn't going to be overlooked by others in the Allerton family. Vampires were brutal and cold-blooded, but they were loyal.

"There's no question of whether or not I'll tell Damon," I said bluntly. There were times and jobs when I'd have to keep things from him, a fact I knew well. This wasn't that time and this wasn't that job. "But if you think this is going to make things all nicey-nice, well...you don't know Damon."

A quick laugh escaped him—it sounded rusty, like Abraham wasn't used to laughing. I could imagine he wasn't. "On the contrary, I know him...rather well," Abraham said after deliberating on his words. He scraped the nail of his thumb down his jawline. "Samuel and Annette were very much alike. I had to clean up more of his messes than I care to remember, just as Damon spent a great deal of time cleaning up after her. We came into contact quite often."

The idea made me frown.

Damon's comment rose to my mind: *Allerton's one of the few that I don't immediately want to skewer.* I was running it through my head as Abraham rose and made a lazy circuit around my office. He paused at my weapons wall, studying them in much the same way I studied the swords that decorated the wall in Chang's office. He slid his fingers along the chain of the three-section staff I was determined to master.

"Trust me when I say that I don't see Damon making 'nicey-nice' on anything," Abraham said, his voice wry. He moved away from the staff and eyed the military sabre that took up position next to it. "Can you use all of these?"

I didn't answer right away. I was too busy thinking about just *what* it would look like to see Damon making *nicey-nice*. It was really kind of baffling. Shoving it into the forget-about-it file, I rose from my desk. "I've got a rudimentary understanding of every weapon I own, at least, or if I don't, I learn it." I lifted a shoulder. "It's all about breaking down the style, or understanding it. I'm very good at that."

A smile curled his lips. "I imagine you are. Perhaps one day, we could spar."

A hot thrill raced through me. He'd just spoken my language.

I inclined my head. "Maybe. I usually work with one of Damon's lieutenants, Doyle." I didn't elaborate on the connection between them. "He's got an interest in blades as well. Maybe you can join us—or Justin."

"I think I'd enjoy that." He turned to face me, then. "Justin will not be pleased to have me involved in this. He will not have any say in the matter."

I glanced at the envelope I had to open. I needed to get on that. But for now, I crossed my arms over my chest. "Just how involved do you plan to get?"

My head was officially throbbing.

If I had any more shit thrown at me today, I was going to just lock myself in a room, preferably a bathroom with a giant tub and a pool of bubbles, while I pretended the rest of the world just didn't exist.

Particularly the canny bastard in front of me.

"Ain't happening." Justin lifted a shoulder in an elegant shrug, his green eyes glinting with a mix of feigned humor and a polite *fuck-you*. "Sorry, Abe. Tell Icarus we'll be on the look-out for anything affecting vampires, but we've got other issues to handle and we can't be distracting ourselves with leeches."

"Justin—"

"Abraham." I waited until he looked at me. "Can it."

Justin's self-satisfied smirk barely had time to form before I caught the edge of my desk and rattled it with enough force to catch his attention. "Justin? Shove it."

He gave me a blank look.

Baring my teeth at him, I said, "Don't give me that look. You need to stop showing him one hand and me the other. This is too big and it affects *all* of us. Are you going to tell him or do I need to do it?"

"Kit." His voice a low throb, Justin kicked his feet off the table.

I ignored him. "Abraham, have you ever heard of a *hospital*? Someplace where non-humans can go to get cured? Or at least, they are offered the promise of a cure?"

He waved a dismissive hand through the air. "Such places have been rumored to exist for decades. But there's no cure for simple existence. It's like curing a man of being a man, or a tiger of being a tiger."

"Exactly." From the corner of my eye, I could see Justin had turned away and moved to the window. His spine was a line so tight now, I thought it might snap. "But people are stupid. They'll believe what they want—or *need*—to believe, won't they? And people are greedy and cruel and will make insane, impossible promises to those who need to believe."

As a strangled sense of quiet felt, I focused on the things I couldn't hear or see. On the uneasiness coming from Justin, on the disbelief I sensed from Abraham, followed by an odd sort of revelation. That *a-ha* moment. Like pieces of a puzzle suddenly connected in his mind.

The blistering fury that punched through the room caught me off-guard and I found myself lunging across the room just in time to shove in front of the vampire as he tried to grab the witch.

"Why?" Abraham demanded. "You *knew* we were searching for answers to those missing among us. *Why* did you keep this from me?"

"Back off," I said. My skin crawled from the inhuman pulse of his rage. It was a scream inside my head and even though everything in me knew he wasn't a threat, I still didn't want to be here.

Justin could tell, too. Whether it was because he knew me so well or because of what he was, he sensed something. He sidestepped, trying to keep me from being caught between them, but I wasn't going to have them going at each other's throats, possibly literally in Abraham's case, in my office.

Gritting my teeth, I whirled and caught Justin by the front of his leather jacket and spun.

It was unexpected enough that he didn't brace until it was too late and he flew halfway across the floor to land awkwardly on the couch. "Stay," I bit off.

He was already tensing to rise and I swore. "Justin, if you two give me even a *second* to think you'll get stupid, I'm going to cut you both."

It wasn't Justin I should have worried about, though.

Abraham moved around me, his focus on Justin.

He went still at the feel of the blade pressing into his neck.

"Enough." I had it clenched so hard, it hurt from the tension. "We need to sit down, sort this out, figure it out. It's not going to happen if the two of you are speaking with your dicks and testosterone instead of your brains." I nudged him a little farther with the blade. "And you're letting hunger speak instead of common sense. Get it under control."

"Sorry."

It was nearly two hours later.

Abraham had listened—Justin had finally talked. I don't know what made him listen and I don't know that I cared. I only knew that I was tired, and I wasn't even done.

Not by a long shot.

Maybe I couldn't expect Damon to make nicey-nice, but I did have to tell him.

Once I did that, I could consider the idea of a long, hot bath.

At Damon's.

I'd never been comfortable with the idea of soaking in a tub. It left me too vulnerable. Sitting in a tub, naked, nobody else in the house.

But at Damon's…

Justin shifted next to me and I dragged my attention back to the present—and away from the tub in my dreams. "I know," I said quietly. I looked over at him. "There's no more hiding on this, Justin. You're not rushing into this alone. You're not pulling the Lone Ranger deal and getting yourself killed."

"Well, to be fair, the Lone Ranger had a partner."

I frowned. "If he was called the *Lone* Ranger, why did he have a partner?"

"It was a Native, named Tonto."

I ran that through my head and then discarded it. Some things in human culture would never make sense. Among them the self-mutilation they called cosmetic surgery, the mad rush of sales they had on the day after Thanksgiving, and their strange fetish for romanticizing non-humans even as most of them would go out of their way to cross the road if they saw us walking down their side of the sidewalk.

Why write stories about things like *The Vampire and the Virgin Vixen* or *The Shifter and The Siren* then freak out if you actually *see* one sharing the same curb space?

Don't ask me. People are just odd.

"Well, then you're getting a new partner," I told him. "The Lone Ranger and Kit."

"Hi-ho, Silver," Justin muttered. He skimmed a hand back over his dreads and then reached up, his hand closing into a fist as he bumped it against the glass. The magic in the wards recognized his touch—it should. He'd created it after all. "There's something you need to know."

"Really."

He slid me a look at the deadpan tone.

"You think I don't know when you're keeping secrets by now?" Arms crossed over my chest, I glared at him. "I know you, man. I know when you're keeping secrets and I know when you're holding back. Right now, you're holding back a secret the size of Mount Everest."

"Well, it's time to go climbing." He tipped his head back. "I've got reason to believe there are NHs involved in whoever has been setting up these abductions, Kit. *Good* reason."

Those words made my gut run cold.

I sucked in a breath and turned away from the window. Linking my fingers behind my neck, I focused on the floor. Before Abraham had left, Justin had made him give an oath: *Whatever we learn on this job, whatever we do, you have to keep it to yourself. You willing to give a blood oath on it?*

Blood oaths were serious business.

Abraham had agreed, albeit reluctantly. Apparently, he worked with some autonomy so more than likely it would cause him no problem, but the whole *my bond is my blood* shit is just messed up.

But I understood now.

It wasn't the just the *blood* Justin had been looking for.

If Abraham was involved, he wouldn't have been willing to agree to an oath, especially not a blood oath.

Plus, I doubted he'd hunt Justin down.

Justin was known for being a bulldog.

Grim knowledge ate at me like a cancer. "This goes deeper than Saul, then."

"Much."

The weight of that response was staggering, so heavy I felt like it would bow my shoulders under it and I wondered how Justin had managed to carry it so long. "Word about this will get out," I said quietly. "Whoever is behind this will learn you're involved and they'll come after you."

I looked at him as I spoke and saw the feral grin curling his lips. "Let them."

The man was pissed.

I can't say I blamed him.

I wasn't happy either.

I slid my eyes to the trunk tucked under the weapons adorning my wall and thought maybe I'd start carrying a few of the more…subtle weapons. There was a ring. One subtle flick and it would send poison or a paralyzing agent through the veins of whomever I happened to touch.

"Why?" I asked quietly. "Why do you think this and who is involved?"

It was late. I was tired. But when Justin made me an offer I couldn't refuse, well…I said yes.

"What happened to 'me big tough witch, me handle Saul, silly girly?'"

From under the veil of his lashes, Justin's vivid green eyes looked amused. "I'm pretty sure I said *I am a* big tough witch *and I can* handle Saul, *silly girl.*"

I flipped him off.

He flicked my finger.

"For the record, the main was…well, is…" He grimaced. "What we just discussed. NHs being involved and I don't know how far it goes or who all is involved." Mouth tight, Justin said, "You can't discuss this with Damon, Kit. You can't."

"If you think *Damon* is involved—"

"I *don't.*" His hand slashed through the air, an emphasis to his flat statement. Striding to me, he bent down until our gazes were level. "I'm doing the same thing you always do, Kit, so stop giving me shit. I'm following my gut and my gut says the fewer people who know, the better. No, I don't think he's involved—matter of fact, I *know* he's not involved. The idea is *laughable.* But if he knows, he'll start acting different. Your boy, Kit, is not subtle. He'll start looking for things. He'll say something to Chang and even though they are good and even though they can keep quiet, the people behind this aren't *good,* they are artists. They've been doing this *right* under our noses for who knows how long."

He paused, letting all of that sink in.

And I realized he was right.

Damon would give me time, *maybe,* if I asked. But not a lot.

I couldn't blame him. Already, I felt guilty as hell knowing that I was going to stay quiet about this horrible, awful thing. And I knew it was the only way we could do it, if we wanted to catch those responsible and shut them down.

"You get it, don't you?"

I looked up and met his eyes. He was closer than I'd realized and as I stood there, the green of his eyes darkened while his pupils spiked.

My heart lurched.

● ● ●

A strange realization hit me and I realized something crucial. Something vital.

Oh. Oh, no…

I went to back away.

Justin reached up and brushed the tips of his fingers through my hair. Panic seized me. It wasn't that terrified panic. I knew he'd never hurt me and I knew he'd never cause me pain. This was that oh-shit-what-do-I-do panic.

Slowly, I reached up and caught his wrist, tugging. He twisted his hand until our fingers entwined.

"I miss you," he murmured, his voice rough.

"Justin…"

A harsh noise shuddered out of him. "Every day. Even when I was gone, I missed you and I kept telling myself I needed to come back, but it just didn't seem like the right time and then I *did* come back and you were with him. The first time I saw you together, I was like…"

I backed away, fighting the urge to cover my ears.

And still Justin spoke. "…'okay, this isn't going to last,' so I waited. I kept telling myself it wouldn't last. But you stayed together."

He sounded so confused and the pain in his voice hurt my heart.

Closing my eyes, I rubbed my hands down my face. "Justin, I'm not what you need," I whispered.

"Don't you think that's more my call?" he asked.

I laughed, the sound brittle in the strange, waiting silence. "If I was what you *needed*, you never would have been able to leave as easily as you did," I pointed out. "You needed me because you wanted to fix me, because I was weak and needy. When I stopped being that, you didn't need me as much. Maybe you *wanted* me, but that's not need."

A look of hurt crossed his face, but I didn't let myself soften. "Face it, Justin. You wanted to fix things—people. You wanted me because I was weak…because I needed you. Damon loves me because I'm strong."

We didn't ride together to find Saul.

Justin took his bike and I followed him, doing my damnedest not to think about that odd interlude in my office.

I couldn't even remember the last time Justin and I had talked about anything that…personal.

We hadn't been lovers in close to five years. Roughly a year after he'd joined Banner. We'd been very much in the off-phase for much of the past year or so and after one-near explosive fight, followed by absolutely explosive sex, we'd decided we needed a cooling-off period.

He'd left town a few weeks later on a case and when he'd come back, I'd been in a sort-of relationship with another freelancer—a mercenary. Justin hadn't said anything about it when he ran into us at Drake's. We'd shared a beer, the three of us, and then he'd left.

The next time *I* saw him, he'd been wrapped around a vampire with breasts almost larger than her head. Justin might have drowned in her cleavage if he hadn't been careful. I hadn't felt anything when I saw them together. *Anything*.

I tried to imagine how I'd feel if I saw Damon in that situation…

The molding on my steering wheel cracked.

Forcibly, I loosened my grip, uncurling my fingertips one by one.

Okay, so there was no question. What I felt for my friend was nothing compared to what I felt for my lover.

And there was no question—I wasn't going to be able to tell Damon about Saul. I probably would have figured that out on my own, once I thought about it. Damon would start removing heads—with his hands—if he started digging around for information and people didn't yield.

And there was *nooooo* way in hell people in this part of town would yield to a cat.

We'd left International a while back, taking a series of turns that had led us to East Eldritch. We were now in an area known as the Abyss. You could find a mix of heaven and hell and everything in between. There were shops—I guess we could call them that, if we wanted to be generous—that sold the not-entirely-legal brews of garden witches. On any given corner, I could find offshoots who'd decided they'd just give up trying to make a real living and sell drugs instead.

If a girl knew how to look, there were serious treasures to be found in the Abyss. Most of my good weapons came from here. I could see Charnal's store— Charnal was one of those weird offshoots I couldn't quite place. He wasn't human, but he wasn't a witch and I didn't know what else he was or wasn't. One thing I did know—he knew weapons and he knew them well.

If I'd been coming here to see Charnal, I would have been happy.

But I wasn't.

So I was...tense.

People died in the Abyss.

Magic flowed in strange ways here, too—and there had been a time when somebody had died here...and hadn't stayed dead. I'd been standing nearby, talking to Charnal when it happened. Talk about freaky.

A sexless gray-skinned creature had separated itself from the herd of onlookers, watching as the corpse tried to pick up the blade it had dropped only minutes earlier, as it had been run through by a bigger, stronger male. The dead thing's hand hadn't wanted to work. The gray thing had calmly led it back to where it had died, smeared its own blood across its brow and spoken to it.

It laid back down.

A moment later, it closed its eyes and was once more, still. Dead, truly, that time.

I still didn't know what the grey thing was and I'd spent a decent amount of time researching it. We parked less than a hundred feet from where it had happened. I shivered, chilled at the memory of it.

If I never saw an animated corpse again, it would be too soon. Nothing as creepy as seeing a body moving when there was nothing inside to pilot the actions.

Justin joined me a few minutes later.

"Your friend Saul lives in the Abyss," I said neutrally, still staring at the spot where the thing's blood had pooled so thick and wet.

"He *frequents* these parts." Justin craned his head, staring at the place where I stared so hard. He couldn't see anything. The blood had long since been cleaned away or faded by the elements. But could he *feel* it—the bone-deep...*longing*?

"And where does he frequently frequent?"

Justin smiled and gestured to the bar just to the right.

Howlers.

"Wow." I clicked my tongue. "*That* is original."

"I'll be sure to pass your compliments to the MacDonald." He winked at me. "He's part owner."

With more than a little dismay, I eyed the old-school sign, done in neon, with a wolf hanging over the door and the name of the bar spelled out over its snarl. The *e* was going dim and the buzzing noise that accompanied it made me think of a swarm of gnats waiting to descend.

"I would have thought Dair could afford better."

"Oh, he can. He just believes in spreading his dollars around." He winked at me. "Last I heard he had invested in an upscale whorehouse, too."

That didn't surprise me. There was money to be made in flesh. "Does he really expect to make money here?"

"Oh, there's plenty of money to be made here. They water down the liquor, and if you're buying it here, you don't care how cheap it is." Justin shrugged again. "There's also flesh-work going on in the backrooms. It's not as fancy as it is elsewhere, but it's still here. That's where we're gonna find Saul."

"Ugh." I fought the urge to shudder. I could already imagine how many showers I'd need to make myself feel clean once I walked through a place this dirty— especially if they were using it for sex work. I didn't have anything against whoring as a trade. Not in general, at least, if the whore was cool with it and if she—or he—was treated well. But plenty were forced into it and plenty *weren't* treated well. Also, dives like this were *filthy*. I could smell the blood and the sweat—and yes, now that we were close, the earthy, musky scent of sex, a fine film that clung to everything. Alcohol was a pungent kick that blended the whole miasma together.

Yeah. I was going to have to drown myself in the shower to get this stink out of my pores. Aside from alcohol, the scents were a trigger of things I worked too hard to forget. Blood, pain, fear...the desperate wish to escape it all in the only way I knew how.

Filthy pig...your mother should have strangled you with your cord.

Justin's hand, hard and firm, came down on my shoulder, squeezing with near brutal strength. I let myself take that one moment before I stepped away. He always seemed to know. When I looked at him, I saw the knowledge in his eyes. "Let's get this done," I said softly. I wanted out of here already and we hadn't even started.

As we walked inside, an air of despondency settled around us. Below it was something that whispered of the damned, as though the people who came inside Howler's knew that once they crossed that threshold, they might as well just settle down to die. The point of no return—it lay somewhere inside the Abyss. It might even be here.

Justin took the lead and I was happy to follow along behind him. A dozen eyes cut our way. Most of them skittered off as soon as they took our measure. There was no denying what we were and while I might not look terribly intimidating, the sword at my hip wasn't there for show. Nobody with half a brain was going to dismiss Justin. He looked every inch of what he was—a warrior witch.

I saw one man straighten slightly, eying Justin for a long moment before he shifted his attention to me. His gaze lingered on the blade before skimming the rest of me, from my head down to my boots—some might think it odd that the boots would catch much attention, maybe, but people in our line of work don't run around in a pair of beat-up tennis shoes. The boots on my feet told a story almost as detailed as a blade.

When he looked back at me, he lifted a chin in greeting and then did the same to Justin. As he turned back to his drink, I caught sight of the staff leaning against the bar.

"Chuck," Justin murmured.

I glanced at him.

"His name's Chuck..." Then he grinned. "Actually, it's Charles Andrulis. He's a mercenary. Human, believe it or not. Decent guy." He ran his tongue across his teeth and then leaned in. "He's got a thing for taking jobs nobody else will touch and he loves the underdog."

"A human mercenary…in the Abyss." I wanted to stare at him, the same way I'd first stared at the turreted towers of Cinderella's castle. The same way I'd stare at any novelty.

I didn't let myself.

"Come on." Justin nudged me toward the far back. "Let's go sit."

My skin crawled at the idea of sitting in one of those booths, but I breathed an internal sigh of relief when Justin used a bit of his magic to cleanse the area. It cost him nothing and made me breathe easier. I'm not exactly a germophobe, but I'm pretty damn close. I stood at his side, facing over the bar as he placed a hand over the table. He'd done this a hundred, or probably a thousand times and it never ceased to amaze me how simple it was for him, to simply *will* the energy that came from everything around him into doing what he wished. Magic takes practice and control, but he'd turned it into an art.

The truly strong witches are like that.

We hadn't been sitting there more than a few minutes when the human mercenary approached us. He nodded at us both and gestured at the booth. "Mind if I sit down?"

In response, Justin got up and moved into the seat next to mine. Andrulis took the now-vacated booth, and for several minutes, we sat there staring at each other. Eventually, a sleepy-eyed server made her way toward us. Her muttered, "What can I get ya?" had very little enthusiasm in it. I guess I couldn't blame her. I was about to tell her I didn't want anything when Justin told her, "Bring me two Redkins."

She shifted her vague, brown eyes toward Andrulis. He lifted his pint toward her, still full. She nodded and moved to the bar.

"I hope whatever you ordered wasn't expensive." I skimmed a look around the bar. "I don't think I trust my immune system enough to drink anything from here."

Andrulis laughed.

Justin grinned. "Trust me, the amount of alcohol in a Redkin will kill any microbes. Also…they serve it in a bottle. The envies would kill them."

"Yeah, but will I have a stomach lining left?" At that moment, I didn't care what environmentalists thought. I cared about the millions of germs creeping around me.

"Yep." Justin settled back in the booth. "You'll even thank me for it. It's good stuff. Brewed here in the Abyss, so you can't find it anywhere else. The maker won't sell it outside this area."

I wasn't sure if that was an endorsement or a warning.

While we waited for our drinks, Andrulis asked, "What brings you to the Abyss, Justin? You're not around these parts too often anymore."

"Neither are you," Justin replied. He lifted one shoulder. In the dim lighting, the silver on his sleeves reflected a muted light. "I'm looking for Saul. He been in?"

For a mortal, Andrulis was very good at hiding his emotions. But no human could possibly hope to compete with the likes of what I was used to. I caught the faint flicker in his pale blue eyes, the minute tightening around his mouth.

Under the heavy miasma of scents clouding the air, I caught a new one. The slightly-acrid souring of the man in front of me. Body chemistry told a lot about a person, and his reactions just told me everything I needed to know. Charles Andrulis did not like Saul.

I filed that away. Since I hadn't made up my mind about Andrulis, it wasn't a lot of information. Yet.

"Why're you looking for him? Any information he can get you, I can do the same for a lot less." His lips twisted and he added, "And I do mean a lot less. People don't die when I extract information, unless they deserve to die anyway."

Yet another piece of information for me to file away.

From the corner of my eye, I saw Justin's reaction. I also felt how he tensed. I don't know if Andrulis saw it or not, but it was enough to make me wonder.

"Right now, I'm not looking for information," Justin said. "I just want Saul." His voice had noticeably cooled. His normally vivid-green eyes had gone to ice. The expression on his face was that of a man the wise did not cross.

Andrulis saw it all and I watched as he took it in. Something that might have been appreciation flickered in those pale blue eyes. Under his breath, he muttered, "Finally screwed up there, did you, Saul?"

A human wouldn't have heard that low comment. Even though we were in a dive with more than a few non-humans, I doubted if anybody more than a couple of feet away had heard him, Andrulis was so quiet. But I had, and I couldn't help but wonder just what had Saul done to fuck this guy over.

Andrulis scraped nails over the light growth of facial hair darkening his cheeks. "I've seen him today. Seems to me he came in looking for his normal girl. She wasn't here. So the bartender back there—his name's John—offered one of his other girls. He's in one of the backrooms with Marcia." His eyelids drooped while a smiled curved his lips. "Gotta admit...I don't get why she's here—she doesn't really fit in the life, but maybe I'm wrong. He got her price."

"Thanks," Justin said. He might have said more, but the server appeared with two tall, frosted bottles. The bottles were clear and the liquid inside was an odd cross between orange and yellow, not quite the pale amber of any number of brews. Actually, it was unlike anything I'd ever seen before. Damn if it didn't look like it glowed in the dim light. I was supposed to drink that. I don't know if I wanted to drink something that glowed.

She slid the two bottles in front of us and Justin slid a few bills in front of her. The money disappeared even quicker than she did and we were once more left alone.

Once more left the relative anonymity of Howler's, Andrulis resumed his thoughtful contemplation. "If y'all need some help, I'd be more than happy to oblige. Saul owes me some blood." As he spoke, a feral light glinted in his eyes.

Although this man was human, I found myself thinking I wouldn't mind having him at my back. I also did not want him coming *at* my back.

Justin's amused grin did nothing to change either of those thoughts. "Charles, my man, I think I got this, but if things change, I'll definitely look you up."

"You do that." Then he shifted his entire focus to me.

Some people are just born old.

Like Colleen. In reality, she was thirty-nine. She had almost a dozen years on me. But there was something within Colleen that was older—much older. Her soul, perhaps. She had a feel to her that made you think there was nothing you could do or say that would throw her, surprise her. She could just take it all in stride.

The man in front of me gave me the same impression.

Even though he'd likely be dust in the ground before I ever showed the first sign of aging, he had that wise beyond his years look to him.

"I know you," he said.

"Do you?"

"Maybe not personally." He shrugged. "But I know who you are."

"I'm afraid I can't say the same." It wasn't until the words came out that I realized how rude it sounded, but it was too late to take it back and rather than stutter or stammer out an apology, I just brazened my way through it, staring him down while he chuckled into his tall pilsner.

When he didn't seem offended, I mentally breathed out a sigh of relief. Closing my hands over the bottle, I took an experimental sniff. The server had twisted off the caps before she brought them out and the fumes all but singed the hairs inside my nose. Immediately, my head started to spin. "Wow."

A slow smile spreading across Justin's lips, he took a long, deep draught of his and then thumped it on the table. "That's how you do it, Kitty."

"Yeah, if you wanna stumble and fall on your ass." I took a slower drink, tentative and quick. Anybody who wanted to bolt back something in a place like this, more power to them. But me? I preferred to walk out of here—not be carried out.

The taste of Redkin lingered on my tongue, even as it hit my belly and exploded in a loose rush of liquid warmth. It started to spread through my body with every pulsation of my heart. Oh…oh…that was nice.

A sweet buzz settled in my veins and I eyed the bottle I'd put down. One taste. Just one taste had hit my head like this. "Wow."

I found myself reaching for the bottle again—

Something hummed inside.

Reluctantly, I curled my hands into fists. No. No, I didn't want that sweet, *false* liquid warmth. Not right—

"That stuff is dangerous," I said, shaking my head.

Justin winked at me. "Told you it was good."

"No. Not *good*. *Dangerous*." I reached out and shoved his bottle away, too. "What

● ● ●
167

did they do, coat the glasses with candy crack?"

"Hell, Kit." He looked both exasperated and amused. "I'm not Tate. I'm not Doyle. I don't need an intervention."

"Another few drinks of that and *I* might need an intervention."

Justin started to laugh, but it faded as he caught sight of the look on my face. A raised, furious voice from the bar had me glancing away from his face for a moment before I looked back.

"I'm serious." I went to reach for the bottle. My fingers brushed the neck as a scuffle broke out up front.

In the span of time it took me to pick that bottle up, the scuffle went from an awful fight and in what seemed like mere heartbeats, a body flew across the air and smashed onto the table in front of us.

Or rather, the table where we *had* been.

My body had taken over and I'd driven my feet into the floor, shoving back. The empty booth behind us, the table, all of them had toppled and we were now roughly five feet back from where we had been.

And I was still holding Justin's Redkin.

The only reason I even noticed *that* was because of the way the shifter on the table seemed to focus on it.

The look was almost comical.

Really.

Cocking my head, I shifted the bottle to the left and his gaze swung to the left. I brought it back and his gaze followed—then he stopped, his attention cutting upward to my face.

The whole interaction lasted seconds.

But it had been seconds too long.

"Justin?" I murmured softly.

"Yeah."

There were times when it was just poetry to work with somebody who knew you like yesterday. Today was one of those days. I passed the drink to Justin and moved to block him, drawing the blade at my hip.

I readied myself to hear something from the bartender but to my surprise, he was leaning against the surface, arms across, a smug smile twisting his lips. Wonder what had *him* so happy.

The blast of magic warmed my back as the shapeshifter sank lower. Another pulse of energy rippled into the air.

"Out of my way, little girl."

Inky black rolled across the gaze of the creature in front of me, followed by a wash of black that flowed under the man's face as he paced closer to him.

I swung my blade between us, warming up my wrist as I kept my body between the wererat and Justin.

"Now why would I want to do that?" I asked him.

"So I don't fuck you up?" he offered.

"Hmmm." I pondered that. "Decisions."

He lunged, leading up with upper body and I waited until the last moment to twist away. My blade slide across his soft belly, parting flesh like butter and his howl went from enraged to pained as the silver hit his system. I chanced a look out of the corner of my eye and saw that Justin had produced a vial from somewhere and some of the contents of the brew were now inside it. In the next blink, that vial was tucked away in his vest.

The hair on the back of my neck prickled and I swung my head around just in time to see the rat lurch in my direction once more. When he struck out, it was with one meaty, huge, *human* fist. By the time it connected with the space where I had been, it was furred and deformed and clawed.

Too many shifters were used to fighting with nothing more than their strength. Pair them up with somebody who actually knew how to fight—and who knew how to compensate for their greater strength—and they were stumped. The punch threw him off balance and I moved in, brought the butt of my sword down on the back of his head with all my strength. Something cracked and he groaned, swayed.

Without waiting a blink, I took his legs out from under him and he crashed into the ground. I used the blade to skewer him, pinning him to the floor like an ugly, giant, overgrown bug.

* * *

The fur that had been bleeding across his form froze at the insult of silver striking his system. He whined in pain. "Hurts like a bitch, I bet," I said cheerfully. He thrashed and then stilled as the movement sent fresh bursts of pain spinning through him. Placing one booted foot high on his spine, I pressed down. "You might want to be still."

He lapsed into motionlessness as I looked up, skimming the room with a hard stare.

The server was cowering near the bar.

That despair seemed to ooze from her pores.

Andrulis' shadow fell across mine and a moment later, Justin joined him. "Justin, I think we'll have to have a talk with this gentleman," I said.

"I figured that." He came up next to me and I held still as he pulled something out of his pocket.

I recognized it a moment later—cuffs, designed specifically for creatures like the one beneath me. Titanium and silver, reinforced by magic—with a surprise inside.

I leaned a little harder on the blade buried inside the trembling rat. "Boy, you picked a bad, bad day to go slipping people some funny shit in their drinks. My friend is a mean one."

He tensed, but he couldn't do anything with the sword that skewered him. The silver effectively weakened him to the point that he couldn't twist free without ripping through bone or flesh. Plenty of shifters could do that, but he wasn't high-level enough. When Justin knelt down, the rat started to whimper again, loud, sniveling noises that were almost embarrassing.

Andrulis must have thought so, too. He thumped his staff loudly on the floor next to the rat and said, "Shit! You sound like a little boy hiding from the monster in the closet. Grow some balls."

I bit back a laugh and stepped back, watching as Justin closed the cuffs. I braced myself and couldn't stop the wince as the spell inside them also activated.

Silver punched through the rat's wrists, coming out of the cuffs, thin spears of it that immobilized him and made sure he didn't attempt to rip free. If he did, he'd shred his flesh. At the same time, thin strands snaked up his arms, twisting around his upper body, all but mummifying him.

The cuffs were Justin's, made much thicker than typically needed to be and the outer layers were held together by magic. His magic. Once they were clapped into place, the magic was activated and the end result wasn't much different than a straitjacket made of silver.

While Justin finished dealing with him, I evaluated the current situation.

Fear choked the air.

Two servers gathered near the bar, all but clinging to each other, while the others stood in various positions watching with expressions that ranged from amusement to bewilderment to boredom. Those, I wrote off. If they knew what was going on, they'd be scared. So I focused on the ones reeking of fear.

One of the servers actually *flinched* when I looked at her.

I pretended not to notice and continued to study the rest of the room.

Somebody slunk close to the side door. He probably thought he was subtle with it, but there was nothing subtle about the antsy way he shifted from one foot to the other, or the way he beat out a nervous rhythm on his legs, his hands impromptu drumsticks.

Andrulis glanced casually toward the door then back at me.

My gut remained silent, so I thought, *What the hell.* I gave him a slight nod.

There was one other.

He sat at the bar, back to us, like he was completely unaware of everything going on. He was so aware, however, I would be surprised if he hadn't taken notice of my bra size. He had dense black hair with a thick stripe of white running through, just slightly off center.

When I took one step forward, he lunged for the front door.

Everything happened at once.

Drummer Boy raced toward one door while Stripe took the other.

I flung a dagger, watched as it buried itself in the door just an inch past the man's shoulder. He paused for a split second and I used that second to palm another dagger. As he neared the door, I threw again—a larger dagger, practically a small sword. It went through his upper shoulder and he screamed as it pinned him

● ● ●

awkwardly to the wall. I strode toward him as he jerked against it.

I didn't worry about him dislodging it.

He wasn't human, but he wasn't shifter or vampire, either. That made him less of a threat. Offshoots were rarely as powerful as the other breeds of crazy that populated our world.

"You." Lifting my blade, I pressed the tip of it to his throat. His struggles stopped. "Why were you running?"

His response was to spit at me.

I saw it coming and dodged to the side in time—barely.

That was so damn nasty. Why did people do that?

I pressed harder with the blade. "Try it again, and I'm going to ventilate your throat," I warned him.

"You can't touch me," he said, panting. "You got no idea who I work for. I'm untouchable."

"Oh, really?" I dragged my blade across his throat and watched as blood welled. The crimson streak of it made me smile. "I just touched you…you want to run home and tell Mommy?"

"Maybe we should," Justin suggested as he joined me. The silver on his sleeves was sparking bright and hard. "I gotta admit, I *really* want to know who his mommy is, Kit. Think she'll let us join them for dinner?"

"You find out who I work for and you just might *be* dinner."

Justin's smile was vicious and bright. "Oh, perfect."

He struck out.

The magic hit, hard and fast.

The man sagged.

I had to catch him before he tore the hell out of his muscles, pinned to the wall like a macabre butterfly the way he was.

"What t' fuck's goin'…"

The voice came from the door and I whipped my head around to see who it was, although the way the words abruptly went silent, I had a bad, bad feeling.

CHAPTER THIRTEEN

Saul Tremble was an average man. Almost uncommonly average, if such a thing were possible. He had hair of a dirty, dishwater blond and eyes of indiscriminate hazel-brown. His face was neither round nor square and his jawline wasn't soft enough to look weak, but it didn't have the kind of firm edge that would make him stand out.

He stood a good five foot ten, if I had to hazard a guess, and I pegged him to weigh about 180. He wasn't overweight, nor was he uncommonly skinny—or fit.

The *only* thing about him that stood out to me was the fact that *nothing* stood out.

Oh, and the fact that he practically *exuded* panic.

When he caught sight of Justin, a light flared in the back of his eyes. A game smile curved his lips, though, and I watched as he lifted a hand in greeting. "Greaves, man. What are you doing down here in hell? I didn't think the Abyss was your speed."

Justin bared his teeth in a mockery of a smile as he turned to face the man we'd come here to find.

So maybe he'd found us, but I was still going to call it a successful night.

I caught the hilt of my blade and managed to yank it one-handed from the wall while I continued to brace Stripe. Once the blade was free, I let the son-of-a-bitch go. He hit the ground with a muffled thud. A bloody streak decorated the wall where he'd stood.

"Looks like you had a run-in with Dally." Saul smiled. It was a little more confident than the last one. Since Justin hadn't killed him yet, I guess he felt more secure.

● ● ●
173

That just proved what an idiot he was. Justin wouldn't kill until he had what he needed.

"He's a sad little dickwad," Saul said, still talking, his voice too laidback and easy to call it jabbering—but he wasn't waiting for a response and his gaze didn't linger in any one spot, either. "Likes to rough up the girls." He shot me a look. "He get too rough with you, honey?"

For a second, the words didn't process. Then I had to fight not to pick my jaw up. Did he mean—

"I need information," Justin cut in, his voice iced.

"Yeah, yeah." Saul looked around, eyes bouncing over the two servers who still hovered near the bar. They wouldn't look at him and I saw a muscle pulse in his jaw, watched his eyes flicker before his gaze slid back to us. "Sure. I tell you what, we'll just grab us a booth—"

"Can't be here. Confidential." Justin's hands hung loose at his sides.

Saul nodded. "I'll just go get dressed then."

He turned.

Justin moved to follow.

I could hear how Saul had picked up his pace, his bare feet slapping on the wooden floor. Justin disappeared through the door. Then he swore and I could hear him all but running.

I rushed for the door and then stopped.

Justin partially blocked my view, but I shifted a little more, just enough to see around his lean body and what I saw made my brows go up.

Saul lay sprawled on the ground, head turned toward me, a dazed look on his face. There was a woman standing over him and I looked at her long and hard, trying to make sense of what I was seeing.

"Marcia."

She cocked her head, not saying a single word.

I glanced to the side and saw the bartender, a man who was almost ridiculously pretty, standing there. "Please tell me you didn't injure him too grievously, love."

"No." She nudged him with her foot, her nose wrinkling. "He still breathes."

● ● ●

174

After a moment, she added, "And he'll be able to talk. For a while at least."

She looked at me, then, and the green-gold of her eyes flashed to wolf-green.

"That should have been more useful."

We watched as the black van pulled away, driven by Marcia. John was in the back with Tremble—apparently, his partner had too much of a temper to be trusted around the skin trader. They'd taken him out through the back, although it seemed a wasted effort. Absolutely nobody in the Abyss would pay any attention to anything that didn't involve their own neck.

"Think Dair hired them?" I asked softly.

"No idea." He hesitated for a moment and then said, "Probably. Or at least he knows they're here. I've heard of them. They play by the rules so they wouldn't have been digging around in the MacDonald's backyard without his authorization."

Although we'd been *this* close to grabbing Saul, Marcia and John had been circling in on him for weeks, and the bottom line was…we wouldn't have gotten him away from two alpha wolves if we'd tried.

Those alpha wolves, though, hadn't minded sharing info. They wouldn't share a *lot*, but we got the gist of it. They'd been hired to investigate some *problematic issues*— that sound so very like a wolf, uptight and proper—and their search had led them here. To Saul.

"It wasn't a total waste," Justin said when I turned to look at him.

I snorted. "Well, no. We know he was involved. We know he had been under suspicion. But what else do we know that we hadn't known before this?"

By unspoken agreement, we turned and started down the narrow alley, away from Howler's.

"I don't know yet." Justin shrugged. "But we'll figure it out. They also promised to keep us apprised of any information they got from him."

"Think they'll actually *do* that?"

He glanced at me. "Yep."

"It still feels unfinished." But there was nothing to be done about it. They'd been there first; they'd taken him down and that's the way the game was played. Honor among thieves and bounty hunters and fellow problem-solvers. I turned and walked away.

Justin fell into step with me. "He wasn't working solo on this, you know."

"Yeah." Through my teeth, I blew out a short puff of air. "A couple of them were all nervy when we were there. We need to pay them a visit."

"I'm surprised John and Marcia weren't more keen to move on them as well," Justin said quietly.

"Maybe they just saw them as pawns."

"Pawns or not, they played into a dangerous game—on their own. They should have been dealt with."

We turned the corner, our destination the car we'd parked a couple blocks away from the bar. Both necessity and common sense dictated it. The road in front of Howler's had been pocked with potholes big enough to swallow a car. I could see the smooth gleam of Justin's ride just ahead of us.

I stopped. "We need to…"

The words died in my throat as my ears caught a noise—so faint I barely heard it.

I couldn't miss the scent of blood, though. It washed over me and turned my stomach.

It froze me. For just a split second, it froze me.

Then I launched myself forward.

I felt Justin reach out for me, heard him shout my name. I ignored him, my entire focus gathered on the building tucked between the two taller ones—the one that looked like it was only waiting for one final shove before it tumbled down into nothing but walls and rubble.

Howlers. That stink was coming from Howler's.

I didn't even pause when I reached the door, just slowed enough to shoulder it open. I slammed my hand against the wall, searching for the light switches while the coppery, sweet scent of blood clouded inside my head, choking me.

Light flooded the room just as my boot heel hit something slick and wet. My stomach lurched horribly.

Don't look down. Don't look down. Don't look down...

But of course I did.

I looked down and found myself staring at something thick and rubbery, almost ropey. Gorge rushed up my throat as my brain supplied the name to what it was I'd just stepped in.

To what it was that was flung with almost childish glee across the entire part of the bar.

All those trivia facts about how many feet and yards there are of intestines in your gut...I guess they really can be stretched out end to end to cover a football field. Or at last enough to be thrown around a room like bloody surreal holiday decorations from hell.

I heard movement behind me and immediately flung out a hand to stop whoever it was.

"What the..."

Recognizing Justin's voice, I lowered my arm.

"Somebody didn't want them to talk," I said woodenly.

My gaze landed on one of the bodies—this one was mostly intact, save for the disturbingly destroyed skull. Somebody had all but ripped the top half of the head off. I'd seen the injury that had resulted from that before, from somebody grabbing a person and savagely wrenching their mouth open, breaking the jaw—and other things.

The person who'd received that injury had been a shapeshifter—a youth under Annette's brutal hand. He'd survived it.

This woman had been human.

She, of course, hadn't.

"Somebody didn't even want them to scream."

I was less than a mile from home when I got a message from Damon.

I miss you.

After the grim, fruitless hunt, those simple words brought a much needed warmth to the hollowness inside my chest.

We'd hunted for the killer—and it had only been one. Justin had been able to learn that much, but not much else. I tried to find a trail to follow, but there just wasn't anything and by the time twilight rolled around, I was so fucking tired, I couldn't have tracked a child leaving a trail of bread crumbs.

But those three words eased the ache in my heart, changed my plans from a long hot shower followed by a boring dinner and an even more boring evening where I made notes and muttered and complained to spending the evening with Damon. A long hot soak in his tub, a decent meal that I didn't have to cook, and maybe I'd even bounce some things off him, wait for that weird connection in my head to happen. Things always connected for me. They did.

I just had to wait for the right thing to make them connect, or the right sound, or…well, even Damon.

I responded back. *I miss you, too. You busy?*

Not if you're available.

The response made me smile and I tossed the phone back down onto the seat next to me after I told him I'd be at the Lair later. Forty minutes—tops.

A half mile from home, I had to amend it to *an hour—tops. If I'm lucky.*

A vampire was trailing me.

I was almost certain it was Abraham, but I had to be certain.

I gave it another moment for my body to adjust and sure enough, I could feel it. Abraham, just like any other vampire, felt *other*. They were the most different among NHs. Human once, then not, they could mimic emotions, but they rarely felt them.

There is something different about each of them, though, and I'd come to recognize Abraham.

Sighing, I parked my car and waited there as he came to land in front of me in a gathering of shadows.

They'd faded by the time I climbed out of the car, my hand gripping the sword I'd pulled from the passenger seat. "We have got to stop meeting like this." I paused and then added, "Really. I do have an office."

● ● ●

178

He ignored that comment. "I hear you caught Saul Tremble."

"Yes." Rubbing my thumb along the grip of the blade, I said, "I was surprised you didn't show up. You've got a habit of doing that."

"I was...resting."

In a crypt or coffin? I bit the words back but they still danced on the tip of my tongue.

The cool look on his face told me that he had a good idea at my thoughts anyway. Smug, creepy bastard. I really didn't like that I liked him. Scowling, I rested the sheathed tip of my blade on the pavement and propped my other hand on my hip. "You here because you're lonely or you got a reason? Because if you're just lonely..."

"I've got a healthy respect for life and limb," he said, his voice filled with wry humor. "I can't decide what would be more dangerous—you with a sword or your man with his temper."

My man. There was no contest. But I appreciated the fact that he didn't just toss me out with the bathwater.

"Why don't you tell me what you need to tell me, then?" I asked.

"In a hurry?" His nostrils flared. "You smell impatient."

"That's because I've been working all day and I want to get a bite to eat and crash."

I wasn't even lying. I just didn't plan on crashing *here*.

His lips twitched again, his near black eyes glowing. "Very well. It concerns Icarus." He looked around, those insightful eyes taking in everything, be it a bit of shrubbery or a car or a cat creeping across the ground as it stalked a mouse. A moment later, we both heard the mouse's final squeaks. The cat won tonight. They often did. "I have information that might be...important."

I lifted a brow.

His mouth tightened. "Must we discuss it in the open?"

"Most of the people who live here are working stiffs," I told him dryly. "They couldn't care less about what I do—no, wait. Scratch that. They prefer not to *know* what I do."

"Good. Then let's keep them in the dark… and discuss this elsewhere."

Elsewhere ended up being inside my apartment.

I *can't* believe I was letting the undead into my place.

At the same time, I took it as one of the biggest victories I'd made since I'd walked away from that icy fortress on the mountainside. I'd found it in me to trust myself again. This wasn't about trusting Abraham—under the instinctive fear, my gut already knew he wasn't a threat, but I had to get under the fear.

And I was doing it.

Still…

I didn't offer him anything.

Vampires could take food or drink—it was a misnomer, one likely spread by them, that they could only imbibe blood. But I didn't keep blood on hand and I didn't see the point in wasting what I had when he'd only be taking it out of courtesy.

"Okay." I propped my blade up against the nearest bar stool and took up position right next to it. Yeah, I'd decided I could probably trust him, but I was still a paranoid bitch. "Why don't you fill me in on just what is going on?"

Abraham stood in front of the couch, his eyes on the weapons I had there. It seemed he and I couldn't get past our mutual fascination with weapons. His gaze roamed over the curves of the Sais I had on the wall. They were old, too old to use, but too beautiful to keep hidden away. "It's an ugly thing that's happening, Kit. Very ugly."

My instinct was to fire back something full of sarcasm and grim humor. I grabbed that instinct by the neck and strangled it. "Yeah." I nodded in agreement. "It is."

He didn't even look at me. Head lowering, he focused on the polished tips of his boots—good boots, I couldn't help but notice. They'd hold up to a long, hard hunt.

"Icarus was supposed to meet a young vampire by the name of Trident. He had lost much of his family and he wasn't…thriving in his current circumstances."

The note in Abraham's voice made everything inside me freeze. But I didn't say anything.

"Trident hailed from the Marlowe family and he was…well, to be blunt, he was the whipping boy. He was strong, though, one of their pillars—or he would have been, had they nurtured it. Icarus won't share the details, but he tells me that he was to meet with Trident. They were going to…discuss things." Abraham drew the words out and when he lifted his brow at me, I heard all the things he couldn't say.

There was trouble in Marlowe house.

"It's uncommon, but there are ways for one vampire to shift his bloodvow to another vampire's line. Icarus will not confirm this, but I believe he was trying to bring Trident into our house." He was quiet a moment. "It would be just like him. Icarus was fond of saving the lost."

"Was he?"

He flicked me a look. "Very. In our world, Kit, having goals keeps you grounded."

I wondered if that meant *sane* or *human*. He said nothing else and a grim silence stretched out.

"What happened, Abraham?"

"We can't really say…not exactly. Icarus knows he arrived at the designated spot. He knows he was there—and that Trident wasn't. At least Trident wasn't there initially. Whether he ever arrived…" Abraham shrugged. "We cannot say. Icarus heard a noise. He tells me he didn't recognize it at first, but days later, as he was imprisoned, he understood it. It was the sound of an arrow."

He flicked me a look as my blood turned to ice. "It's an unusual sound, Kit, the noise an arrow makes as it cuts through the air."

"What happened next?" I had to force the words out. Not many people used a bow. I could count the number of people I knew who used a bow and arrow on one hand—and still have fingers left over. Of them, I was the best.

"He doesn't remember." Abraham's expression was dark and grim. "He heard the arrow, there was pain and darkness, and then he was in the place where you found him. Whatever was on the arrow drugged him and we believe that is what kept us from sensing him, and him from reaching out to us for help. They continued to drug him, injecting him with a yellowish substance. The effects of it cleared within twenty-four hours and we could once again sense him."

Abraham looked away. "Icarus never saw Trident. But…"

The clawing in my gut only increased at his hesitation. "But what?"`

"Trident is no more. When I went to speak with him, I was told he'd become unstable and had to be eliminated." Abraham inclined his head. "Naturally, as I am not of Marlowe house, there is little more I can do, few angles I can pursue. But Icarus doesn't believe it—not what they say about Trident. He tells me the youth was too strong. Too stable. He wouldn't have become unstable. He would have been as Icarus was. As…"

He hesitated.

"As you are."

He said nothing, but I knew I was right. Something about him simply felt…different. Too close to human.

"So where does this lead us?" I asked softly.

"To an unpleasant place." Abraham folded his arms across his chest and although the light in my living room was bright, the shadows around him seemed to strengthen, cuing in on his moods. "If somebody was watching them, aware of their meeting and knew that Trident wouldn't be at that meeting—or perhaps they mistook one for another…"

My brain took over.

It spelled a whole hell of a lot of trouble.

"You still think this is related to Saul?" I whispered.

"No." Abraham's expression was troubled. "Marlowe House rarely deals with mortals on any level. Very few vampires do."

"It's not nice to play with your food, right?" I quipped in a feeble attempt at humor.

"No." Abraham's response was so deadpan, I couldn't tell if he was joking or not. "It isn't."

Chapter Fourteen

I had several different truths running through my brain and I didn't like any of them.

First and foremost…there were NHs out there, and probably some trusted humans, who were selling us out. I—or rather Justin and I—had already arrived at the conclusion with Saul, but it was bigger than just one or two individuals.

That big, ugly, raw thing sat in my gut as I drove to Damon's, taking with me nothing but the weapons I figured I'd need for the next day or so. It was clear I still had gear there waiting for me, so why worry about packing?

Although darkness had fallen, the space around my parking spot was brightly lit and I hadn't even climbed out of my car when I felt him. I smiled, despite the grim truths chewing at me. I'd have an escort on my way in—no. *Two* of them.

I used my hip to bump the door shut, already scanning the area.

I still didn't see him until he'd practically pounced on me.

The young man in front of me was ridiculously beautiful. Pale blonde hair in an uneven cut framed his face. It was uneven because he was too lazy to have somebody who knew how to handle scissors deal with it and although he was certainly vain enough, he was so damn pretty, nobody was likely to care if the strands were rather lopsided. It suited him, in a weird sort of way. You really didn't expect to see a tiger sitting still for a haircut anyway.

Doyle's blue eyes were vivid and bright—happy, even as he caught me around the waist and swung me around. Over the past few months, some of the darkness had faded from him. Some, not all. The natural exuberance that had emerged recently made me wonder who he would have been if tragedy hadn't punched him in the face so early on.

"You've been too busy," he said in lieu of greeting. "I haven't been able to kick your ass in a week. I've had to fight with Scott."

I snorted. "You can't kick my ass...*yet*. And you're just irritated because Scott's boring now."

"True," he said, shrugging. If they went muscle to muscle, Scott might be able to beat Doyle, but as far as skill went, Doyle had outreached the older shifter and they'd been training with weapons. Before he'd been changed, Scott had been a martial arts master and had some skill with a few weapons. Doyle had already eclipsed him and then some.

I bumped my fist against his shoulder. "If we can, we'll spar before I leave for work."

The brilliant grin that lit his face fired a response within me and because of that, I was smiling when I shifted to face the other man striding toward me. He didn't rush with the pent-up energy that still drove Doyle.

He moved with the lazy, easy grace of a predator who seemed to know he could *make* the world wait for him. And damned if he wasn't right. I'd sure as hell wait.

Why not?

The view was worth it.

My heart was racing by the time Damon joined me near my car.

When he reached out to take the bag from me, I didn't argue.

When he dipped his head to brush his lips against mine, I sighed in pleasure.

And when I heard somebody address him, I gritted my teeth and kept the insults trapped inside.

He didn't respond. Not even to tense.

Since he managed to pull it off, I figured I could do the same. Slowly, I reached up and placed my hand on his cheek, angling my head to the side as I opened my mouth.

She said his name a second time, but he continued to ignore her. He'd make the world wait for him, and she was no exception.

I heard a low growl of a voice—Doyle. He wasn't all sunshine and rainbows, a fact I well knew.

When Damon curved his arm around my waist and tugged me in closer, I didn't give in to my normal urge. That would have been to break the kiss and pull away. We were in public, for crying out loud—at the *Lair* of all places and now I was going to have to walk through that place with his scent practically clinging to me.

Instead, I opened my mouth deeper and when he stroked his tongue along the curve of my lower lip, I bit him.

A low rumble of a purr emanated out of him and it made me shiver.

That was when the kiss ended.

He pulled away and I sighed in wistful regret.

He cupped my cheek and rubbed his thumb over the curve of my lower lip. "I missed you."

"Missed you, too." I pressed my hand to his. "Been busy…this case…"

I grimaced.

He nodded and stepped aside. "We'll go in. You can sit down, relax. You probably need a night off."

Yeah. I probably did. But I wouldn't take it. "No time."

There was another reason I'd headed over here and she'd just conveniently placed herself in my way. Shanelle Maguire looked right through me as she focused her lovely, dark eyes on Damon.

That was fine.

I didn't plan on doing this out here anyway.

I slid my hand down and linked it with his. As his fingers folded over mine, Shanelle's gaze flicked downward.

"Did you need something, Maguire?" Damon asked, his voice blunt.

"Yes…Alpha." She gave him a look that was the picture of the perfect soldier. Composed, unreadable while her voice was modulated with just the right amount of respect.

And yet…

It was there.

Some hint of fury or disgust—whether it was a glint in her eyes or an undertone in her voice or just something I caught coming off her, I couldn't tell. Whatever it was, she hid it well, but I knew as well as I knew my own name, she had about as much use for me as she'd have for a used handkerchief.

She glanced around, shifting from one foot to the other. "May we discuss this…elsewhere?"

Cats came and went and more than a few shot us curious glances.

Damon opened his mouth and I could already see the refusal on his lips. I tightened my hand and tugged.

His muscles tensed and he blew out a breath as he dipped his head, turning his body toward mine to block her view. It was just the illusion of privacy and we all knew it.

"I've got questions I need to ask about Georgia," I said quietly.

He stroked his thumb along the back of my hand. "Can they wait?"

"Not forever," I replied, lifting a brow at him.

"Forty-five minutes."

I nodded.

He squeezed my hand and we started to walk. "You may come to my quarters in forty-five minutes, Shanelle. Doyle will escort you."

I heard her sharp intake of air.

Damon did as well and he stopped looked back at her. "Is that a problem?"

"No, Alpha." She gave him that same perfect smile.

I saw the flash in her eyes, though. One that hinted at fury.

He'd gotten to her with that one. He'd gotten to her bad.

We were still in the hall leading to his quarters when I realized why he'd wanted time.

I could smell it from here and my belly started to rumble.

"Oh, man." I picked up the pace and Damon laughed.

"You'd better not eat it all," he said.

"That's lasagna. You're always fussing about how real food is meat. Lasagna is pasta."

I shoved through the door and then came up short, my heart stuttering to a halt

• • •

as well.

Candlelight turned the room golden. The long sturdy table that too often ended up being the focus of hard talks and even harder decisions was now bedecked with a white tablecloth—linen, I thought, although my knowledge of the finer things was sorely lacking. Candles graced almost every flat surface, their flickering glow turning the room into a dance of shadow and soft light.

Silver-covered serving dishes awaited us and flutes that might be real crystal reflected back the light.

"Wow." My throat clogged up. "What's the occasion?"

"You." Damon came up behind me and wrapped his arms around me, his lips brushing over my cheek.

My bones melted. Just melted, right there. If he'd been forced to catch me to keep me from falling to the floor at his feet, I wouldn't have been surprised. His stubbled cheek rubbed against mine as my heart started to beat once more, a hard, heavy rhythm.

I covered the hands at my waist with my own.

"You don't by chance know what happened to Damon, do you?" I asked, my throat tight. "Big guy, looks a lot like to you."

He chuckled. "Don't worry. That son-of-a-bitch is still around here somewhere."

"Good." A ragged breath escaped me.

"Come on. Let's eat. I was going to draw this out, but…"

I grimaced. "Sorry."

He moved out from behind me and dropped a hard, fast kiss on my mouth. "Don't be. You've got a job to do and you're doing it."

"Never let it be said that you don't know how to romance a girl, Damon." I thought I might have to waddle away from the table and wasn't *that* a sexy image?

When he went to offer me more tiramisu, I pushed his hands away. "No, no, no…I'm going to pop if I eat any more."

He caught me around the waist and pulled me onto his lap.

Something I hadn't noticed until he led me to the table—as large as it was, the two settings had been placed side by side, only a few inches away. And now I was literally on top of him.

It wasn't a bad place to be. Sighing, I curled my legs more comfortably around him, bracing the soles of my boots on the rungs of the chair while he cupped my hips.

"You were supposed to be dessert," he said.

"You are not putting me on that table and eating anything off me." I wrinkled my nose. "Ain't happening, pal."

He laughed softly. "I had something else in mind. But for now…" He reached for something behind me. "Here."

I looked down and found him holding a simple wooden box.

"What's this?"

"It's a present. Well, sort of. More like a question, because if you say yes, I'm the one who gets the gift."

Something about the way he phrased that made me nervous.

Really nervous.

Slowly, I flipped the top of it up.

Confused, I stared at the small bit of a thing inside. It looked like a computer chip more than anything else, barely the size of my thumbnail. "What's this?"

I jolted when the thing spoke back: "Please identify yourself and speak slowly for voice print identification."

"Ahhh…"

Damon just stared at me.

Frowning, I said, "Kit Colbana."

"Verified. You now have open access to all areas of…"

As the voice droned on, my ears started to roar. Carefully, I closed the box. "So what's this?" I asked quietly as my blood thundered in my ears and my hands went slick with sweat.

"I want you to move in. To live here." Once more, his hands went to my hips, kneading the skin there in that absent, restless ways he had. "If you're not sure, if you want to think about it, that's fine. If you're not ready—"

I leaned in and kissed him.

I'd always been one to go with my gut.

Yes, I'd take time.

Yes, I'd think about it.

But just then, the only thing I wanted to do was kiss him.

The knock came forty-five minutes after he'd told her to come to his quarters. Forty-five minutes, exactly. If it had been forty-seven, she probably would have been told to come back later.

As it was, I was fumbling my shirt back into place and Damon slumped at the table with a look of sleepy hunger on his face that made me want to bite him.

He wanted me to move in.

"I'll…" I moved away from him before I jumped on him again. "I'll think about it."

He nodded as though that was exactly what he'd expected.

"Come on in, Doyle," he called out.

I glared at him. My hair was still probably standing up—a quick glance in the mirror across the room verified that and my face was still flushed.

Damon flashed me a grin. He'd done it on purpose.

Shanelle came into the room and her nostrils flared. Her gaze landed on me, then him. "Should I come back?" she asked, each word icily polite.

"Nope." Damon reached for the glass of wine left over from dinner. Over the rim, he eyed her. "What did you want, Maguire?"

Doyle sauntered deeper into the room and wagged his brows at me. I flipped him off. His grin widened. While he flopped down on the couch, I returned to the table for my own wine. I'd need about fifty glasses before it had any effect, but at least it would help how dry my throat had gotten.

"Scott has me on sentry duty."

When I reached for my wine, Damon reached for me, skimming a hand up my back. I heard the silent message. *Stay.* Whether it was a command or a request, I didn't know, but I knew what he was doing. I'd wanted to make sure Shanelle knew loud and clear that Damon wasn't up for the claiming. He was spelling it out in the clearest way he knew how—by making sure our dual claims for the other was imprinted on our skin.

"I'm aware." Damon angled his head to the side. "He asked where to put you and I told him that was a position where you'd done well in the past."

Her mouth opened, then closed. "I did well in that position *fifteen years ago.* I'm not a *sentry* anymore. I was one of the highest ranked enforcers—"

She snapped her mouth shut when Damon rose from his chair.

"You were," he said, his voice brutal and cold. "And then you left. You've been gone a long time, Maguire. Plenty of others stuck it out and plenty of stronger ones stood between the weaker ones and the monsters. You weren't one of them. You want to be worthy of being one of *my* lieutenants? Then you start from the ground up."

Her entire body went rigid, all but trembling in her fury.

"Is that all?" Damon sat on the couch, settling back in that familiar, slumped, casual sprawl, but his eyes were hard.

"Yes, Alpha. I'll be certain to prove myself." She went to turn.

I caught Damon's gaze.

He rolled his eyes.

"Hold up, Maguire." He rose as she turned back to us. I could see a muscle pulsing in his jaw. He didn't like this. At all.

I'd told him earlier I'd have to talk to her without *him* there, because she wouldn't take her focus off him and it made it impossible for me to dissemble the truth if she wasn't responding to me.

"Kit has questions about your kidnapping," he said finally, folding his arms over his chest.

Her gaze slid to me. "Then she can read the report that was filed with the Assembly. It gives all the pertinent data, although I fail to see why she cares."

"She cares because I've hired her to get to the bottom of what's going on." Damon rocked forward slightly—there was the impression of a giant cat, preparing to pounce. "She's got questions. You'll answer them."

"Is that an order?" Her eyes rolled to gold and I caught sight of her animal. Wildcat. Small, capable. Deadly.

"It is."

She dipped her head. "Very well."

Damon glanced at Doyle and jerked his head. They strode to the door and Shanelle's gaze tracked them. It wasn't my imagination that I saw the faint smile forming in her eyes.

It faded when Damon paused at the door.

"Shanelle."

It was the first time he'd used her name and her eyes widened fractionally.

"We worked together a fair amount of time," he said and the words were easy, almost companionable. But menace leaked from him, choking the air. "You know what I do to people who piss me off—what I do to people who harm what's mine. I suggest you keep that in mind."

As he disappeared through the door, a muscle pulsed in Shanelle's cheek.

I smiled at her. "Won't this be fun?"

She flicked a look at me and then moved to the chair nearest the fire—the one farthest from me. Worked for me.

"Get this done, please," she said, her tone snide.

"How did they take you down?"

She frowned.

"When they found you—Atlanta, right? Damon said you were last seen in Atlanta. So how did they take you down? You're no low-level wolf. One or two people aren't going to be able to manage it."

She inclined her head.

"No." Her mouth went tight then and she looked away. "But I never saw who did it. I don't even *know* what happened. There was a pain…" She reached up with her left hand, going over her shoulder to touch some point on her upper back. "Here. Then darkness. I woke up in the place where you found me."

"Was it Night?"

She lifted a brow, giving me an appraising look. Then she shook her head. "No. I've been drugged with Night before."

It was my turn to focus an appraising look on her. Just what had led to *that* occurrence, I wondered? But I wasn't here to chit-chat with Damon's ex. "Any idea what it was?"

"No." Shanelle wrinkled her nose. "I recognize some of the ingredients, because they shot me up with it several times. I smelled belladonna and foxglove—or at least it *smelled* like belladonna and foxglove, only more potent."

Her gaze slid to my neck—for the quickest fraction. The tattoos twining up my neck started to burn, almost as if in reaction.

"The chemical signature was unique." She pursed her lips. "It's not wholly natural—the belladonna and foxglove were part of the drug, but there were other things in it as well. I'd recognize it if I smelled it again. It took roughly twenty-four hours for it to clear from my system. I was due for another injection not long after you arrived. Had you come earlier, I might have been unable to shift without impetus."

"What sort of impetus?"

"What do you think?" The words were scathing. "They used pain—torture. But adrenaline is one of the key factors behind the change. If I was angry enough, scared enough, I would have been able to shift, but reactions would still be slower."

"So this shit lingers even after the shift?" I asked, worry twisting through me. That was bad. Very bad. Usually a shift will heal wounds and it *should* chase any aftereffects of drugs from the system.

"Yes." Lip curling, she echoed my words. "The shit lingers after the shift."

Chewing on that a moment, I stared hard at her.

"Is that all?" she asked.

"No." Rising, I moved toward the closet that had been outfitted for me to store my gear. I kept her in the corner of my eye, taking a ridiculously circuitous route around the room. But there was no way I was giving this woman my back. "Right before you went night-night in Alabama, did you hear anything?"

She was quiet and I turned to face her fully.

The harsh frown on her face carved deep lines into her face as she rose from the couch. "What do you mean?"

"Did you *hear* anything? Anything unusual? Anything weird?"

"The air whistled," she said. That glow was back in her eyes.

Lovely. "Would you recognize it again if you heard it?"

"Yes."

Taking a chance, I turned more fully to face the closet and used my body to shield the action as I freed the strap that held the Glock in place. I hoped I wouldn't need it, but she was strung tighter than the bow that waited for me in its case.

"Good." I pulled the case out and gave her a brilliant smile. "Let's go outside."

Damon hadn't gone far—he was leaning against the wall but as the door slid opened, he straightened, looking at me. "Get what you need?" he asked calmly as Doyle moved to position himself at my side. Guard position. There was a feel in the air he didn't like either. The boy was becoming wickedly astute. I don't think Damon quite picked up on the same thing I did, but he wasn't quite as driven by his instinct the way I was.

"Almost."

Shanelle stood a few feet away. I gestured to her. "I need her to listen to something."

Damon had brought in targets and there was no denying they were there for me. He was already doing everything he could to make it easy for me to be at home here—to *feel* at home.

I could have told him all I needed was him, but when I caught sight of the new gym—something clearly designed more for me than for his wolves—my heart melted.

"Nice," I murmured.

• • •
193

"Glad you like it." He folded his arms over his chest. "It's been…well…" He jerked a shoulder. "I had it ready for Christmas, but…"

He didn't continue. I didn't need him to.

But I did wonder.

Had he planned to ask me to move in even then? Back before…

One hand clenched into a fist and I forced the memories out of my head. Moving on, I told myself. I was moving on.

As Shanelle wondered around the room, her mouth a tight, flat line, I put the case for my bow on a nearby table. He'd even gotten practice blades. Ignoring them, I opened the case and pulled the bow out.

Shanelle was staring at me when I turned around.

"Listen." That was all I said when I chose a target. The gym was long and skinny, definitely long enough for a lazy round of target practice, although I tended to prefer moving targets. I didn't need one for this demonstration.

Shanelle's frown deepened as I let one single arrow fly.

She sucked in a breath.

"That the sound?"

Her gaze shifted to me. That was the only movement she made for a span of tense seconds. She stared at me like she wanted to see straight through me—or maybe inside me. Remove the layers of skin and bone and peer at everything. It was an unsettling sensation.

"Yes," she said after a taut moment. "That's the sound."

Perfect.

We had a pattern, at least. And now we had at least some idea of what the person taking these people down could do—they could use a bow and arrow…and they hunted some big, mean-ass game.

"Have you asked all your questions now?" Shanelle asked, her tone growing pissier by the second.

"Ooooohhhh, no," I said, shaking my head. Now I needed to ask so many more.

• • •

194

Back in Damon's quarters, my bow stored, I folded my arms and returned Shanelle's glare with one of my own. "I need to know more about where you *were*."

Damon was in there this time and his expression was thunderous, but he remained silent as Shanelle replied tightly, "I've given you this information. I was in Atlanta. I stopped for food."

"Where?"

She opened her mouth, then closed it. Vaguely, she waved a hand. "Some dive. Just a *dive*. You know the kind of place people go if they don't want to be noticed? That's why I went. I've been through Atlanta before, stopped there before. That's why I went this time. I didn't want anybody to notice me."

"Were there others there? Anybody you recognized or knew?"

She opened her mouth, another biting response on her lips, but then she stopped. "I don't know. Maybe the regulars? Seems like I'd seen a few of the customers in there before. Like they were just there all the time. But I can't be certain."

"What's the name of the place?" *Please let it have a name.* Some dives don't. Legally, they might, but I can't think of how many places I know by location—*the rec club on Bart Street. The bar over on North. The strip club on Green.*

My head was already hurting at the prospect of going to Atlanta, but if that was what I had to do, then okay.

"Fangs." She curled her lip. "It was just called Fangs. Sounds more like a blood bar, but there's this wolf in the window with these giant teeth, so you know it's for people like us. Shifters and the like. And...yeah. I might know them. Might not, but I might."

Fangs. My mind was whirling as I started to connect things.

Fangs. Howlers. Both Icarus and Shanelle had been taken down by arrows—something that would incapacitate them, but not kill. Arrows would be chancier on creatures *not* vamp or were. But hey...there was drugged booze for that, right?

Lots of loners went through dives like that. Shanelle was right on the money there. People went to places like that because they didn't want to be recognized or remembered and very often, they weren't.

"Were you able to eat before you were shot or did it happen on the way in?"

"After," she said, her voice losing some of the tension. "Why?"

"They watched you," I murmured. "They were *watching* to make sure you were alone. That you didn't have people joining you, people who'd look for you."

She didn't respond to that. I took a deep breath. "Okay. One more time."

She did, and this time with a lot less bitchiness. I committed it all to memory, word for word. When she was done, I asked more questions, trying to dislodge more information or shake free another memory, but there was nothing there.

I'd gotten everything I was going to get.

I actually remembered to say *Thanks* on my way out the door, too.

I shot a message to Justin to call me and then I called a number I really didn't like to call.

Call it a personal dislike, but Megan of the Wolf Pack just rubbed me the wrong way. Oh, she was friendly enough, when she wanted to be and she could hold her own in a fight—she *should* be able to, because she was the Alpha's right hand man. But we just rubbed each other wrong.

"Better be important, Colbana, it's late and I got a date with a book and a bubble bath," she said, her voice blunt.

"Wow. Aren't we all warm and fuzzy?" I said.

"Yeah. I'm a bunny rabbit. Want to see my teeth?"

I could practically see her baring them. "Nah. If I'd wanted to do dental inspections, I would have gone into dentistry. Listen, when I was there talking to you and the MacDonald, I asked for information on disappearances. You been able to run any of that info for me?"

She was quiet a moment. "Some. Not a lot. Most of what we have is just after the fact stuff, because people are just gone. The only wolf we know for a fact that *did* disappear was Drake—you helped him get out. But he's…"

Alarm bells screamed inside my head. "He's what?"

"He's dead. I had to put him down a couple of days ago, Kit."

I stopped in the hallway, shoulders slumping as I thought of the angry, scarred man. I'd told him I'd get him out…

Fury screamed inside me. "Why?" I demanded, not hearing the ragged snarl in my voice.

"He was losing control." Her voice gentled. "The trauma. The attacks. Everything he's gone through…it all but killed me to do it, but when I went to check on him and see how he was, he didn't even know who I was. He attacked me. It was me or him."

Numb shock settled in and I moved over to the wall, leaning against it for a moment before I slid down to sit on the floor. "What…" I cleared my throat. "Did he have family? A wife? Was anybody brought in to try and help?"

"Drake was moving to join the Pack. He was a loner from upstate New York. No family. Nobody. It's harder for them to hang on when bad things happen. A lot of things are harder when you're alone."

Yeah. They were.

"I gotta go," I murmured. Disconnecting, I lowered the phone into my lap and stared at nothing.

CHAPTER FIFTEEN

"He's not the only one."

I met Justin's gaze over the table. It was early—too early, but I'd managed a few hours of sleep. Now I was fueling myself with caffeine. Damon had already stuffed me full of food with a bacon and cheese omelet—he'd all but hovered over me until I'd cleaned the plate, too. But coffee...what I'd really needed was more coffee. I couldn't get decent tea here. They thought it came in *bags*.

Justin had joined me at the Lair for coffee and he now sported a nice, shiny black eye. Really, if I'd been thinking straight, I would have kept him and Damon apart for a little longer. Damon could have done a lot more damage—although Damon had ended up scorched and singed around the edges. Sometimes I think they liked hurting each other. Justin seemed quite content with his black eye, though.

"Not the only...what?" I asked although judging by the creeping dread in my gut, I already knew.

"One that died." His mouth went tight. "Rihall. She was one of the witches."

"Please tell me she wasn't the one who'd escaped," I said, my hands closing into fists so tight they ached.

"She wasn't." A vicious smile curved his lips. The look on his face was one of grim satisfaction. There was no other way to describe it. "That's Lila and she's staying with the house down in the 'Glades...and Paddy is with her. Between Paddy, Tate and Serene, it will take an act of God or a force of nature to get to her *now*."

A soft sigh relief escaped me even as the guilt gathered and grew. "Who was it, then?"

"Teah." He took a healthy swig of coffee so hot, it had to burn his tongue, but he didn't show any reaction. "She seemed fine—almost stable. Pissed off...man, was she pissed. Teah was warrior-born. I thought she'd be okay. I went to talk to her yesterday and she'd been found shot through the heart. Bullets." His mouth was grim, tight. "They shredded her heart to a pulp. I've got a friend in forensics who's going to try to get me whatever info he can from the ammo, but I don't expect we'll get much."

"Somebody is silencing them."

That meant they knew something—or somebody *thought* they did.

The idea was enough to turn my gut to stone, but at the same time, it meant we were getting closer.

Was it because we had Saul? Or at least, we'd gotten to Saul. Whether or not he was still alive was anybody's guess.

"I need to know when Drake died," I murmured. "Teah died yesterday—we grabbed Saul midday."

"She died later." Justin jerked a shoulder. "I haven't called for the TOD. They should have the time of death soon, but if I had to estimate, I'd say she was killed in the early evening."

"Enough time for somebody to know something was up with Saul, that he might have talked."

"Or maybe they were already cleaning up," Justin said. He stared into his coffee cup. "We just don't know."

No. We didn't. So now we had to dig around for more answers, and ask more questions.

I sipped my coffee. "I'll call Megan, see when Drake died."

"Let me handle it," Justin said. "She likes me more."

Judging by the curl of his lips, I took that to mean something else. "She likes you or she wants to get in your pants?"

"Hmmm." He ran his tongue across his teeth, eyes glinting. "I think it's a mutual sort of thing. Anyway, she'll be more likely to talk to me. She'll just screw with you—and not in the fun and sexy, *Kit, can I please watch?* kind of way either."

I made a face at him.

He winked at me and then went back to the business at hand. "I'll go by his house. Maybe I'll luck out and find…something."

● ● ●
199

The lighthearted teasing was familiar, but for some reason, it wasn't as comfortable as it used to be. He was convinced he still loved me. Hell, for all I know, he still did. I knew there were still feelings there. *I* had feelings. He'd been my first love, my first lover, one of my first friends and even now, if everything went wrong, I knew without a doubt, he'd be the one person who'd have my back no matter what else was going on in the world.

Damon would always have the clan to think about as well—as he should. That was part of being a leader. He'd be a shitty leader if he put his girl in front of the clan and I knew there would be times when I'd have to come in second place. I knew this and I was aware of it.

The security Justin represented was undeniable. But I didn't *love* him. Not like he needed.

Not like he deserved.

And I didn't know where this was going to leave us.

Forcing my attention back to the matter at hand, I asked, "You think you'll have any luck at Drake's? It's not like he was grabbed there."

"No. But everything points to this being a job where these people were chosen." Justin shrugged. "That means they were watched—or at least people knew who they were. Drake, for instance. Somebody knew enough about him to know he wouldn't be missed for a while."

"No family," I murmured, remembering what Megan had told me. "He wasn't a born shifter, was he?"

"Nope." Justin scraped a finger across the table. His green eyes were grim. "He was changed not long before the war started. Lost his entire family. His mother was labeled as an NH sympathizer while his brothers became human supporters in the war. They were some of the first to die. He pretty much hated this existence."

"I can see why," I said softly. I looked out the window. "Civil war all but tore the United States apart once and civil unrest continued for a long time after. It started all over again when the world discovered us. People never stop finding excuses to kill each other, do they?"

"No." He pushed back from the table, reaching for the shades he'd put on the table. They were the same metallic silver as the threads on his sleeves and he slid them into place, hiding his gaze.

"How's the eye?"

The grin on his face was pure evil. "It hurts."

"Was it worth it?"

His only response was a faint laugh. "I'm gone. Need to get out to Drake's, then head out to find Megan. I'll send an update if I find anything at the shifter's place."

His idea of *anything* was the kind of thing that I'd have no luck with. Justin, being a warrior-born witch, could sometimes hone in on acts of violence. It was a long shot, but if he'd ever had contact with Drake's kidnapper—particularly violent contact—he might recognize something. The right vibe, something. Hell, maybe we'd *really* luck out and Justin would be able to pluck the right connection right out of thin air.

There *were* connections.

We just have to figure what they were—and where to look for them.

"Okay." I nodded. "You do that. "

"You need to tell the cats to stay in place. I think they're safe enough if they stay in the Lair. If you warn Damon that somebody is hunting down the NHs we rescued, he'll put his best on alert." He skimmed a quick look around us. "I don't think I'm dumb enough to try and sneak in here."

I knew *I* wasn't.

"I'll talk to him." There was something else I needed to do, too. My skin crawled just considering it, but I had to do it. I shoved back from the table and busied myself gathering up the cups. Aware that Justin was watching me, I went ahead and just got it over with.

"I think I'll talk to Icarus."

Justin gave me an appraising stare. "Bearding the vampire in his crypt, huh?"

"Why not? Maybe I'll get the answer to that age-old question." I dumped the dishes in the sinks. "Do they sleep *in* a crypt or does a coffin suffice?"

Annoyed, I stood at the entrance to the Lair and listened while Damon finished speaking into his phone.

"She's on her way back," he said shortly.

"Why did she *leave*?" I demanded.

"Because you just now made it clear she shouldn't."

I made a face at him. "Thanks for pointing out the obvious," I muttered, rubbing the back of my neck. A moment later, Damon brushed my hand away and I fought a groan of pleasure as strong fingers dug at the tension building at the base of my skull. "The other cat?"

"Here. Safe." He paused and then added, "Physically, at least. His head…"

I reached up and covered his hand with mine. "Give him time."

Damon dropped his hands and pressed a quick kiss to my neck before he moved away. "I'll keep my eye out for Maguire. Let you know when she's here."

I nodded shortly. "Do that. I have to go. Need to run by my place and then…"

I should have just kept it short and sweet, but knowing the ears in the Lair, Damon would hear about it soon anyway.

"You're going to Allerton House." Damon stared at me.

I made a face at him. "Spying?"

"Not necessary." He jacked up a shoulder in a shrug. "My people heard you and one of them felt like it was news he should share."

I narrowed my eyes.

"Don't get mad at my cats for trying to protect you." He took a step forward and grabbed the front of my vest, tugging me onto my toes. "Be glad I convinced him you didn't need an escort."

His mouth was warm on mine. I sighed into his kiss and then tugged away. "That's something you'll have to work on if I do move in here, Damon." Scowling, I shoved my hands through my hair. "Might need someplace fitted out with soundproofing. Some of the jobs…"

He lifted a brow. "I'll see to it."

"Just like that?"

He brushed his fingers down my cheek. "If I want this to be your home, then…yeah. Just like that." He let his hand fall to his side and I turned away.

"Kit?"

I looked back at him.

The early morning sun painted him with brilliant color, the chilly wind of fall whipping at his clothes. "Be careful," he said softly.

"I will."

The stop at my condo was meant to be quick—in, out. I needed stuff, the kind of stuff I'd take along with me if I thought things would get FUBAR—my favorite phrase from a classic movie that made me laugh every time I watched it.

Fucked up beyond all recognition.

And this job just might push things into FUBAR territory.

I'd already roughed out the gear I'd take and it should have taken me ten minutes—probably less.

But that was before I climbed out of the car and smelled…it.

I flared my nostrils, vaguely realizing I was doing the same thing I'd told Abraham was so annoying, but it did help. I dragged in the air and smelled…

Immediately, I shoved my back against the car. I drew my gun, staring hard at my condo. My nice, innocuous condo that had been all but drowned in a strange little potion garden witches cooked up and sold—if they were brave enough. It was called *hide.*

I had some of it myself, but I didn't like to use it. It itched like a bitch and the only thing it did was cover your scent. It did nothing to hide you physically and nothing to cover the sounds you made. I could take care of being *seen*, but unless I could completely silence myself, it did no good to not be scented.

I'd only used it once or twice—for break-ins.

I hissed out a breath and had to fight the urge not to lunge toward my house. Instead, I focused on my other senses.

A minute later, I began to make my way toward the front door.

Nothing had been taken.

Or at least, if it was, it wasn't anything important.

But my place had been searched—and searched well. The wards had been evaded—not shattered. Justin would have felt that, since he'd put so much of his magic in it. No magical construct is full-proof, though, not even the wards Justin and Colleen had crafted for me, and somebody had gotten past them.

Actually, I suspected it was *somebodies*, although how they'd done it, I didn't know. I could still feel the ripple of the wards—active now. They lay in a dormant state when I wasn't here, only flaring to life when somebody other than me or the few who'd been keyed in to gain entry tried to come inside.

It still took a decent chunk of power to get past—or around or under—my wards and the idea that somebody had done it so easily left me on edge. I kept my blade in hand the entire time, her grip warm in my hand. That curious, empty ache in the back of my head that had once held her voice seemed to pulse, but I didn't let myself think on it.

They'd gone through *everything*. I wanted to bite something as I came to a stop in front of my kitchen counter. They'd even gone through my tea supplies. My *tea*! What the hell?

Spinning away from the counter, I stared at the weapons on my wall. I'd been staring blindly at them for a few seconds when a thought hit me. I sucked in a breath and fury had me leaping over my kitchen counter instead of running around it. In my bedroom, I caught the bedpost and shoved, pushing it too far—

"Oh, man," I muttered, hissing out a breath when the magic there held.

The spell Justin had used on this hidey-hole of mine was the quietest, subtlest magic he could have done and he'd tinkered and refined it over the years, understanding the need to keep secret the things hidden within. The quiet magic hid a devastating spell that would incinerate anything that tried to power through it. Severe consequences, but no innocent child could accidentally *find* these weapons and nobody with any decency in them would want them enough to steal them.

That made any possible thief fair game. These weapons were too powerful to fall into the wrong hands. I didn't even trust them in *mine*.

Both spells, the concealment spell and the destructive one, were powered by the magic of the weapons. They breathed it out, like they were living creatures and the spells fed from that energy.

They were also both intact.

Setting my jaw, I went about disarming the magic and as soon as I removed away the false piece of floor, I was hit with swells of power and whispered promises of death dark and bloody. The blade called Death wanted to come out and play. He'd tasted blood recently and instead of slaking his thirst, it only made him yearn for me.

"Shut up," I said to the blade.

There was no lessening in the power that came off it, but I didn't expect there to be.

The Druidic bow was in there as well, along with the charmed blades and poisoned steel.

Whoever had broken in, they hadn't found these weapons.

Once I had them safely stowed—and hidden once more—I got busy checking everything else.

The rest of my quick search turned up nothing but frustration. I could tell where somebody had gone through my things. My clothes, my damn *underwear* and my papers—what little I kept anyway. They'd even gone through my books. I could tell simply because certain things just weren't…right. A few pages were too neatly aligned, while the spines on the books weren't *perfectly* aligned.

Nothing missing.

But I learned nothing about who'd done it, either and I couldn't linger here.

It pissed me off in ways I can't explain and it also confused me.

Who in the hell would break into my place just to look around?

"You're certain."

I sighed as I pulled my car in front of the gates of Allerton House. Vampires were notorious for keeping their homes gated. Supposedly if you were stupid enough to climb those gates, then you got what you deserved.

I didn't try to climb.

I just sat in my car and waited, using the time to finish my call with Justin. "I'm beyond positive. Somebody was in my house and they didn't want anybody tracking them, that's for damn sure."

He hissed out a breath. "Okay. We'll…shit. Do me a favor."

"What?" I had a feeling I already knew.

"Stay with Damon until this is done."

I closed my eyes.

When I didn't respond, Justin pushed on. "Look, if it's somebody who is onto what we're doing, I want you safe."

"And what about you? They've taken down high levels before, Justin. You're not immune to harm."

"I'll stay at the big house."

My lips twitched as his sardonic name for the local Green Road house. Green Road was a branch of witches—and they badly wanted to get Justin to join their ranks. They would offer a bed to a witch who asked—it was just their way, but they'd also try, yet again, to make him understand why he *belonged* with them.

He'd likened belonging to a house to being in prison.

Thus the name *the big house.*

I pretended to hesitate another moment, but it was for show. Justin didn't need to know that. "You'll really stay there? I won't lie and say I'm not nervous about this thing with my house, but I don't want to be all tucked up and secure if that leaves you as the only target out there."

"I said I'd stay," he said, aggravation coming through in his voice. "We'll go back there later and see what we can learn, okay? I'd do it now, but John and Marcia agreed to let me have a few minutes with Saul before they turned him over to the MacDonald."

"The MacDonald?"

"Yep." Justin sounded bemused and wary at the same time. "He hired them. They won't tell me why, but they did tell me that much. Since I don't expect to get much from him expect what I can scrape or mop off the floor by the time the wolf Alpha is done, I need to get these questions in quick."

"Okay. Call me when you're done. We'll work a time to go by there." I had to admit, the idea of having him go over it made me feel better. He could maybe unearth something I couldn't. A creaking noise caught my ears and I looked just as the familiar dry-bones sensation rolled across my skin.

The gatekeeper has arrived.

"Miss Colbana." The vampire was unfamiliar, the voice rich as butter and honeyed by a drawl that could make cavities form.

"You at Allerton House?" Justin asked as I continued to study the female vampire who still stood in the gates, waiting.

"Yep."

"Be sure to let me know the answer—crypt or coffin."

The woman's brow rose and I knew she'd heard.

"Kiss ass, Justin." Then I hung up and got out of the car.

To my surprise—and dismay—I got the answer.

My escort led me to the door, gesturing where to park my car. She was there before I was, even though I was driving. I never even saw her leave her position by the gates, nor did I see her arrive. *Poof, magic.*

She turned me over to Abraham, who in turn led me up a winding staircase and down a wide, dark hall lit with a gentle gold light.

Vampires, or at least, *this* vampire, slept in a bedroom as dark and elegant as he was. Icarus didn't turn to face me, just stood at the window, staring outside as I took in my surroundings.

The walls were a dark brown, but it wasn't a dull, dun sort. It was the kind that made me think of rich, molten chocolate. There was trim of a pale ivory and it matched the bedding. The bed frame looked like it had been carved from massive trees and the bed itself was big enough for a debauched sort of party.

Somehow, I didn't see Icarus getting involved in debauched bed parties.

The man was still standing quietly by the window, his gaze on something I couldn't see.

"Please tell me none of the family were rude to my guest, Abraham," Icarus said.

"No, Icarus. Of course not." Abraham's voice was soft, as respectful as I'd ever heard it.

"Ms. Colbana?"

"Ah…no." Tucking my hands into my pockets, I rocked back on my heels. To be honest, I'd only seen the two vampires—well, three now—Abraham, the woman who'd met me at the gate and now Icarus. But I couldn't complain, other than the fact that I knew I was surrounded by vampires, even if I couldn't see them.

Icarus nodded and continued to stare outside.

He could have been an English lord from a time gone by, standing there in cravat and waistcoat, staring out over his estate.

"I must say, Kit Colbana, it surprises me that you would come to a vampire's home. You must be very tenacious," he said, finally turning his head to look at me.

"I've been told that once or twice."

"Only once or twice?" A smile ghosted around his lips. His mouth was pale. He didn't have that…sense of life I was used to feeling from vampires. He wasn't feeding. That made me leery.

But his eyes retained their sense of self.

"Abraham, how goes Estella?"

"We haven't had much luck getting her to talk, I fear. She's been feeding from us for too long. Her resistance to mind control is somewhat strong." The vampire at my side flicked me a look.

Curiosity burned inside me, but I kept quiet. I wasn't going to go poking and prodding at things I didn't need to know.

I focused on what I *did* need to know and when neither of the men said anything else, I did. "Master Allerton, I have questions I need to ask you, if you don't mind."

"Please." Icarus gestured to a seat, still staring outside. "Forgive my lack of manners, if you would. My mind is somewhat frazzled today. It's been…upsetting."

What in the hell could upset a *vampire*?

A worldwide shortage of necks?

"Perhaps you should tell Ms. Colbana what has transpired. She's investigating the disappearances that have happened within the cat clan," Abraham said, lowering himself to a chair after I'd reluctantly sat down.

Icarus didn't move to join us.

He couldn't seem to move away from that spot near the window.

What had him so mesmerized?

In the next moment, a scream shattered the silence.

Icarus closed his eyes and bowed his head.

"How many times now, Abraham?"

"It's the fourth, Grandfather."

The title sounded more like an endearment.

"She will not speak," Icarus said, his voice solemn. "It was why I chose her. Her stubbornness was a trait I so loved. I believed she would stand with me, strong through all the long, dark years. But she has betrayed us."

"You are not to blame for her deception."

Unable to stand this conversation I couldn't decipher, I rose and moved to the window. Neither Abraham nor Icarus moved to stop me and I stopped still several feet from the vampire. He was so old, he made my teeth ache, the power in him. He would have to work to keep it contained, and I appreciated the effort he must be making on my part.

Even now, standing a few feet away, the air around him was chilled. I wrapped my arms around myself as I stared outside. It was a large window, possibly six feet across so I had no trouble finding what it was that held his attention.

Although it wasn't a *what*.

But a who.

She'd probably been beautiful once.

Now, though, she was strapped to a wooden pole and blood splattered everything around it. Some of it was old, some of it wasn't. It wasn't hard to see where the blood came from, either.

Internal organs glistened wetly in the midday sun.

It was a misnomer that vampires slept during the day. Only the very young had to sleep for long periods of daylight, but few of them went out in the daylight as the sun did sap their energy. Stronger vampires could overcome that. After all, if you were strong enough to bench press a tank at night but only able to bench press a truck during the day, you probably still felt pretty confident in your abilities to walk out your front door.

But the vampire chained to the thick wooden pole wasn't a vampire.

Humanity still clung to her, although it had been altered. Altered and twisted until it was more an echo than anything else. Servants fell in that strange gray area along with psychics—not quite human, not really *other*. The only people who truly accepted them were their makers. The vampires.

I had a disturbing feeling this woman's maker was standing a few feet away.

As I watched, the blood oozing out of her came to a halt and as the minutes stretched out, I could see that the wound in her belly was closing. It took almost ten minutes—and nobody spoke a word—before anybody down there moved. It was a vampire, a man shrouded in black from head to toe against the sun's painful rays. I watched as he caught the entrails hanging out of the woman. She cried out as he viciously pulled and then cut.

"She'll begin to regenerate new internal organs now," Icarus said quietly. "And in two hours, the injury will be struck again."

I fought the urge to flinch at the cruelty of it.

"What did she do?"

"We learned that Estella, my star, has been feeding information on weak and younger vampires to people outside the family." Icarus turned to look at me now and his eyes were screaming black pits of hell.

Perhaps vampires were able to feel, I realized.

This one certainly seemed to.

"I'm sorry."

"Torture isn't working." Abraham shook his head as I told him I needed to talk to her.

I'd asked Icarus every question I could think of, and then I flipped the questions around and started over, but I couldn't discern anything new from him. And down there in the courtyard, standing in a bloodstained mess of her own body organs was a woman who could give me answers.

"Then we won't do torture. We'll try something else." From the corner of my eye, I kept Icarus in my line of vision. In the back of my head, a weird little voice was shrieking at me: *Vampire, vampire, vampire!* Every part of me wanted to bolt.

I didn't let myself.

Maybe I'd wanted to run every step of the way and maybe I could still feel the inhuman presence of too many vampires inside this house, but I wasn't running away.

"Somehow, Kit, I don't think she's going to respond to *pretty please*," Abraham said, temper threading into his voice.

"Well, how do you know?" I gave him a sweet smile. "Maybe you just need to try…the right way."

I looked at Icarus. "How long was she yours?"

He tore his gaze from the window. I don't know why he was torturing himself like that, but he couldn't seem to help himself. "Almost one hundred-fifty years. Next year would have marked that occasion. I was going to take her to Paris. She didn't know."

I chewed on my lip and went back to the window. "When was the last time you fed her?"

Vampire servants receive near-vampire strength and inhuman healing abilities, all from feeding from a vampire. If they feed often enough, they can extend their lifespan indefinitely. A vampire's blood, I'm told, can be addictive, though, and the more you take, the more often you take it, the more you need it. Wise vampires limit their servants to small, weekly feedings.

"Four days ago." His lids drooped.

I hesitated, because I was now going to risk moving into personal territory. There was quite a bit I didn't know about vampires—quite a bit I didn't want to know. But a bite can be business-like or all about the bedroom and it can range from a sip to a full-course meal.

As though he sensed my dilemma, Icarus smiled. "We shared a mutual feeding. It was always a small exchange. I no longer require heavy blood feedings. Being with my servant provides me much of what I need…or it did."

The words *I'm sorry* sprang to my lips again, but I bit them back.

They made no difference. None at all.

"Since it's been a few days and she's had to use up her reserves to heal herself several times over, she's probably running on empty," I said.

Icarus frowned.

"She means that her power levels are depleted, or close to it." Abraham moved to join us.

"Ah." The confusion on the older vampire's face cleared. "Yes, I imagine she is quite…empty."

We all looked outside. The time was moving closer and closer to the point when she'd be cut open again. She hadn't regained much color, not that I knew how she'd looked before this started, but that chalky white wasn't normal.

"She's as close to her original human state as she's ever going to be." Crossing my arms over my chest, I looked back at Icarus and made the offer. "I've got a friend who's a witch. He's good. Very good. He has ways of getting people to talk that don't involve torture. If she was at full-strength, it might not work, but she's not."

"We've already tried to read her mind."

"It's not the same thing—not the same sort of…magic." I shook my head, unable to explain. Justin probably could, but he'd gone to school, had taken all sorts of magical theory classes. I just knew what I knew—and what my gut said.

"Call him," Icarus said. His features had become remote. "Call your friend and tell him that Allerton House wishes a favor."

"Repeat that."

I sat in my car and did just that.

Away from the scraping uneasiness that was the presence of vampires, I closed my eyes and tried to coax the muscles in my body to unknot. It was just now *really* hitting me what I'd done.

I *had* bearded the vampire in his den. Or in his bedroom, at least. I'd done it. All without a panic attack and all while other vampires hovered far too close. In other rooms, but they'd been there.

I'd done it.

I wanted to puke.

Now I had to do it again.

I knew I *could* now. But I sure as hell didn't want to.

"You heard me. Allerton House found a mole. They want you to charm the info out of her—and I don't mean with your pretty face."

"Got that part," he muttered.

Over the phone, I heard the harsh sound of his sigh. "Fine. I'll head over once I meet up with Megan. We were supposed to…well, never mind. I'll get the info I need from her and then head over."

"Where are you meeting?"

"Howler's. I told her what went down with Saul and she's going in for damage control." He paused and then added, "She seemed kind of pissed about the pseudo-bartender that the MacDonald had hired."

I shrugged and then rolled my eyes. He can't see me shrugging on the phone, now can he? "If she wants to go in and figure out where the mess started, let her. It's not like we can be quiet anymore. Not after what went down with Saul. It didn't stay quiet long anyway."

"Nope." He was quiet a minute. "Okay, I've got the supplies I need. Most of them anyway. I'll need a heat source—the quickest way to make her talk is one of the truth spells and I've got all the stuff I need for that, save a natural heat source. I'm sure they've got something that will suffice in that old mausoleum of a house. Expect me within three hours."

I hung up.

Then just sat there.

The odd itch on my spine had me very, very uneasy.

"I don't understand," Abraham said, following me down the hall. "We need this information—you said it yourself. Yet you now you wish us to allow her to remain as she is—that will let her regain her strength. That could allow her to fight the charm or spell...whatever Greaves will use. What is the sense in this?"

"The sense is that something feels wrong," I said. And it wasn't just the fact that I now had the attention of maybe half a dozen vampires focused on me. Including two very old ones.

Icarus and a quiet, slim woman who looked like the living breathing personification of a fairy tale. With lips as red as blood and skin as white as snow...that's how the story goes, I think.

Their power was so massive, I thought it might crush me into the floor, but I mentally squared my shoulders against it and soldiered on.

"Explain." Abraham folded his arms over his chest.

"I *can't.*" I shoved a hand through my hair. This was why I didn't like working with people who didn't get me. Abraham might understand certain things about me, as I now understood certain things about him, but he didn't get *me*. The things that make me what I am.

"Abraham."

He looked at Icarus.

"Let it be." Icarus inclined his head and met my gaze. "Please. Take Abraham with you."

He slid a look at the woman standing next to him and she nodded. Her voice was a slithering whisper across cool, soft skin when she spoke, "We'll see to it that Estella receives no further punishment until you return with the witch. We, too, want answers."

"Thank you." I turned to the door. Riding in the car. With a vampire. Again. I paused just before I slid outside. "Ah…if you would, make sure you keep only the most trusted with her. Somebody is hunting the people who have information. We don't know who is involved or how far it goes."

Complete and utter terror screamed down my spine at the looks exchanged between Icarus and the woman at his side. She inclined her head and lifted a hand. It seemed to me she was gesturing at nobody but a man separated himself from the others and moved closer. He immediately went to one knee, capturing her slim, pale fingers in his. The kiss he pressed to them was tender. "My queen."

The devotion in his words was creepy. When he rose and placed himself at her side, I caught a glimpse of his eyes. Another servant, yes. But he no longer had anything remotely human in him. He'd been feeding from her so long, they might as well be one.

"This is Gunther," she said, her eyes still on my face. "He has been with me since I was still mortal, my most trusted companion. He will watch over Estella."

He bowed his head—to *me*. "No harm shall come to her until my lady wishes it."

I don't know if that was supposed to reassure me or not.

I headed out and when Abraham fell into place at my back, I let him stay there. If you had to have a devil at your back, better the devil you know.

I called Justin from the road.

He didn't answer, so I left a message and then called Chang.

"To what do I owe this pleasure, Kit?"

"Uh…" I frowned. His infinite politeness sometimes made me feel like an ass when I just plunged feet-first in with my demands. "Hi. How are you doing?"

He chuckled. "Well, I'm in the midst of some bloody business—"

There was a harsh whine that abruptly ended and I had the feeling he meant *bloody business* literally. "Is this a bad time?"

"Of course not." Chang sounded almost appalled that I'd asked. "This business can wait. Now tell me what you need."

From the seat next to me, Abraham sat in a seemingly relaxed pose, his hands lying open on his thighs, his gaze hidden behind an overlarge pair of sunglasses. He wore a long, hooded coat that covered him almost completely but that was the only concession he made to the late afternoon sun. "I'm heading out to meet Justin. I've…" I momentarily gritted my teeth and then just said it all in a rush. "I meant to mention it last night, but things got sort of crazy with Shanelle. I assume you know what all happened."

"Yes." His tone was neutral. "Why don't you just tell me who is in the car with you?"

"How do you know anybody is?"

"I heard something move."

I shot a look over and realized that Abraham *had* moved—one hand. He'd moved one hand to smooth a crease in his trousers.

"As I cannot hear this person's breathing or this person's heartbeat, I'm going to assume you have a vampire with you."

"Hello, Chang," Abraham said, a grim smile on his lips. "I was saddened to see that you decided against selling me the katana."

A low chuckle drifted over the phone.

The muscles in my spine relaxed somewhat. "I hope that means you're not going to alert Damon and try to send out the cavalry. Allerton House has asked for my assistance in resolving the mystery behind Icarus' abduction. It's all tied together. Abraham has been assisting Justin and me in the other matters so it makes it neater to just work together."

"I have no say in how you do your job, Kit." He made a low noise in the back of his throat. "I believe I'll talk with Damon. Considering the events of the previous evening, it's understandable why this…slipped your mind. But none of that is why you called, either."

"Stop reading minds, Chang. It's not attractive." I stuck my tongue out at the media panel. "Listen, the cats who've gone missing…Shanelle was at a bar—Fang's. Did any of the others go missing near a club or a bar? I'm looking at low-rent places. Dives."

"Actually…"

There was another one of the pitiful, gagging whines—and it was *wet*. I heard a strange sucking sound and my mind conjured up a hundred images to go with that noise.

"Tell me, Barry."

Barry? I blinked at the sound of this—a shapeshifter named Barry. For some reason, it didn't inspire the fear.

I scowled, listening to Chang's voice and trying to make sense of what was happening on the other end of the line.

"Just what happened at The Viper's Pit?"

I sucked in a breath. Next to me, Abraham tensed. That name was notorious. The Viper's Pit was one of the biggest hellholes around. It attracted anybody looking for a bit of pain and it didn't matter if you flashed fang or grew fur. They even had witches darken their door, as long as the witches were into that sort of thing.

People didn't go to the Pit because they were looking for a cheap beer and some quiet to watch a game.

"I…" There was a wet, thick cough and when the man spoke again, his voice was clearer. "I didn't know he was the Alpha's, Chang. I swear. I thought he was just some loner passing through."

The sharp yelp made me flinch. "Oh, Barry." Chang's sigh sounded sincerely sad and full of regret. "You're not answering me. We'll have to do this—"

"Don't! Please, please don't!" The panicked scream had me tightening my hands on the steering wheel. "I can't talk. They'll kill me. You don't know what they are capable of."

I checked the mirror and cut over, listening to horns blast as I slid through the traffic. I grimaced at Barry's words. Clearly the idiot didn't know what Chang was capable of. The man was death in silk suits.

A symphony of screams and whimpers followed. From the corner of my eye, I saw Abraham listening with a great deal of interest.

When the noises faded away to whimpers, Chang said, "We'll try this again and hopefully you'll keep in mind who the real threat here is. Let me give you a hint, Barry. It's not some nebulous *they*."

For a moment, the only sounds audible over the line were pained, broken mewls.

But then Barry spoke. "I only got one name."

He said it and my blood went cold.

For a few awful seconds, my blood went to ice and my hands were so slippery, I couldn't grip the wheel worth shit.

"Chang."

I heard his voice, but I couldn't make sense of the words. Nor did I care. "Call Damon, then call the MacDonald. I need men at a bar called Howler's. I need them now."

I disconnected the call and tried not to panic.

"Kit, what is—"

"Shut up," I said through clenched teeth. Blood roared in my ears and I could feel my heart in my throat as I put in another call to Justin.

When he didn't answer, I put in a final call.

She didn't answer, either.

But when it rolled over for a message, I left one.

"Megan, if something happens to him, there's no place on earth you can hide from me."

Chapter Sixteen

"Megan isn't an uncommon name. Are you so certain it's her?" Abraham asked as my car went screaming around the final corner.

I hit the brakes with enough force that the seat belt cut into me but I ignored it. "I'm so certain."

"How?"

I climbed out of the car and he did the same, staring at me hard over the roof. "Icarus has bade me to come with you—what you didn't hear was the command to watch over and assist, which I shall do, but I'd like to know if I'm going to cause ill will between the pack and my House."

"You won't. You know how your kind can smell blood?" I looked away from him, staring around me. Compared to the scene from just a day ago, the street Howler's sat on was almost deserted. I almost expected to see a tumbleweed come rolling down the street toward me. "My kind can smell trouble…and danger. Just trust me."

Somebody darted across the street in front of me with a quick, furtive look over her shoulder. A glorious black eye spread down across her cheek.

Fear all but leaked out of her pores.

It added to the overall atmospheres.

We started toward the bar, but Abraham went still after less than three spaces. "I don't believe it," he murmured.

"What?"

He didn't answer directly. Instead, he tipped his head back, taking in the air. I heard the audible inhalation and I fought the instinct to just walk away from him, giving him a few seconds to figure out what he'd tasted in the air. "She was here," he murmured, shaking his head. "Megan Banks was here. She no longer is. Neither is…"

He paused and then looked at me. "Neither is Justin."

I strode across the pocked and pitted excuse of a sidewalk. Fury bubbled inside me and my skin itched. Magic hovered in the air and none of it was pleasant.

Violence clung to the area like a bad stink and I knew when I went inside I was going to find evidence of bad, ugly things.

Megan was dead.

She didn't know it yet, but she was dead.

I was going to kill her. I don't know how—it would probably take more silver than I had on me—possibly the rocket launcher I'd been thinking about getting to burn down Jude's ass while he still rotted in the ground. Overkill, maybe? That wasn't a problem for me.

"What—?"

I sucked in a breath and the effects of remnant magic hit me like a sucker punch. Too much magic and it hadn't been finished. That was bad. Very bad.

Justin didn't leave his magic running wild like that.

There were different kinds of magic—there were charms and spells, which by their nature *had* to be finished to even work, but there were other forms of magic, too. Like the elemental magics, fire and wind and water and earth. Leave earth magic unfinished and an entire continent could collapse upon itself as an earthquake tore the world apart. Unfinished fire magics had been known to cause devastating fires— some of the worst wildfires had actually been caused by witches with pyro skills. They just hadn't realized it.

There's also just the manipulation of energy—something the strong witches excel at. That's all about intent, will and skill, a witch bending energy to his will and controlling it.

Controlling—then *releasing* it.

There was remnant magic in here, the kind that would have been gathered for something. But it hadn't been used and it was just…waiting.

Waiting, while already colored with Justin's powerful intent, will and skill—but no target. It swarmed around me, recognizing another magical creature, but I couldn't control it.

Red washed over my vision and I stumbled. Cool hands gripped my elbows. I couldn't stop the instinctive flinch and I batted at Abraham's hands. "I'm fine," I said. The edged note in my voice belied my words, but I wasn't about to fall down.

It was just the magic trying to latch onto me and be used. As it realized it had no outlet in me, the intensity of it faded away.

I breathed through my nose and fought to steady myself. My blood was hot, pounding too quick through my veins as everything in me reacted to the fury of an angry witch and the fear of a desperate shifter, but fear was an old friend of mine and anger…well, we were practically soul mates. Wrestling the demons under control, I took one more breath and waited for the rest of my head to settle. Magic was a potent drug—one I was glad I didn't use.

Slowly, I lifted a hand and the air currents, charged with the unused magic, twisted and twined through the air. "You need to call Banner—have them send a witch. Tell them they need to do a discharge. They'll know what it means."

Abraham was quiet for a moment and then he moved away.

That left me alone to focus.

They hadn't been gone long and Justin had all but rattled the foundations with whatever magic he'd been doing here.

I could do this.

My hand itched.

I am aneira.

My heart is strong.

My aim is true.

My blood is noble…

I let myself fall into the mantra that had been beaten into me.

My enemies cannot hide themselves from me. My prey cannot escape me.

I don't know how I stood there, mind empty of everything but those words. Slowly, I sank into an unnatural state of calm. I don't even remember closing my eyes, but suddenly, I was brutally aware of everything. My heartbeat. The scent of the blood—two different blood scents. The stink of booze mixed with sweat and desperation and anger and desolation. The air currents stirring along my skin.

And the magic that continued to wrap around me like a lover.

It *clung*.

It *tugged* on me.

Follow, it whispered.

Follow…

It had been an age since I'd had to track like this. But there was no doubt I could do it.

I focused on that tug in my gut and shoved open the door to Howler's.

I didn't hear the footsteps, but I knew I wasn't alone.

Abraham said nothing and for that I was thankful.

The place had been destroyed.

My mind cataloged everything for future reference even as a calm mental voice made a checklist of everything that already had an easy explanation. There was damage to the bar, signs that somebody's head had been smashed into it, along with streaks of blood—the scent of it too close to human to be anybody's but Justin's, but right next to that, I could see scorch marks.

It would take a lot more than a dented head to do Justin in.

He was made of sterner stuff than that.

Slowly, I turned, taking in everything.

He'd burned her. Under the heaviest scent layer of blood, I could just barely smell the stink of something burnt. I needed Doyle or Damon. One of them could get a better idea of how badly she'd been hurt. But for now, I used what my eyes and brain could piece together.

One table was smashed completely. There were pieces barely large enough to use as toothpicks now. That wouldn't be the case if Justin had slammed her into it, unless she'd shifted or if he'd thrown her into it using his magic. If she'd thrown him into it that hard, there'd be traces of his blood and I didn't smell any there.

I closed my eyes and breathed in again, breaking down the scents as much as I could.

So much blood. So much of *Justin's* blood.

The door behind me opened and I whirled around, my sword already drawn.

Abraham had moved like liquid darkness, placing himself between me and the newcomer.

Damon.

His eyes rolled to green-gold as they landed on Abraham, his lips peeling back from his teeth in a snarl.

"Damon." I tried to keep my voice steady.

I tried so hard but at the sight of him, reality hit me and I could feel my control faltering.

Damon's gaze shifted from Abraham to me.

He moved around the vampire and came straight to me, his arms coming around me for a quick, tight hug. Then he moved away. It was a good thing, because if he'd stayed much longer, I would have grabbed on and the storm building in me might have broken.

"I'm going to kill her," I said as he moved to stand in the middle of the room.

Damon's gray eyes came to mine and a small smile twisted his lips. "Of course you are." Then his lids lowered and he tipped his head back.

I left him to it.

He could break down the scent trail.

I was tracking Justin.

They found me miles away from the Abyss.

I closed my eyes and slid back into that semi-trance state. It had come easier that time, easier, quicker. I didn't remember leaving the bar.

I didn't remember anything except that voice in my head. The one that murmured, *Follow...follow.*

Magic and I weren't easy bedfellows. I had my own subtle forms, there was no denying that and I could recognize magic—recognize it well enough to even know *whose* I was feeling, if I was familiar enough with the person.

And Justin's magic had been all over Howler's.

An angry, pissed-off sort of magic, the kind to both attack and defend and I was following the tug of that now, but it wasn't an easy fit.

Trying to follow a magic trail was sort of like a trail of dust motes…and fire ants. It itched and burned and every instinct in me screamed to stop.

Needless to say when two men came bearing down on me, I wasn't in a good mood.

Damon was the one brave enough to grab me by the arms when I didn't slow down.

"Let me *go!*"

Instead, he hauled me off my feet and shook me like I was a ragdoll. "Wake *up!*" he snarled into my face.

"I am awake!"

Then I blinked and looked around.

Okay, I was mostly awake. Blowing out a shaky breath, I said, "Where am I?"

"You crossed out of East Orlando city limits nearly ten minutes ago," he said, his voice unreadable. "I had to track you. You went outside and I stayed inside, figured you were just prowling around. But you took off." He stopped and ran his tongue across his teeth. "You don't generally move that fast."

"I…" The itching, that driving *need* to keep moving grew stronger and I had to fight the urge to jerk out of his hands and take off running. "It's just…"

Damon's hands smoothed up, then down my arms. "Take a deep breath, Kit. Breathe, clear your head."

I scowled at him even as memory worked free.

Justin would have said that.

Clear your head, Kitty-kitty…focus on the prize.

"You going to be my coach or something?"

"Or something. I was around when Doyle had to do this…" A dark look entered his eyes and he laid a hand on my cheek. "Once upon a time."

I covered his hand with mine. *Doyle…*

Doyle. And Justin. Justin had helped Doyle find me. "Help me find him," I whispered.

"I will." Then he smiled, his hard face softening. Damon gave my ear a quick

● ● ●

tug. "But you don't really need me for this, Kit. You know how to do this. You've done it before and you learned how on your own. You just have to stop reacting…and *think*. What would *he* have done to her? What is going on with him and where are you going? Where is your gut taking you? Are you following *her* …or him?"

He cupped my face in his hands and pressed his brow to mine. "Climb inside their heads, Kit. It's what you do."

I vaguely aware of Abraham coming up behind me and there were shadows behind him. Others. Too many others. Dimly, I realized who it was—knew the feel of their presence stinging against my shields. Chang. Doyle. Scott. Others I didn't know.

I ignored them.

Justin…

I let it play out in my head, my imagination kicking in—how much was imagination, how much was just an educated guess…how much was just *bullshit*…

My mind sketched it out.

Justin going into Howler's.

Would she already be there?

Yes.

It was the MacDonald's place and she was his second. She would have gone in and cleared it out. No witnesses.

That would have made Justin leery.

He would have shielded up, hard. But subtle.

Then…

They were sitting. Close.

Was he already suspicious?

He might not have been—

No. That's not right.

Justin is a suspicious bastard by nature and I hadn't smelled the recent presence of others, nor had Abraham mentioned it. There had been no blood from others, no bodies. Howlers hadn't exactly been hopping the other day, but it had been far from empty, too. Yeah, the very emptiness would have made him very, very curious and

Justin's curiosity isn't a soft, pretty thing.

They were sitting down.

She attacks—*hit him somehow*, I thought, forcing myself to separate the rage. She hit him and it hurt him, but not enough because he lashed out with one thing that makes just about *any* creature freak.

Fire.

It wasn't enough to kill, just enough to let him regroup.

He hadn't wanted her dead, because if he had, he could have just flamed her ass to death. He wasn't a natural born pyro, but again, with a witch of Justin's power level, it's all intent, will and skill and once he had the flames going, they wouldn't have gone out until he wanted them to.

So he'd wanted her alive.

For information.

Yeah, made sense. It was a gamble, of course, and one that hadn't paid off, because Justin was hurt, missing now, and she had him.

Shifting my focus to her, I tried to put myself in *her* head.

If she got him out of Florida, he was dead. But that was a big if. The state line was a couple hours away, unless she flew and that wouldn't be possible without authorization—she was a known NH. Flight was restricted for NHs and authorization was required. She could try for private, but that took time and she had very little.

So that required she drive through territory that was either populated by humans or mostly under the control of the cats.

Damon's people would be on the lookout and she'd know that by now. Megan would be desperate. If she was found out, her Alpha would destroy her. There wouldn't even be skin left by the time he was done. She'd reduced herself to the same level as Saul—a skintrader, somebody who sold out her own kind.

Why?

"Doesn't matter," I muttered. Although it might—

"No." I shook my head, uncaring of that fact I probably looked insane to everybody who was watching. Staring at nothing, pacing, muttering to myself and generally looking like a madwoman.

The *why* might matter, later. But right now, the *where* mattered.

The big obstacle. Get Justin out of Florida.

He'd know that, so he'd have to fight that.

But if he was hurt or unconscious—

It hit me then.

That was it.

I dropped my hands and spun around, practically launching myself at Damon. "Colleen. I have to get to Colleen."

He closed his hands around my wrists. I'd grabbed the front of his jacket like I would shake him but really, I was just trying to ground myself. "Okay." His gray eyes, calm and unshakeable, held mine. "Why?"

"That's what he'd do." I drew in a breath and suddenly, I felt like me again. The panic eased back like it had never been and I could think. "You asked me what he'd do. Justin knows if she gets him out of Florida, she'll get him to whoever is collecting the bodies for the hospital. So he'll ward himself...no. That's not right. He uses wards, like those at my office to keep things *out*, but he can do similar magics on people. I don't know what they are, how they work, but I've seen him use his magic to keep *people*. One guy, we thought he'd rabbit on us before we found proof so he just use some sort of spell to keep the guy contained in the area where he normally lived and worked. He got nervous and tried to run—but he could only run in circles in that area. Justin can do that to *himself* and it would hold, right up to his death."

"So why do you need Colleen?" Damon passed a hand over my hair.

"She can help me lock in on him." I flexed my hands. "I'm trying to do that now, but I'm fried. I can track him down eventually but that could take hours and we don't have that time to waste."

He smoothed a hand down my hair. "You're moving pretty well on your own."

"*No.*" Frustrated, I shook my head. "I'm not. I'm not as good at this as I need to be. All the magic he'd pumped into the air has me jumpy and I'm nervous... I *need* to go to Colleen's."

Need.

227

Had to.

Colleen lived too far away.

Personally, I understood.

Really.

But not today.

Today, I wanted to get her on the phone and *yell* at her, shake her, for insisting on living more than thirty minutes outside the city.

Of course, I tried calling her to tell her what was going on, but she wasn't answering and I couldn't leave a message—*messaging service is unavailable at this time*. I'd yell at her about *that* for sure.

Then I wanted to turn my fury on Abraham as he dropped down out of the sky, landing in a crouch, one fist planted into the earth. Dust rose up from the impact of his abrupt landing. He strode around to the door and before Damon could speak, he said, "She's there."

Well, of course—

"Megan Banks," he said, clarifying. His gaze flew to my face. "She's at the witch's house. Your friend. When you couldn't reach her, I flew ahead to check on her. Megan is there."

My heart seized.

"Talk." Damon demanded.

"Greaves is there as well. I smell his blood, but I dare not get any closer for fear of alerting her," Abraham said, speaking quickly, not bothering to look back as a car came to a stop behind Damon. Other cars laid on the horns. Damon had just stopped in the middle of the road. Scott strode toward the back of the second car and stood there. I could see him, a human-shaped wall in a three piece suit, arms folded over his chest as he stared down at the road.

If a car came barreling down the road at him and decided not to move, Scott would just move it himself.

When a shiny black sports car slowed down in front of him, my shoulders went tight and one by one, the others turned their heads.

• • •

The MacDonald climbed out of his car and came toward us, each step slow and deliberate.

Three of his men moved in unison at his back.

Megan's absence was another stab in my heart. Part of me still hoped I was wrong, despite what everything my body—and the others—could already tell.

"What is going on?" Alisdair MacDonald asked softly. His gaze flicked to mine, one straight black brow going up. "What was the meaning of the call I received earlier, Kit?"

"Megan's gone fucking nuts," I said, fear and fury eradicating any diplomacy I would have normally shot for.

The shadow at his right took a step forward. "Use care how you—"

Chang stepped between us.

I'd barely noticed him.

And *care* wasn't in my vocabulary right now. Baring my teeth, I glared at the puppet. "I'll use *care* after I'm done shoving my sword up Megan's ass." Then I shifted my attention to Dair. "She has Justin."

Dair's eyes flashed gold and he shot out a hand just as the soldier at his side went to move forward.

Chang was resting on the balls of his feet, almost like he was *hoping* the wolf would attack.

Apparently I wasn't the only one spoiling for a fight.

"Why would you say this?"

"Because I was at the place where it happened," I said, fighting the trembling that threatened to overwhelm me. "I might not be able to break down the scent layers like you can, but my nose doesn't suck. I smelled her, I smelled him and the magic in the air almost knocked me off my feet—I'm *still* choking on it. She attacked him and he fought back."

"How do you know he didn't attack her first?" Dair asked.

But he knew.

I saw it in his eyes.

"Because he went there looking for answers," I said. "And if Justin had attacked first, she'd be dead. Justin knows what a high level wolf is capable of. Hardly anybody knows what a warrior witch is capable of until they've fought one. If she had any idea what she was taking on with him, she would have put him out with the first blow. She didn't and she missed her shot."

While Dair processed this, Abraham took a step forward. "I caught traces of blood, Alpha MacDonald. The witch bled first—he also bled the most. Your second bled some, but not a great deal. She was burned, as well. I find no fault with Ms. Colbana's theory."

"Except of course it requires that I believe my top person has betrayed me," Dair said, his voice icy.

"You already know she has," I said quietly. "That's why you hired outsiders when you started to suspect things were wrong at Howlers. You got even more concerned when the wolf Drake died."

He didn't answer.

But the look on his face spoke volumes and we all saw it.

"I'm leaving," I said gently. Then I looked at Damon.

If Megan had hurt Justin, a man who could—and would—break bones—what would she do to a woman who couldn't defend herself?

Chapter Seventeen

The whisper of Colleen's wards brushed over my skin like a warm hug from an old friend.

The magic here knew me.

It knew me. It welcomed me.

And it spoke to me.

That hug *clung* to me and didn't let go, because the wards were living, breathing extensions of Colleen's magic and they responded to her emotions. Her emotions were full of anger and helplessness and fear and I felt all of them, all over me as I crossed the creekstone path that led to her front door. Glass sparkled in the sun and I fought not to let my expression change even when I caught the scent in the air.

More blood.

How much had Justin lost?

Was he even conscious?

I hit the door with the side of my fist. Hard. "Open up, Coll. I need your help! Justin's hurt."

I was going to fake my way through that door. Damon and the rest of them had stayed a mile back. They could hear me—just faintly, if I screamed and they could be here in minutes. I was banking on the protections in Colleen's house to give me those minutes—well, Colleen's protections *and* mine. The protection that came in the form of the mean-ass Glock I had holstered to my thigh. The protective strap was off, but most people wouldn't notice. Cops, other weapons aficionados, sure, they'd notice. But Megan was her own weapon. She didn't put a lot of stock in what she'd once called my *toys*.

My hands all but itching to draw this particular toy and make her eat every last bullet inside.

There was a faint sound from inside—I heard it, a low grunt. "Come on, Colleen. I hear you moving around in there. I need your help, damn it!"

A few more seconds passed before I heard her voice. It was low and rough and I heard the pain in it. "Kit, I'm sorry, but it's not a good time."

"Too fucking bad!" I hit the door again. "Didn't you hear me? Justin's in trouble. I *need*...wait. Colleen...?" I let a small note of the fear inside me infuse my voice. "Are you okay?"

I sucked in a breath, made it louder than it needed it to be.

Megan was in there. I could hear her breathing—actually, if I strained, I could hear *three* different breathing patterns.

One of the reasons I always downplayed just *what* I could do was for moments like this. People always assumed I was closer to a human or witch than anything else, and if it was Justin standing on the porch, he wouldn't have heard Colleen's breathing, much less three distinctive sets of respirations.

"I'm fine," Colleen said, and her voice was steadier.

I imagined Megan had given her a good reason—probably was holding her hand right at Justin's throat, ready to rip it out. Although I had to wonder—why hadn't she just killed him? It would be easier.

Worry later. Rescue now.

The gist of the plan was to get inside and make sure she stayed away from Justin and Colleen. Then...

Well, the cavalry expected me to stay a nice safe distance away while they dealt with the wicked wolf.

Not happening.

"I'll be there in a moment, Kit. I've been..." Her voice hitched. "Sick."

"Oh." I rolled my eyes. Sometimes I debated on whether or not I should tell Damon and Dair that they'd be wise to educate themselves and their respective peoples about the other races more, but I did so much better when the other NHs were uninformed. If Megan was half as smart as she liked to think she was, she'd know not to give that lie to Colleen. Strong witches like Colleen didn't really get *sick*. Their bodies healed everything short of normal aging and severe injury. "Okay. I'm really sorry…"

As the shuffling footsteps drew closer to the door, I slid my Glock out, angling my body to the side so I could block my weapon-hand from view.

I slid the safety off just as the door opened.

The sight of Colleen's pale face and red-rimmed eyes made my heart lurch.

She was alive.

Alive, and unharmed.

And Megan was right behind the door.

Even if Colleen hadn't let her gaze slide to the right, I would have known.

I met Colleen's gaze as I moved inside, encircling her with my right arm for a quick, tight hug as we stood in the door way. I continued to keep my left hand shielded.

"You said Justin was in trouble." She murmured against my ear as she hugged me back and I could feel the minute trembling of her body.

"Yeah. We'll make it okay, though." I gave her one last tight hug. "That's what I do, right?"

She eased back and she darted another glance to the door.

"You've still got your wards, right?" She had lowered something. I could feel it—the air here was different and it only made sense. She didn't know Megan, but she'd allowed her in, probably because Megan had Justin. Megan would have said he was injured or something. She was Dair's right hand—although she was probably fired now—she'd know the major players in the area, even if they had little use for witches.

Colleen's wards were designed to protect her against attackers. Although she couldn't defend herself, her wards were designed to defend her against threats. Justin had worked with her, using his own magic to pump them up so the wards themselves would step in and do what Colleen couldn't do.

But a threat had gotten through so Colleen had altered or lowered one of the wards, even if it was something as simple as allowing somebody unknown onto her property.

"My wards…" Colleen frowned.

● ● ●

233

The door squeaked.

"What's the one…armae?" I pursed my lips, fumbling over the unfamiliar word. I stared at her hard.

Armum. Latin for shield. Colleen liked Latin.

Her lids flickered in answer.

Drop it, I mouthed.

"I can do better," she said. She shot out a hand as the door was torn open. I grabbed her and we both hit the floor. "Blood, Kit!"

The confusion cost me a precious second, but I drew out a knife and whipped it across my neck—yes, my neck. It was a shallow cut and I didn't have to worry about it making the grip on my sword slippery. Colleen snatched the knife away with a grim shake of her head. She also swiped her fingers through the blood on my neck and flung them on the ground with a whisper, some unintelligible word that made no sense to me, but as the hairs on the back of my neck rose, I caught the intent.

It was a shield spell, something quick and dirty and it would last—

Megan threw herself at us and howled long and loud as she came up against an unseen wall.

She was thrown back and hit the far wall with devastating strength.

Blood-red cracks appeared in thin air before me and then, with an odd shudder of air, like a death sigh, they melted away.

The shield spell was gone.

Megan was already pushing away from the wall, shaking her head as though to clear it.

Colleen sliced the knife down her palm.

She couldn't wound me—or anybody else—to save her life, but she could slice and dice herself just fine.

I stared at the hot blood welling out of her palm. Magic all but *wept* out of it and I was so fascinated, I didn't have time to prepare myself. She slammed her open, bleeding hand over the shallow cut in my neck.

"*Defensori!*"

I tensed just as her magic flooded me. It punched through me and lit me up.

● ● ●

I was on my feet in the next blink, as though I had wings and it was none too soon because Megan launched herself at me. She was human when she first started to move.

Flesh began to melt away into fur and muscles began to realign, bones popping and breaking in a vicious shift as she changed forms.

The one and only time we'd ever had any physical contact, I'd broken my hand on her hard-as-rock face.

She'd been human that one time and she could have broken me easily.

If we tangled while she was in wolf form, I'd be shredded. I leaped into her, blade extended.

I felt the impact of her weight as I brought my sword up.

Smoke rose up to fill my nose, the silver in my blade scorching her flesh. She growled in response, her body stiffening from the reaction, but she didn't pull away.

That's the difference between a true high-level wolf and those who just think they're bad asses. A high-level wolf can fight through the pain of a silver-wrought wound.

The rest just curl up and whine.

I really wished Megan would have just curled up and whined.

I wrenched the blade around, trying to widen the injury and she caught me, her claws sinking into my flesh. My skin began to burn as the virus ripped into me. She yanked me back and hurled me away.

I hit the wall and came down hard. My teeth were still rattling when I lifted my gun.

A strangled noise—something between a yelp and howl—escaped her when I shot out her left kneecap.

We both struggled to get upright first and I glared at her as she shot a rage-filled gaze my way.

"You're done, Megan." I was already panting. Never go head to head with a wolf, not if you can avoid it. "Dair knows."

A snarl built in her throat and the rage ate up every other emotion in her eyes. "I'll kill you."

"Did you really *think* you could get away with killing Justin, killing a witch of the road…me…and not be found out?"

She rolled onto her knees, her breathing as ragged as mine.

She punched a fist into the floor, her hand going through the boards. I leveled the gun at her bowed head. *Shoot. Just shoot…*

They'd be coming.

Might already be pounding toward the house even now. This would be done in seconds.

Once Dair got here, it was done.

She was done.

But I had to know.

"*Why?*" I demanded.

She surged upright, a howl ripping out of her. She leaped through the door and I bounced up, my body screaming. I had to know.

"Kit!" Colleen screamed after me, but I ignored her.

Megan hadn't even made ten yards before her knee went out, the silver in the bullet slowing her ability to heal. She must have sensed the inevitability of it and she shifted back to human. Her body healed with the change and she lurched upright, spinning to face me. Naked, strong and beautiful, she should have looked like a warrior goddess, blood still streaking her body.

But the desperation gripping her changed everything about her and even the threat inherent in her very being was altered by it.

She stared at me for a long moment and then spun on her heel, her body a blur as she ran away.

No.

It's not cool to shoot a person in the back. I try to be a fair person and I won't fight dirty unless I have to.

So I shot her in the lower leg and blood and meat exploded out as the bullet tore the limb apart.

She went down with a scream and I knew she'd stay down—for a few minutes at least. She'd expended too much energy healing herself and shifting. She couldn't do it again so soon. Gun in one hand, sword in the other, I approached.

My ears picked up the sound of footsteps—quiet rustles as they flew over the grass and I swallowed.

"It's done," I said again. "Dair's almost here. Tell me why."

She was silent.

Circling around her, keeping a wide distance between us, I lifted the gun. "Next time, I'll shoot you in the back—several times. I'll sever your spine, Megan, and I use silver. You know that. You can feel it by now. If you're lucky, the scar tissue won't interfere with your ability to walk or run. But you'll heal *slowly* and *painfully*."

"*Heal?* I'm already *dead*. If Dair knows…" She laughed and the sound was bitter and broken. She lifted her head now and stared at me through a mess of bangs and blood. "Just kill me already. There's no point to this."

"I will kill you—and I'll be quick about it. But I want *a fucking answer*."

She roared, the sound inhuman. She lunged at me, fueled by fear and the desperation that had driven her this far. Although she only had one good leg, it was strong enough and she still had two good arms.

And one of them had done a partial shift, fingers elongating as black claws slid out from where her nails had once been.

I don't know who was more surprised by what happened next. Me…or her.

Blood geysered out from the stump where her monstrous hand had been only a fraction of a second earlier.

She fell to the dirt on her knees—but she only managed to balance there for a second before she went over onto her side. Dumbfounded, she stared at the stump of her lower arm as blood pumped out in a fountain.

She grabbed her arm just above the wrist as she rolled to her back.

Then she threw back her head, the noise that left her throat was more scream than howl and it chilled the blood in my veins.

The sound was still dying in the air when she awkwardly rolled herself to her knees and one hand. Her lower leg was already regenerating and if she had time—minutes even—she'd been healed.

But she didn't give herself minutes.

● ● ●

She leaped at me.

I sensed movement behind me but I ducked to the side.

I know my speed. I know my strength. I've never moved that fast in my life and I've never struck out with that strength. She went down with a force that spun her around and I leaped on top of her back, driving my blade in through her back, then through her chest, down deep into the dirt.

Magic rippled in me, made me shudder as Megan jerked away. The place on my neck where I'd cut myself, where Colleen had mingled her blood with mine and forced her magic into me, it stung.

What the *hell* had Colleen done?

Megan struggled to jerk away, but the blood pumping out of her veins, coupled with the poison that was now circulating *inside* her from the silver left her weakened.

I dropped my weight down onto her, shoving my knee into her back, close to where my blade skewered her.

I grabbed her hair, the long, shining, silken banner, and jerked her head up.

Her eyes met mine, tormented and full of pain. "Dair..." she whispered raggedly.

I looked up then and saw them all, gathered around us in a loose circle.

Doyle had a smug, shit-eating grin on his face and Dair's soldiers stood at his back with their jaws locked. The rest of them, I couldn't read their expressions for anything, although I could *feel* Damon—something that was pride and fear and relief and...I rolled my eyes.

The man was a walking sex bomb.

Dair stepped forward, dragging my attention to him.

Okay, *him*, I could read.

The wolf pack's Alpha was all but trembling. The look in his eyes was one that spoke of heartbreak as much as rage.

Megan closed her eyes and started to weep.

"Why?" I demanded as he continued to stare.

"They..." She shuddered, her body spasming as pain from the silver wracked her system. "They gave me...no...choice. A few...strays. They leave the..." She started to cough and half screamed as it sent more pain lancing through her body. "They'd leave them...alone. If I helped. It seemed...a safe bargain."

A growl worked its way out of Dair's throat.

She flinched at the sound and then gasped as the movement drove the silver closer to her heart.

"Who is *they*?" I demanded. "And who would *they* leave alone?"

She wasn't looking at me, though.

Her gaze locked at Dair.

He took a step forward. "I'll get the information out of her. Please allow—"

She wrenched herself underneath me.

I recognized her intention but too late.

In the next second, before anybody could stop it, she heaved her body to the left—and completely shredded her heart on the sharp edge of my blade. Reflex had me jerking up, pulling my blade free, but it was too late.

Megan was dead.

Dair closed his eyes.

CHAPTER EIGHTEEN

Damon was the one who found him.

Justin, battered to a bloody pulp and barely breathing, was in the bathroom of Colleen's house and while I watched, my lover lifted my friend as though he were a fragile, broken doll.

Now, as I stood at the foot of the bed, Damon waited behind me, a silent presence.

We watched as Colleen worked.

And I prayed.

I don't know that I've ever prayed before.

I don't even know what—or who—I prayed to.

But I had to do something, because with each fragile beat of Justin's heart, I could hear him slipping away.

When his heart slipped, I spun away and pressed my face against Damon's chest.

His hands came up and rested on my hips.

Memories flashed through my head.

The first time I'd ever seen Justin—the dumbass had been getting the shit kicked out of him in the alley behind TJ's. *His* idea of an interrogation.

"Well, you look like a little bit of nothing. But you went after a rat pack and helped bring them down. There's gotta be something to you."

Something to me? He'd been the first one to think so—the first one to make me *want* to think so.

A million other memories blurred through my mind—a job we'd taken because Nova had said, *I think you'll like the payout.* And we'd found nearly twenty grand buried under the floorboard in the house of the guy we'd hunted down.

That time up on the mountain, when he'd come for me.

"Justin. You…are you here?"

"Yeah, Kitty-kitty." A weak attempt at a smile. *"Did you ever doubt it?"*

And he hadn't just *come* for me—he'd brought an entire fucking army.

I tightened my fingers in Damon's shirt. "He can't die, Damon. He's my best friend. He can't…"

Damon pressed his lips to my temple. "I know, baby girl. If he does, I'll just have to haul his ass out of hell and throttle him for you."

I would have laughed. But I was too afraid I'd start to cry.

So I just stood there, breathing in Damon's scent and letting the memories swarm me while Colleen funneled her magic and her healing into Justin's broken body.

"Bruised spleen, bruised kidneys, both lungs are punctured, perforated intestines, nine broken ribs…" Colleen grimaced and passed a hand down her side. She took a deep breath and gave a long look at her patient. "Subdural hemorrhage and his heart is bruised as well. She almost pulverized his chest. Must have punched him hard enough to break every bone—had he been fully human."

She slid me a look. "Apparently, she's uninformed about the differences between warrior witches and the rest of the people out there."

"Let's keep it that way," I said, rubbing the heel of my hand over my chest. I stared through the door at his pale, gaunt form. "Will he make it?"

"He should." She leaned against the door frame opposite me, exhaustion in every line of her body. "If he doesn't, it's not for lack of trying on my part. And…if he doesn't, I'll find a way to make him suffer for it even if he *is* dead. I didn't work that hard to put him back together just for him to die on me."

Her voice went husky and tight.

I slid her a look, but she wasn't facing me.

I reached down and caught her hand.

She squeezed mine.

"Where did the goon squad go?" I asked.

It startled a laugh out of her.

"Only you would call some of the scariest sons-of-bitches I've ever seen *the goon squad*, Kit." She let go of my hand and then shifted to put her back to the door. Sliding down, she rested her elbows on her upraised knees. "I think Damon and his men are close by. Hunting...or just running. Although one of them probably went to the store. Damon opened the freezer and told me I have no meat here. Apparently this is problematic for him."

I smiled. "Yeah. He thinks if it doesn't bleed, it's not really food."

A look of mild disgust crossed her features. "I've never been inclined to go vegan, but that image is almost enough to tempt me."

Chuckling, I leaned back against the wall. "He's always fussing at me to get more protein." The wall didn't seem to help much, so I decided to follow Colleen's example and I slid down the wall as well, groaning as my body screamed at me. Although I'd gotten off pretty damn light, I still felt every second of the fight with Megan—particularly in my back. That short, unscheduled flight across Colleen's living room had done nothing for my spine.

Thinking of Megan, I sobered. "And the MacDonald?"

"He left." She looked away. "He was very...grim."

"Grim. Yeah." Drawing my knees to my chest, I hugged them tight, trying to ward off the chill. "I can understand that."

The question that had haunted me all these hours burst out. "Damn it, Colleen, I don't understand. Why did she do this?"

"I don't know." She rolled her head against the wood of the door and met my eyes. "Even if I knew the reasons, I wouldn't know, Kit. But I don't know the reasons. I don't have any answers."

She sucked in a harsh breath and then spat out, "I *hate* her. It's this huge ugly thing inside of me and I want it out, but I can't get rid of it. Why did she hurt him, Kit? Why?"

The venom in her voice took me off guard and I blinked, staring at her, and for the first time, I saw something...more.

● ● ●

Oh, hell.

"Coll?" I whispered.

Her gaze flitted to me and then away. "Don't," she murmured, shaking her head. "I can't...I can't talk about it now."

She came to her feet, her movements harsh and jerky, unlike her normal graceful motions. "She hurt. Tell me you made her hurt..." She screamed and spun away, shoving her hands through her hair. "*Damn* it."

Quietly, I moved up behind her. She was tense, tremors wracking her entire body. Slowly, I slid my arms around her. "You don't want to ask those questions," I said softly as I hugged her from behind. "This isn't who you are. You can't carry that poison in you, no matter how mad you are, no matter how scared."

She started to cry.

A few seconds later, so did I.

Evening gave way to night in a thundering torrent.

Justin hadn't moved.

Damon told me Dair's men had taken Megan's body.

Chang was gone but I hadn't even noticed his absence until he came through the doors, four of Damon's enforcers at his back.

Two of them carried grocery bags. I guess Chang wanted to make sure there was meat for everybody. They moved straight into the kitchen and Colleen followed them with a frown. It's a dangerous thing, messing around in a girl's kitchen. Even more dangerous when that girl is a witch.

The other two moved to stand guard at Justin's door and that had me turning to Chang.

"What is going on?"

Chang gestured to the couch. "Kit. Please. Sit." He softened those words with a smile. "You look exhausted."

I wasn't exhausted. I'd cruised past exhausted and sailed straight in zombified territory some hours ago. It was possible that if I sat down, I wouldn't get back up and I didn't want to sleep until I had news—news about Megan or news about Justin or news about...*something*.

"I have information," Chang said, as if he'd read my mind.

Sulking, I flung myself down on the long, wide couch, tucking my body up against Damon's.

"How is Justin?" Chang asked.

"I don't know," I said waspishly. "When he's done being all comatose and shit, you can wake him up and ask him."

Chang looked away.

Aww, hell. Sighing, I rubbed my hands down my face. "Chang, shit. I'm—"

"Please don't apologize," he said, his voice gentle. But when he looked up, his eyes flashed—and stayed—green. The pupils slitted, going feline and his voice lowered to a rougher growl.

Next to me, Damon said something.

I blinked, not catching the words.

Chang responded in the same language and then he looked away, shaking himself like a bird settling his feathers. When he looked back at me, his eyes were normal. "Please, don't apologize. This...travesty lies at our feet. Ours, Dair's, perhaps even at the feet of the Witches Council—even the Assembly."

Confused, I straightened, settling my weight on the edge of the couch, rather than against Damon. "What are you talking about?"

His lips twisted. "It all came from within our ranks. All of it. We never saw it."

The faceless Barry now had a face—or at least *something* of a face.

He lay in a bloodied mess of limbs and torn flesh and silver pinned him to the floor in four places. Enough silver to keep him not just restrained, but trapped in his human form. They weren't just relying on the blades pinning him, though.

He was also chained and I had a good idea of where Justin had gotten the idea for his cuffs.

Blades skewered his wrists. If he tried to rip his hands out or dislocate a bone, he'd have to cut his hand through completely. It had to be torturously painful. But I felt no pity as I hunched down in front of him.

"Talk," I said quietly.

He just opened his one good eye.

The other was battered shut. He had done some healing—or I assumed he had—so I didn't want to think about how bad that eye had looked earlier.

"I told...them..." He stopped and licked him lips. "I told them what I know. Just...kill me."

Leaning in, I asked, "Do you want to die?"

His eye shone wetly at me. I could see the plea there. *Yes.* The answer was yes.

"You won't," I said, shaking my head. "I'll ask Damon, real nice like, if he can keep you alive for *weeks*...maybe even months or a year."

He started to cry.

A few months ago, I'd wondered if there was some part of me that had broken, ruined beyond repair, during those two weeks at Jude's. Torture can break the mind, warp the soul. I felt nothing as I watched him cry.

"How many did you help capture?" I asked. He didn't answer but I didn't ask him to. "You sit there wailing and expecting pity, but you turned over your kind to be brutalized and tortured. For *what?*"

"We..." He sucked in a ragged breath. "We didn't have any choice."

"There's always a choice." The words were bitter. "Sometimes the alternatives suck, but there's always a choice."

"They wanted test subjects," he whispered, voice shaking. "It was...find them some or they'd just...take them."

The tremor cleared from his voice and he jerked against the silver pinning him, as though he'd indeed rip through it. I eyed him narrowly and reached for the Glock. I pulled it out and watched as his eye widened—with hope. He swallowed, though, when I shoved it against his groin. "I'll blow them off," I said softly. "Keep it up and I'll do it. You'll sing soprano for the rest of your life—however long it may be." I leaned in and said, "I won't let you heal, either. I know a way to make all mutilations permanent."

● ● ●
245

"You wouldn't." He stared down at the gun pressed to his balls, almost mesmerized. "You couldn't."

With a shrug, I said, "A year ago, maybe not. But I'm not who I used to be."

He shot me a look—and went still.

"We had no choice," he said again.

"You always have a choice."

"And what would you have done?" he half-spat. "You don't even know what it's like. You have no clan, no family. You're alone."

I didn't let the words hurt. They weren't true. I *wasn't* alone. Not anymore. I hadn't been alone for a very, very long time. "I would have found the person who made that *deal* and made them choke on the words. And I would have buried them in a hole so deep, they'd never be found. And if it was more than one, then I'd just settle myself in for a long, long hunt." I leaned forward. "You could have gone to Damon. You could have. But you didn't. Just like Megan didn't."

He flinched.

I nudged harder. "Start to talk…now."

"A quick death."

Damon's eyes narrowed on me.

Clenching my jaw, I looked away. "He gave me the information I needed. He did give it to me. Make it bloody if you want, but…"

Blowing out a disgusted breath, he nodded. "The things I do for you," he muttered.

I wished I could have smiled, but I felt too battered inside.

"Did that help?" Chang asked, drawing my gaze to the others in the narrow, hall. It was grim and dark, made of cinderblocks painted black and the uninviting atmosphere seemed fitting for pain and torture and misery.

Scott and Doyle were there as well, although I wished I'd asked that Damon have them leave.

They both looked at me with something akin to…apprehension. I'd probably be doing the same. I felt half-mad—not remotely like myself.

Was this who I'd become then? Could I do the things I'd threatened Barry with and still live with myself?

Yes.

I tightened one hand into a fist. In that moment, I wanted to cry a little. I'd fought so hard to stay...*human*. Or at least walk a line far from the monster too many non-humans had become and here I was, teetering on that precipice.

"Doyle, Scott. Go."

Damon jerked his chin at the entrance to the underground cells. I hadn't even known this space was down here and I wanted *out*, up in the fresh, clean air, away from the blood and death that crowded my senses.

"You're still you."

Startled, I looked at Damon. Then with a frown, I turned away. "Chang's supposed to be the mind reader, not you Damon."

"I don't need to read your mind to understand that look in your eyes, Kit," he said softly. Then he shrugged. "Besides. I heard what you said. I don't need to be a mind reader to know you're torn up over this."

"But I'm *not*." I gripped the gun, squeezed it tighter and thought about the fact that maybe, just maybe, I could have done what I'd threatened.

"If you weren't," Chang said gently. "Then you wouldn't be standing here looking so torn."

Anything else I might have said was interrupted by a hard knock. Scott opened the door without waiting for a reply although he dipped his head in deference to Damon. "Alpha, my apologies." His gaze came to mine. "There's a man here to see you. A *human*. He says you met at Howlers. And he has some information he can only give to you."

If I'd expected Charles Andrulis to show up with all the answers wrapped up in a tidy package, well...clearly I'd expected too much.

He didn't have a package.

He had a phone.

He stood in a room where I hadn't been before and Chang had led us there, assuring me that the room was soundproofed and completely suitable for a private discussion.

Damon hadn't come with us.

He'd still been staring into the cell and I had a feeling there would be the bloody, painful death I'd asked for soon, if it hadn't already happened.

As the door closed behind Chang, I stared at Charles. My gut said I could trust him and he'd willingly surrendered all weapons at the door. His gaze dropped to mine. "They let you in here armed."

I lifted a shoulder. "They must like me."

"They must," he said, nodding. He drew a thumb down his stubbled jawline. "I was threatened with evisceration when I was led to this room."

I mentally swore.

He cocked a brow. "Seeing as how that could be a death sentence if I wanted to make a case out of it, they must *really* like you."

"Are you?"

"Am I what?" A guileless smile curved his lips.

"Going to make a case of it."

"Naw." He laughed, long and hard. "Of course not. I respect a man who makes it clear he won't tolerate his friends being harmed." He shrugged and turned away, his phone still on the table in front of us. "That big guy—former military?"

Scott. "You'd have to ask him."

Charles turned back to me. "More important matters." He nodded at his phone. "You might want to look at the pictures on there." He leaned forward and pressed his thumb to the screen and it flared to life. "You know a lot of NHs dismiss any human on their turf. A woman could walk naked down Bart Street and not so much as have a single person look at her, so long as she's human."

True. "Point being…?"

"Point being…" He smiled. "It's useful, how blind people are to me sometimes. Like when I was at your place the other day. I stopped by because I'd heard some…disturbing intel. About the wolf pack."

I clenched my jaw. "Stop beating around the bush."

He shrugged. "I've got a visit with the wolf Alpha in a bit. Have more info to share, but this…"

He shoved the phone across the table to me.

I caught it and scooped it up, staring hard at the images.

I sucked in a breath.

"She didn't see you?"

"Like I said. People are all but blind to me. My own camouflage." Charles smiled at me, but I barely registered it, too busy staring at the image of Shanelle Maguire striding down the walkway that led around the back of my condo.

Shanelle.

CHAPTER NINETEEN

I heard them coming.

I didn't hang up the phone.

Colleen continued to speak in low, soft tones.

She was no longer alone with Justin.

Damon had sent two of his trusted enforcers, but that wasn't enough for me. I put out calls to the Green Road. There would definitely be witches tied into this, I had no doubt, but some Houses were less susceptible to this level of evil. And even if whoever these sons-of-bitches were managed to get a warrior to go turncoat, it wouldn't be possible to find one who could hide such wrongness from her house. This kind of thing stained the soul in a way no witch could hide.

Colleen had given me two names, people to ask for and I'd been comfortable with them—I knew them both.

But some of the stirring in my gut settled as our conversation concluded. "He's waking up. The worst was the swelling on his brain. His energy was split between holding his protections up and healing him which is why he's still not responding much, but I can feel him stirring, deep inside. He'll be okay, I...I think." The words wobbled and she cleared her throat before she finished speaking. "No. I *know* he'll be okay."

"Yeah. He's too stubborn not to be." Relief made me queasy, but I didn't have time to indulge in it, any more than I had the ability to reach through the phone and drag Colleen in tight for a hug.

Showtime...

I could hear the rumble of the Challenger's motor as he pulled into the parking lot and cruised to a stop. I could see it, the gleaming black paint as Damon stopped next to my shiny new bullet of a car. Doyle's was next, and although I didn't see that one, I recognized the feel of him.

And Chang.

Scott wasn't there.

He'd left his other top men back at the Lair, on what I guess was his version of high level alert. Nobody out and nobody in who wasn't clan. If anybody had even one iota of doubt, the person went into lockdown—a.k.a. *a cell*—until Damon cleared them. He wasn't taking any chances with his people.

I supposed we could have done this back at the Lair, but it felt wrong. This was my case. I wanted to do it on my turf and that was something I guessed shifters, of all people, would understand. Shanelle clearly did—and she didn't like it. She gave me a pissy look as Chang none too subtly marched her inside. He didn't touch her, but the body language was there all the same.

She clutched her phone in one hand and was dressed in sparring clothes.

I must have interrupted training.

Her gaze cut to Damon's and I could all but see her fighting for control. He bared his teeth in a smile. "You got something to say?"

"No, Alpha."

I could practically hear her grinding her teeth as she spoke—it was an obvious lie and we all knew it.

"Why don't you go ahead and say it?" I said, settling more comfortably in my seat and stretching out my legs. I was going to take a page from Damon's book and try the lazy, I-don't-give-shit attitude. As I slumped, I reached for the gun I'd placed in my lap earlier.

She was standing in the perfect position for me to put a bullet in her leg, should I need to—and she wouldn't even know until it hit her, thanks to the barrier of the desk.

"Say what?" Her eyes spat fire.

"Whatever it is you're biting back." I shrugged and flicked Damon a look. "Maybe he can give you a pass on that. We're kind of on *my* turf right now." His lids flickered and I could all but here his mental snarl. *The things I do for you…*

But he gave a lazy shrug. "You got something to say, Maguire, here's the one chance you get—but I'd suggest you *be nice.*"

She opened her mouth, then shut. Finally, in a cool, modulated voice she said, "If your investigator needed information from me, I don't see why she couldn't have come to the Lair for it instead of having me dragged in here. *First* I'm ordered to return to the Lair—and not long after I did that, I'm ordered to leave—as is, no chance to change out of my gear or shower. If it was that urgent, it seems like it would have been easier for her to come to me. Or she could have simply stayed at the Lair. She had been there earlier."

"Well." I shrugged. "What can I say? When I'm working, I like my own space. You want to sit down?" I nodded at the seat across from my desk.

"I'll stand." She folded her hands at her back, military-style. "Shall we begin?"

"You familiar with Megan Banks?"

Her lids flickered. I saw the truth there. She canted her head to the side and lifted one shoulder in a slight shrug. "The name's familiar."

"She runs with the wolves."

"Ah…" Now she smiled. "Brunette. Tall. Ballsy."

"Not so much now. Now she's sort of dead."

Her pupils spiked. "And this has…what, exactly to do with me?"

"Know a guy named Saul Tremble?" I asked instead of answering.

She lowered her head, staring at the floor. "What's with all these questions, investigator?"

"Well, that's the answer right there. I investigate. That means I look for answers and usually it requires that I ask questions, poke around…"

She slid me a look from under the veil of her lashes. "So why poke at me?" She glanced around, but the look seemed to take in something beyond the room. "I've been here a few days. And these disappearances go back a lot farther, don't they? How do you expect *me* to know anything?"

Now the smile turned mocking. "It's possible I could have been of *some* use…I proved useful in positions I've held in the past, but it seems I've been relegated to nothing more than a sentry." Slowly, she lifted her head and studied me. There was a whole world of antipathy in that gaze. "Sentries can only do so much, investigator."

"Guess you expected to come back in high on the food chain." I shrugged. "Can't blame that on me."

I tapped my pencil on the table. She was uptight. I could see that, could even *feel* it, in the edged anxiety that all but colored the air around her, but she wasn't *afraid*.

All the others had been afraid.

"What do you know about the hospital?" I threw it out there on an impulse, hoping I'd see nothing but a blank expression and I could just write her off as a dead end.

Why in the hell do I even *bother* to hope?

Her physical reactions were perfect. Everything was on key and she managed a confused tone when she parroted back, "Hospital?"

But it was in her eyes.

They truly are the windows to the soul.

And I looked inside her eyes and saw the truth—she knew something.

I suspected my physical reactions were as good as hers—and that she saw something in my eyes, too.

Her body subtly tensed and for the first time, I sensed the first edge of fear. *Real* fear.

She shifted, as though bored and lifted a hand to brush at her hair. With the other, she held up her phone and glanced at it, a casual gesture. Even the way her thumb swiped over the screen was casual.

Alarm screamed down my spine.

"Stop!"

I lunged over the table, but it was too late.

Her phone clattered to the floor as Chang grabbed her and threw her to the ground, one hand shifting—for one split second, I stared, fascinated, at the dense, black fur. He moved and the angle of the light changed. I thought I saw spots dance across the darkness of that clawed monstrosity of a hand.

"Alpha?" Chang said as he muscled the struggling woman to the ground.

Damon looked from her to me.

He took a step closer and crouched down in front of Shanelle. He stared at her for a long moment and then jerked his head at Chang.

Chang stepped back, his hand already melting back into its human shape. He cracked his neck, shifted his shoulders and once more had his urban businessman façade back in place. Son of a *bitch*, what a façade it was, too.

Shanelle slowly pushed herself onto her hands and knees, blood trickling from wounds already closing. She stared at the floor. "This…" She swallowed. "I'm not involved in it, Damon."

I scooped up the phone, staring at the obviously encoded message. I had no idea what it was, no idea what she'd sent, or who she'd sent it to. Flipping it out, I showed it to her. "Who did you contact?"

She gave me a disgusted look but said nothing.

Chang held out a hand and turned the phone over. From the corner of my eye, I could see him tapping away furiously, brow furrowed. I moved closer. "What are you involved in?" I asked bluntly. "How do you know about the hospital? How is Megan involved? Saul?"

She went to look away.

A low growl made her freeze.

Slowly, she darted a look at the man still crouched in front of her. Whatever she saw on Damon's face wasn't pretty because she paled and then looked back at me. "I'm *not* involved with it. I've…" She stopped and swore, hot and furiously. "*Fuck*," she conclude.

She went to push back onto her heels, but shot a look at Damon and froze once more.

I turned her words over and over in my head, but I couldn't find the *lie* in them. I wanted to feel the lie, wanted to hear it. I couldn't see Damon's face without moving so I shot a look at Chang. He wasn't looking at the phone now—he was studying Shanelle and then, as if he'd sensed my gaze, he looked at me.

She wasn't lying.

"Damon."

He didn't move but I know he was waiting. "Can you let her up, please? I…" I swallowed. If I was wrong about her, then who the hell *was* involved? "I've got more questions."

Hell, I had more blanks in my theory now than ever before.

Damon rose slowly. "Get up, Maguire. And you better start talking. Those questions Kit has? You're going to answer." He didn't give her an *or else*.

As she came to her feet, I knew it wasn't necessary. She'd already heard it.

She wiped at the blood still gleaming on her neck and then looked around. I was surprised when she moved to the chair, dropping down on it like her weight had become too much to bear. "I'm not involved," she said again. Then her shoulders rose and fell on a sigh. "But...yes, I'm aware of it."

She flicked her blue eyes my way. "I knew Saul Tremble was one of the men grabbing people for them. I did *not* know Megan was involved..." She paused and tilted her head to the side. "She was involved, wasn't she?"

"You tell me."

"If I had to hazard a guess, then yeah. She was involved. She wasn't the first high-level they dragged into this, but she sure as hell had the highest rank. Second in command...shit." Shanelle dragged her hands down her face.

"Son of a bitch," I whispered. "You've been *investigating*."

When she looked back at me, her gaze was direct, and for once, void of most of the apathy she'd directed my way once she figured out who stood between her and Damon.

"I'm here on business for the Assembly," she said in a neutral voice. "That's public knowledge."

"So did *they* hire you or is that just a cover?"

"I have a real, legit job to accomplish for the Claw," she said, lifting one shoulder. She tossed a look at Chang. "You're not going to break the encryption on it."

He gave her a cool look and went back to whatever techno-magic he was trying to work on the phone. I love technology, but I don't understand it. He could play with the phone all he wanted.

"You need to worry about yourself, not your phone," I advised. Then I paused, a thought occurring to me. "Unless of course you sent some secret message telling the people you're working with to blow up my office."

"Damn." She curled her lip. "I knew I'd forgotten something."

That bitchy reply made some of the muscles in my neck loosen. Grabbing the file that held the pictures I'd had printed from Charles' phone, I tossed it across the desk and watched as the images spilled out. "Since you aren't going to confirm whether or not you're investigating, then maybe you can explain this."

"They look like pictures."

A few feet away, Damon shifted his stance and that subtle movement drew her gaze his way. It was just for a split second, but I saw her swallow, watched the way her hands tightened in her lap.

"Why were you at my place?"

She drew in a breath. Her gaze darted once more to Damon and then back to me. "That's a question I think I could probably answer, but if I do, I suspect I'm dead in seconds."

"If you—" An ugly snarl escaped Doyle, who'd been silent the entire time.

Damon caught the younger man's arm. "You aren't the kind of person to come at somebody's back, Shanelle," he said, his voice pulsating with rage. "And you knew Kit wasn't there. She was with me that night. It only stands to reason you were looking for something. What was it?"

Shanelle flexed her hands wide.

She opened her mouth, but whatever she was going to say was interrupted by a pretty little chime that came from the phone in Chang's hand. He eyed it and then looked at Shanelle. "I believe you have a message, Shanelle."

She slicked her hands down her pants and I could see the damp trails left by her palms.

As Chang came toward her, she went rigid and I wasn't sure who she feared more—Chang or Damon.

She shot it a look.

"What does it say?" he asked gently.

"I don't know. The code…" She stopped.

"Take the phone."

Shanelle's gaze bounced off him, then Damon before finally landing on me. I tried to read the expression in her eyes, but I couldn't. Slowly, she reached out a hand and brushed her thumb down it.

Another weird little tone came from the phone. *"Identification."*

In response to the automated request, Shanelle said, "Agent Maguire." She then rambled off a series of number and there was a pregnant pause.

Agent?

Her gaze ran over the message.

I wonder if she had time to read it before Chang took it away.

"Clever," he murmured. "Voice ID and the code are all that's needed?"

"No. Those are just two of the layers." She shrugged and looked away. "If you want to know more about the toys, you'd have to ask the higher-ups."

I'd love to.

"I'd rather talk about why you were at my house."

Her mouth went tight and then she gave a short nod. "You were on the short list. We knew there was somebody who had considerable trust who was covering up some of the disappearances, as well as setting up loners and other misfits who wouldn't be missed if they were just gone one day." Her throat worked as she swallowed and I could see her body tensing. It wasn't me she was afraid of. "Your name came up on the shortlist. I was there looking to see if I could find anything to tie you into Blackstone."

I blinked. "Blackstone...?"

"The hospital."

"You thought *Kit* was responsible?" Doyle demanded, striding up from his position by the door to glare at her.

She met his gaze stonily. "I had a job to do."

"She saved your ass, you stupid—"

"Doyle," I said. I was pleased at how calm my voice sounded. "She did the same sort of thing I would have done."

He looked like he was biting back a slew of words—all of them ugly—and then he turned away, staring hard at me. "You got her out of there. I don't know what exactly is going on, but I heard some of the rumors, heard the rumblings. You sprang her from some place and she *still* thinks you could have done it?"

"Doyle, think." I had to admire her persistence in seeing it through. "I was asked to help by my best friend. For the sake of argument, let's say she was *right*—that I was involved. Would I really risk having anybody look too closely at me by acting out of character?" I hitched up a shoulder. "Justin needed my help. Of course I was going to give it."

It was a nasty thing, though, knowing some people thought I could be doing this. "For the record, I am *not* involved," I said clearly. I stared at her hard as I spoke.

She lifted a brow.

I couldn't force her to believe me.

"You weren't our first option, but you were…available," she said after a moment. "I was working to clear who I could so I could move on to the next. That was my job."

"Was Megan on the list?"

"No." Shanelle cleared her throat, looking frustrated and embarrassed. "We'd considered her and then set the idea aside. Whoever was doing this went after those with weaknesses to exploit. Megan has no family. Her loyalties are to the MacDonald and the pack—or we thought they were."

Oh, Megan had a weakness. I just didn't know what. Or *who*. I thought about what she had said, right before she'd shredded her own heart on the silver in my blade. *They* would leave *them* alone. Swearing, I slammed my fist down on my desk and stared at nothing. Who were *they*—

Chang made a disgusted noise under his breath and tossed the phone down. It clattered on the scuffed table that sat under the window as he tucked his hands into his trouser pockets. I found myself staring at him, at the clean lines of his profile.

Chang…

Chang was to Damon what Megan was—or *had* been—to Dair.

Chang's loyalties lay to the clan, although he'd walk away from the clan in a moment if Damon asked him, I suspected. But there was another—or well, a *collection* of others.

The kids.

As if he'd felt the intensity of my stare, Chang turned his head and met my eyes. I was right. I knew it. "Megan…" I pushed away from the table and turned to look at Damon. "I saw her the other day. I was grabbing groceries and she showed up. There was a kid—a little girl. Megan said she was there to get a cub and it was that girl."

"Yeah?" He shrugged. "Megan more or less looked after the young in the pack. It was…"

His words trailed away as he made the same connection. "Kids." Woodenly, I turned away. "If you're being straight with me, then I think that's how they got to Megan. They promised they'd leave any stray kids alone, as long as they had adults."

"It stands to reason." She inclined her head. "Now that I have a name, I can change the angle of the investigation, dig deeper. But if Megan is dead and Saul is in custody, then you have the main problems." A ghost of a smile curved her lips. "The vampires already found their rat."

I thought of the woman I'd seen being tortured.

Estella.

"There could be more," I said.

"Could. And there likely are a few lackeys I'll dig up." She glanced at Damon and I heard the unspoken *if I'm alive*. "But it will take them time to replace the people they've lost. They must be very careful."

"Yeah. I imagine it takes work to find somebody who'd turn against their own." I sucked in a breath, trying to stop the anger that tore gouges through my self-control. "Offer up strays for slaughter or we'll take your kiddies. Son of a bitch."

The heat of rage built so hot and fast, I was amazed my skin didn't show burns from it. Moving away from the near suffocating rage that encompassed them, I took up position behind my desk.

I didn't sit.

I couldn't.

"Would she have done it?" I asked quietly.

"Yes." Chang slid me a look, eyes flat. "For the children, she would have."

• • •
259

I studied him for a lingering moment.

He wouldn't have.

He'd have found another way.

Chang inclined his head and I knew yet again he'd figured out just what I was thinking.

"I'll tell Dair," Damon said, his voice tight. "It...it won't help much, but at least he won't have to think she betrayed them all for nothing."

Focusing on Shanelle, I asked, "Who else was on the list?"

I wanted their names, because my mission was now to hunt them down and make them all pay—for the kids, because I had no doubt they'd grabbed some along the way—for the people we hadn't been able to save, and even for Megan. She'd made an awful choice, but in some way, I understood.

For the children, she would have.

Shanelle hadn't answered and I let some of my anger bleed into my voice. "Names." Then I frowned. "And you know what? I want to know who in the *fuck* you're working for and how *you* got involved in this."

The low, muffled purr of an engine filled the silence that stretched out while Shanelle and I engaged in a staring contest. I ignored it until it continued to grow closer and closer—

"Kit. You have somebody...dude, that's Amund," Doyle muttered.

I felt him now, that familiar presence that whispered *vampire*. And...no. I thought I'd felt something else, but with the sucker-punch of power that came from an undead more than a thousand years old, I don't think it would be *possible*.

"Another car," Chang said quietly.

Shanelle sat quietly in the chair now, her face blank, void of all emotion.

"What's going on?" I asked her softly as I heard yet a third, then fourth car pull into my parking lot.

When she didn't answer, I strode to the door. "Back up. I need to activate my wards—"

"You're not in danger...Kit." It was the first time she'd said my name and I shot her a look over my shoulder to see she hadn't so much as changed position.

"But if you want your questions answered, you should speak to them."

A series of car doors opening, then shutting filled the silence.

I rested my hand on the locks. They were the keys to the wards Justin had designed for me and I put a whole hell of a lot of faith in them. Blowing out a breath, I looked at Damon. He stood with his feet spread wide, thumbs hooked in the front pockets of his jeans.

Doyle was pacing, long, restless strides.

Chang had his head cocked, a smile on his lips that spoke of some vague entertainment.

Slowly, I let my hand fall from the locks. As I sat down, I laid my Glock on the table and cracked my neck.

There was a polite knock. People tended to knock on my door rather than just come in, something I'd never quite understood. Damon nodded to Doyle and the younger shifter opened the door, quietly stepping to the side so that the first thing Amund saw was me—holding a gun leveled on the doorway.

"Really, Ms. Colbana. That's not necessary." A smile ghosted around his lips as he stepped inside.

"So…he's your boss?" Clenching my jaw, I struggled not to snarl as I shifted my gaze back to the vampire. "That mess at the party—were you behind it?"

"Of course not." He flicked a look around. "Such a spare place. Oh, and I'm not her boss. I just…worked to make certain things went more smoothly once it was clear we needed eyes on the ground."

As he came near, Shanelle rose from the chair.

He took it without speaking and she took up position at his back. Bodyguard style. Not that he needed one.

"Certain…members of the Assembly have been aware of Blackstone for some time," he said, without preamble. "We didn't connect the disappearances to the hospital until a witch out of Blue Sky had a vision." His mouth twisted in frown. "It was…brutal."

"Yeah, people being grabbed by their own, kidnapped, tortured, that's pretty brutal," I muttered.

"No," he said, shaking his head. "The vision. The witch…it killed her. Or I should say the *visions*. After the first one, she kept returning, looking for more intel."

The modern word sounded oddly out of place, in his strangely formal voice. He paused, clearly thinking on something that disturbed him. "She stumbled into the mind of somebody being tortured and the shock of it…" He looked away. "It's believed the shock killed her. She slid into a coma and died three hours later. But she was the one to link these disappearances to the hospital. Since then, we've used the tools at our disposal to find those who've been helping."

He smiled then. "Shanelle was one tool. Justin Greaves…yourself, you were another."

Shanelle stiffened.

So did I.

"Justin didn't get his information from the Assembly," I said, rising from behind my desk.

"No." Amund made a pretense of studying his nails. "I believe he got that information from a man you both know—Nova." He slanted a cunning smile at me. "Nova is very receptive to tactile triggers. It simply took the right…trigger."

"You manipulative son of a bitch."

He waved a dismissive hand. "Live as long as I have, watch what I have watched. Know that the people who trust you to keep them alive are being slaughtered—then complain to me about the methods I use to protect my House— and not just *my* House, but all those who'd suffer under the hands of those behind this…*hospital*."

His voice grew colder and harder and the shadows around the room deepened, responding to his rage.

"Assemblyman Amund," Damon said, his voice a low pulse.

Amund continued to stare at me for a long, pregnant moment. I felt each beat of my heart and was keenly aware of the pulse of my blood as it pumped through my veins. His lids drooped lower and then he closed his eyes.

The moment shattered and Damon moved, not being at all subtle as he placed his body between me and the vampire.

Amund's lids lifted and he focused on Damon with a smile. "Don't start showing me your claws, Alpha Lee. I'm not threatening her." He gave me a polite smile. "You've questions. Ask."

I didn't ask how he knew. It seemed obvious enough that I *would* have questions. "I want to know how deep this goes. I want to know who is suspected to be involved. I want to know how many people have disappeared, where they disappeared from and when. I want names. I want dates."

Amund's eyes widened as I continued to tell him what I wanted. I didn't include what seemed obvious to me—the heads of those involved on a silver platter.

When I finally wound down, Amund was eying me the way he might study a particularly confusing puzzle. "Indeed," he murmured.

I shrugged. "You asked me what I wanted. I told you. Whether you give me the information or not, I don't care, because I'll find it." And I'd start collecting heads on my own.

"Hmmm." He tapped a finger to his lips.

"Who all knows about this?" I asked. "Is there any suggestion anybody on the Assembly is involved? Is there—"

"Enough." He lifted a hand as he rose and moved to the door.

What the *hell?* Was he really leaving without answering a damn question? Not even *one?*

But all he did was open the door and wait.

A few moments later a figure appeared in front of him, a man, clad in a coat that seemed rather extreme for the brisk November air. He wore a hat pulled down low on his face, paired with large, dark glasses, as if to block the sun, but he wasn't a vampire.

He was just a man.

"You wished to meet Ms. Maguire's boss," Amund said as he shut the door behind the man in front of him.

The man lifted his head and looked around.

"You sent Maguire here." I studied him as he studied my office. He looked familiar, but I couldn't figure out why. Of course, with the hat, the giant glasses, I could only see half of his face.

"In a fashion." He smiled and it was the perfect smile, warm and open and honest—the kind that said *trust me*.

I hated that kind of smile.

His voice was just the same, warm and open and honest—the kind that invited you to pull up a seat and listen to anything and everything this man had to say, even if he was just telling you the story of *The Little Engine that Could*.

I *definitely* didn't trust that kind of voice.

When he glanced at Shanelle, she bowed her head in deference.

"Shanelle was sent here with my approval," the man said, reaching up to remove his hat, a lovely grey fedora. I watched as he stroked it with his hands. Perfect hands, even. Long-fingered, blunt nails—neatly cut, but not manicured.

Everything about him seemed just perfect,

"We needed answers, Ms. Colbana. You see…Blackstone isn't just looking to grab a few stray non-humans from the street and experiment on them for kicks. Their purpose goes deeper, but until recently, they'd convinced nearly everybody— Banner, their backers, even much of their staff that they were simply there to help those who *wished* for some other alternative."

"Alternative to *what?*" I tried not to spit the words out as I stared at the top of his bowed head. "*Living?* A vampire is a vampire—a wolf is a wolf. That can't be undone."

"No." He reached for his sunglasses now and looked up.

I sucked in a breath. For one split second, I saw it—a flash of silver, the sort of color that no mortal eyes could ever duplicate and then his gaze was human. Eyes a lovely shade of amber, but just…human.

I'd seen it, though.

"You're not human," I said quietly.

"No." He smiled, a politician's perfect, self-deprecating smile. "I'm not. And that's a closely-guarded secret. I'm sure you can understand why. Just as I'm sure you can understand my…desire…to resolve this matter."

He watched me closely, as if waiting for something.

I nodded, unable to do anything else.

"Very good." White teeth flashed in a brilliant smile and he smoothed a hand down the elegant, raw silk of his red necktie. "Very few know the truth and we must keep it that way, which is why I'm here, and why Shanelle was answerable only to her contact within the Assembly—and me. I hope all of you will keep this to yourself." Then he looked around and blew out a breath. "Ms. Colbana, you could do with some more chairs in your office.

"Now," he said. "We should talk, because while I understand we caught a few of the key players down here, this is far from done."

"No," I said faintly. "We're not done."

He nodded, and I gaped as the President of the United States moved across my office, paused in front of my battered old couch and then, with a satisfied smile, sat down.

ABOUT

J.C. Daniels is the alter-ego of author Shiloh Walker. She has been writing since she was a kid. She fell in love with vampires with the book *Bunnicula* and has worked her way up to the more…ah…serious works of fiction. She loves reading and writing anything paranormal, anything fantasy, and nearly every kind of romance.

Once upon a time, she worked as a nurse, but now she writes full time and lives with her family in the Midwest. She writes romantic suspense and contemporary romance, and urban fantasy under her penname, J.C. Daniels. You can find her at Twitter or Facebook and read more about her work at her website. Sign up for her newsletter and have a chance to win a monthly giveaway.

Also, look for J.C.'s next book, FINAL PROTOCOL, a science-fiction romance, coming in summer 2015.

Curious about her works as Shiloh? Read on for look at her Grimm's Circle series, urban fantasy romance, fairy tales, guardian angels…what more could you want?

Greta didn't get her happy ending her first time around. And now that she's a Grimm—a special kind of guardian angel and official ass-kicker in the paranormal world—romance is hard to find. Besides, there's only ever been one man who made her heart race, and the fact that he did scared her right out of his arms. Now Rip is back. And just in time too, because Greta needs his help.

On a mission he knows is going to test all of his strengths and skills, the last person Rip expected to see is the one woman who broke his heart. Working together seems to be their only hope. But when faced with a danger neither of them anticipated, the question is, how will they face the danger to their hearts—assuming they survive, of course.

Candy Houses

What's more believable? That Gretel was an unhappy, orphaned girl, or that Hansel and Gretel skipped merrily through the woods, leaving a trail of breadcrumbs as they walked in hopes that it would lead them back home?

Come on. Even back then children weren't idiots. Throwing bread on the ground usually results in something trying to eat the bread.

Hans might have been stupid enough to try a trick like that, but I certainly wasn't. Besides, if my parents had been deliberately trying to get rid of me, there's no way I would have kept trying to find my way back.

The Brothers Grimm never asked me, though. It was the popular version that got recorded for the ages, not the real one.

The real one involved things even uglier than a woman sending her children off to starve in the woods. I guess the real one had a happy enough ending, though, now that I think about it. Hans died, my stepmother left me alone, and I didn't have to live my life in fear.

Yes, Hans died. That's probably what led to the story ending up in a Grimm fairy tale.

It wasn't long after his death that my stepmother went a teensy bit crazy. Okay. A lot crazy. People would hear her rambling like the madwoman she was. Back then, people didn't really get insanity, if you know what I mean. They thought she was possessed, or that she was a witch, communing with the devil and demons and that was what led to her ruin.

Maybe that's where the idea of a witch came from. It certainly didn't have anything to do with Mary.

Mary had been…different.

She saved me. When she took me in, bought my "services" from my stepmother for a few pieces of silver, she saved my life.

But it came with a price. Nothing is free in this world. Not now. Not then.

* * *

Not ever, I'd guess.

So you want to know the price? Well, think of Buffy. Yes, as in Buffy the Vampire Slayer. Think of her, more or less. I say more or less because I'm both more and less. Less because I don't come with the super strength. I'm a little stronger than the typical person, but I can't send a man flying through the air when I punch him.

That's okay, because I can knock a man to the ground and that's perfectly sufficient. I also don't come with visions or prophecies. Much to my disgust, there's probably no Angel or Spike in my future, either. I'm not petite. I'm not blonde. I'm not beautiful.

I'm just me.

So definitely less on some front.

But more on others…because…well, there's more. Nobody looking at me would ever realize just how much lies below the surface. They'd never believe the things I've seen, the things I've done. The lives I've taken. The lives I've saved.

I don't have super strength, but—well… I guess you could say, I'm hard to kill. And man, oh man, have people tried.

Old age won't kill me, because I don't age.

Injuries won't do it, because my body has been blessed with the ability to heal from even the most mortal of wounds, a bit like the vamps from Buffy in that aspect. If you cut out my heart or take off my head, I'll die. Maybe drop me inside a vat of acid, but that sounds really painful.

Kind of gross too. Actually, it all sounds kind of gross. It's even worse in reality. I've had to cut out hearts, and I've had to take heads. Never had to resort to acid…

Find out more about the Grimm by checking out Candy Houses in ebook or The First Book of Grimm in print, written by J.C. Daniels' alter-ego…Shiloh Walker. Information available at www.shilohwalker.com

HUNT ME

Published by Shiloh Walker

Editorial Work by d.y.m.k. productions

& Sara Reinke

HUNT ME

Enjoy this free short story, written by J.C. Daniel's other half...
Shiloh Walker

CHAPTER TWO

"Hello, gorgeous."

The low, rich purr of her voice was enough to have Drew Quentin shifting in the miserable, busted chair. He also had to fight the urge to smile as he reminded himself he'd decided to ends things with Dakota Coulter.

He wanted her, he was halfway in love with her…and she refused to so much as give him her damn phone number.

He could have handled that.

But the cop in him was a little bit disturbed by the fact that Dakota Coulter had a past that was just a little *too* mysterious. Oh, her background check held up—too well, actually. Something about her had his instincts quivering.

She wouldn't open up for him.

"Drew?"

He closed his eyes. "I'm here, Dakota."

"Having a rough night, sugar?"

The compassion in her voice all but gutted him. *Damn it.* This would be so much easier if she didn't care—so much easier if he wasn't in love with her.

"Yeah, you could say that." He rubbed his temple. He shouldn't have answered the damn phone. But shit, it wasn't like he could avoid this forever. He looked up and saw Nicole staring at him. Nicole Halloway, the local DA with the pretty blue eyes, sweet smile and dynamite body.

She was there, she was steady. She was the reason he needed to break things off with Dakota. He liked Nic. Cared for her—a lot. There was an attraction there, too, one that could maybe become more. But not if he was obsessed with a woman who wouldn't ever hang around for longer than a night or two.

"I guess you're not up for meeting me after work, huh?" Dakota sighed. "That's cool, sugar. I understand. I'll look you up—"

"No." He continued to star at Nic. He had to get this done. "We can meet. I…I've been needing to talk to you anyway, Dakota."

Now Nic's brows arched up over big blue eyes. So far their 'dates' hadn't been

● ● ●

much more than a cup of coffee, a quick lunch. She knew he'd been seeing another woman, knew he wasn't going to get serious until he'd been able to break things off. It was time he did that.

Even if it did feel a little like he was ripping out his own kidney with his teeth. Or even his heart.

Sighing, Dakota ended the call.

Something in Drew's voice had her heart aching.

"We need to talk, huh, lover? Yeah. I've heard that line before." Then she tipped her head back, staring up at the nighttime sky. Granted, she hadn't heard it much in recent years. Not since she'd slid into a crazy little world where vampires, werewolves and other things went bump in the night. Sometime back in the 70's, she thought.

Yeah. She smiled absently, some echo of fondness trying to lift the melancholy settling over her heart. But it wouldn't budge. She'd been kind of happy about coming to Asheville. Now? Not so much.

She was a Hunter without a territory or Master. Her random circuit had her rambling all over the east coast. She often ended up in this area, and she'd been just fine with that. Because this area held a lot of appeal for her, namely in the fine form of one Asheville city detective…Andrew Michael Quentin…Drew.

Drew—the cop who was getting ready to dump her.

She glanced down at her clothes, remembered she'd planned to change before she saw him. "Screw changing."

She was going shopping.

If he was going to dump her, she was going to show him in vivid, glorious detail what he was missing.

Maybe it would make her feel better.

Although she wasn't particularly counting on it.

The splash of murderous red on her nails didn't do much to lift her spirits, but

Dakota was pleased with how she looked, at least. The dress might have been a bit overdone, but red looked good on her. It clung to her curves, stopped just a bit short of her knees. And she could still move.

She'd passed on the really cute Jimmy Choos with the ankle straps, settling on a simpler pair of heels. She could run barefoot without falling. Even though falling wasn't likely, running flat out in heels wasn't as easy as people might make it seem in books or movies.

On the job, Dakota was practical, and even if she was taking some time to get dumped, she was still working. The only time she wasn't working was when she crashed in her cabin up in Maine or when she got pulled into Excelsior for one thing or another.

The life of a Hunter.

Sighing, she made one last study of her reflection, pulling the brush through her dark brown hair. It curled around her mostly naked shoulders, the ends coming down to drape around her breasts. She looked good. She was honest enough to admit that. She looked good…like a woman who wanted a man to *know* it, too.

"Damn it." She swallowed and turned away from her reflection, determined not to spend the next hour thinking about this. Next hour, minimum, because even though she wasn't meeting Drew until midnight, she'd be circling around the city. Circling around, watching things. Making sure she wasn't being watched. There were paranormal creatures aplenty here.

Every damn time she came through, she had to settle trouble. None of it was *bad*. If it had been *bad* in the *major* category, a bigger bad-ass would be here.

Dakota had yet to grow into full bad-ass potential.

But she was good enough to play cop and if things got bad, call in the big guns. Part of playing cop meant being careful.

The life of a Hunter.

A damn lonely life.

"So. You're breaking things off." Nic stared at him with a thoughtful frown.

"Look, you know, you don't have to do this. I…I can tell you've got feelings for her. And it's not like we're ready to move in together or anything. All we've got so far is a couple of casual dates and…"

He caught her around the back of the neck and pulled her close. When this woman started babbling, as adorable as it was, this was the only way to stem the flow of words. She gasped against his mouth and then sighed, moving closer. Her lips parted for him and she slid her hands inside his coat.

"Hmmm." She hummed under her breath as he lifted his head. "What was that for?"

"To make you be quiet a minute." Pressing his brow to hers, he stroked his thumb across her damp lower lip. "I know I don't have to do this. But things with me and her aren't ever going to change, and I don't like where they are. I *like* where things are with us. We *can't* change while she's in the picture. Those casual dates won't go any further until things change, right? So we change them."

I *change them*, he thought.

She wrinkled her nose at him. "That shouldn't sound so sweet. But it does." Nic rested her head against his chest. "Call me when you wake up?"

"Yeah." He stroked his fingers through her hair, the silken blonde strands glinting in the harsh, fluorescent lighting. "You want me to follow you home?"

"No. I'm good. I've got paperwork to finish up. I'll have somebody walk me out." She stroked a hand down his cheek. "You need to shave, baby."

Then she pecked him on the lips and turned around, her heels clicking on the floor. Just before she disappeared around the hall, her phone rang. He could hear her voice drifting down the hall. When she suddenly snapped, "Son of a *bitch*!" it made him grin.

He was still shaking as his head as he turned to grab his stuff. But the grin had faded by the time he hit the door. He had thirty minutes.

Thirty minutes to figure out how in the hell to tell Dakota Coulter good-bye.

How did he tell this woman he loved that he was leaving her because she wouldn't hang around for longer than a day? Hell, he hadn't even told her *loved* her.

If she asked why he was ending it, did he tell her he didn't entirely trust her?

● ● ●

274

And that he'd rather have the sweeter, quieter woman who was *there*…even if he didn't want her *quite* as much as he wanted Dakota?

Rage vibrated inside her. She hid in the darkness, clinging to the shadows she'd just learned to call, because she had to get control. Yeah. Dakota was being dumped. For another woman. She could smell the other woman, even above the smoke, the alcohol, the food…and that lovely, male scent that was uniquely Drew's.

Now it was for another woman to enjoy.

Mine.

Everything inside her screamed it. But she pushed it aside. Yeah, she had feelings for the guy. She'd had them for a while, but Drew was human.

Dakota was a vampire. Her heart might still very well be human, but she'd stopped being human forty years ago. Tears pricked her eyes. She blinked them away. Nothing like leaking blood-tinged tears to really freak him out. She waited until she knew her eyes would be normal. Even though she knew they hadn't slid from their sheaths, she checked her fangs with her tongue.

He didn't know. Oh, he knew she had secrets. She could see it in his eyes. She had no doubt that was part of the problem between them. But what could she say? *Honey, I'm a vampire. I'll be around as often as I can, but…*

He was a mortal who wouldn't even believe in her world. She'd always known it would have to end. Now it was time. As she slid from the booth, she released the shadows. She saw the way he stiffened when he saw her, caught off guard. She allowed herself a small, pleased smile. She'd seen him looking for her, and he was a cop—he'd have looked *well*.

But nobody could hide like a vampire.

She came to a stop in front of him, smiled at him lazily, careful to keep her mouth closed. Now that she was closer, she could smell the other woman more clearly and she wasn't going to risk losing that oh-so-precious control.

"Hey there." He bent down to kiss her, not that he had to bend much with the four-inch heels she wore.

● ● ●

Dakota turned her head to the side so that his lips brushed against her cheek. Her heart shuddered in her chest and she eased backward, avoiding his gaze as she headed toward the bar. "I need a drink," she said over her shoulder. Not that she expected it would do her much good, except maybe the familiarity of it. She'd have to down a vat of it before she could really get tanked.

She slid onto the stool and called out to the bartender. "Hendrix and tonic with a cucumber slice! Make it a double."

"Sure thing, beautiful." His smile flashed white in his dark face. White…with rather sharp teeth. She rolled her eyes. Bo was a shifter. It was one of the reasons she liked this pub. He was a decent sort. If she had to slip out sudden-like, he'd help cover her retreat. As he brought the drink down to her, he focused on her face, his nostrils flaring a bit.

"You're unhappy, Hunter." he said, his voice too low for Drew to hear. That didn't keep him from trying. He slid onto the stool next to her, gaze narrowed on Bo. The shifter ignored him, stroking a finger down Dakota's cheek. "I don't like to see a pretty Hunter unhappy."

"Can't be helped." She smiled brightly. Then she reached out and patted his hand. In a voice just as low as his, she said, "Now stop trying to piss him off. This is going to be hard enough, 'kay?"

Bo stared at her, then, with a sigh, he walked off. She took a sip of her drink. Distracted, she glanced around and saw a business card somebody had left on the bar. It had a phone number on it. For some reason, it made her even sadder to see it. Somebody else had struck out tonight.

Taking the business card, she absently started to fold it up, turning it into a neat triangle. She kept fiddling with it until Bo slid a Guinness in front of Drew.

Dropping the business card, she took a healthy drink from her glass and then turned, crossing her legs as she studied Drew's face. His gaze dropped, quick as a wish, to her legs and then shot right back up to her face. Oh, yes. It was over.

He reached for the business card, unfolding and it smoothing out the creases. "You did that the first time I gave you my number."

"Habit. You know that by now." She shoved her hair back, staring at the familiar lines of his face, memorizing them. Over, it really was over. Damn it, she had to get out of here before she started to cry. "Look, let's just get it over with, baby. I'd rather not listen to whatever pretty speech you put together."

The thick fringe of his lashes drooped over his eyes. "What exactly do you do for a living, Dakota, read minds?" he asked, his voice conversational. Or it would have been, if he hadn't been raising it to be heard over the noise in the bar. One hand, long-fingered and callused in just the right way, closed around his glass.

Dakota sighed. It wasn't the first time he'd asked, although she knew he wasn't really asking, this time. "Baby, you know what I do for a living. Security consulting. We've had this discussion before."

"Yeah. And I sell bridges in Arizona." He took a deep drink from his Guinness. "Do I even need to spell this out or did you already piece it together?"

"Why don't you just save me the details, Drew?" She tossed back the rest of the drink and slid off her stool, ignoring the concern in his eyes. "I hope she makes you happy, cop."

Without saying another word, she headed off toward the back of the bar. She heard him behind her. Almost started to turn—she wouldn't mind one last kiss. Something to give him to remember her by. But something prickled along her spine.

There was a whisper of warning, those instincts that made her what she was. Part of those secrets she'd kept hidden from Drew. As much as she'd love to give Drew that farewell kiss, she knew she couldn't. Once more, duty called. She was needed.

She shot Bo a look. He wasn't a Hunter, but sometimes she suspected that was because he'd chosen not to be.

Their gazes met. With a subtle jerk of his head, he nodded to the backroom. He'd cover her, let her leave in secrecy, in silence.

As she slid away from Drew, he played interception.

One last time. Because she wouldn't be seeing Drew again.

It all but ripped her heart out to think about it.

"What the…?"

Okay, he'd come here to break things off, but he'd wanted to say good-bye, damn it. Was there a fucking reason he couldn't say good-bye?

Oh, hell, no. He was going to at least do that. She might not be what he needed—even if she *was* what he wanted, but he would have good-bye.

"Hey there, buddy…"

The bartender, moving with an eerie silence that was almost as disturbing as Dakota's, stood between them. Drew tensed, his eyes narrowed. "Step back."

"Can't do that, cop." Then he smiled, quick and easy. "Not unless you got a good reason for tearing off into the backroom of my business. You give me a reason, then sure, I'm happy to let you. I'm a law-abiding citizen, you know."

"How about you just let my girlfriend go back there and she's upset?"

The black man reached up, scraped his nails down his cheek in a thoughtful, lazy manner. "Well, you see, the problem there is this…she isn't your girlfriend. Not any more at least. You just broke things up. Got another lady waiting for you, too."

"That's none of your business, is it?" *And how the hell did you know that?*

"Your girlfriend? You?" The man shook his head. "Not a bit. But Dakota, well, she's a friend of mine. She walked away. That means she's done. Let her go. Go on now, man. You got your own path to follow, don't you? Doesn't seem to include her anymore."

His golden eyes glimmered in the dim light and for a minute, Drew would have sworn they glowed. The man's face seemed something…other. But then the moment passed and the bartender smiled. "You gotta understand, man. I just don't like the idea of a cop roaming around my place without a reason, but even less…I don't want you upsetting her any more than she already is."

"That's why I'd like to *talk* to her."

"Talking to her after you ditched her for another woman isn't going to make her feel better." Now he stared at Drew as though he was the stupidest man on God's green earth.

It didn't help that maybe Drew even felt that way.

It also didn't help that Drew had the weirdest feeling he was making a huge mistake, walking away from Dakota. But she wasn't what he needed…

• • •

Isn't she…?

No. What he needed was the pretty, petite blonde who didn't have a thousand secrets, who answered his phone calls, and who would *be* there. He didn't want to put a ball and chain on any woman, but he'd sure as hell like to have a woman in his life who was around more often an once a month, once every two months…less.

Sighing, he shifted his gaze past the other man, staring at the closed door that separated him from Dakota. "You need to go check on her then. Make sure she's okay…hell. I don't know. I just…"

"I've always been there when she needed me. Today's no different."

As the cop finally left, Bo said, "Marin."

His second, a small, sleek woman, appeared at his side. The top of her head barely reached the middle of his chest. She was one of the meanest bitches he'd ever met in his life—he absolutely adored her.

"Yeah?"

"Watch the bar for me. I think I'm needed somewhere."

She sighed and pushed her pink-streaked hair back from her face. "Dude, you keep insisting you're no Hunter."

Bo smiled. "I'm not…I'm just worried about Dakota. She's a friend. If she wasn't, I wouldn't worry unless it was going to present a problem for us."

His small pack was just now getting established here. He wouldn't risk it.

But he wouldn't be much of a friend if he ignored that tingle on his spine, either. Dakota had problems coming her way. He didn't know what they were, but if it was something she could handle, he wouldn't be feeling this way.

"I'll be back."

As he slipped through the back door, Marin made a face at him.

CHAPTER TWO

Somebody was going to die. Dakota tasted it, felt it. Could feel it clogging her throat and she wanted to kick her own ass. It didn't matter that she hadn't felt anything earlier. It didn't matter that she hadn't realized anything bad was going down. What mattered was that she hadn't been doing her job. She had been with Drew.

Now somebody was going to die. She knew she wouldn't get there in time to stop it. She could feel the blood. Taste it. It hung in the air like a cloud.

Idiot. Stupid, selfish idiot. What had she been thinking?

It was thicker now, the stink of death, thicker as she drew closer to the building, and when she started up the fire escape, it was almost enough to choke her. She heard them. Voices, whispering. A grunt. A soft, broken moan. The air is thick with the stink of violent, angry lust.

Calling on the shadows, she wrapped herself in them, hiding. Distantly, she was aware of the fading, faltering pulse. The woman, she was dying. *I'm sorry...*

The window was open. Dakota hesitated. *How do I get in?*

How had feral vamps gotten in? Had the woman invited them? There was some truth to the rumor vampires could only go where they were invited—a person set up a home, set down roots, it gave him a bit of protection. Their protection started to fade, though, when the owner died. This owner wasn't gone—yet.

Dakota wasn't going to wait until it was too late. Focusing her mind, she reached out. As she did it, she prayed. As the ferals were too far into the blood lust, they wouldn't be aware of anything else. That was bad for the woman, the better for Dakota. She was clinging to life, but only barely.

Hey, sweetheart. Invite me in. I'll get rid of them.

She felt a flicker of surprise from the woman—followed by desperation, determination. This woman wanted to live. Even though her body strength was waning with every drop of blood loss, clung to life. *Help me. Help us...*

Us...? Dakota frowned. Then she took a deep breath, trying to filter out the sense of blood. Death, that faint sense of food and something else... another scent, one she knew, hauntingly familiar and tugged at her senses.

And something—stronger, so strong, it threatened to overpower everything else.

Death. Not a woman about to die, the people who had already died.

She didn't need to wait for this woman to invite her in.

The people who lived here were already dead.

Out of habit, Dakota took a deep breath and gripped the knife she had lifted from Bo's backroom. The Kel-tech was wicked sharp and specially made, with enough silver in the blade to make any vampire very, very sorry.

The first one, stupidly standing with his back to the door, didn't survive for more than a few seconds. She plunged the knife into his back as savage jerk of her wrist, shredded his heart. He was dead before he hit the floor.

She stared at the remaining vampire where he remained crouched over his victim. "Get up." She stared at him and twirled her knife.

His eyes, dazed, all but drowned from the blood lust, stared at her. Dakota took one step toward him. Snarling, she said again, "Get. Up."

He might be lost to the blood lust—barely more than an animal. But even animals had the instinct to live. As he came for her, Dakota braced herself.

Screw it.

Drew tried to tell himself that, tried to tell himself it didn't matter. They had ended it. That's what counted, right? They had even ended it without an ugly, dramatic scene. To be honest, he'd expected some drama. She just seemed the type.

Maybe he should be happy.

Fuck that. He wasn't happy. Damn it, she'd just walked. How in the *hell* could she just walk? Two years and this was how it ended?

Okay, so yeah, he'd ended it, but...

"Shit."

He couldn't forget that no matter what, Dakota it made him feel like nobody else ever had.

• • •

"Shit." He shoved a hand through his hair. "Not supposed to be doing this. Not supposed to be comparing them. Not supposed be thinking about Dakota, not anymore."

His future needed to be with Nicole. He knew that. She was what he needed, and pretty close to what he wanted. At least what he thought he wanted. He should call her. He needed to see her—yeah. Go see her. He always felt better after he saw her, after he talked to her. Once he did, maybe this emptiness inside would go away.

Frowning, he saw the messages on his phone. It was from Nicole. When had she sent it? He tapped the screen to bring up her message.

Had to go check on a client. If you're free, might be in your neck of the woods in an hour. Don't know about you, but I could use the company.

"My neck of the woods?" He scowled.

A cold chill ran down his spine. He needed to see her. He needed to be there. Right *now.*

"Bastard." His worthless body fell to the ground and although everything inside her screamed to get to the woman, Dakota paused to make sure the heart was completely destroyed. It was.

She checked the other corpse and heaved out a sigh. Both dead. Good. Job done. *Shittily* so, but still done. Moving over to the woman, she crouched at her side and did what she could to stop the sluggish flow of blood.

"I'm sorry. I'm so sorry. I should have been here sooner."

There was no response. She was fading. Taking a deep breath, Dakota blinked back the tears, tried to think. Once more, something about the woman sent tugged at her. Familiar, very familiar. Dakota hadn't met her before—that much she knew. But she had smelled her before. And there was something else, no, someone else.

"No. Oh, no."

Her already bruised heart began to shatter. Her voice was thick with tears as she spoke. "Hey, sugar. Listen, we don't have much time. I can help you—if you want to live, I can help. It can be weird, and may not be a lot of fun, especially at first. But I can help. You have to tell me you want to go. Do you want it?"

• • •
282

It was law. No Hunter was allowed to bring another over unless the person wanted it. No, this woman didn't entirely understand what Dakota was offering her, but if she wanted to live and if she was willing that was enough. Focusing, she waited.

Hello. Screw *acceptance*—it was a demand.

You help me, damn it. Now…

From the roof, Bo saw the cop coming. Although he wasn't surprised, he sure as hell was irritated. "Don't need this mess."

There was a reason he preferred to leave the Hunters to themselves. They got involved in things they shouldn't. They tried to save those they shouldn't. They tried to help every damn body and half of them couldn't even help themselves.

Like Dakota, for instance. Poor girl, down there doing her best to save the cop's girlfriend. Yeah, Bo knew who was in the apartment building. The woman didn't live here, but her scent was all over the place. She was here, and she was here often. And because she was, he also smelled the cop.

Dakota wasn't to blame for a couple of ferals making a snack out of the pretty lady. She'd done her job, dealt with them. They wouldn't kill another woman, another child.

He was pissed off, and yeah, he did feel guilty some poor human had suffered for it. But that was the way of the world. Monsters preyed on the weak. Dakota would let the guilt eat her up, and because she had a connection to this victim, it would be that much worse.

And here comes the cop. "I do not need this." Leaping off the roof, Bo landed lightly on the fire escape on the floor below.

Sighing, he ignored the sarcastic voice in his head reminding him that he didn't have to be here. Yeah, he did. Dakota was a friend. She had trouble coming her way, trouble with a capital T. He didn't leave friends hanging.

CHAPTER THREE

Hurry, hurry, hurry.

It was a scream in his head, a song in his blood. Drew lived by his instincts. Like the time he had first seen Dakota— sauntering down the street, all sexy curves, feline smile and attitude. Instinct had demanded he follow, just as his instincts had screamed *mine.*

Right now, his instincts screamed *danger.* They screamed *death.*

Everything looked normal as he tore into the Hendersons' apartment building. Nothing looked off. Nothing sounded off. But something was—the hairs on the back of his neck stood up, adrenaline crashed through him and every muscle inside him was loose, ready for action. His phone was silent. He had called Nicole twice on the way over. She always answered, at least when she wasn't working.

He knew this apartment building too well. One of the elevators never worked. The other was slower than smart, and it broke down often. He took the stairs. Five floors up—it only took him minutes, but it felt like years.

Nic…

The Hendersons lived at the very end, the two-bedroom apartment housing a family of four. Up until past fall, it had been a family of five. The oldest had run away and gotten involved with a criminal type. When she had tried to leave, the bastard that killed her. The family had proof of their daughter's involvement, though, and they had gone to the cops.

Was that why Nicole was here? He didn't know. All he could think was…*Be safe, please be safe.* And because he didn't trust that to be enough, he prayed silently, *please, God, keep her safe.*

If any of those thugs had gotten to her, Drew was going to tear this town apart. He wouldn't rest until every last one of them had been arrested and put behind bars.

He reached the door, hesitating.

He couldn't wait. He knew that. He couldn't wait… and neither could Nicole.

● ● ●

Dakota heard the footsteps. More than that, she knew she wasn't alone. Recognizing his scent, she ignored him. She couldn't lose focus right now.

"Come on, sweetheart. You need to take more." She held her wrist to the woman's mouth and when she fought to turn her head away, Dakota held it in a merciless grip. She hadn't done this much to lose her now. The problem was that Dakota wasn't overflowing with blood of her own.

A master of the obvious, Bo decided to emerge from the shadows and point that out. "Baby, you know you haven't fed enough to be doing this. You barely have enough blood to walk out of here."

"I'll be fine." Staring at the blonde's face, she thought she saw a bit more response, some animation there. A split second later, she felt the response as the wounded woman started to draw on her wrist.

Behind her, Bo sighed. A second later, the rich tang of shape-shifter blood filled the air and Bo's wrist appeared in the center of her field of vision. "Feed, Dakota. You and me got about three minutes before we have company. And trust me, they aren't bringing us tea and cookies, either."

"What...?" She scowled, but she wasn't looking at him. Staring at the door, she narrowed her eyes.

"Feed. Now. Her cop is on the way and what do you think he's going to do when he sees this mess? I'll deal with the bodies and I'll handle the blood—throw enough chemical shit on it that no lab in the world is going to be able to get anything useful out of it, especially not vampire DNA. But you and her, you have to be gone..."

She didn't wait another second. As the woman fed from her, Dakota seized Bo's wrist with her free hand and closed her mouth around the wound there. It was already healing, but that didn't matter. Her fangs pierced his skin and the rich, ripe taste of his blood flooded her mouth.

It wasn't even a minute before Bo rested his other hand on her scalp. "Enough, baby. We didn't have three minutes. Our time is up—that cop of yours is fast. And damn quiet for a human. He's already on almost on this floor."

In under sixty seconds, Bo had scattered the chemicals needed to break down the vamp DNA. Another ten seconds wasted as he gathered the bodies of the dead vamps. In another fifteen seconds, he was out the window. Dakota gingerly pulled her wrist from the woman's mouth, grimacing as she fought to continue feeding. Already hungry—that was a good sign, Dakota supposed. Showed strength.

As she gathered the woman in her arms, she looked up and as Bo looked back through the window. "Go on. You need to be out of sight more than I do. I don't have anything here to come back to, in the end. Your life is here, though."

He nodded. "I'll keep in touch."

He was gone in another blink.

Dakota started toward the door, cradling the whimpering woman in her arms. Soon, she'd fall into the deep, dark slumber that would dominate the next few hours. It would give them some time to get safe—and they needed to be safe—

Shit.

She heard the footsteps. And she could smell him.

Don't look, don't look dontlookdontlook!

Lunging through the window, she peered downward. Five stories. She could jump that. The door behind her opened. Foolishly, she glanced backward. Her heart leaped into her throat as she saw Drew. Their gazes locked.

Then he looked down and saw the woman clutched in Dakota's arms.

As he pulled his gun, the shattered pieces of Dakota's heart shriveled. There wasn't anything even left to heal now. "Don't move," he warned.

She shifted to the side, using her body to protect the woman she carried. And then she leaped.

Still unable to believe what he'd seen, Drew took off running for the window. This wasn't happening—

He wasn't going to find Dakota crouched on the fire escape, carrying a bloodied Nicole around like a ragdoll. It wasn't happening—wasn't, couldn't be. He was seeing things...

The fire escape was empty.

Scrubbing a hand over his face, he turned and looked around. Maybe he was seeing things…?

Except the Hendersons' apartment was a bloody mess—very, very bloody. There was a faint, odd smell in the air—something like bleach, but not quite. Remaining by the window, he reached for his phone.

He'd call this in. Then he'd call Nicole again.

He hadn't seen what he thought he'd seen.

He hadn't.

If Dakota had been here, she'd either still be on the fire escape or if she'd been *able* to haul Nicole down the fire escape, he would have either seen her climbing down, or seen them both…no. He couldn't even make himself think of that image.

There was a logical explanation for all of this. There had to be. Nicole was at home, or she was out with a friend, or something…Dakota wouldn't *hurt* anybody. She didn't even know who Nicole was, right?

There was a logical explanation, and he'd find it.

Except there wasn't one. And he couldn't.

Twenty-four hours passed and as those hours ticked by, Drew was aware of too many fucking weird things.

All of the Hendersons were dead. The children had been killed in their sleep, the father's head had been all but ripped off, and the mother had been raped, her throat practically torn open.

Nicole was missing. Her phone, her coat, her keys, all of them had been found at the Hendersons' apartment. Her car was parked outside, just down the block. When he tried to track down Dakota at her 'security firm' he'd been told she'd turned in her resignation early that morning, as well as relinquishing the key to the apartment they had furnished for her. They were terribly sorry but she hadn't left a forwarding address, promising she'd come by to pick up any needed paperwork in a few weeks— was there any way they could take a message? Naturally, they told him, they'd cooperate in any way they could.

Warning sirens were already screaming in his head.

What in the hell is going on?

Eyes gritty, head pounding, Drew pored over the lab reports, trying to understand what he was seeing. It was just a rough preliminary and it was likely about as conclusive as anything he was going to get, too.

The blood that had been found in the living room was messed up. Contaminated with something, the techs had told him. Something similar to bleach—that made him think of what he'd smelled.

But they couldn't identify the compound. They also didn't think they'd be able to process the blood. It was breaking down on them—*it's like sludge, Detective. We can't even get a blood type—never seen anything like it.*

"You know, you can't work this case."

Looking up, he met his lieutenant's eyes. Then he looked back down at the reports. "I'm not working this case. I'm reading these reports. That's not the same as working this case."

"Just like you calling and hassling the lab techs isn't the same. Just like you doing door to door isn't investigating?" Anna Reid lifted a graying brow as she studied him. Sighing, she settled herself on the seat in front of his desk. "Drew, I know this is hard. But you can't work this. And you need to take a few days off. Go home. Clear your head."

"I can't." He couldn't clear his head…every time he even closed his eyes, he'd seen Nicole. Suffering—screaming. Shit, earlier, he'd dozed for maybe twenty minutes and had the most fucked-up nightmare. Dakota had been torturing her. Holding Nicole down on a bed—

"I *can't.*"

"You don't have a choice." She rose from the chair, lingering for a moment. "Go home. Take a few days. I promise, if there's anything new, I'll call you."

CHAPTER FOUR

Go home.

Yeah. She could make him go home, all right.

But the lieutenant couldn't make him stay. After another one of those fucked up dreams hit him, Drew left. Driving around aimlessly. Until he wasn't—until he realized he had a direction. On a road heading north out of North Carolina.

Drew didn't know where he was going, but he knew he had to go somewhere. He stayed off the highway, sticking to the smaller roads. When he came across a small town, he figured he'd stop and get some gas, maybe grab a bite to eat although he wasn't hungry.

But instead of searching for a gas station, he found himself slowing down in front of the small hotel. He wasn't sure why.

It didn't look like much. The units were set up in groups of twos or threes.

The beds would be rock hard, the water pressure would suck, but it would be cheap.

"What in the hell am I doing here?" What he needed to be doing was calling his lieutenant, seeing if there was any progress. Or maybe heading back to town and doing his own investigating. He could stay out of the way. Nobody had to know what he was doing.

Instead of doing any of that, he turned into the parking lot of the little hotel.

Because he knew he needed to, though, as he parked his car, he grabbed his phone. A quick call to his boss, Anna Reid would only take a couple minutes. And he suspected if he didn't call, it would make her suspicious. He didn't want that.

"Lieutenant." He climbed out of the car and shut the door, leaning against it as he studied the hotel. It looked even more humble up close. "Has there been anything new? Have we found Nicole yet?"

"Sorry, Quentin…there's nothing new. She hasn't been seen or heard from. You know I would call you if I had news."

"Yeah. You know I can't just sit around twiddling my thumbs either, waiting for you to call me. I had to at least check."

"Yeah. I was surprised you hadn't already called. I was getting kind of worried—thinking you were out doing something stupid." She paused. "You don't plan on doing something stupid, do you, Drew?"

He ran his tongue along his teeth. *Something stupid?* Hell. He just might be getting ready to do that. He didn't know. His skin was itching something awful and his instincts were screaming.

"Nah, I want to keep my badge. Keep in touch."

He ended the call and tucked the phone in his pocket. Blowing out a breath, he started toward the office. Although he had no clue what he was going to say once he got in there. *Hello... I'm a cop. I live a few hours away from here and the night before last, I broke up with my sort-of-girlfriend and less than an hour later I saw her hauling my other sort-of-girlfriend's body out of the window of an apartment. They disappeared right in front of me. Nobody has seen them almost forty-eight hours. Now I don't know why I'm here. But I feel like I'm supposed to be. Any idea why?*

Yeah, that would get somebody's attention. Just not the kind he needed.

Okay, so he wouldn't mention the fact that Dakota had disappeared from a five-story building carrying a woman who had weighed almost as much as she had. She hadn't fallen, because they would've found bodies. He kept that fact quiet from his fellow officers—he would keep it quiet now. He would just go with some official line, *investigating a missing persons case... yadda yadda yadda—seen anything suspicious?*

No reason to get descriptive at all.

As he stepped inside the office, stale stink of cigarette smoke wrapped around him like a cloying, embrace. It was going to cling to him, too. Sighing, he moved to stand at the desk.

As the older man ambled through a door behind the counter, Drew rested his hands on the old, stained wood. It was clean, though, cleaned and polished to a mirror shine. There was a smudged fingerprint there. Absently he brushed his thumb across the small smear. When he did, his elbow bumped into a cup of pens, knocking them over.

"Sorry." He shot the owner an apologetic glance and scooped up the pens on the counter. Then he crouched down and gathered the pens that had rolled onto the floor. That was when he saw it. If he hadn't bent down on his knees, he never would have.

A piece of paper, maybe a receipt. Folded into a neat triangle, roughly the size of the end joint of his thumb.

She could never be still. For some reason, it had always charmed him. That wild, crazy energy she had inside her.

The little folded triangle lying on the floor could have been left there by anybody. Logically, Drew knew that. But as he picked it up, that itch along his spine got worse, and his blood roared in his ears.

Slowly, he stood. The hotel manager was at the counter now, a friendly smile on his face. But it faded when Drew pulled out his shield and laid it on the counter.

"Officer. Can I help you?"

"Detective." His hands were sweating, he realized. His hands were sweating, his heart was racing, and he felt more than a little sick. Dakota...was she here? How could she have hurt Nicole? How did Dakota even know about her? "I'm looking for a woman who might be one of your guests. She's about 5'3, mid-thirties, long, dark brown hair. She would have checked in yesterday or today. Have you seen her?"

Something flickered in the man's eyes. He was good—very good. But Drew saw it, that flash, there and then gone again.

With a smile, the man said, "Naturally, Detective, I want to help. But I have a responsibility to my guests as well. You'll need to give me some sort of warrant before I can tell you anything."

Still gripping that small piece of paper, Drew returned the man's smile. Then, without a word, he left the hotel's office. The man had already told Drew everything he needed to know. The rest, Drew figured he'd just take a look around and see if he couldn't find those answers for himself.

Sick at heart, tired and hungry, Dakota rose from the floor. Nicole was sleeping on the bed, if her restlessness could be called sleep. The fever had come on her yesterday, the Change hitting hard and fast.

As hungry as Dakota was, Nicole needed to feed. Drawing her knees to her chest, Dakota pressed her face against them. "I'm not equipped to handle this."

She had never brought anybody over. She knew the basics. After all, she had gone through this herself, and all of the Hunters were taught—they had to be, in case they ever had to make a choice like this. Ideally, this would've been done in a better place. A more controlled environment. Too bad life didn't happen under ideal circumstances.

So Dakota was doing the best she could—the best she could think of was to get Nicole to Excelsior. But first she had to get somebody here so the newborn vamp could feed when she awoke. Which meant Dakota needed to go trolling.

Her destination was the town's single bar. Of course, it involved her leaving the security of the hotel before the sun set. She could do it, tolerate some of the evening sun, but not for long.

Nicole would sleep longer but if Dakota wasn't back fast enough, the baby vamp would rise and hunger would drive her out on her own. She was too young to be able to control it yet. The hunger would drive her to do awful things if somebody wasn't there to help her.

Staring at the tousled blonde head just barely visible under the blankets, Dakota sighed. "This isn't what I signed up for. I wanted to kill the bad guys, that's all."

It only cost him $20 to convince the gas station owner to let him leave his car there. Not bad, and it only took him five minutes to make his way back to the hotel. And he got back just in time to see something that left him rather floored.

No. Just... no.

It was her, though. Dakota. He couldn't see her face—he was too far away. But he recognized that hair, and he recognized that walk. Even with her head down, her shoulders slumped—it was her, all right.

Was she leaving? Did he go back for his car?

But even as he went to do just that, Dakota glanced back toward building behind her. There was hesitation in her steps.

What in the hell...?

As she started back toward her car, suspicion settled in his gut. Suspicion. Fear. Maybe even hope.

The skin on the back of her neck crawled. Dakota had the weirdest damn feeling she was being watched. The wind blew her hair back from her face and the sun was already stinging her skin. She breathed in deep, trying to pick up something on the air—the strong wind was throwing her off, though and she didn't have time to linger if she wanted to be back before Nicole woke. And this wasn't just a *want*—it was a *need*. She *needed* to be back.

So she didn't worry about the strange sensation of being watched. Whoever it was, they were human. A witch, a were or vamp—any of those would have set off her internal alarm in a different way. Since it wasn't that, she needed to focus on the problem of her baby vamp and keeping her fed. Safely.

Maybe God would smile on her and there would be a town drunk. Wouldn't be a tasty treat for Nicole, but a town drunk would be pathetically easy for Dakota to use her not-so-impressive mental skills on and once Nicole had fed, Dakota could wipe the memory away. Nice, simple...

Drew circled around from the back, making sure any nosy managers peeking out from the office wouldn't be able to see him. He'd noted the general location Dakota had looked and it had to be one of two buildings. Her car had been parked closer to this one, too. So he figured this was the best option. But he was wrong. The curtains were partially open. If anybody was using either of these rooms, they were an obsessive neat freak. The same could be said for the next unit. But the one next to it...the curtains were drawn tight. Not even a sliver of the room could be seen.

His gut was a cold, hard stone. He stood there, staring at the door. Images flashed through his mind. Nicole twisting on a bed. Crying out. Begging for help.

Swearing, he lifted his hands to his face. Yeah, he'd relied on his instincts a lot in life. Listened to his gut—sometimes he had hunches that had played out in ways that had been almost spooky. So what if this felt *almost* like one of those things? He couldn't—

Swearing, he stepped back just a pace. Enough with this shit. Blocking everything else out, he kicked the door in. As it went crashing back, he braced himself. If he was wrong—

The sight of the blonde laying in the bed almost sent him to his knees.

"Nicole!"

But she didn't move.

When he ran to her side, tearing back the covers, she barely stirred. As a matter of fact, she barely seemed to be breathing.

Dakota slowed and pulled into the parking lot of the town's sole bar. It wasn't even a block from the hotel, if you cut across the back lots. But since she planned on picking somebody up, using him for a pint or two of blood and then taking him to wherever he lived…well, she'd rather not be *seen* so much. Climbing out of the car, she sighed and stood there, studying the toes of her black leather boots, wishing she knew why she was so edgy.

Wishing—

There was a breaking sound. She tensed and slowly lifted her head. The bottom of her gut dropped away. Vampires had pretty spectacular hearing.

"Nicole!"

That voice…she knew that voice.

Swearing, she took off running toward the hotel. Screw the car. Screw catching attention. He couldn't be *near* Nicole now. And damn it, how had he found them?

CHAPTER FIVE

Her skin was too cool. She wasn't waking up, either. Lifting one eyelid, Drew peered into Nicole's blue eyes, studying her pupils. No reaction—fuck, was she drugged? Sick? *What*—

"Get back, Drew."

Hearing that familiar, low voice, he looked up.

Dakota stood in the doorway, her eyes locked on his face—for a second, they almost looked like they were glowing—

Shit.

"I think *you* need to get back," he told her as his heart split in two. She'd done this. Damn it. She'd somehow hurt Nicole. How could he have misjudged her—?

She came into the room, frowning at the door for a moment and then shifting her dark eyes his way. "Drew…get away from her. It isn't safe."

Drawing his weapon, he leveled it at her. She didn't even blink—damn it, she could stare at him over the barrel of a gun and not blink. Who in the hell was this woman? "You kidnapped a lawyer, Dakota. You've done something to her. You got any idea how much trouble you're in?"

"I didn't kidnap her." She lowered her head, pressing a hand to her temple. When she looked back at him—

Drew stumbled back. Her eyes—*shit*—they *were* glowing. "Get back, Drew. *Now.*"

His legs started to move. He was halfway across the floor before he could make himself stop. Shit. Not right. This was so fucking *not* right. Spinning away from Dakota, he stared at Nicole. "I'm taking her out of here and getting her to a hospital."

I need to call the cops. That was what he needed to do. But his gut told him Dakota wasn't going to let that happen. His gut also told him, though, that she wouldn't hurt him. Maybe she'd hurt Nicole and God knows who else, but not him. Yet. He'd use that to get Nicole safe, and then he'd make her pay—

Returning to Nicole's side, he bent down to lift her, still holding his gun. He

● ● ●

had no chance, though. A hand closed around his arm. Small and feminine…it shouldn't have been so strong. "No." Dakota shoved him back. *Damn it—*

He fell into the wall, hitting it with enough force that it left his head ringing. Swearing, he shoved off it, wobbling for a step before he steadied. "Dakota—" He lifted the Glock he held and that crack in his heart widened, ripping his heart in two. "Don't make me use this."

Her lids flickered. "If that's what I have to do to keep you safe, I will, baby. Please…just leave while you can…"

A strange, whimpering moan rolled through the air.

"Not yet, damn it. It's not sunset…" Dakota swore, her gaze shooting to the bed. Then her gaze cut to him. "You. It's you. Damn it, get *out.*"

If he'd been looking at Dakota, he might have seen the fear in her eyes.

But he was staring at Nicole. Watching her chest started to rise and fall…watching as her eyes opened, revealing glowing eyes of blue. Watching as her mouth opened on a broken moan. Revealing fangs.

"Nic…?"

She turned her head toward him.

He never even saw her move.

Dakota caught her just before Nicole reached Drew. Fast brat. Wrapping her arms around the baby vamp, she pinned the smaller woman. "No, Nicole—you can't. Not now."

"*Hurts…*" Nicole moaned low in her throat. She snapped at the empty air, like it might ease that burning ache.

"I know…shhhh…I know." Dakota stared at Drew's stunned, pale face. *I couldn't have fucked this up more if I tried.*

"Dakota, please." Nicole, begging and pleading, shuddered in Dakota's arms.

"Here." Dakota lifted her wrist. "It's not going to help for long, but it's better than nothing. It will hold you for a few hours." *Long enough for us to get out of here, at least.*

And as Nicole sank her newly formed teeth into Dakota's wrist, Dakota stared

● ● ●

at Drew, wondering if he'd bolt. He couldn't leave knowing what he knew—and she wasn't strong enough to wipe his mind. She'd tried and failed.

What now…?

"What's going on?" Drew asked, his voice tight and rusty as he stared at Nicole, bent over Dakota's wrist.

"What, haven't you read *Twilight*, seen *True Blood?*" Dakota forced a smile, even though her heart was breaking. She didn't know what to do.

Nicole, first. Make sure she wasn't going to attack him. Then she'd figured out the next step.

Although she had an idea. She couldn't wipe his mind, but there had to be somebody who could. He'd thought she'd kidnapped a lawyer—well, she hadn't. She suspected she might be getting ready to kidnap a cop.

"I can't believe you put him in the *trunk*."

It was hours later, nearing dawn and she'd heard this ten times already. Sighing, she shot Nicole a look as she hit her blinker. "Babydoll, I didn't have a choice. He saw us. He knows too much for me to just let him go merrily off. I wasn't able to wipe his mind, either."

"But you put him in the *trunk*," Nicole repeated. "He's a *cop* and you kidnapped him and he's my boyfriend and…"

Dakota sighed. "Nicole. I didn't have a choice. Unless I decided to stick *you* in the trunk, because you can't be that close to him yet. Even though you fed, you don't need to be around him." She made herself smile as she glanced over. "Besides, you've been through enough. You don't need to ride in the trunk."

"And he does? Damn it, he's got to be so worried. You should have let me talk to him."

"I will."

"You will?" Nicole stared at her. "When?"

"Soon." She took the turn. "The school is ten minutes away. There will be somebody there who'll know how to fix this."

She hoped.

She'd knocked him out.

Taken his phone.

Restrained him.

Oh...and let's not forget...Dakota was a fucking *vampire*. At least he was pretty sure she was, even though he hadn't seen her fangs.

When she opened the trunk and his eyes adjusted, the only thing he could think was...*I should have known. I just should have known*—not about this insane shit, but that she hadn't hurt Nicole. He still didn't know what in the hell was going on, but...

"Come on," she said quietly once he was out of the trunk. "I'll get you out of those cuffs. We'll talk. Figure out...something."

Figure out *something*...?

As she pulled the gag out of his mouth, he narrowed his eyes. "I don't like the sound of that."

"Drew, baby..." She shook her head and rested a hand on his cheek. "You really should have just left. Screw that. You should have just stayed *away*."

Yeah. He was figuring that out fast.

His skin crawled as he looked around. Everywhere, he saw people looking at them. And almost all of them moved with that odd, easy grace that Dakota had. Dakota...or Bo. Similar, but not the same.

Fuck, just how much trouble was he in?

"Calm down, sugar. Nobody will hurt you here."

He glanced at her. "Yeah? Somehow I'm not reassured."

A sad smile curled her lips. "I guess not."

"I tried."

Dakota flinched as Malachi came into the other room and sank into a chair. He pinned her with a dark blue stare and she immediately looked down. He freaked her out in the worst way. "Tried?" she asked.

"Yes. I tried. He has a natural resistance, so it's not just you. I can do it, but it would damage his mind."

"No—" She jerked her gaze up, staring at him. Looking past him, she stared through the one-way mirror to where Drew had been placed. Like a prisoner, she realized. "You can't."

He was in there with Nicole now, talking to her, but they weren't alone. Kelsey, the witch who ran Excelsior was in there, along with Shawn Lenning, one of the vamp instructors who stayed at Excelsior. The two of them could control her if the hunger returned. Shaking her head, she looked back at Malachi. "You can't. He didn't mess up—*I* did."

"Dakota…" Malachi gave her a gentle smile. "Screw-ups happen. Something about his mind feels…well, strange. I think he's probably got a bit of psychic skill and that's why he's resisting so easily. Your biggest fuck-up was in not calling for help when things went to shit."

Rising, he turned to the window. "I've enough on my hands now—dealing with a stubborn mortal cop and breaking his mind isn't high on my list. But we can't let him leave here if he's going to talk." Over his shoulder, he looked at her. "You know that."

As he slipped out of the room, she swallowed.

"So…"

Nicole tucked her chin against her chest, staring at the table like it held something fascinating.

"So." Drew, on the other hand, was staring at her bowed head. This was surreal. He was sitting in a room with a woman he'd been dating…and she was a vampire. In another room, just down the hall, the woman he was in love with? Another vampire. Surreal.

"That's Dakota."

Now it was *his* turn to study the table. Yeah. Pretty damn fascinating. "Shit,

Nic."

She laughed softly. "Hey, Drew. Stop looking like you kicked my puppy…or me."

Shooting her a glance, he pushed back from the table and started to pace. "I wasn't very fair to you," he said softly.

"Stop." Nic sighed, slipping him a sidelong glance. "You weren't unfair. I knew you were seeing somebody. I knew you cared about her. I also knew you liked me…I just kept hoping in the end, I could make you like me *more*."

She snorted. "Now if I'd met Dakota earlier? Seen how you look at her?" She shook her head. "You and me, we might have had a chance, if you hadn't met her. But as it is? Nah. We're friends. Hopefully we can stay that way."

He had his own misgivings about that but he wasn't going to say anything. "You think you're going to be okay?"

"Yeah." A smile curled her lips. "It's going to take some adjusting, but I'll be fine. What about you?"

That was something he couldn't answer.

CHAPTER SIX

The way they kept looking at him was driving him nuts.

The big guy, his bald head as smooth as polished quartz, shot him a narrow look before focusing back on Dakota. She had her back to him and her shoulders were slumped.

If he tried hard enough, he could hear them.

He didn't want to, though. He didn't want to think about the insane shit going on. Nicole seemed okay and that was the main thing, now that he knew Dakota hadn't hurt her. He didn't want to...

"—fuck up, you fix it. How you think you can fix this, kiddo?"

Dakota groaned and dropped her head into her hands. "I don't know, Shawn. I just don't know."

"Well. You need to think fast or you'll be the one paying for it. This is serious, D.C. People will die if word of us gets out—what were you *thinking*—?"

Closing his eyes, Drew turned away and started to pace. Damn it, he didn't know what to do. Nobody seemed to want to hurt him—not even that big, red-haired bastard who'd come in on them earlier. Although *something* had hurt—he'd felt something in his head, like somebody was pushing on it.

But nobody had done anything to him—nobody had even looked at his neck. Well, except Nicole.

Still, he didn't see them letting him leave here, knowing what he knew. He could try telling them he wouldn't say anything. And he wouldn't—it would be a danger to both Dakota and Nicole. He couldn't risk that. But nobody here was likely to believe him and why should they?

Damn it, he was fucked.

And worse...so was Dakota.

You'll be the one paying for it.

What had that meant?

Was she in trouble now?

Blood roared in his ears. And as he stared at the floor...once more images

● ● ●

begin to flicker through his mind, rolling like a silent filmstrip, completely and utterly fascinating.

Nicole had told him what she'd gone through—somebody had attacked her. Dakota had found her, but she'd lost too much blood. The only way to save her had been by making her a vampire. It hadn't been fun, either. Bad fevers, like she'd been sick. Seizures. Dakota had been forced to restrain her. Like what he'd been seeing in his head. It was insane...so screwed up. But all of this was insane. All of it. Maybe this was what he needed to do. How things were supposed to happen.

They had taken his service revolver, his phone. But there was one other thing. Feeling oddly disconnected, he reached into his back pocket. The knife wasn't good for much of anything except cutting open boxes and the like—he used it as a letter open more often than anything else.

He figured it would open a vein, too. If it saved Dakota...

The smell of blood was something any vampire would recognize. Spinning around, Dakota stared at Drew's back. He was still standing, but he wouldn't for long—not considering the amount of blood—

"Drew!"

She lunged for him.

"Mother fuck..." Shawn whispered behind her. He was faster than she was, and he reached Drew just as the other man started to sway.

They were on the floor now, kneeling amidst his blood. As Shawn gripped Drew's wrists, easily cutting off the flow of blood, she cupped Drew's face. Okay...he would be okay. He was pale, but that was okay. He hadn't lost that much...

"Damn it, Drew, I told you that nobody would hurt you." She stared at him, her heart tripping a bit in her chest. "What are you trying to do?"

"Save you..." He grimaced and tried to pull away from Shawn. Dark lashes fluttered over his eyes. "They can't hurt you for telling me if I'm one of you, right?"

"Saving me—?" She could smack him. Kiss him. Shake him. "Damn it, Drew. I don't need *saving*. Nobody was going to hurt me."

"They..." Confusion fogged his eyes. Or maybe that was blood loss. "But he said you'd have to pay..."

Shawn frowned. "He's got good ears for a mortal."

Dakota ignored him, swallowing. "It'll be okay. You didn't have to hurt yourself just to keep me out of trouble."

He closed his eyes. "And what if I kind of wanted to be with you, too?"

As her heart did another one of those funny stutters, footsteps sounded outside in the hall. "Healer's here, kiddo," Shawn murmured.

"Be with me?" She shook her head. "But you dumped me. Damn it, no. We're not talking about this. We'll get you healed and then..."

"No. Because if I'm healed, I can't be with you..." He opened his eyes and stared at her. "Can I? Not for real. Not for good. That's why, Dakota. I needed more and this is my only chance for it, isn't it?"

He shot the vampire holding his wrists a look. "Let me go."

"Don't you *dare*," Dakota snarled. "I mean it, Shawn."

The black man grimaced at her. "Dakota...ah, well. It's kind of his choice..."

Shawn let go.

He slept.

For now.

Dakota sat at his bedside, feeling old. She'd slept until an hour before sunset, her body forcing it on her, even though she'd wanted to stay at his side. She was there now and she wouldn't leave until he opened his eyes, and fed...so she wouldn't feel so bad when she beat him.

Damn it, she wasn't ever going to forget what he'd done. She didn't fully understand it, either. She realized he had some disturbed, twisted sense that he'd been helping her, and while it made some part of her heart warm a bit, she *still* wanted to beat him.

"What were you thinking?" He'd slit his wrists. Damn it. He'd slit his damn *wrists*.

She felt sick. Sick at heart, sick in her soul.

She needed answers. She needed...

Him. She needed him. She'd needed him for a very long time. Pretty much from the first night she had met him. The night she should've turned around and walked away. And now look what she had done. How badly she'd screwed up his life.

Absently, she found herself thinking about what Shawn had said—what Drew had overheard.

You'll be the one paying for it... yeah. She guessed she was. But Drew was paying, too. And he didn't deserve that. He didn't deserve any of this.

None of it.

A moan came from the bed. Drew moved restlessly, tangled in the sheets. Rising, she moved to his side. The fever. It was coming back.

He was burning—so damn hot. Was he sick? Had to be...couldn't move, couldn't breathe, so *fucking* hot—why was he so fucking hot? Why couldn't he breathe?

What in the hell was going...?

Pain gripped him, twisted him. Tore at him like it was going to rip him into shreds and just when he thought it would drive him to screams, it eased. And Dakota. He heard Dakota...

It was Dakota, right? Her hand in his, her voice murmuring to him.

But she couldn't be. They were over, right?

Images flashed through his mind—crazy images of glowing eyes, Nicole and Dakota. His mind couldn't process it. Maybe he wasn't sick—he could just be going crazy.

A cool cloth stroked across his brow. And he heard her again, that low, sexy drawl that had driven him mad from the first, now so comforting. He didn't understand her words, but he didn't have to; she was there and that was all that mattered. He wasn't alone. Listening to Dakota's voice, Drew slipped back into sleep. He just hoped she was there when he woke up.

• • •

She was there, all right. She was there. One look at her and he knew all the crazy dreams that had haunted him over the past hours hadn't been crazy dreams. Not unless he really was going crazy.

He opened his mouth to speak but he didn't even manage a word before gut wrenching pain ripped through his belly. Dimly, he heard a knock at the door. But he was too busy wondering if he was dying to worry about it. Doubling over, he tried to breathe through the pain. Then a hand touched his brow.

"You need to feed. That's what's causing the pain."

Feed... what? "Feed. What do you mean—feed?"

"Sugar, you're a vampire now. What do you think I mean?"

He sucked in a breath and that was when he smelled it. Something lush, rich... *ripe.*

Drew was barely even aware of the next few seconds. There was a woman there, and then she was in his arms. It was a blur—a hot, brutal blur. Some part of his mind remained sane, almost horrified. He had to stop, he knew he had to, but he couldn't, he just couldn't—it was so *fucking good*—

And then two hands gripped his head, prying him away.

Snarling, snapping, he fought with whoever it was tearing him away.

That hot, heavy fog. Only got worse. Then somebody was whispering to him. "Calm down, sugar. You can do this—you made it through the worst. You can make it through this, just trust me. Breathe, just breathe. That's it, sugar... that's it."

Sugar...

"Dakota."

A hand touched his face. "Yeah. It's me. I'm here. You with me?"

Misery gripped him. What had he done? "That woman—what...how could I...*aw, fuck...*"

"Come on now. Open your eyes."

He couldn't. Not ever again. What had he been thinking?

"Beth."

"I'm here, D.C." That voice—Drew didn't know that voice.

* * *

Opening his eyes, he found himself staring at Dakota's face for a long moment. Then, he shifted his gaze past her and saw the other woman. She had blood all down the front of her shirt. But she was alive. Alive—how?

"What is going on?" He sat up, looking between Dakota and the other woman.

"Don't you think you've got enough to process right now?" Dakota's eyes, dark and gentle, rested on his face. "Beth, thank you."

"Not a problem, Dakota."

Drew called out after her, but he was ignored. Ignored, and left alone with Dakota. "How is she still okay?"

"We can talk about that later. Right now, we have more important things to talk about. Like me beating you, for example." She jabbed a finger into his shoulder. "What were you thinking? You have any idea what you did to me?"

Scowling at her, he rubbed his shoulder. "Damn it, what are you trying to do— put a hole through me?" Then, giving into the urge, he reached for her. As bad as he had felt earlier, as sick as he suspected he should be, he shouldn't have been able to do it. Hell, he shouldn't even be *alive*. But he pulled her into his lap like she weighed nothing. He actually ended up using too much force—and they ended up on the floor when he lost his balance. That was just fine with him. Fisting a hand in her dark hair, he closed his eyes. "Well, I guess I understand a little bit more about all those secrets you. But, Dakota, security? Couldn't you do any better than that?"

"Shows how much you know." She sniffed. "I do work in security, just not the sort you would think. You still haven't answered me. What in the hell were you thinking? You didn't have to do that—you didn't have to do this. Not for me. I don't think you realize exactly what you have done. This is permanent—it can't be undone."

"What makes you think I would undo it?" Opening his eyes, he stared at her, combing his hand through her hair to toy with the ends.

"Duh." Rolling her eyes, she shifted around. As she did, Dakota grew aware of one thing—Drew was feeling better. A *lot* better. Swallowing, trying not to think about it, she stared at him. "Drew. Two things, one... you dumped me. Two... your girlfriend is here, she's a vampire—you're a vampire—maybe you two can ride off into the sunset and live happily ever after… if you really love her. If you don't, you're stuck in one very long life and you very well may hate it. It's not a fun one, and it can be pretty damn lonely. You shouldn't have done this."

"My girlfriend." He rested his hands on her thighs. He had a look in his eyes, a heated, slumberous one that she knew all too well. "You know, you really ought to tell me how you knew about her. She's not exactly my girlfriend. We were kind of dating, and we were going to get more serious. But…" He sighed and shrugged. "Then the other night happened. And we need to talk about that. About just what *did* happen."

Stiffening, she stood and moved away. "I didn't hurt her. Somebody else did. They've already been dealt with. I got there too late to save her—she was already bleeding out. I did the best I could, and the best I could do was bring her over. I realize it's not good enough, but it was—"

"Hey, that's not what I'm talking about. I know you didn't hurt her. Already figured that much out. It just took me a while."

She shivered as his voice sounded in her ear. Close, very close. He was already so quiet…usually, it took a baby vamp a while to settle into their skin. It wasn't taken him much time at all.

As his hands closed around her shoulders, she set her jaw. "Then what else is there to talk about?"

"Don't you think maybe we can worry about Nicole and everybody else *later?*" He pressed his lips to her shoulder. "Right now I want to talk about you. You're right, I don't fully realize just what I did. But I do know one thing—I did this because I knew it was the only way I could have what I really wanted. I broke things off with you because I didn't think I would ever have that. And as I was, I guess I was right. This sounds crazy, but while you were talking with that guy, I started seeing things—images in my head—I saw me, like this, I knew this was how I had to be if I wanted to be with you. And I wanted that more than anything for the past two years. I just didn't think I'd ever have it—*that* was why I ended things."

He tugged on her shoulders, forcing her to turn around. "I leaped before I looked. There is no doubt about that. Am I going to regret it? It's possible. But the only way that will happen is if I did it for the wrong reason—I did it for you, because I think you feel the same way about me that I feel about you. I love you. I've been in love with you almost from the time I met you. I just didn't think you were right for me, because of all your secrets." He grimaced and reached up, probing his mouth. "I wasn't prepared for this kind of secret, though. It wasn't you the needed to make some changes. It was me. And I've done that. So... am I right or am I wrong? Did I do it for the wrong reas—"

The rest of the sentence never made it out of his mouth. Dakota lunged for him.

He caught her in his arms.

"You idiot…" She muttered against his mouth. "You stupid idiot. Yes, damn it. I love you."

He groaned and trailed a hand down her back, toying with the hem of her dress. "Good." His other hand, he wrapped around her waist, locking her body against his.

She rocked against him, pressing closer, but it still wasn't close enough. Questions, demands, everything else faded from her mind. The two of them had plenty of time to talk, to figure the rest of things out. Right now, a bigger need dominated her mind.

"You know what, sugar? It's been like…three months since I've seen you naked." She caught his lower lip between her teeth and tugged. "That's way too long."

"Is it?" He caught the hem of her short black dress and pulled—too hard.

Dakota heard fabric tear and she might have been irritated, but the befuddled look at his face distracted her. "You'll have to get used to it…you're stronger than you were." Shrugging out of the remains of the dress, she dealt with her bra and panties, lifting a brow at him. "I like my pretty stuff in one piece."

He was still staring at the ruins of her dress. With a look at his hands, he looked at her. "I didn't…I mean…"

"Shhh." Catching his hands, she brought them to her breasts. "That's some of the stuff we need to talk about. But later. Touch me. I won't break or tear, I promise."

"But…"

"Touch me." She moved closer, crowding closer and going to work on his jeans. "Just touch me…please. Damn it, I thought I wouldn't have this again, be with you again."

She could feel the burn of his hunger, too, a purely physical hunger now. But he was worried…*that* she could scent, wrapping in the air around them. Staring at him from under her lashes, she smiled. "Drew…you should know…I play dirty."

For a vampire, lust and the desire for blood often went hand in hand. Her fangs had been threatening to emerge; now she let them. As she rose on her toes to kiss him, she bit her own lip just before she pressed her mouth to his.

He stiffened, went to jerk away. Chuckling, she clutched him tight. "Baby…you can't hurt me this way."

"Dakota…"

"You won't hurt me."

He shuddered. Then, with force that would have bruised her had she been human, he hauled her against him. There was barely enough room between them for her to push his jeans out of the way. She managed though. He sucked on her lip and the sensation was so damn erotic, it drove her *insane…*

Tearing her mouth away, she gasped, "Bed."

"Fuck the bed," he growled. He lifted her up.

And then, without waiting another second, he pushed inside.

Oh…hell…

Groaning out his name, Dakota gripped his shoulders, sinking her nails into his shoulders. Her head fell back and dimly, she found herself thinking, it was damn good thing she didn't *have* to breathe…because she couldn't.

Strong hands gripped her hips, dragged her up. "Look at me."

Forcing her eyes open, she stared at him, into those beautiful eyes that had haunted her dreams for the past two years. Curling arm around his neck, she pressed her brow to his. "I love you."

"Yeah?" A slow, heated smile curved his lips. "I love you, too…"

His hands curled into her ass as he turned and took a few steps, until she had the wall at her back. "I'm not going to break a wall, am I?"

Dakota laughed. "If you do, you won't be the first…" She gripped his hips with her knees. "Now stop talking. Make love to me already."

"Bossy…bossy…" His eyes glowed as he pulled back.

Then he surged back against her, deep, hard. She cried out, arched her back. He did it a second time, a third, as he worked a hand between them and stroked his thumb over the hard knot of her clit. Hot, liquid delight burst through her. Her heart ached for him and the pleasure, even as it tore into her, it remade her.

"Mine…" he muttered against her neck. "Finally mine."

"Always. I always was, sugar." Arching her neck to the side, she pressed him closer…she needed…

As he sank his teeth into her neck, they both exploded.

Fuck…"I bit you."

His head was still reeling. Shuddering, he lifted his head and stared at Dakota's neck. Then he gaped at he realized the holes were closing. "I…fuck. I bit you. And you're healing."

"You bit me…and I loved it. Now take me to bed," she said, her low, raspy voice smug and pleased. "And maybe this time, I'll bite you. Later on, we can have that talk…"

"But…"

She pressed a finger to his lips. "Later. We have plenty of time to talk, sugar. We need a night just for us…"

Dazed, stunned, he looked back at her neck. Then into her eyes. She was smiling. Didn't look worried at all. Shit. She was right.

"Yeah." Dipping his head, he whispered against her mouth, "You know what…yeah."

Printed in Great Britain
by Amazon